A
PHỞ
LOVE
Story

A PHỞ LOVE Story

LOAN LE

SIMON & SCHUSTER BFYR

NEW YORK LONDON TORONTO SYDNEY NEW DELHI

SIMON & SCHUSTER BFYR

An imprint of Simon & Schuster Children's Publishing Division
1230 Avenue of the Americas, New York, New York 10020
This book is a work of fiction. Any references to historical events,
real people, or real places are used fictitiously. Other names, characters, places,
and events are products of the author's imagination, and any resemblance to actual
events or places or persons, living or dead, is entirely coincidental.
Text © 2021 by Loan Le
Cover illustration © 2021 by Alex Cabal
Cover design by Laura Eckes © 2021 by Simon & Schuster, Inc.
All rights reserved, including the right of reproduction in whole or in part in any form.
SIMON & SCHUSTER BOOKS FOR YOUNG READERS and related marks are
registered trademarks of Simon & Schuster, Inc.
For information about special discounts for bulk purchases, please contact Simon & Schuster
Special Sales at 1-866-506-1949 or business@simonandschuster.com.
The Simon & Schuster Speakers Bureau can bring authors to your live event.
For more information or to book an event, contact the Simon & Schuster Speakers Bureau
at 1-866-248-3049 or visit our website at www.simonspeakers.com.

Also available in a SIMON & SCHUSTER BFYR hardcover edition
Interior design by Tom Daly
The text of this book was set in EB Garamond.
Manufactured in the United States of America

First SIMON & SCHUSTER BFYR paperback edition December 2021
2 4 6 8 10 9 7 5 3 1
CIP data for this book is available from the Library of Congress.
9781534441934 (hc)
9781534441941 (pbk)
9781534441958 (ebook)

This book is dedicated to:

My parents Phung Le and Dong Pham
I love you so much

My sister An Le
I love you and I'm proud to be your little sister

My brother Dan Le
I love you still.

AUTHOR'S NOTE

Before escaping the country, my family lived in Nha Trang, a gorgeous coastal city in south central Vietnam. I grew up speaking the southern Vietnamese dialect, but given Nha Trang's location, some words may reflect a mixture of central and southern regions. For example, I call my dad *Ba* and my mom *Mẹ* while some readers might call theirs *Bố* and *Má*. The food featured in this novel also reflects the dishes that are commonly eaten in my family.

CHAPTER ONE

BẢO

Hoisin sauce is not paint.

We need a sign that says that, because our customers don't get it. Today's latest work is a misshapen star on the wall. A five out of ten, if you ask me. The kid's parent probably did a double take, snatched the bottle away, then paid the check and left before Mẹ could notice. To be honest, it's not like the sauce makes our wall look worse; it's just hard to wipe off when it dries. But I try, I really do—sometimes. Maybe.

Various relatives from both sides of my family judge me from their water-stained portraits that hang around the restaurant.

I sit down and look ahead at the five booths I still need to wipe clean, but this heat's unbearable and the main fan, the good fan, died last week. Break time. I brush off grains of rice that cling to my apron. Later, I'm sure I'll find a few that somehow end up under my socks at the end of each shift. On the opposite side, my best friend, Việt, goes at the same pace as me. His ears are plugged up, probably to block out the *Paris by Night*–like soundtrack blasting from the back room, songs on repeat about the Vietnam War, love, war, poverty, war.

Việt is the most chaotic neutral person I know. On any other day he wastes time by raving about the latest criminal-investigation show he's gotten hooked on. I consider that a trade-off; he's the one who suffers through my fascination with strange words. Once I was wiping down a front window from the inside, unknowingly overriding his work and adding more streaks than there were to begin with. I'd been mentioning the word "defenestrate," which made him calmly threaten me with that very word.

Ba stands behind the counter, punching in numbers at the cash register, then piercing receipts onto a spindle. I think he finds the routine satisfying.

The front door opens, the bell shattering the slowness in the restaurant, ushering in more sticky hot air. My mom's voice whips two other lingering, taskless waiters to attention, and I snatch up the towel and wipe off bean sprouts, leafless stems of herbs, and straw wrappers shaped as tiny accordions. Mẹ charges across the room. She drops her plastic shopping bags in the path toward the kitchen, a storm on her face. Everyone clears the way for her; they know Mẹ's mood. But Ba's expression is as indifferent as his look in their wedding pictures from the 2000s: Stone. Cold.

My mom slaps down a crumpled piece of paper before him. "Anh, do you know what they're doing across the street?"

Without looking up, speaking to his calculator, he asks, "Did you get more sriracha sauce?"

"On my way back, I saw these ugly posters all over the place."

"There was a sale. Did you get them on sale?"

It's always like this, their conversation misaligned, a *not much* to a *how are you* question.

"Lampposts, windows all over Bolsa Avenue!"

Glass shatters in the back kitchen. The line cooks start blaming each other, Spanish and Vietnamese mingling together. My guess: Bình did it. That guy sucks at his job more than me.

Mẹ ignores the noise. "Two-for-one. Two-for-one bowl of phở. *Trời ơi.*" Only one family can get her riled up like this. She pauses. "They're trying to steal all our customers. Why isn't Anh worried?"

Ba snorts. "Their phở is not good. They never have enough salt." Now *that* I can't verify. I've never stepped foot into the Mais' restaurant. Because what happens? Apparently my mom will cut my legs off.

Maybe they had one of the waiters pose as a customer. . . .

Mẹ nods, dialing back her worry. After a moment, she says, "Two-for-one phở. Who wants to have phở *lạt*?" She laughs at her own joke about their phở's blandness. Ba joins, too.

Lately their preoccupation with the Mais has ratcheted, probably because they keep hearing about the changes the other family's been making, changes that seem to be in direct response to our adjustments. We'd recently added new wood grain blinds that block out the sun—just because it looks like they replaced their blinds, too.

My mom zeroes in on me. *"Con đang làm gì đó?"* She side-eyes my tables. "Why are the tables still dirty?"

"I'm not finished yet."

"Why not? He's done." Mẹ points to the opposite side.

I look across the room at Việt—

And blink. The tables are shining, and the mirrors are fingerprint-less and—yes—hoisin-less. Kid's like an Asian Flash. "Oh, c'mon," I mutter.

"Giỏi quá!" she says to the traitor.

"Cảm ơn," Việt answers without a trace of an accent even though he was born here.

My mom turns back to me. "Hurry up!" She jabs a finger at me. "And fix your hair! It's so messy." I can't help it; my hair has a mind of its own.

The poster that Mẹ showed my dad floats to the ground in her wake. Curious, I pick it up, passing by Việt. Making sure my mom's a good distance away, I elbow him. "Suck-up."

Việt lands a punch to my stomach. "Lazy."

I pretend not to die; he's always been stronger than me.

Việt goes into the back room. I look down at the flyer. I'm not sure how anything like this can be considered ugly. It's awesome. There's no other word for it. Just really cool—some kind of collage of old and modern Vietnam: a woman wearing a traditional silk white dress and rice hat winking at a camera. You can see the sun and beachline—reminding me of Nha Trang, my parents' home-town—blazing behind her. An airplane flying above the woman spells out in the clouds OH MAI MAI PHỞ: TWO-FOR-ONE DEAL. With this kind of advertising from the Mai family, my parents should be worrying about *our* advertising. We don't have a Linh on our team.

I glance out the window. As if this poster summons her, Linh appears from Larkin Street's direction. She rushes into the restaurant, her flyaway hair alive, her large canvas bag, which she hauls everywhere, hitting her long legs. Over the entrance and below a pagoda-style eave hangs a South Việt flag just like ours—yellow with three red stripes—and it flutters in greeting to Linh. She's always a colorful blur—going to class, dashing down La Quinta's hallways when the bell lets out, running into the restaurant at 3:30 p.m.

I see her, but I know close to nothing about her. Maybe it's a good thing she's constantly moving, because if she ever stopped, we might have to talk to each other. And we haven't done that since we were kids.

Hypothetically, a Buddhist temple is not a place for insults or threats or a potential bloodbath.

I've gone to temple sporadically throughout my life, but the day I met Linh is the most memorable, for many reasons, aside from running into the rest of the Mais and being *thiiis* close to seeing bloodshed before Ông Phật.

Before meeting Linh, I'd never seen another seven-year-old kid stab paper with a crayon. Repeatedly. We were in the kids' room where the *chùa*'s volunteers babysat kids as the parents went to worship or at least get a moment of silence. Mine were catching up with friends upstairs. There were tables with finger paint, macaroni, glue, and paper, and another table with crayons and markers. I'm not sure why—maybe because it was less work—I went for the crayons.

The other kids sat so far away from Linh because they were afraid she might turn on them. But the look on her face was calm and concentrated—satisfied, even—and when she made sure all of the crayons were completely dull, she raised her white paper in triumph. I was closest to her, so she showed it to me.

The dots formed a complete picture: green grass, a yellow sun, and a red-and-blue swing set.

"Wow," I said, like any six-to-eight-year-old Asian kid with a bowl cut would say.

"It's the playground at my school," she answered proudly.

"Can you draw Spider-Man?" Because back then, that was the only thing that mattered to me.

"Maybe. I can't remember what he looks like. I need something to look at."

"I have one! I can get it!" I'd brought along my Spider-Man backpack, but it was upstairs in a cubby with our shoes. We raced out of the room, escaping the volunteers, who didn't really try to catch us. Up on the main floor, the temple membership was serving bowls of phở *chay* and a white-haired lady waved us over for a bowl of vegetarian soup.

Linh took her bowl with everything that my family always

taught me to use: hoisin sauce, thai basil, and bean sprouts. That told me she knew phở; she *came* from phở. It was confirmed when we both tried the phở at the same time and said, "BLECH." Salty as hell. We left our bowls, quick, then moved on to our destination.

Running, that's what I remember. I was chasing a girl I barely knew, but I really wanted that Spider-Man drawing. Before we could get to my backpack, though, Mẹ's sharp voice rang out. The one that still summons centuries' worth of furious Vietnamese mothers. I froze. Our families stood on opposite sides of the room, where Buddha was at the center, accepting gifts and praise from the visitors. Linh and I were caught in between. I waited for Buddha to come alive, chime in, like a referee, and bellow—while the ground vibrates forcibly—"Ready, set, FIGHTTT!"

But nothing like that happened.

Linh's mom took one step forward, like she was marking her territory. Her eldest daughter and husband were just behind her.

"Đến đây," my mom said to me. I thought she was angry at me for running in a temple. I couldn't say no and when I was with her again, she gripped my hand tight. Ba hung back, and I remember being confused by the fury barely contained on his face, so different from his usual passivity.

After that, they all but dragged me and Linh away from each other.

"You still haven't finished your tables."

Ba's voice from the front desk snaps me out of my memories. I'm still standing by the windows, but I notice the sky is a bit darker and the lampposts are starting to turn on. The din of inside chatter fills my ears.

"Why do you have that flyer?"

"Sorry," I say. "I was thinking of how ugly it looked. Mẹ's right." I walk to the nearest trash can, hand poised over it.

The story of me and Linh at the temple could have been kept as a carefree memory, lost and dusty like an old book in the basement. And I did actually forget about it; she was just one of many kids I'd run around with and never saw again—best friends for an hour or two, instead of forever.

Then Linh's family opened their restaurant across from us five years ago, and I knew it was her. I knew she still drew, because she carried her portfolio with her everywhere, the size of it almost as big as her body.

I also knew that I couldn't go anywhere near her without risking my mom's wrath. Disdain was clear in my mom's voice whenever she talked about *that* restaurant, as if it were a person.

I heard that restaurant underpays its staff.

That restaurant is connected to a gang; they just moved from San Jose, after all.

That restaurant blackmailed Bác Xuân, pushed him out of his business.

That last reason might be why the neighbors didn't accept them so easily at first. Bác Xuân had basically helped the area flourish, connecting fellow business owners with the right people. Beloved, you can say. I don't think my mom's circle of friends made it any easier for *that restaurant*—social wolves who ran various businesses in the area: like Lien Hoa BBQ Deli, nail and hair salons, and even one travel agency. Back then advertising wasn't really a thing, so the good word of one of these women? Certified. You either get a *dở ẹc* or a *cũng được,* the latter being as close to great as you can get in terms of Vietnamese praise. Their group is led by Nhi Trưng, an older woman who constantly liked to brag that her name bears a similarity to one of the female military leaders to rebel against the Chinese domination centuries ago—as I discovered on Wikipedia. As if that was supposed to impress people these days. I think of her as the General, though the real-life Nhi Trưng was the general's daughter.

She had a special reason for hating the Mais; she'd always liked Bác Xuân's spot and said it'd gotten the most traffic. I bet she was planning to go for it right when the first opportunity came up.

Luckily gossip changes and some attention spans are short. Now the Mais' restaurant has become a fixture just like ours. But that doesn't stop my mom's competitive streak.

My parents—my mom, really—have now perfected the art of non-encounters, knowing their schedule right down to when they close and when they leave. In a way, their schedule has become ours. We're background characters in each other's stories.

As I look at the poster in my hands, though, I wonder if it's possible for us to change up our scripts. What would happen if our families came face-to-face with each other like that time at the temple? What would me and Linh say to each other?

"Tại sao mày đứng đó vậy?"

"Sorry!" I shout to my mom. Back to work.

I fold up Linh's poster and pocket it, not knowing why.

CHAPTER TWO

LINH

"Maybe I just won't take the SATs again. Maybe I'll just drop out right now and become the next best American novelist."

I give my best friend, Allison, my *You're annoying me again* look, since this is the third time she's interrupted me as I worked on my latest sketch. "C'mon."

"No, really. What's the point of the SATs? There's no real-life application that we can get here." She twirls her curly hazel hair with a finger. Her foot kicks my left ankle. "And your legs are in my space again."

I fold them just a bit more, but there's not much I can do in this booth. "You're going to do fine. They were fine the first time around. So what if your math scores aren't perfect? They're still great. And you'll ace the writing part, Ms. Editor in Chief. I know it."

"And you're going to ace all of it. Because you're Linh fucking Mai," Ali says. She pretends to take an angry slurp of her *cà phê sữa đá*, condensation leaving a puddle next to her. Since middle school we've always had iced coffee to get us through the mountain of homework we have. Senior year just started but I already feel as if I'm buried.

Some of my coffee spills onto the table, soaks the edges of my cream-colored sketch pad. I don't clean it up. Ms. Yamamoto is in my head, saying, *If you want to be an artist, you'll need to get messy.* I focus on my sketch.

Downtime at the restaurant is actually a nice time to draw. The empty seat next to me balances my Prismacolors. My eraser, an ugly blend of all the colors I've been using, sits beside them. The sketch isn't going that bad. The assignment: *Draw your memories.* Instructions: *Why the hell should I tell* you *what to do*? Or at least that's what Yamamoto always says to our art class.

I'm drawing a beach scene, remembering the time Ba taught me how to float on my back, and where Mẹ taught me how to "cook" with sand—or play make-believe as I dug concave dents in the sand, poured water in them to make *bánh bèo ngọt*, a sweet steamed treat you can hold in the palm of your hand and eat.

My older sister, Evelyn, stayed under the shade of our umbrella, reading—of all things—a book about the human skeleton. Guess who's now majoring in biology at UC Davis?

The tip of my colored pencil breaks as I shade an area under my beach umbrella.

"What is it?" Ali says, reaches over her SAT book to touch the picture—but I quickly slap her hand away. "*Jesus*, you're a beast when you're drawing, you know that?"

I pull back my sketch pad. "It's not ready yet." And it won't be if I keep losing focus, or let Ali distract me with her talking.

And that's what she does best.

Luckily, I'm used to it. Ali is a fixture in the restaurant after school, and for years, it was me, Evie, and Ali, and nothing really changed, unless you count the fact that now Ali steals the last egg roll, always shooting me an impish grin.

There was a time for a year when her parents were going through a divorce, and as strong as she was, home was more like a battlefield. The divorce eventually happened, and everything's more stable now. She's back to being the Ali who likes my artwork so much that she always has to take a peek at it. She says that one day we're going to dominate the world—her as a writer, me as an artist.

"What's with your dad today?" Ali tips her chin toward the front of the restaurant, where Ba takes up his own booth. The light from the front windows streams in, turning his normally salt-and-pepper hair a blinding white. He's writing the checks for the week, but keeps looking up at the Nguyễns' restaurant. Best guess is that he's keeping an eye on the Nguyễns. Ba's weird like that.

"I dunno."

The Nguyễns can't *not* see him. My dad isn't the most discreet person or the stealthiest; every part of him—his walk, his breathing—

makes noise. My mom, though, is the opposite. She slips in and out of any social gathering, from any room, any conversation, like a ghost. But she's loudest when she's cooking; the spices and flavors in her phở, *bún bò*, and *bún riêu* are her way of announcing, *I'm here*.

Our plan to do a two-for-one deal combines Ba's talent for advertising and Mẹ's cooking, or so Ba claims. But I'm already dreading the flood of people who'll come. We're understaffed as it is; we had to say goodbye to three servers who were seniors off to college. We hired replacements, but only one of them seems like they'll last.

Before I realize it, Ba appears at our table. He sets down a plate of hot, crispy egg rolls that Mẹ sent out from the kitchen. Ali literally *ooh*s, like she hasn't eaten a gazillion in the lifetime we've known each other.

"*Cảm ơn*, Ba."

He reaches for my sketch, appraises it. "*Con vẽ này hả?*" he asks evenly. I nod and he dips his chin in acknowledgment. I know he sees I can draw. He wouldn't have asked me to make the flyers if he didn't at least approve of my work. "Did you do your homework already?"

"*Dạ*, Ba."

Ba nods, satisfied, and walks back into the kitchen.

There used to be a time where I brought home every single art project in elementary school and middle school, and they would take it, hang it up. A picture of flowers in a vase still hangs in the kitchen by the in-and-out door. I knew they were proud.

But high school is different. In my freshman year, regulars would come in daily, updating my parents on their kid who went to Harvard, or won a prestigious award, or graduated with honors, or bought them a house. That was when my parents really started paying attention to my grades—the ones that actually mattered and could get me into a good school.

Toward the end of junior year, I'd brought home a physics exam that I aced and it was only because I studied without sleeping, abandoning an art project I had at the time. The test was worth too much. Mẹ had mentioned it to a regular customer who mentioned a niece who was good at physics and now works as an engineer. Somehow that idea has stuck, and my parents have been pushing engineering as a path for me ever since.

I'd never seen them look so eager.

"Have you told them yet?" Ali pulls me from my thoughts. She is watching me. She's one of the few who can guess my moods, read me instantly.

"About coffee with Quyền Thành? No, it's pretty much all set. I can't back out now."

My parents don't usually ask for favors from regulars or their friends. Here's how it goes: If something is broken in the restaurant and a friend offers to fix it, they protest. That same friend shows up with a toolbox anyway, and my parents grudgingly let them in. When all things are fixed, my parents offer to pay them, but their friend protests and argues all the way to the door.

In that case, an envelope of money might mysteriously end up under their doormat, or in a pocket of their jacket they might hang up inside the restaurant.

But my parents had pulled in a favor when Evie was deciding

among schools, and called a few friends of friends to help weigh in. This time they used up another favor, arranging a coffee meeting with that niece who was an engineer. They tell me it's a chance to ask questions and learn more about "my future."

How can I say no?

"Con," Ba calls for me. He's halfway into the kitchen but he gestures to the front where a family of four are waiting to be seated. I slip into my role as waitress, something I've done since freshman year—and even before that. When we'd just opened the restaurant, I remember tagging along with other servers, armed with my own notepad and pen—or was it a crayon?—the customers indulging me with smiles.

"Table for four? No problem. Just follow me." I lead the family to one of the center tables, until Jonathan, the most competent of our new hires, easily swoops in.

I slip back into my booth with Ali. She's chewing on the end of her pencil, stuck with an article she's writing.

It kills my parents, even now, to have Evie a day trip away instead of at home. Evie was the better server out of us, calm and cool under service. Orderly. Mẹ never had to tell Evie to fill up the napkin dispensers or the bottles holding *tương phở*, because they were probably already filled.

And she's definitely more charismatic, like Ali, with the other customers. It's unsaid, but I know, in the way they ask after Evie, that some longtime customers must be disappointed to have me replace her—me who would much rather be in my head or in front of a canvas. They tell my parents how proud they should be of her.

15

"She'll be a doctor in no time," these customers say fondly. Then they look significantly at me. "And maybe you can be the same."

Perhaps in other families it would have worked out. I mean, me and Evie are only two years apart, but if anyone didn't know better, we might as well have been raised under two separate households.

Mentioning that I want to major in anything remotely creative? Impossible. Back in freshman year, when the idea of doing something with art just came into mind, we had a regular who had one daughter who couldn't be more perfect. Straight As, active in everything in her life, her hair always in a perfect bun. She was also one of the best seniors on the dance team and naturally decided to major in dance at college. Supposedly, the dad was more lenient, hence why she was even allowed to, I don't know, *live* after announcing her decision. Her mother's reaction, though, stays with me: "I want to die sometimes! She'll be poor her entire life. It'll never work out."

And my mom just consoled her as if she had lost a child, agreeing with every word. The woman and her daughter used to be close; now the girl's a choreographer and rarely comes home. Whenever her mom drops by the restaurant, loneliness comes off her in waves.

Now I glance around the restaurant, my eyes landing on the familiar parts that make up a place that's been like a second home for years: our red shrine greeting customers; our private shrine in the back room, where the ceiling is black with soot after so many years of joss sticks lit for worship; the people who come here for breakfast, lunch, and dinner, people from way back, like Mẹ and Ba's refugee camp days, who apparently remember everything about me as a child, even if I don't remember them. I mix them up half the time.

Nothing is bad. Nothing is *wrong*, really.

But it doesn't feel enough. There's something urging me to go a bit farther than here. Am I just being selfish?

Ali has gotten up to stretch her legs. She stands by the window with Ba and has started talking to him. Leave it to her to talk to someone who doesn't like to talk unless he has reason to. Off-and-on charisma. Ali laughs at something, but Ba looks serious. I leave my sketch and join them, curious.

"I can always sneak in, you know. Pose as a customer and steal some recipes."

Ba doesn't answer right away. It even looks like he's considering. I roll my eyes. "Ba, no way."

Anything the Nguyễns do, we have to do better. They knock down their *chả giò* price to four dollars for two rolls, we have to do three dollars and fifty cents for the same number of egg rolls. They have five flavors of *sinh tố*; we have six flavors. I'm never sure who's winning.

My parents are still trying to catch up to the others in the area, like the Nguyễns, still cognizant of how hard it was to open a new restaurant in the place of one that had, for all purposes, looked successful.

I remember Bác Xuân, the previous owner, coming over to our old San Jose apartment whenever he had a free weekend—stopping by after seeing his only daughter and his four grandchildren. The oldest, Fay, is getting married later this fall. I remember the slow way he'd shuffled inside and given a satisfied sigh as he sunk into our only comfortable La-Z-Boy chair. He told my parents he wanted to retire and that his daughter, a coworker of my mom's from a nail salon where she used to work, would rave about my mom's phở.

If you make good phở, you can open this restaurant, he'd said.

Things happened so quickly after that. We moved. I transferred schools. The restaurant opened . . . and suddenly I was only a few feet away from that boy who'd asked me to draw him a Spider-Man. It would have been a good coincidence, and I could have made a friend—if only it wasn't made clear that I should never step near their place.

"Gia đình đó thì dữ lắm, lại rất là xấu."

"But how are they mean?"

"They don't pay their staff anything. They owe their suppliers too much money. They—"

"Just don't ever associate with them." My mom had cut my dad off, rarely doing so.

I know Vietnamese people like to judge one person based on the whole family, and to my parents, the Nguyễns are the worst, but Bảo is a mystery to me. There, but not. In four years of high school, with more than 2,500 students, we haven't had one class together. As if our school administrators know of the rivalry and have conspired to keep us apart.

And high school will be over before I know it and we'll lead even more disparate lives.

"Mr. Mai," Ali says in a mockingly grave tone, "I am more than happy to spy on our enemy if it helps the restaurant biz. Just tell me when." She goes back to the booth to pack up. "Think I'm about to head home now. I'm on deadline." She puts on her backpack, groaning at the weight of her books. She stops by the pass-through shelf and pops her head in. "Can I take home some broth, Mrs. Phạm?" Pro tip to getting on my mom's side: Address her by her maiden name, which she kept instead of taking Ba's. "My mom's *dying* for her next phở fix."

Perfect pronunciation, thanks to me.

It's like you're confused and asking, "Huh?" except there's an f.

Oh. Yeah, I get it. In the pitch that kind of loops around, right? But it's also like if you're swearing and saying, "Fu—"

Okay, yeah, you got it.

In Vietnamese, my dad mutters in awe and confusion about how he's never seen a *mỹ trắng* —a white person—eat phở so many times a week.

I hear my mom's pleased smile in her voice. "Of course!"

Her hair tied in a loose bun—with a pencil, which I can't ever figure out how to do—Mẹ appears from the back, wipes a hand on her apron. She offers Ali a plastic cylinder filled with our signature homemade chicken and beef bone broth.

Ali beams at her. "Awesome. Thanks so much, Mrs. Phạm!"

We both watch Ali leave the restaurant until Mẹ gushes, "Allison is so *dễ thương*!" She's proud that I have a friend who likes her cooking.

Ba shakes his head. "*Con đó khùng.*" I laugh. According to my parents Ali can only be cute or a bit weird. I'll take my dad's side this time.

"You're not eating?" She points to the egg rolls.

If I say I don't have the stomach for it now, she'll be worried. "Yeah, working on it." Remembering Ba's reaction to my sketch, I close my pad and stash it in my backpack, rustling the paper tucked inside.

Ms. Yamamoto gave me that flyer two days ago. It's for an exhibition at the Asian Art Museum that will only be there for one night and morning. Chang Dai-Chien's piece will be displayed, donated by his living family members. He'd been one of the first to elevate ink painting and traveled all around the world before focusing on perfecting the art of Buddhist paintings. Yamamoto thought I'd be interested. She's always telling me how it seems I like capturing memories—rather than something posed—in my artwork.

"Just check it out," she said, as class was letting out. I was already late for work and ran out the door after grabbing the flyer with a quick thanks. But as I looked at it on the walk from La Quinta, I knew I couldn't miss out on it.

Mẹ disappears, then returns from the kitchen with her own bowl of phở. She likes to eat before the dinner rush. My insides sigh at the smell: star anise, cinnamon, the earthy tones of chicken and beef bones. She dresses it with shredded thai basil and fresh bean sprouts, a spritz of lime here and there, and finishes it with a generous swirl of hoisin sauce, glossy under our lights. A work of art.

"Beautiful, isn't it?" She inhales, a small smile on her face. Mẹ's loud when she's cooking—and she's happiest when she's eating. And I love her for it. I always want her to stay this way.

She gets sad sometimes—mornings when she doesn't let the sun in, leaving the window shades closed so that only slivers of yellow peek through. She buries her head in her pillow, both temples dotted with dabs of *dầu xanh* to soothe her headache. I hate the smell.

It reminds me of sickness and tummy aches, because that's what they used on me as a kid. Ba cooks on these days. Dinner is always a simple *canh sườn bí*, which always has less salt than it should, and never measures up to Mẹ's cooking.

It's worst whenever it hits the anniversary of her escape in 1983 or when a relative's death anniversary is just around the corner. Mẹ's story about her boat escape to the Philippines is the stuff of nightmares. I grew up listening to these tales. I'm not sure why—a lesson, maybe? Like in a *hey, listen to the hell I went through so you can have a good life* kind of way. But should an eight-year-old have dreams about a pitch-black sea and a boat packed with thirty-nine people, including crying, starving babies?

It's not depression, I don't think. Sometimes, she checks out. That's all. Like she's remembering something and can't get it out of her mind.

It helps when she calls my aunt, her older sister by six years, the one who stayed behind in Vietnam. She'd planned to escape with my mom in tow, along with their older cousins. But the officials had gotten to her, so she pushed my mom ahead, trusting their cousins from there on. They eventually made it to a camp in Palawan, Phillipines. My aunt wasn't held back in Vietnam for long, and might have bribed her way out.

But she understood then that she wouldn't be as lucky the second time.

Mẹ says I remind her of Dì Vàng because we both like to draw and sketch. My aunt had visited us when we lived in San Jose. I was five. I remember thinking she was like a colorful painting come to life, and when I saw a Kandinsky painting in my sophomore-year art theory class—one of his *Compositions*—I thought: *This is her*. Kandinsky had always talked about a connection between himself and the viewer, how the role of the artist was to not only excite the senses but trigger the viewer's soul. Colors and soul—I saw that in my aunt.

When my mom and my aunt get on the phone, I know things will be okay. They took care of each other back in Vietnam—since my grandparents had passed away when my mom was eleven—and they still take care of each other now. The almost nine thousand miles between them is insignificant.

Mẹ smiles as a young couple comes in—Vietnamese, by the way she greets them. Ba shows them to a table. Charisma on. He's already pushing the upcoming phở deal by handing out my flyer along with the menu. Dad's latest marketing scheme might work, but it's going to be hell working during those nights. It will track in a bunch of other Vietnamese people, who were trained by their chopstick-wielding mothers to eat what's in front of them, *then* eat some more even if they're full.

The sight of the flyer tickles something in the back of my mind.

"When is it again?"

"Hmm?"

"Phở Day." *Or whatever you call it.*

"September thirtieth, remember? We'll need your help that day."

Until three weeks ago, we were down three waiters and waitresses. Julia, Kingston, and Huy were a grade above me and left for college. But to say that the new workers were making things easier would be a complete lie. Jonathan was just okay. Lisa, the hostess, gets flustered too easily. And Tài has slippery fingers.

I lean back in my chair. Some of the air in the padding squeezes out.

Of course it's September thirtieth. The same day as the exhibition.

"Is Evie coming back to help?" My sister texted the other day and sent me a long string of pictures of her dorm room, a selfie with her new roommate, and a sunrise view of the campus after a morning run.

Maybe if she comes back, she can help out like she used to and I can sneak out. . . .

My mom frowns. "Con, you know your sister is busy with school."

What about me? I'm busy. I have other things to do. I have a life.

But I can't say those things. "Yeah, right, I remember now."

Mẹ sighs as she mixes up her phở. "I know this is not the best situation. I know this isn't how you want to spend your time." I try protesting, but she only adds, "You are not so hard to read. Your face always tells me everything. I just know.

"But we want this to go well. We need it to go well. Or else your father will be grumpy for days." She glances over at Ba, who's taking a couple's orders to the kitchen.

There's no way I'll be able to see the exhibition. No way at all.

I tuck a strand of hair behind my ear. I bite into my egg roll. Soggy.

CHAPTER THREE

BẢO

I regret many things in life, and I know I'll regret many more at the rate I'm going. But my number-one regret *now* is taking journalism as my elective. Astronomy, the easiest class any senior can take, was already filled up. Việt was lucky enough to get in. I thought journalism was the second easiest. Since freshman year, *Hawkview*'s been filled with crossword puzzles, sudoku games, and What's the Difference? games, and always ended up stuffed in toilets or cafeteria trash cans.

Then Allison Dale became the editor in chief. I swear she's tougher than any staff member at the *Los Angeles Times*. She's not even *in* this class—she has study hall last period, which means she can technically leave school early, but doesn't. Even though this is our first journalism class, Allison's already expecting us to chase news stories from things like the chess team embezzling money from their joint fundraiser with the checkers team—how Allison sniffed that lead out, I'm not even sure.

The adviser, Ben Rowan, should step in more often, but he seems more like a glorified babysitter. Rowan lets Allison run everything on the newspaper. He's the kind of guy who looks like he says "sorry" a lot.

We're at the tail end of our editorial meeting about assignment statuses. I take the back seat at this meeting and try not to fall asleep, since it's the end of the school day. But a part of me is still recovering from being accosted by theater nerds at the club fair during lunch period. Traumatic. They were demonstrating some circle game in the quad, but to me, it looked like they were trying to summon demons. Other clubs were less intimidating. Apparently there's a new TikTok club? I even managed to dodge the Vietnamese Student Association.

The president, Kelly Tran, still hasn't forgiven me for oversleeping and missing one Saturday service day during sophomore year. Actually, it was three.

The newspaper room used to be an art room, so the walls have posters about journalism ethics and one blow-up portrait of a younger Woodward and Bernstein posing together—not sure where that came from—but also a deep sink with an annoying drip and leftover jugs of neon green and yellow paint from last semester. Macs surround the perimeter of the room, all asleep. I'm basically silent because I don't have anything to show. I forgot my article about upcoming school field trips.

Kind of.

The truth is, I started to write it. I really did. I'd talked to the people Allison told me to seek out: the bus drivers, the teachers, and some random students that she found somewhere, and I jotted down everything they had to say—nothing interesting, of course.

But the moment I started to type them out during the last class, my words stopped making sense. I remember thinking in that moment: *What's the* point? *Will anyone read this?* Then my words and sentences froze onscreen until nothing was coming out, and I was stuck trying to find a way to string them together into something remotely reasonable.

Meanwhile, everyone around me was zoned in, typing without pause, putting their stories into those "pyramids" or whatever that Rowan had taught us when we first started classes.

So I say that I "forgot" my article, and Rowan just sighs—

Did he just write Loser *on his pad?*

Honestly, I don't know where Allison gets her energy from. What does she eat? What did her parents *do* to her? She stands at the center of the desks, which are flush against each other in a perfect square. She's more like a lion at the zoo looking out at gawkers. Her hair is in a braid. I think of Katniss Everdeen.

She squints at me. Of course she knows that I lied, that I actually hate writing. Why isn't she saying anything? I squirm. I see her at school with Linh in the hallways. What if Linh talks about me or my family—and what stories has she heard? Maybe she and the rest of the Mais throw darts at pictures of us. That could explain why Allison looks like she's devising a way to meticulously murder me and stash my body.

"Fine. Since you don't have anything to write about, I'm putting you on proofreading duty. Do you have an *AP Stylebook*?"

I shake my head.

Smack. Allison tosses me a tome that lands on my desk.

Fingerprints smear the glossy front cover. "Thanks," I mumble. Awesome. All I've ever edited was our restaurant menu where the letter *s* mysteriously dropped from plural nouns. I just added them back in if I thought they looked weird.

Finally, Allison's focus shifts to another kid named Ernie, who smells like wintergreen gum even though he never chews gum. He fiddles with his round glasses that are down to his nose. Looking at him makes me feel anxious.

"Ernie, you're two days late with the article on the recycling scandal. Where is it?"

"Mr. Allen hasn't gotten back to me." From what I remember, Mr. Allen, the marine biology teacher, was caught putting trash into his recycling bin—by Allison herself. That's a "scandal," apparently.

Allison sighs. "Did you talk to him?"

"I e-mailed him."

"I want you to chase him, okay?"

"O-okay," he stutters.

"Wait for his class to let out. Show him that I have proof that he broke the rules."

"Hang on, Allison, you saved the contents of a *recycling bin*?" Rowan interjects.

She looks confused. "Yes, why?"

Is she for real?

Rowan starts laughing but he hides it behind a cough. "Good. A journalist always needs to back up their claims." He shakes his sleeve up to show his wristwatch. "Why don't we finish the meeting now and get right into it? Bảo, here's something for you to start proofreading. Try to finish it." He offers me a manila folder, which I get up and take.

Try?

Asshole.

We still have more than a half hour left and Rowan doesn't think I can get through a five-hundred-word article. Oblivious to the insult, he retreats into his office abutting the newsroom.

Allison pushes away a desk with her hip, creating an exit. She pulls aside Luigi, the managing editor, so she can come up with a way to fill what used to be the comics section. Apparently the comics artist showed up to one class, was given an assignment by Allison, and then switched over to graphic design class.

I dive into Allison's article about bullying issues and how our statistics compare to nationwide statistics. She knows how to write, knows when she's said enough, knows when to punch the details. She's good. She quotes Hal, the janitor who's one of the main advocates for stronger anti-bullying policies because he sees it happening all the time in the hallways, and Allison writes him so well that it's like he's right there in the room, leaning against his mop, a watchful eye on bullies.

I only fix a few commas and start a new paragraph when one of them looks too long. At the last sentence, though, I stop. I read the sentence over and over again and it just feels . . . weird to me. I can't put my finger on it, so I let my pen linger there, a red dot bleeding through the page. But still, it's one word. One word won't ruin a piece. And Allison's probably not going to like the fact that I'm questioning—even if it's a small bit—her article.

The hallway bell dismisses us, thankfully. Allison is yelling out the next deadline for articles. When she walks past me, I hand back her article.

"It's really good." Then I'm free, but not really, since I have work.

"Wait."

I turn.

"You're lying." She peers at the paper . . . at the red dot that I left. "You hesitated here. Why?"

It's unnerving to see a girl my age use the same withering glance as my mom.

"I don't know."

"What do you mean, you don't know?" she demands.

Now she's annoying me. I snatch the paper back and stab at the paper. "Maybe cut this word and replace it with an adjective. I just think you need a stronger one. Plus the word is repeated earlier in the article."

A long pause falls between us. I swear I hear the clock ticking. *Did I just say that?* "Thank you," Allison says. She looks like she's trying not to grimace.

I grab my things. My adrenaline's pumping, like I just finished a mile. I feel good—being right about something for once.

I'm the only one left in the room, so I leave . . . before running into someone.

"Sorry!" a girl says.

Linh.

"Uh, no that's fine." My mouth feels numb. I can't find any other words to say because of the way she's looking at me, wide-eyed, indecisive—everything that I'm probably feeling right now.

I do the only thing I can think of:

I run away.

CHAPTER FOUR

LINH

"Hey, what are you doing here?" Ali asks as she leaves room 436 with her backpack. Strands of her hair have escaped her braid, but she hurriedly brushes them aside. I didn't expect to see her because I knew she had study hall; she should be home right now, which makes me jealous even thinking about it. I would have given anything to have a break before going to work. A time where I can just think and not be around people, like I am all day.

"Grabbing paint for Yamamoto," I tell Ali. When I'd gotten to the studio upstairs, she shouted from the back, asking me to drop by the old art room downstairs because she left behind a few things during the move.

Thinking everyone had emptied from the room by now, I walk through the door . . . until I collide with Bảo. His eyes widen.

"Sorry!"

Why do I sound like a squeaky first grader? He's a head taller than me, which shouldn't surprise me—puberty and all—but having always seen him across the street from the restaurant, I never noticed his height.

"Uh, no that's fine." He slips past me, then nearly bolts down the hallway, away from us. Away from me. Which shouldn't bother me so much, since I would probably do the same in his shoes, but it does. I glance at Allison to see if she noticed the weird exchange—she usually does with things like this—but surprisingly, she's watching Bảo, looking like she has something to say.

"I'm not sure I like that kid."

"Bảo?" I spot the canary-yellow paint by the sink and grab it while Allison talks at me.

"Yeah, him. On one hand, he's clearly lazy and doesn't give a shit about journalism. On the other hand, he found a mistake in my article that even *I* missed."

"Oh, wow, he found a *mistake*," I say mockingly. We walk down the hall together, toward the art room. With school letting out at the end of the day, it's chaotic. Elbows and shoulders crash against me, and the smells of Axe, sweat, and sweet Victoria's Secret perfume hit me all at once. Loud rap and pop music float from the earbuds of my classmates. Teachers fast-walk with their heads down and dodge students TikToking random sketches.

"I'm serious! It's been read, like, three times by Rowan. Bảo has a good eye. But I don't think he cares—or knows. Which is annoying."

"His parents own that restaurant across from me, you know." I've told Allison about the feud in general, how it doesn't really make sense and all that, but I've never really mentioned Bảo. Or our time at the temple together. Some things aren't worth mentioning; they sound and feel better as memories locked inside your brain.

"No way! He's *that* Nguyễn? No wonder you guys freaked out." I smile. I knew it; even if she didn't react in the moment, of course she'd catch that. "That's a tragedy. He's kind of cute. And he's taller than you, which is good."

Good? She doesn't explain why. "One minute you say you hate him—"

"Obviously you're not listening. I said I don't *know* if I like him. But I know how to appreciate someone's aesthetics."

"Aesthetics?"

"C'mon. That hair?"

Silently, I agree.

Yamamoto's room is a forest of easels, with white canvases of all sizes, their pictures all works-in-progress. This side of the school gets the best lighting, not only for drawing, but also for feeding the hanging plants by the windows. Yamamoto is closer to the back and sits cross-legged on a stool, yet manages to look completely relaxed. Her nose practically touching the canvas, she dabs whatever she's working on with a wet sponge. She has a streak of forest-green paint on her cheek.

A tattooed Asian wasn't a familiar concept growing up, so meeting someone like her was so cool. She's not posing, either; the tattoos fit her. She can say the word "bullshit" in a classroom without a problem.

"Here you go," I say, handing her the jug.

"Ah, perfect. Canary yellow, just what I need." She sets it down on the ground. "How's my old lair lookin'?"

"Weird to see all the computers there. And the room looks smaller."

"That's what I think too. You know, even though I complained a lot last semester, the move was actually a good thing. Look at all the space!" She opens her arms wide. I laugh because I love it when she smiles. Not that she's so serious in class, even if she has the authority to be. But when it's just us, she acts like an older sister—sans the weird, unnecessary biological facts Evie likes to point out.

She claps her hands together. "Okay. Give it here."

I let her see my homework assignment again. I ended up finishing it after work, at midnight. That's when I usually do my art—with a desk lamp as my only light source and bass-heavy electronica thrumming in my ears. It makes me feel peaceful and zoned in.

"So are you going to the exhibition?"

Left turn.

"Wait, what?"

She sets down my sketchpad and I follow the movement. Suddenly the conversation is turning to me.

"At the museum I mentioned. It'd be good for you. You should really go."

"Um, yeah. I think I will." I bite my lip at the lie.

"Your parents don't know, do they." A statement, not a question.

The flyer that I made floats back into my mind, September thirtieth haunting me. I sigh. "No. I still haven't asked my parents."

Yamamoto knows a bit about my family and what it's like to work at a restaurant, since she's lived some of it. Her mother owned a Japanese fusion restaurant for half of her childhood before retiring. But because her parents were also artists on the side, she can't truly relate to my dilemma.

I lean in on my elbows, listening as she continues with her critique. Yamamoto shares the same language as me. No one else in my life can teach me about light and shadow and how they fall on objects. Ba's unlikely to sit still long enough to watch shadows. He'd only think of it as wasting time. *Ba không có thì giờ!* Which is actually his usual excuse for things he'd rather avoid doing, like fixing something broken at home or running errands for the restaurant. My mom *loves* that.

And the few times I've talked about art class with my mom, there's some words and feelings that I can't translate into Vietnamese. Like, orange is *màu cam*, but then there's also burnt orange and cider orange. Direct translations don't work.

My phone vibrates in my pocket, bursting the bubble ensconcing me and Yamamoto. "Ugh, sorry, I'm late for work."

"Okay, but wait." Yamamoto crosses the room to her desk and removes a packet from her drawer. "I know I've mentioned this before, but I wanted to make sure you don't forget about it."

The Scholastic Awards. Each year, high school students submit their best works in art and writing. There are local awards, then there are national ones called Gold Keys, judged by the best in the business, and the winner gets recognition at Carnegie Hall in New York, and even some scholarships.

"I'm telling you. Keep your eye on this. You have a chance."

"Really?"

Yamamoto smiles. "Absolutely. And, hey, maybe it'll help your parents see the value in what you're doing. They can't say no to money. But first step: Just make sure you check out the exhibition, okay? I know you have a lot of things riding on you, but I don't want you to forget about yourself. About what *you* want. This is *your* year."

"Yeah, sure." Dread sits at the bottom of my stomach, and her heavy gaze on my back pushes me through the door, out into the hallway.

CHAPTER FIVE

BẢO

"*Con ăn như mèo*," Mẹ says. According to her, I'm eating like a cat right now. I look down at the meal before me: a nearly finished *bánh xèo* in a bowl, floating in *nước mắm*—my fifth serving in twenty minutes. Other times, Mẹ accuses me of eating too much like Ba.

Three hours ago, my parents were in the kitchen checking on their Powerball numbers, their concentration resembling scientists working toward a breakthrough cure. After each ticket failed to yield winning numbers, they placed it in a pile that goes into the "everything drawer" in their bedroom. *Everything*'s there: keys with no locks to fit them in; nail clippers; prescribed medicine for their high cholesterol (which they trade sometimes, and I'm pretty sure they're not supposed to do that); and pictures of me at various ages. Mẹ had glanced through the kitchen screen door. "Oh look, it's raining." She nodded to herself. "A good day to have *bánh xèo*."

"Ah," Ba said in agreement, before striking out another losing ticket.

And here we are.

Why does *bánh xèo* taste good when it rains? Every time I ask my parents they always start to explain—"*Tại vì . . .*"—and then something else grabs their attention. I've come up with my own explanation. I'm not sure there's a scientific reason, but I do know that *bánh xèo* tastes like a good fire when the outside pavement is wet, the air ripe with earth and cement. I found a word for that smell: "petrichor." In this kind of weather, nothing tastes better than rice flour, made yellow by turmeric powder, cooked crisp, packed with chewy pork belly, shrimp, bean sprouts, in one megabite.

Thinking that we need another batch, Mẹ disappears outside in her raincoat, fishing out another piece. She noisily slides the screen door open, returning with a giddy smile. A perfectly cooked *bánh xèo* sizzles on the plate. My body a half hour ago would have been like, *Oh* yes. She gestures for our bowls, filled with salty *nước mắm*, and lets those babies sink in.

Ba gestures for it, chewing on his piece, as if to say, *Lay it on me, woman.*

"How is school going? College applications?" Mẹ asks.

Nonexistent, my brain answers, but I say, "Good."

We'd done our road-tripping last year, visiting mostly state schools so that it's cheaper. My scores might be able to get me into some of them, though there aren't any guarantees. At least my parents know that.

"Just make sure your grades are steady and you don't go under."

"Sure."

Mẹ lets out another sigh.

"Con, do you have any idea what you want to do? What major yet?"

"Mẹ, that's, like, a year away."

"But isn't it better to know now?"

"Plenty of students go into college undecided. It's perfectly normal."

"Dì Nhi"—the General—"said her son knew right away that he wanted to do premed before going to Stanford."

"Premed's not a major, though."

"I know! But what I mean is, he knew what he wanted to do."

I shift when I realize I'm sitting exactly like my mom, one leg bent on the chair. I stretch out both legs and cross my arms. But then I notice that's how Ba sits.

"A year will come quickly," my mom continues.

"I'm thinking of a lot of things." Strangely, today's journalism class pops into my mind. The feeling of my grip around my pen, seeing the changes I made on the page, the moment I made Allison shut up for once. I haven't felt this way before.

"Thinking is not the same as doing!" She leans back and turns to Ba. "Anh, tell him."

"Ừ," he says in agreement. My mom stares at him reproachfully, probably hoping he'll say something more inspiring.

She gives a long-suffering sigh. "Mẹ wonder what Việt is planning to major in."

Given his attention to criminal TV shows and his near-obsession with getting into forensic science class, I'd figured that was his intention. But he hasn't really said anything, even though it shouldn't be an issue with him. The kid doesn't study and has probably never studied, because his pores just absorb all the knowledge on a page. "I don't know. Ask him next time you see him."

"Việt is so smart." My mom nods in approval.

"Brilliant," Ba agrees.

"His parents must be so proud."

Not for the first time, I wonder if my parents would be happier to have him as a son. Their eyes are practically glazed over at the mention of him.

Annoyed, I say, "Maybe you can adopt him, then."

"Con," my mother says, her voice turning sweet in a way that bugs me. Pleading, almost. "We just think you can do anything. And you have to *cố gắng*." She pauses to inhale.

Here we go.

"You know, con, when we die—"

"Mẹ—" I plead.

"When we die—"

"In, like, fifty years!"

Mẹ talks louder. "Ba Mẹ just want con to be able to support yourself. But that means trying." She gestures to her and Ba, who nods like he's confirming, *Yes, I will die, son.* "Con don't know how lucky you are. When Mẹ arrived in this country back in 1982, Mẹ was three years younger than you. Only *mười bốn tuổi*! *Không biết* what was going to happen. But Mẹ learned. Mẹ adapted. Same with Ba. We trusted our education and we only want you to do the same."

I duck my head, eating the last bit of *bánh xèo*, and feeling like the biggest asshole. But low blow, using her escape story. I can't really say anything in response to that. How can I, when she mentioned everything she'd lost? Her home, plenty of relatives—including her older brother, who attempted escape before her, but died during the passage.

In rare moments, she would say that I look like him, like Cậu Cam. We have the same hair, she says. I can tell how much it hurts her to mention him because she either goes silent or quickly moves on to mention something else. I never know what to say when that happens.

Before my mom goes on to talk about her night of the escape— the last recitation having been one hour and forty minutes long—I relent with an "Okay. Okay. I promise I'll focus." I breathe in. "I'll do better."

Mẹ brightens and shares a look with Ba, her guilt trip a success. It's like I solved all her worries—past, present, and future. "You can be anything!"

"Maybe a doctor," my dad offers, finally edging a word in.

. . . *with the most malpractice lawsuits*, I finish as I carry my plates to the sink.

My mom starts clearing away the other dishes, and she's already on to the next task on her list, a nonstop machine. She asks me if I want to take anything to school tomorrow. *No? Why? It wasn't good enough?* I relent and tell her maybe a few pieces of *bánh xèo*, sans fish sauce. Turning to my dad, who's still digging away at his teeth with a *tăm*, she reminds him that they'll need to wake at five in the morning to receive Việt's parents' delivery, so the alarm needs to be set. Ba tells her to stop reminding him: *Bà nói điếc lỗ tai.* Which only means she'll continue to pester him to purposefully get on his nerves. Her type of revenge.

I leave them, the thoughts about my promise to them—*to do better*—running rampant in my mind.

CHAPTER SIX

LINH

One of my earliest memories of learning Vietnamese at home and at the temple with other kids has to do with a traditional folk poem. If I close my eyes, I'm back in that basement room, surrounded by our teacher's singsong voice, loud over the overhead ceiling fans fighting off a July heat: *Công cha như núi Thái Sơn / Nghĩa mẹ như nước trong nguồn chảy ra . . .*

I was more enthralled by the image that went with the folk poem: a towering, majestic mountain wrapped inside a delicate fog. Father. A pool of glistening water gushing from the same mountain. Mother. The next lines talked of honoring their labor and love; the lesson was clear enough: Everything I do is in their reflection.

Now alone in my bedroom, I lie flat on my back, staring at the ceiling fan turning at the slowest speed possible no matter how far right I turn the knob. I thought the room would feel more spacious since I wasn't sharing with Evie anymore, as I've done for sixteen years. That I can decorate however I want, make it however messy I want. But my body became used to another person in the room, and any desire to rearrange things is forgotten.

Anyone walking in would see two distinct personalities—one wall immaculately decorated with cute thrift-shop finds—Evie can sniff out discounts like no one else's business. My side, while it might be just as clean, holds years of my artwork, no rhyme or reason to the colors, from drawings showing my childhood obsession with goats and llamas, to my more recent work.

On my Picasso desk calendar, I marked the thirtieth but somehow didn't mark Phở Day. I trace it with my finger—it's not the end of the world if I don't go. I know that. But am I giving something up? Missing out?

I sit up quickly and my vision spins. Sometimes when I think too much, I make myself sadder, which doesn't help at all. I find refuge in art, escaping thoughts like this, to regain control when life throws another obstacle my way. When I work, magic happens; for a few hours at a time, the world just slips away. I don't have to listen to customers comparing me to Evie. Any worries about upcoming tests or working a shift at the restaurant—that all takes second place in my mind. My attention fixates on an image or an idea that doesn't exist just yet, and can't exist without me.

I first saw art in action when my family and I took a trip to

Huntington Beach. We were walking along the boardwalk; I was still young, because I remember holding my mom's hand when *it* happened. A small crowd had formed, a sketch artist ensconced inside, his canvas before him. His muse, a little boy, sat in a chair, feet dangling. The boy tried and failed to look serious as the artist captured his likeness on the canvas. He kept grinning at his parents. It was only five bucks for a portrait, yet the artist treated him like the most important being in the world.

I stayed there the entire time, counting the artist's deliberate strokes. My mom waited alongside me, half interested and half ready to move. We would have if only we hadn't reached the end of the boardwalk.

The artist's still there these days, though his hands look more shriveled and sun-spotted than they did over a decade ago.

I breathe out, letting go of my memories, replacing my thoughts with a nicer reality: *Maybe no one will show up and I won't need to work that night. Maybe my parents will be in such a good mood that they'll let me go.* Their moods are always good indicators of whether or not I can do anything. *This is your year*, Yamamoto's voice says in my head.

I'm choosing to believe that can be true.

Our home has only one floor, with a long hallway connected to each room. I pad lightly across the tiled floor to the opposite end, where Mẹ and Ba's room sits.

At the door, I hear only whispers. I'm seven again, eavesdropping on my parents like I used to with Evie. Evie would be right across from me, mouthing, *What are they saying?* because she was never the stealthy type, didn't have good hearing, and completely sucked at reading lips. Through the slit of the door, I see my father lying prone, shirt off. In the morning, he's usually half naked, baring his stomach, and wakes up before everyone else, then shuffles through each room, lifting up all the window blinds.

Mẹ stands next to the bed, a tube of Bengay in plastic-gloved hands. She scolds him in Vietnamese. I lean back against the wall, out of view.

"You should have let someone else carry it. You're not young anymore, Anh."

"Hmm? One of our cooks? They can barely lift anything. I'm the only one who lifts things back there."

"The only one," Mẹ repeats sarcastically. "Are you sure?"

Ba, ever the stubborn one, answers, "Yes." He hisses as she slathers Bengay on his back. She then tells him calmly that if he keeps complaining, she'll actually break his back. I hide a smile even if I don't have to. Ba stems his protests and Mẹ takes off her gloves. I hear her go into the bathroom, the creak of the mirror as she puts back the Bengay.

"Will we need to hire someone for the day?" Her voice echoes. "I can ask Duy-Loan's cousin to work."

He doesn't answer right away, as if he's waiting for her words to subside. "We have Linh."

He says my name like I'm the solution. A flash of anger courses through me. Why do I always have to be the solution?

"You know we can't afford more people," Ba continues. "I think it will be fine. I can still help."

Wait. What does he mean?

"If you say so."

They haven't told me about any financial problems. My stomach drops as I remember how anxious my mom looked yesterday, the hope in her voice that the special will work. Of course. But then I remember they wouldn't have told me something like this. They don't want me to worry about things that *they're* supposed to be worried about. Typical.

Later, sitting down for dinner at the kitchen table, I smell the Bengay, but Ba doesn't complain, only winces as he slowly sits down at the head of the table. I slide over our bowls, which Mẹ just filled with rice—mine full to the brim, while hers is half. She eats the side dishes more than the rice.

"*Mời Ba ăn cơm. Mời Mẹ ăn cơm,*" I say before we start eating.

We don't immediately talk, each of us lost in our thoughts. Our chopsticks ding the sides of our bowls. The waves of steam from the *canh chua* rise up, swirled away by the ceiling fan. It's one of my favorite dishes—sour soup, but not the kind sold in Asian restaurants. It's made sweet from pineapple chunks, and balanced out with simmering tomatoes and tamarind. Mẹ asks if I want more catfish. I shake my head.

I swallow a clump of rice and muster as much eagerness into my voice as I can. "Phở Day will be fun."

By Saturday, Ba's back problems are worse, and now he can barely move. Mẹ and I leave around noon to start prepping for the rush, but before we do, Mẹ reminds Ba not to do anything too strenuous.

Ba lies across the living room couch, TV remote in hand, which is his preferred state whenever he has time off, but he wants to work tonight. As much pain as he's in, he's still thinking about the restaurant.

Mom's having none of it.

He continues his protest in Vietnamese. "No, you need me tonight. Who's working the stand?"

"Lisa."

Ba snorts. "Lisa! She doesn't know how to do anything!" Lisa's been working for us for three weeks, a replacement for the outgoing seniors.

Mẹ answers, "Ba say that about her all the time. And Jonathan—"

"Everyone, basically," I mumble. "And you're the one who hired them."

Ba just glares. He lies back down, staring at the ceiling.

"But what if something goes wrong?"

My entire morning was spent alone in my room, preparing myself for tonight's rush. I was so tense that I couldn't concentrate, couldn't even sketch in my note pad or pick up a brush. Ba complaining throughout the house didn't help things.

Yet now, I hear the genuine worry in his voice, the worry that everything he had masterminded would undo itself.

Mẹ pats his head as she passes by, keys in hand. *"Đừng lo."*

The simple truth is that he can't get up; all three of us know this. He falls silent. Or more accurately, Mẹ silences him by shutting out any response with the front door.

◇ ◇ ◇

One thing that people forget when they're yelling at waiters or complaining about meal prices is the realities of how much prep goes into the menu. It's hours. I learned that the hard way when I was young, hanging out in the kitchen, waiting for Mẹ to be done because she said she was "only doing prep." *Only doing.* No. That meant watching the outside go from incandescent yellow to midnight blue with specks of white from the street lamps. But it was fun back then. I always had my crayons with me. The waiters and line cooks took their turns watching after me or cooking up something sweet—caramelized plantains sort of became my drug. Evie took it upon herself to refill all of the hoisin bottles.

Now in the kitchen, my mom has two large pots cooking on the stovetop, all containing the broth for tonight. Four small pots sit on the prep table, ready to be reheated once the orders come through. Mẹ strides with purpose in the kitchen while the other line cooks chop green onions, limes, and jalapeño peppers, and wash bean sprouts and Thai basil that makes the anise in the phở broth pop even more. It's all a rhythm; they follow the beat set by Mẹ because they've done this for forever. She's the most methodical in the kitchen, though whatever method she uses here can't be replicated or measured. It's instinctive. My art and her cooking are kind of the same, when I think about it. Our hands move before our brains. But I never say this out loud, because the retort would be: "But will it support you?"

"How's everyone on the outside?" she asks when she notices me watching by the door.

I double-knot my apron strings, then sweep my hair into a

high ponytail. "Good. Everything's in place." Servers are setting out the soup spoons, chopsticks, and sauces.

Mẹ wipes her forehead with the back of her gloved hands. "Good," she repeats. I wonder if she's trying to make herself feel better about tonight. Like I am.

The first wave of customers are young college students. Lisa greets them, clumsily grabbing the menus. I hope she can pull it together before the real challenge begins.

Within a half hour, our tables are booked and a line has formed, a sight that would make Ba giddy—as giddy as he can get, at least. Instead, my body pings with a sense of foreboding. As I move to table six with plates of egg rolls, a chatty group of three passes by, Jonathan leading the way. He mouths, *Help!* before plastering on a fake smile to the group, who seat themselves at table eight—which I'm sure is reserved.

I make a beeline toward the booth and sort through the table management system. I'm right. Lisa comes back from seating another group, playing with her hands. She does this when she's nervous. "Lisa, did you check the system just now?"

"Why?"

"Table eight. Someone had a reservation and we were going to seat them there."

Lisa glances down and blanches. "I'm *so* sorry, I didn't see it!"

I tamp down my instinct to shout, like Ba would. "Just find a way to fix it." I turn sharply and control my breathing. It's not my usual job to greet the guests, only serve them. Lisa will need to do it.

Passing by table four, I see a little kid, age six or seven, reach for a bottle of hoisin while his mother chats with a friend. I summon the Mai and Phạm women's stare—*Mày đang làm gì?*—and the kid retracts his hand. As he should.

The sound of pots and pans from the kitchen grates on my nerves, threatening to send a headache my way. But there's nothing I can do to stop it, so I hand in my orders, then circle back to the stand to make sure Lisa hasn't messed up again—I can't help it.

If possible, the line outside has gotten longer. More college students. Families. Couples. They stare back at me as I pop my head out, a sea of eyes reminding me of a surrealist painting.

"Uh, excuse me, miss," a guy wearing cargo shorts asks. He's third in line. "How long will it be until we're seated?"

"About a half hour."

"Half hour, whoa." He sends a look to his friend who stands behind him.

I tamp down my annoyance as best I can. "As you can see, it's quite busy now."

"This is ridiculous," he mutters to his friend.

"We apologize for the wait, but there's nothing more we can do."

"What's taking so long?"

The. Nerve.

"Hey! We're having a special! So of course there will be a line!" I snap. The guy reels back for a second, rendered speechless. He's too shocked to be angry. Before a mortified apology can slip past my lips, Lisa sidles up to my side, taking control of things. She shoots me a concerned look and says a few things that I can't make out. The fact that Lisa needs to save me pisses me off even more.

I stalk back to the kitchen. Pine for the art exhibition. I pretend I'm there right now—me with other patrons. Whenever I'm at a museum, seeing the work of geniuses before me, I imagine a cloud of quiet reverence settling over me. In the room, there's a bunch of people looking to art for answers, who examine pieces just to *feel* something.

One day, I want to be that artist who sees this, who knows that what she created made them feel completely content, filling a void they didn't know they were seeking.

I want to be there . . .

. . . but I'm here. The ticket machine pushing out food orders at crank speed yanks me back into my reality. Its chirping will stay in my nightmares forever. From the dining room, Vietnamese, English, Spanish, and other languages and laughter swell up, crashing into me like a tsunami wave. The back room now feels like a sauna.

"Con?"

My mom pops her head out when she realizes no one's picked up the three bowls of phở she just placed at the window.

"I just need some air," I say.

"But—"

"Just one minute!" I say. Using my whole body, I push through the back door, my mom's question chasing after me.

I duck into the alley. I don't care that it smells like fish and sewage or that the ground might be dirty; it's the best sanctuary I can find in the moment. I slide down, bring my legs to my chest, and rest my forehead on my knees. *Breathe, Linh. Breathe.*

I'm not sure how long I sit there. At least I'm alone. At least no one's here to see me fall apart like Jenga pieces.

"Um, hey."

I peer down at the scuffed edges of red Converse.

Oh no.

CHAPTER SEVEN

BẢO

It's always hard to work when your best friend is summarizing a rerun episode of *Law & Order: SVU.* Even when we're not in the same area, Việt's shouting across the room.

"You always know it's the good-looking celebrity guy who's the perp." He uses the term like he's a well-seasoned cop.

"Uh-huh."

"I just wish that for *one* episode, the perp would be the ugly one. You know?"

"Yeah."

"I mean, the *moment* John Stamos came on screen, I was like—*hello*, it's him. The bad guy."

We're running through our checklist of things to do at closing at ten, only a few minutes away. Cold items in the fridge. Cutting boards washed down, then turned over. Each bottle of hoisin and sriracha sauce filled. Eduardo, one of the line cooks, fist-bumps me on his way out. He's usually the last one to go and first to show up every morning, on the dot. He sends me a rictus of pity, having been on the receiving end of Việt's recap before.

Việt has his quirks—his obsession with all the weirdest police procedural or forensic science shows and his near-perfect ability to quote the dialogue from them—but I can't imagine Việt without them. He's been in my life for that long. His parents and mine would get together at the restaurant—mostly after the shift ended, or when Việt's parents were done delivering supplies to various restaurants—to unwind or rant about other store owners in the area. Heineken would come in at some point. While the adults talked, we'd sit underneath the tables trading imaginary stories—playing cops and robbers—sharing toys with each other. Sometimes we didn't even need to talk.

I thought him joining the cross-country team in freshman year would be the end of Việt and Bảo. That he would find more coordinated friends who didn't wheeze after running a quarter of a mile. But I was still his best friend.

And as Việt launches into another recap, I think: *For better or for worse.*

The night passed easily, the two of us having already established a rhythm with the other servers. Mẹ had put a line cook's mom, Trần's, in charge of the kitchen so she didn't have to come in. It's different with the server situation, though. She's pairing me up with Việt

55

because we know each other and make decent partners. She trusts Việt to do his job, as well as make sure I do mine. The concept's not perfect: We're the same age, and letting him watch over me makes as much sense as letting a horse and a pony run the show. But somehow it works.

Trần's mom leaves before us. I make sure the front is locked from the inside. As I'm closing the blinds, I see Linh's place is packed with customers at ten. Just for today, for that special, it's staying open for two more hours. A line wraps around the corner. Something that I'm sure our place has never seen before. I'm glad Mẹ is home tonight or else she'd come and just sit here and spy on people coming and going, scaring not only their customers but our own.

Việt joins me to peer through the blinds. "What people do for specials." He shakes his head. "We gotta one-up them, man."

"How?"

"Put something special on the menu."

"What else should we make?"

Việt shrugs. "Mom's always telling me your mom makes the best *bánh xèo*—why not work with that? Like an anything-you-want-in-your-crepe kind of deal. I mean, my mom has talked multiple times of poisoning her to get the recipe. Which could be effective, if you think about it, since your mom needs to taste a lot of things in the kitchen."

I glance over at my best friend. His mom's known for being hawk-eyed and competitive. She didn't get to be one of the most sought-after suppliers by doing any favors. But poison?

Việt backtracks. "But she won't—you know, poison her. It was a joke."

I can't ever imagine his mother—or his father—joking.

"That's appreciated," I reply dryly. I almost drop my blinds. Then a blur bursts from the back door.

Linh. She escapes into the alley. "What the hell?" The customers waiting in line watch her go before facing frontward again—shrugging or just shaking their heads. I glance back at Việt, who'd already gone back to the kitchen. He notices no one had thought to restock the fridge with beverages yet.

"That was probably Trần's fault," I say, still distracted.

That alley's one-way. Where could she possibly go? And why was she running?

"Of course," Việt scoffs, the sound distant, before reemerging with a carton of Arrowhead and kicking along another one half full of different sodas. He crouches down to start filling up the fridge's compartments. My attention alternates between him and the alley. "You gonna make me do all the work here?"

Linh's been out there for a while now. Three minutes?

I've never worked so fast. We recycle the leftover boxes, turn off the lights, then go outside to lock up. As Việt pulls down the doors over the storefront, I turn toward the alley, imagining Linh there, no one knowing where she'd gone. What made her run away?

An unnamable feeling washes over me—similar to when I was looking at Ali's article, knowing, *just knowing*, there was a piece that did not fit. I'd tried to pass it over without fixing it, until Ali confronted me, forcing it out of me.

This time, though, maybe I can fix what's wrong . . . whatever that is.

Right on the dot, I get the ten o'clock text from Ba—but really from Mẹ—asking if I was finally on my way home. My thumbs hover over the keypad, my vertical bar blinking slowly.

"Take the long route home," I tell Việt.

"Uh, why?"

"Because I'm going to need to buy some more time, and I don't want my mom wondering why I'm late getting home."

"Why are you going to be late?"

"I can't really say." Because even I don't know what I'm going to do.

Việt regards me in silence and I imagine that he gets the intensity of his stare from his mother. He's not going to do it. He's going to ask why and what I'm doing, and Linh's never going to get out of that alley.

"Tell her you stopped by my house to get a copy of a homework assignment. I'll cover for you."

I blink. "Really?"

"Yeah." He shrugs. I've never been more thankful for his laissez-faire attitude. "But you're gonna have to tell me later what's up."

With a small wave, he's off. I quickly type out my excuse to Ba, who answers with a simple "Okay." And I know it's really Ba, because his answers are always short and right to the point.

Just before I hit the opposite street, I think about turning around again. *What am I doing? Maybe this is a bad idea to come over here.* It feels like I've just walked past enemy lines and might step on a mine.

But now a few feet away from the alley, I hear her whispering, "Keep it together, Linh! It's not the end of the world." She's crouching, breathing deeply, forehead to her knees.

I clear my throat when I'm in front of her. "Um, hey. Are you okay?"

"Um, yeah." She sounds like she's about to cry. I shuffle my feet.

"I didn't mean to bother you. I'm Bảo, from across the street. I don't know if you remember me, but we met that one time—" I stop. It was ages ago; she wouldn't remember. I was just a blip in her childhood. . . .

"I remember you," she says slowly, blinking a few times. The question of why I'm here sits heavy between us.

"Rough night?" I ask, my voice catching slightly. Why do I sound like that guy in about every romantic comedy? Next thing I'm going to ask is *Wanna talk about it*? "I mean, it seems like things are busy over here."

Linh sighs. "It's just hectic in there. My dad hurt his back, so we're short one person. I couldn't breathe for a moment, and totally just ran out on the customers." She adds, almost to herself, "I feel so useless right now." She sounds miserable. I don't have to know her to know that.

I crouch down to her level. Linh inches away instinctively, but she doesn't leave. I try to find the right words to help her, to make her feel better, but who am I to do that? I'm mostly a stranger to her. Before I can get a word out, Linh inhales deeply.

"Never mind." She furiously wipes away her tears. "I'll have to go back inside."

Back when we were kids at the temple, I could have gone to any other table, sat with any other kid. Instead, I ended up with her. I wonder if it wasn't just the crafts that drew me in, and if it was also her, Linh Mai, in the zone, in her natural habitat. So sure of herself, while other kids were only fooling around and passing time.

This isn't the Linh I remember.

I look at the alleyway door, imagining that it would lead us into a kitchen. I assume her mother is in the kitchen, cooking, delegating tasks to the other cooks—just like mine would. That's her domain and unless an issue manifests, she usually stays there during serving time. Linh's mom wouldn't have a reason to go up front. A plan starts to form in my head. An impossible one that I hesitate to even voice. "I can help?" I clear my throat. "I mean, I can help you. You know, with customers and stuff. Just for tonight."

"But your restaurant—"

"Closed a few minutes ago."

"I don't know if my mom—" She pauses, though I know what she's suggesting. "I just don't know."

"It's a win-win. I won't need to be trained," I try to joke.

She cracks a smile, but it disappears. "If my mom or my dad were hearing this, they'd think you're just trying to spy on us."

That type of thinking echoes what my mom would say. It's the same kind of gossip that's passed around by my mom, the General, and her Vietnamese watch group. The truth of it pierces the bubble enveloping us; the noise from inside the restaurant intrudes.

I'm instigating some sort of plan that Linh clearly doesn't want to take part in. I shouldn't have even come. Annoyance runs through me—at Linh for bringing up this confusing feud when I was only trying to help; at me for thoughtlessly running into this whole situation that had nothing to do with me—for reasons

I'm not capable of understanding right now. I should just go back, return to our separate stories as background characters in each other's small worlds.

"I'm not trying to spy. And I'm not my mom *or* my dad. I'm just . . . Bảo." I back away, shoving my hands in my pockets. "You know what, it's okay. Sorry for bothering you and for butting in. Good luck."

Tomorrow, when Việt asks where I'd gone, I'll make up a shitty excuse.

Tomorrow, everything will be back to normal, this encounter between us erased from our minds.

"Bảo, wait." I pivot at my name. "Are you really serious? About helping me?"

The despondence already clouding my mind eases just slightly. She still sounds distrustful, but there's a note in her voice pulling me back. I retrace my steps, standing in front of her just like before, and I offer my hand—my sweaty hand. "Tonight I'm Bảo Nguyễn, some guy just trying to help out on what's clearly a stressful night."

She stares at my hand, shaking her head slightly, realizing how ridiculous it is for me to do this in some alley. Still, her hand, showing traces of washed-out paint, accepts mine—and releases.

Linh wipes her hand on her jeans.

Great.

"What's the plan?" she asks.

"I can serve in the dining area. Your mom's probably cooking in the back, right? She won't even see me. And the waiters—" I stop. *Shit. I haven't thought of that.* At our restaurant, Bình and the others have suffered hours of my mom's rants—about them, about customers, and especially about the Mais. They've been indoctrinated. So it's likely that Linh's fellow servers have gone through the same thing. They *could* recognize me.

"We have new waiters," she adds quietly. "Which might work in our favor."

She looks away for a second. Then she pulls back her hair. I'm shocked by how long it is as she hurriedly ties it all up, not caring that some strands have escaped. As the moonlight hits her, as I see the tightness of her jaw set in determination, the fierceness in her eyes that makes me breathless for a second, I realize—

The Linh from the temple is here.

She draws back her shoulders, looking like she's ready for battle. Which I guess is accurate. "Okay, let's do this."

We're doing it. We're really doing this.

Please work out, I think, as I follow Linh inside.

The smell of phở is ubiquitous. If I close my eyes, I'm back inside my family's restaurant. We're in a narrow hallway where employees store their bags and jackets. To the right is the kitchen, bustling with the clang of pots and pans, water running, shouts from the line cooks. Linh gestures for me to crouch as we get to the serving window. A woman's voice calls her name.

Without warning, Linh shoves me back and I backpedal into the alley.

"Jesus," I mutter as I regain my footing. Is everyone stronger than me? I need to work out.

"*Dạ*, Mẹ! I'm good. Sorry, things were just . . ." The door cuts me off.

A pause. For one frightening moment, I imagine her mom emerging from the kitchen, kicking the door open—as my mom would do—and seeing me, recognizing me on sight.

Brandishing a pair of chopsticks.

I know what Vietnamese mothers are capable of doing with chopsticks. And my butt cheeks definitely remember '10 when I drank ginger ale for dessert without asking Mẹ and Ba first.

A few seconds later, Linh pulls me back in by the hand. "Sorry," she whispers. I nod numbly, my mind suddenly still, feeling her hand in mine again. She looks down, then snatches her hand away.

Trying to push past the awkwardness, I say, "I'm ready. Just tell me what needs to be done."

"Follow me. Act normal."

I crouch-walk past the window again. The moment I walk into the dining room, I regret every step that I'd taken to get here. Though the front-of-house staff might not recognize me as the enemy's son, they're going to notice a new guy miraculously starting on the job when they needed the help the most.

But I'm wrong. They're busy with their tables; one guy shoots past us, muttering that he'd forgotten the drinks. Linh brings me to the reservation system to teach me the layout. We use the same system, I realize, and my mind zones in, keyed to the language we've grown up with just a street apart from each other. It's not as hard as I thought it would be, the restaurant practically being a mirror of ours.

Unbidden, Linh's earlier insinuation and my mom's accusing

voice come through: *They spied on us to learn our ways!*

I shake away that thought. Not helping. Unlike our restaurant, though, whose walls and floors have seen better days, this one has a grand statement wall with mirrors and art that might have been done by Linh. I feel a flicker of jealousy before Linh pulls me back to reality.

"I'll stick around in the back of the room to keep an eye on the food coming out. Just look for me—if you don't see me, I'm at the window and will probably need to get dishes out. But if you hear the bell and I'm not there to grab whatever's ready, just come find me."

"Got it."

"Linh?"

I freeze, not turning for a second. A girl our age steps in front of the stand. She's wringing her hands, eyes beseeching Linh. "I'm so sorry about earlier. I should have remembered to check the reservation, but now everything's fine, I think."

"It's fine. Mistakes happen, but thanks for fixing it, Lisa," Linh answers quickly, already grabbing my arm, but the movement catches Lisa's eyes.

"Wait—have you been working this whole time?" Lisa asks, more curious than suspicious.

"Yes, I was . . . prepping in the back." I glance at Linh, who gives me the barest of nods. "But her mom noticed things were getting hectic, so I'm just jumping in."

"Oh, thank God." The girl smiles like I just saved her life.

A customer steps up to ask for a table, allowing me and Linh to escape.

"Nice!" she whispers. I hold back a smile as she points me to table four by the statement wall, a couple looking to order dessert.

Working at a restaurant over the years, the customers themselves become a pattern, types with issues and demands you learn to manage. I always spot the let's-do-something-different-tonight crowd—the moms who think they're being adventurous by deviating from ladies' night at Olive Garden. They're always asking for our opinion: What's the crowd favorite? What do *you* suggest? What's the most *authentic*? Ignorance is the same no matter where you eat. When I do bother to give answers, they don't even take my suggestions.

There are assholes who come in as a party of eight and expect to be seated within five minutes; Vietnamese women dressed up way too fancy for this type of restaurant, like Bà An who comes on Tuesdays—*"Bà ngu,"* my mom spits out whenever she comes in—and people who didn't learn how to use chopsticks at a pliable age, but make a valiant effort, only to search helplessly for a server so they can flag down forks and spoons.

Then, there are customers who don't even need to order; they walk right in—or at least shuffle in—a tide of gray and salt-and-pepper heads, and my parents know immediately what they need. Most of the time, these people and my parents go way back, some even from the refugee days. It's all easier for us; they're the least fussy of the customers.

Tonight, I'm not spotting any here, maybe because they'd know to avoid this huge crowd.

If I have an order in there, Linh slides it down to me to grab. I'm an hour in and I swing to the back to get my next order. Linh's there, elbows on the order table, speaking to someone in the window. She spots me and her eyes widen, which tells me to hide, and I step back into the eating area, out of view.

". . . another order of *gỏi cuốn*?"

"Yeah, third order for the same table."

"Third!" Her mom sounds delighted. She addresses one of the cooks, joking, "What did we put in there? We're doing good, yes?"

"We're doing awesome, Mẹ!" Linh answers, catching my eye again.

She smiles briefly before bringing her order to the table.

In my section, I field questions about the menu, but that's no big deal since we sell similar food items. Customers ask me how many shakes we sell, and of course that's five—

Wait, the Mais have six?

"Excuse me, can I get another order of *chả giò*?"

"Sure, let me just—"

Oh shit.

"Frank," I breathe.

Frank's five years older than me. His mom used to work at the nail salon on the same strip as us and we'd suffered through hours of their lunchtime gossip by playing games on his Nintendo DS, which I'd never owned. But they'd moved somewhere else and I hadn't seen Frank in years.

We're at a standstill, lost for excuses as to why we're both in a competitor's restaurant. We start speaking over each other.

"I'm just helping out a friend—"

"Don't tell your mom I—"

"But it's no big—"

"I just wanted some *chả giò*!"

We blink at each other.

My shoulders relax when I see Frank looking sheepish. His group of friends watch the exchange, amused. "Look, I know your mom would have my ass if she knew I was here. Well, first my mom would. And I'm not sure what *you're* doing here, but I won't tell if you won't."

In any other situation, I'd laugh at the idea that a grown-ass man is still terrified of getting in trouble with two Vietnamese mothers. But now's not the time. "Deal," I say.

"Thank God. I've been craving these egg rolls. They're the best in the area—er, I mean, no offense to your mom."

Good decision.

Apparently Linh was watching us, and as soon as we pass each other, she leans in, a hand on my elbow. "Everything okay?" This is the third time she's touching me, and I'm finding that I don't mind at all. I was lucky and partly thankful that my mom has the skills to intimidate people even if they don't live in the area anymore.

"I think so."

Time passes quickly. Customers have finished and left at a steady pace, allowing the line to grow shorter and shorter. The deal has probably given the place a profit. I remember my mom's snide comments about the Mais' phở, how it's all too bland, but from the smiles on the customers' faces as they leave, I'm sure that's not the case.

We have five tickets left at this point. The restaurant closes soon, at midnight, and my time here will end. Maybe we'll never see each other again after tonight. Maybe this will just be a fluke incident. But I don't think anyone can deny that we made a good team.

From across the room, over a sea of heads and laughter, I catch Linh's eye.

We got this.

I sneak out once the servers have said goodbye to the last customers. Linh gestures that she will follow in a few minutes. I wait by the alley while cleanup happens. The back door opens now and again as some of the bus boys dump the trash or empty boxes. They see me, but just nod indifferently, not caring that some weird guy is just waiting there in near-darkness.

Linh appears at the alley's opening having gone through the front. She's carrying her messenger bag. "My mom's just cleaning up a few things. You're safe."

Out by the curb, some feet to the right of the restaurant's facade, we wordlessly sit down. I watch her shoulders move as she breathes, until I realize I've timed my breathing with hers.

She speaks first. "Tonight was . . ."

She trails off, a smile playing on her lips. My brain has gone to mush. More strands have fallen out of her ponytail and I get the urge to move them out of her face, behind her ear. They shine, like the hair of a violin bow just polished.

My hand rises of its own accord. Linh freezes; her body stills, then my brain yells, *WHAT ARE YOU DOING?* And my hand goes off course and before I realize it . . .

I pat her shoulder.

CHAPTER EIGHT

LINH

Did he just pat my shoulder?

CHAPTER NINE

BẢO

"We were awesome today!" I say with more enthusiasm than I have in that moment. I look down at my knees, my face burning. And I'm pretty sure I'm sitting on gum. After not hearing anything for a few seconds, I risk a glance at Linh—and feel light-headed when I see her smiling. We lose it, our laughs echoing down the street, vibrating with the other late-night sounds. Ecstasy.

CHAPTER TEN

LINH

Okay, so that pat on the shoulder was weird, but I forget it soon enough.

"That was intense!"

Bảo laughs, a deep, husky kind of laugh—God, what a nice sound.

"I thought I was finished when your mom called you—"

"And Lisa came by—"

"Then that guy Frank who I did *not* expect to see there at all!"

We're like little kids full of sugar. Or like the kids we were back at temple. This time we didn't get caught. "Never thought that would work," I say after calming down. The smell of rain is faint in the air. Couples stroll past us, their shoes squeaking. Cars crawl by. "But we did an awesome job." I register the parts of us that are touching—our thighs and shoulders.

I'd shut down his offer before and watched him close up and turn his back on me. Waves of regret overcome me, not only because of what I said about him spying on us, but because I was ashamed that he was only trying to reach out to help and I denied him. He didn't have to check on me. He could have gone home just like every other week. But he didn't turn *his* back on *me*.

I sneak a look at him now. Bảo stares the opposite way, resting his forearms on his knees. He's, well, *hot*. He doesn't have a bowl cut anymore. There's quietness to him as well, reminding me of my mom when she's concentrating on a new recipe—the opposite of the energy around Ba or Ali. I shift, discomfited by these unexpected emotions warring inside me. We don't know each other. *We can't.*

"Thanks for tonight." I gesture toward the alley. "I'm not usually like that, you know. Freaking out."

"It's cool. I'd be like that if our restaurant was ever that busy."

"It wasn't just that." I exhale. "There's this exhibition I wanted to go to. I just found out about it recently, but then remembered it fell on the same day as this whole thing."

"Oh."

"Yeah." I'm rubbing my thumb against the bump on my middle finger—made callused after years of resting my pencil against it—not understanding why I want to explain everything to him in the moment, or if he wants to hear it. "I was going to ask my parents if I could have the night off. But my dad hurt his back, and like I said before, we're short-staffed."

"How do you feel now?"

I'd wanted to run far away. I'd wanted to be anywhere but in that restaurant. Then Bảo reached out to me, looking so solid, so earnest, and just one touch shocked me so much that I had to pull away. It seems silly to think about it now . . . but he was real! He was right there, and now right here.

"I'm okay," I answer honestly. "Now, at least."

Bảo nods. "That's good. I mean, tonight was challenging, and you survived it. And there will always be another exhibition." He pauses. "Was it some kind of avant-garde exhibition?"

"Avant-garde?" I say teasingly. "Wow, most people default to cubism. Picasso."

"Sorry, who?" Then he smiles and shrugs one shoulder. I forget what I'm thinking about for a breath. "I know nothing about art. I just thought 'avant-garde' sounded smart."

"You *almost* convinced me."

We smile at each other, not knowing what to say next, which I guess is expected. We haven't had enough time to work out a true rhythm in our conversation.

"Shit, I think I just saw your mom by the window." Bảo scrambles to his feet, brushes off his bottom. I remember now— this isn't supposed to happen. "I guess that's my cue to leave," he says, walking backward toward Lemare Street.

"I'll see you around?" I call out.

Did I just—?

He nearly trips over a raised part of the sidewalk and shoots me a sheepish smile that makes me woozy—even though I'm still sitting down. "Definitely! Let's not wait another six years, though."

And he's gone.

The door rings as it opens. Mẹ is behind me, locking the doors. "Who was that?"

"Someone was just asking for directions."

Mẹ smiles. She looks younger than I've ever seen her.

Any other day, she would have pestered me about who I was talking to, but she's too elated. She lifts a bulging plastic bag. "I'm bringing home *chè Thái*. Three for all of us."

"Nice." I stand up and snuggle under her arm when she gestures for me.

She presses her nose against my cheek and squeezes me tight, like she used to when I was younger. She'd say she "just wanted to eat me up."

Today went well. I want to paint us just like this.

"C'mon," my mom says. "Let's see if Ba is still alive at home."

Ba forgets about his back pain the moment we unlock the door. The television shuts off. My mom dangles the bag of desserts before him like she's a baiting dog and he shoots her a mock expression of anger before taking it and undoing the knot. This isn't the first time we've had dessert at midnight. When me and Evie were younger—and probably still too young to stay home by ourselves—we would fall asleep on the couch, curled up against one another, waiting for them to finish at the restaurant. They'd bring us leftovers—always something sweet.

We're missing one person now, but we still move in unison toward the kitchen.

"Did it work?" Ba asks almost warily. Playing with his hesitation even more, my mom ignores him. She digs into the drawer for spoons, closing it with her right hip, grabs ice from the freezer, and crushes it in a ziplock bag with a pestle. She pours the ice into three cups, then spoons the *chè* over it: coconut milk, sweet, plump longan pieces, cubes of grass jelly that snap under your teeth, red-dyed tapioca pearls made from water chestnuts. It's one of my favorite summer desserts—and one of the best late-night desserts to have without feeling so guilty.

She's taking too long for Ba. "*Bà này*," he says, and clicks his tongue with real annoyance. He just wants to hear about tonight.

Finally, Mẹ gives in. "It was perfect."

Ba accepts the spoon handed to him. Then he just nods. He tries to hide it, but I can tell by the way he's straightened his posture that he's glad to hear it. "Of course it worked. It's all because of me."

My mom smacks him on the shoulder. "*Ông quỷ*, this wouldn't be possible if the food wasn't good, and that's because of me." She sends me a shining look. "Not to mention Linh, who took care of the front and the customers."

"Of course. This is Linh we're talking about."

I smile weakly. If they were able to read my thoughts, review all the events from tonight, they wouldn't be praising me. I wouldn't be able to explain how I didn't want to work tonight. How I wanted to give up. And of course I can't do that, shouldn't do it. It'll ruin just about everything.

CHAPTER ELEVEN

BẢO

"Infestation." The word is usually negative, referring to bugs or something else that causes illnesses, but it accurately describes how thoughts of Linh swarm my mind lately. Yesterday after school, as I was wiping down tables, my thoughts drifted to Linh and last week's encounter. Then, noticing I wasn't doing any work, Mẹ whacked me good on the head, propelling the image of Linh—hair tied up like that night and that damned smile—from me. Việt laughed, watching me recover. He knew what was distracting me because I'd already given him a recap in our forensic science class together, waiting for our teacher to get here.

"Linh Mai."

"Yes."

"You talked to Linh Mai."

"Yes."

"Linh—"

"Okay, you can stop saying her name like that."

"It's just hard to believe. You actually helped the enemy."

"Do *you* see her as an enemy?"

"Yes, but that's what I know your mom would want me to say." A slow smirk began to form on his face. "The question is: Do *you* see Linh as the enemy?"

"I never did," I answered quickly, almost marveling at the truth of it. Việt arched an eyebrow, which I'd never seen him do.

"I still can't believe you actually talked to her. I never thought that'd happen. I mean, way to go!" I was somewhat amazed and bolstered by his enthusiastic reaction . . . like he was cheering me on.

"You're strangely happy about this. Meanwhile, I'm dead if my mom ever finds out about this."

"I don't know. It's just . . . you're taking a risk. Going out of your comfort zone. And you don't usually do that."

All of this was true, but it was something I'd never heard coming from my best friend.

Now, I'm debating the possibility that my school schedule is conspiring to keep me and Linh separated. When I do "see" her, it's just the usual flash of her hair as she turns the corner. I can never seem to find her during passing time or lunchtime.

A nagging thought comes to mind: What if Linh's actually dodging me? Did something happen after I left her? Maybe her mother *did* see us and told her off. Maybe Linh agreed not to speak to me because of that. It's not hard to imagine what she's heard about me and my family over the years.

A few minutes before sixth period—journalism class—I reach into my locker to exchange books. Allison basically said she was "a bit" disappointed by the quality of our recent articles, so there's going to be a long lesson on how to write. Is Rowan ever going to step up and remind Allison that she's still a student? I mentally and emotionally prepare myself, when I sense someone next to me. I close my locker.

My day hasn't completely gone to shit. "Linh. Hey."

Linh leans her shoulder against the lockers. "Here." She hands me a carton of chocolate milk.

Her hair's down past her shoulders, longer than I remember, and she looks like the Linh post-Phở Day instead of the one I'd checked in on in that alley. My throat feels dry. "What's this for?"

"I didn't get to it at lunch but didn't want to throw it away. Consider it a small token for helping me out last week."

"You really know the way to a guy's heart." *Okay, Bảo, okay! That was smooth . . . maybe?* We start walking. I try to remember if I'm actually going the right way. "How's it going?" That's the question I ask after a WEEK of thinking about her?

"Good, I'm glad it's almost over. I feel like it's been one assignment after another." Linh then grimaces. "APs especially."

"How many do you have?"

"Three."

My stomach clenches. Three? And she's still alive?

"Plus I have to work tonight."

"I do too. Maybe we'll see each other?" I say this as casually as possible, not wanting to seem like I'm suggesting anything other than, well, just seeing each other.

"Sure, maybe I can help out this time," she says conspiratorially, adding a smile. I'm feeling the effects of it—maybe it's because she's so much clearer under the lights—a nice faintness that I've only felt after waking from a long, good nap.

"There's no chance we can get away with that again," I say weakly, half as a joke, until it registers that isn't a joke. It's the truth. Things just worked out over at Linh's, but he can't ever expect that to repeat.

Some of the laughter leaves Linh's eyes, and we walk in quiet silence, our bodies remembering to feel unaccustomed to each other's company. That feeling, back when I thought she'd rejected my help, takes over again, until she says, so quietly that I might have imagined it:

"That's sad to think about . . . because we worked great together. Like we were meant to be partners."

Partners.

Yeah, it sounds right to me.

Eager to just keep talking until we can't anymore, I ask more about her classes. She asks if Allison is *still* attending our classes instead of using her study hall time to go home. She seems to talk about Allison with a teasing smile, so I don't tell her that I'm truly terrified of her in certain moments.

We make it to journalism class, where—no surprise—Allison

sits in Rowan's seat, next to her the biggest Blue Bottle cup of iced coffee I've ever seen. In a disorienting move, she smiles at Linh. She looks different when she does that.

"Hey, lady!" Her eyes fall to me, then flicker over to Linh. If possible, her lips widen. "Didn't think I'd see you two together."

Linh clears her throat. "Ali, I told you about how he helped me out last week? Right?"

"*Rightttt.* That was sweet of him. Well, good timing that you're here. Because I have an idea." *Ali* spins in her chair before rising like a villain who finally settled on a plan for world domination.

"Oh no," Linh says, earning a glance that is both withering and playful from Ali.

"So, in one of my classes, some girls were complaining that their boyfriends are taking them to all the wrong places. Boring vibe. Expensive, etcetera, etcetera. So what if we created a whole new beat for the newspaper? Assign a reporter to visit new places that any high school student can go to *and* actually afford, and tell the real deal about it."

"Will restaurants let us do that?" We're not exactly the *Los Angeles Times*. Who cares about what someone from La Quinta says about their establishment?

"I'm sure I can spin something," she tells me confidently. "It's basically free publicity for the restaurants."

"Okay, yeah, it's not a bad idea," Linh says. "Do you have someone in mind?"

"Good question." She points both fingers at me. "Bảo, I'd want you on this beat."

In what way does any of this sound good or helpful to the newspaper? Me who's been delegated to proofreading duties. Me who consistently gets Bs on his English Lit essays.

"Why me?"

"Because you're better than you think you are, as much as it pains me to say." Ali watches me closely; there's a gleam in her eyes telling me she likes that she can shock—and disturb—me with her compliments. "And Linh, you can help, too."

Her eyes shift to me. "Um . . ."

"Hear me out: Bảo puts words to the scene, rates the food, describes it. Since he grew up in restaurants like you and knows food, he should *hypothetically* be capable of doing this—"

"Hey!" I interject.

"—and you can sketch the environment. Or paint it. I've watched you sketch for years, Linh. You'd be perfect for this. The newspaper desperately needs your talent. It needs something entirely new." Her voice has taken on a tone I've never heard from Ali before—something more earnest. She's turning a bit softer, gifting me a glimpse of her normal self, and of their friendship.

Linh looks away, deep in thought. She said she was taking three APs just earlier, not to mention juggling after-school work at the restaurant. I'm brought back to last week, seeing her in that alley alone, looking overwhelmed, looking lost. Something inside had pulled me toward her then. I just knew I needed to see if she was all right.

That feeling rises again, and the words are out before I can stop them. "I'll do it."

The girls look at me—Ali, triumphantly and maybe even a little approvingly; Linh just confused.

I know there's a lot against me. It'll take away some of my weekends, most likely. But as long as my parents don't find out *who* I'm working with, this project might work. "And for what it's worth, Linh, I know you'd be awesome for this, too."

"I don't know if I can do this. It's not just the workload—it's the fact that I haven't done something like this, let alone had my work published in a newspaper. What if I just *think* I'm good and it turns out I'm not?" Her question comes out quietly, laced with uncertainty.

"Yeah, no," Ali counters immediately. "I don't think anyone could think that. I've seen what you've done ever since we were twelve."

"And the flyers. They're great!" I interject. "If anything, it's another chance to show just how good you are."

"Linh," Ali says. "You have two people here saying you can do this!"

"How—" She pauses. She's aiming that half-said question at me. I read her mind like that night. We're part of a long history; we might not be directly involved like our parents, but nothing can change the fact that our families and our restaurants are considered rivals.

So I keep my answer simple. "We can make it work." We have *worked* together and it turned out great. Because it wasn't anyone's family against someone. It was just me and Linh then. I want to believe that can happen again.

After a few beats, Linh looks away. "Let me think about it some more."

"That's not a no, so yay!" Ali claps her hands together and hugs her, then turns to do the same to me before remembering herself. Linh still appears unsure, maybe a bit exhausted in her thoughts, but she still musters a smile.

When we're alone, Linh says, "Ali only asks for help when she absolutely needs it. So you've earned some Ali points."

"That's good, because I was in the negative for a while."

Linh heads off to her art class. When the last of my classmates walks in, Ali closes the door, game face on. The lights dim abruptly, freaking some kids out, but it's only Rowan being complicit in whatever torture Allison has cooked up for today. Turns out I don't really care about that. Linh and I might get to be partners.

I open the chocolate milk carton and sip from it. *Partners.*

CHAPTER TWELVE

LINH

Of course, when I was walking with Bảo, I didn't mean to give the chocolate milk to him. I didn't finish it at lunch, felt guilty throwing it away—my parents' voices reprimanding me—so I carried it for my next class. Then I saw Bảo at his locker, and before I even knew it, my legs were carrying me across the hallway and suddenly: chocolate milk. If Ali saw that, she would've never let me live it down.

I dip my brush into a jar of water, washing it of cadmium yellow. Yamamoto's voice is on background as she talks to the class, weaving in between each student to check on their work.

Bảo has snuck his way into my brain for the last few days. I turn into a mess every time I see him, which is more than I can ever remember. There's a theory that we've talked about in my psychology class called red car syndrome, where you hear or see something once, like a red car, and suddenly you see red cars everywhere. I don't remember seeing Bảo so many times in the hallway—or maybe I've trained myself to see past him—but I've turned a corner several times before pivoting in the opposite direction. Just the other day at work, while my dad was passing along details on where to meet Quyền Thành, which happens to be today, I was sneaking looks at the window, hoping to catch sight of Bảo through his. My mom wondered aloud if I should dress up for the interview.

"Linh."

Could we really work together?

Had Ali planned to pair us the moment the idea came to mind, or was it after I told her about Bảo and Phở Day? I make a note to bring it up later.

"*Linhhhh.*"

But the question is: *How are we ever going to do this?*

"Linh!"

Yamamoto is right by my ear. I yelp and my brush falls out of my hand and clatters on the floor. Classmates, now busy packing up, snicker. Yamamoto stands before me, arms akimbo, but while other teachers would be pissed off, she only appears amused, a stampede of questions probably in her mind.

"You know, I've seen you get lost inside your brain before, but never like this. I mean, you were *far* gone," she says teasingly.

Blushing, I hurriedly fold up my tarp and place my canvas on a tabletop by other day-old canvases. Just a bunch of fruits in baskets and flowers—beginning paint classes. I wash my brushes with an odorless thinner—I hate the citrus kind—before wiping them dry, then running them under water with some linseed soap. The usual next step is futile. I wash my hands until most of the paint has disappeared. I've stopped worrying about the rest on my fingers; it all eventually just fades. The bell rings and I push my way out into the hallway.

Inside my jeans pocket, my phone buzzes. I have a half hour until I have to meet with Quyền Thành, learn about the *fascinating* world of engineering.

"Hey, lady," my best friend says casually at my locker. But I know her better and read the gleam in her eyes. She wants to talk about Bảo. I don't think she'd ever been more excited than after hearing me tell her about Phở Day. "Wow, I didn't know he had it in him," Ali had said in mock surprise.

"How was art class?"

I roll my eyes at her. "Is that the question you really want to ask?"

"No, but I'm a journalist. I have to throw out questions to warm you up. But now that you mention it: What do you think? Are you going to work with Bảo?"

"Ali."

"C'mon, it'll be *fun*."

"Wouldn't use that word."

"What would you use?"

"Full of dread. Confused. Perplexed—"

"That's a synonym." She waits for me to switch out my textbooks, smoothly catching one that jumps out at her. She reads the title before shelving it. "Psychology—well, that's saying something."

"My question is: How the hell will this work? Our families hate each other. We know *nothing* about each other. I feel like I'm breaking several rules just by agreeing to this—"

She holds up two hands, telling me to slow down. "I already worked out the first question. I'll just find restaurants that are a little farther outside the radius of where your parents tend to go. Aren't you always telling me that your parents or people they know never eat out because your mom—"

"—says she can make anything at home." Evie and I used to beg our parents to take us to McDonalds for Happy Meals.

"Exactly." She signs the number two. "Second, I'm well aware of this feud. I don't get it, but I'm not supposed to. But it's your families who despise each other. What about you? For once, let's just remove the whole family situation—if it's just you and Bảo standing across from each other, would you say that you like him?"

"It'd be very easy to like him."

She smiles knowingly. After a few seconds of delay, my words catch up to me. My face warms up. "Seems like you already do like him." She pauses dramatically. "Maybe even more than that."

I close my mouth, reaching out to shut my locker door that dangled between us. The afternoon rush around us seems more muted than it usually is, the crowd flowing naturally around us.

Like him.

My phone buzzes again. Fifteen minutes until the meeting.

I don't have time for this right now.

Ali nods in agreement, like she's just read my mind. "Things like this don't really wait for you to catch up. Like the way you end up drawing something you never intended to draw. Just think about it: When you *like* an art piece, how much of it is thinking and how much of it is feeling?"

There are artists and fans interested in artwork on an intellectual level; they consider the message of the piece, the intention of the artist, the connotations of the time and place of its creation. Yamamoto's one of those artists, which makes all of her lessons interesting. But I'm different from that—in art that I like, in the pieces I create. It's always a memory or feeling that I start with. Ali knows this by now.

"You're using way too many art metaphors today."

"How else will I actually get through to you?" Ali nudges me by the shoulder and we walk outside together, heading to her car. She'd told me she would drop me off at a nearby Starbucks.

A jock runs by, jostling me as he tries catching up with his teammates off to practice. The buses full of students depart one by one, leaving little trails of smog. Everything's moving, but, somehow, inside me is still.

"Why don't you just feel things out?" she asks me finally as she unlocks her Nissan, and we slide into our seats. "There's so much in your life that you can't control, Linh, as much as I *totally* want things to be different for you. So maybe you can use this chance to

do something for yourself. Forget everyone—your family, Bảo—
this is about you. No rules but your own."

I buckle my seat belt. A reminder pops up on my phone: ten
minutes until my coffee with Quyền. Without words I show it to
Ali, who brushes the notice away, saying there's no reason to worry.

"I thought you didn't like Bảo," I finally say.

"I said that I didn't *know* if I liked him or disliked him. But
he has an eye for words. I think he's better than he realizes."
She makes a right but too widely, and she needs to adjust before
straightening in the lane. "You know, I feel like I can write a whole
human-interest piece about you, Bảo, and your families."

"I strongly disapprove."

"Can you imagine the headline?" To my horror, she releases her
hands from the steering wheel, doing what I'll now call the Banner
Move. "Two students from rival families and restaurants? Like
Romeo and Juliet—"

A car honks at us and her hands snap back onto the wheel.

"Just drive."

As I walk into the restaurant after an exhausting half hour with
Quyền Thành, I try to gather enough enthusiasm to convince my
parents they didn't waste a favor on me. Even though they did.

Quyền Thành had shown up before me. She sat straight-
backed, on a stool no less, her badge from the firm proudly pinned
to her chest. She was on her laptop looking focused as she sent off
e-mail after e-mail. She wore a gray business suit—which I won't
mention to my mom because then she'll despair, "I knew it! You

should have worn one to make an impression." While Quyền was petite and smaller than me, the strength of her handshake took me by surprise. Her eyes, framed by black thick-rimmed glasses, were strikingly clear and I felt that she was somehow scanning my body for answers.

I had questions that I looked up the night before, pulled off some college website about informational interviews. She had clear, precise, straightforward answers; I had to wonder if she was used to doing this type of favor.

She was a mechanical engineer but she was "told that I liked art," and knew tons of friends who were "into that thing, but it's not really My Thing."

Our meeting was interspersed with inconvenient pauses, long sips of cold coffee, and me finding it hard to maintain eye contact because I was afraid she'd see the truth about how little interest I really had in engineering.

By the end of it, though, she smiled sympathetically. She even hugged me as I thanked her for her time.

"I know I bored you."

"No, I—"

"You're sort of easy to read."

I hate my face. But Quyền Thành just laughed. "Trust me: You're not the only one who's had to suffer through hearing about my work. As much as I love what I do, I know it's not for some people." She was being so nice that I wish I could have pretended to feel something. But as Ali mentioned, that's not the way I work—I either have to feel something . . .

Or I don't.

"Some advice. I don't think I'd enjoy this career as much as I do if it wasn't *mine*. And what I mean by that is it's something I can claim as my own. If my parents were forcing me to be a physicist, I would not be okay. So, do you have something that's *yours*?"

I don't nod or answer, still hesitant to prove how I've wasted her time. But maybe she saw something in me because she merely nodded, saying, "Good. Then protect it."

We parted and she promised not to say anything to her parents.

Back in the restaurant, my parents don't jump on me right away about the coffee interview. Instead, Mẹ is wrangling a box free from tape. Ba is sitting in a corner booth that my mom banished him to. While his back is better, he's still wearing his back brace and looks completely miserable, like a dog in his flea cone. I set down my backpack and slip into Mẹ's booth, inching closer for a look at what's inside the box. It's a flower vase, cerulean with specks the color of the jade bracelets she and just about every woman in my family wear. When I was younger, I thought it was something every Việt woman had to wear, some rite of passage.

"Whoa." It's handmade, that's for sure. "That's so cool. Where's it from?"

"Dì Vàng." Mẹ sighs. My aunt always seems to evoke that kind of sigh from my mom. She hands over the vase; I weigh it, feel the slight bumps alternating with smooth curves. I took a pottery class once in freshman year but couldn't control the speed of my spin, or get the clay into the shape that I wanted. But Dì Vàng does this for a living, which is mind-boggling to think about, something I can only dream of.

She likes sending my mom things, and I know Mẹ likes them, as much as she doesn't approve of her sister's career choice, since she displays them everywhere: the mantel under the TV, the night-stand in my parents' bedroom. I have an elephant-shaped piggy bank that Dì Vàng made for my fifth birthday and hand-delivered when she was last in America.

Since the Vietnam War, and especially after the fall of Saigon, which was what forced our family to scatter, most of my extended family relocated to Washington, Louisiana, Florida, and Texas. It wasn't exactly cheap to fly over here, and the government has strict rules, so my aunt must have made the right friends to be able to visit for a little while. I imagined how cool it'd be for her to live per-manently nearby and how she could teach me more about her art.

I'd asked my mom why Dì Vàng didn't want to just move here.

Mẹ just waved her hand. Her usual gesture and non-answer. "I've tried to convince her, but she says she's happy there." Then my mom turned her attention to something seemingly more important, ignoring my question.

She and Ba tell childhood stories about Vietnam all the time, but they often conflict with each other: the good times, when Mẹ talks about running carefree along the beach with her friends, the sun rising behind them, or when Ba would play soccer with American soldiers stationed nearby. Then there are the dark days—funerals, saying goodbye to family members, losing everything on their way here. It's something I can't ever understand.

"Aren't you supposed to be working?" Ba says grumpily from his booth. Mẹ and I roll our eyes, then pack up the vase again ever so carefully. "Ah, your coffee meeting!" she suddenly remembers. "How was it? Isn't Quyền Thành so nice?"

"She was really nice. Really helpful." I pick at the flap of the box the vase came in. I wonder if she can pick up on the dullness in my voice.

Mẹ nods approvingly. "Perfect. It's all working out."

Just like Phở Day. Just like anything that doesn't make them worry too much.

As I'm tying up my hair, readying myself for my shift, Ali's words from earlier came back to me.

There's so much in your life that you can't control. . . . So maybe you can use this chance to do something for yourself.

Something just for me.

I take out my phone and text Ali.

CHAPTER THIRTEEN

BẢO

I groan the moment I walk into work. My mom and her circle are planted in one of the side booths, cackling about something. The General's telling the story, her face pink with laughter. I'm sure this is *after* she brags about her son at Stanford and her *other* son at MIT, both of whom rarely come home.

"The meats they use are never fresh! One day I'm sure they'll poison their customers."

"You shouldn't say things like that," one of the women says while laughing, her voice nasal.

"But it's true. I swear. I'm surprised *that restaurant* is still standing."

Of course that's why they're laughing.

Biting back my disgust, I quickly walk to the back, though not before registering my mom's laugh, dimmed compared to the General's. I wonder—considering how much she talks shit about the restaurant to me and my dad—does she really want Linh's family gone that much? Does she truly want the other restaurant to fail so badly?

I nod absentmindedly at one of the line cooks, Trần, who goes into a series of coughs as he breaks down cardboard boxes. Eddie's prepping vegetables, his knife-chopping at warp-speed. A pile of onions takes over the prep table and newly washed aprons sit nearby for the taking.

Before, I would have let these thoughts slide; they were normal things to hear. Not now, though. I remember Linh, her near breakdown in the alley, the pleasure in her mother's voice as she heard how customers complimented her cooking.

Maybe there's good reason for the Mais to hate us.

"God save us," Việt groans as he enters the kitchen, backpack hanging off one shoulder. "Bà Nhi's voice gives me the worst headaches."

I smirk. I call her the General, but Việt calls her by the term usually reserved for older people. *Bà Nhi, bà quỷ.*

"At least she's going to leave soon."

"How would you know that?"

Việt swipes through his phone. "My mom says she heard from Tracy's cousin's uncle that Bà Nhi's planning to get a nose job. So she has an appointment." It takes a minute for me to connect the dots. "The uncle at Star Nails." Still doesn't help, but if Việt's mom is the source, I'll believe her. She's judicious about the people around her.

Trần, still dealing with the boxes, coughs so hard that spit flies from his mouth.

"You okay, man?" I ask.

"Ugh, I've been so sick. But I can't miss out on work. Got some bills to pay."

My mom comes into the kitchen. *"Mày bệnh hả?"* she asks Trần. She doesn't wait for an answer. Despite the usually threatening-sounding *"mày,"* she steps closer and rests the back of her hand against his forehead. "Why are you working? You are burning up."

"But—"

"Go home. Sleep."

"I know but I kind of need the money and—"

"Go home. You will get the money." She pivots on her feet and heads to the stove where broth simmers in two pots. "Here, take some of this home. It'll be good for your throat. *Bệnh mà còn đi làm.*" She tsks. Then she calls him an idiot.

Again he tries to protest, but Mẹ steamrolls over him. She won't take no for an answer. Giving up, Trần thanks my mom as he backs out of the kitchen.

A few years ago, Trần's wife had had their first daughter, but she couldn't take off more work—her company didn't have maternity leave—so on certain days, Mẹ let them leave the baby in the room with air-conditioning. The other servers and I would rotate shifts, poking our head in. Ba had worn the baby monitor on his belt like it was some fashion accessory. But my mom mostly looked after her, cooed at her in a pitch I'd never heard from her.

I watch now as my mom gives Việt a to-do list for today, her voice sharp and leaving no room for arguments. This is the mom I see all the time. But she's also the type of person who'd give a sick man a container of broth, who'd babysit a kid at a busy restaurant.

My mom is still a kind person, even though she hangs around the General, and listens to jokes at the Mais' expense. She has to be.

It's 8:00 p.m. on the dot, and I'm finishing up to go home to do homework. My mom made a point to let me out early even though the shop closes at ten.

I spot Linh's door creeping open. *That's right. She also leaves at this time.* She's too busy stuffing something into her messenger bag to notice me at first. A week ago, I'd count the seconds until she was gone. Today, though . . .

Risk. Once I think about it, I've never really taken a risk. But I'm taking a risk today. Seized by an emotion I can't place, I'm out my own door in a split second.

"Hey, Linh!" I shout.

Alarmed, she looks up, then her expression melts into recognition. She says something, but a beat-up sedan decides to struggle through at the exact moment, dragging away her words. We smile when it's gone. I realize my parents also have a clear view of us enemies fraternizing with each other.

Getting the same idea, Linh gestures to a spot out of window view. She's tied back her hair into two small buns, exposing her face so that when she's smiling at me, like now, her left dimple shows. My stomach does a dismount. I recover and smile back as best I can.

"So, there's this boba place that I love," Linh says, as if we're just continuing a conversation. "7 Leaves."

"Yeah!" *Hold back, Bảo.* I clear my throat. "I mean, I've gone there all the time."

"You wanna meet there? We need to figure out some sort of plan if we're going to work together."

"We are?"

"Yes. I've decided, why not have some fun?"

My heartbeat spikes in excitement. "Yes, a plan." Apparently I can only say monosyllabic words. "I mean, that sounds great. Copacetic."

I wince. *I just said that, didn't I?*

Luckily Linh laughs. "Meet you there in an hour? Just want to change. I smell like fish sauce."

That gives me an hour to get ready. I probably smell like fish sauce too.

I sniff myself.

Yep.

Once Linh disappears around the corner, I bolt in the opposite direction toward home.

I will be "studying with Việt." The normal translation is that we'd just play games at his house. But now that's changed. Việt texts me that I need to pay him each time I use him as my cover. When

I respond with a GIF of Stephen Colbert lifting a certain finger, Việt merely sends back a kiss emoji. But really, any activity that was Việt-related was okay in my parents' book and they barely acknowledged me as I flew out of the house, Mẹ occupied with a Korean drama because she's all about the drama. Ba waved me aside, more preoccupied by his bowl of warm, sugary *chè xôi nước.*

Linh is outside 7 Leaves, her hair free around her shoulders, dressed in jeans and a white tee.

I never thought walking to the cashier would cause an internal freak-out, but it did. I order milk tea while Linh orders a strawberry. *Do I pay? I should pay, right?* The counter person, some twentysomething bored-as-hell guy glances between Linh and me, looking like he pities us. Awkward teenagers, he must be thinking. Then he sighs out loud. Definitely thinking about us. Just to relieve us from his gaze, I pull out my wallet and the cashier nods almost approvingly, like, *Good on you, bud.*

"You didn't have to do that."

"Consider it payment for the chocolate milk the other day."

We get our drinks and sit down at a table sandwiched between two others: one table with a couple, Chinese from my guess, who act all lovey-dovey with each other, and another table with a grandpa sleeping on a stool—impressive—wearing a fishing hat, a black vest over a plaid long-sleeve shirt, and beige cargo shorts. A fisherman who doesn't fish. The cashier says something, but the grandpa has zero reaction. Probably the owner or the owner's father.

The upside of meeting here is that it's easy to see who's here and who's not. Especially if anyone is a part of Mẹ and the General's group.

The seat beneath me is chilly. My stomach gets jittery the moment we sit down together. The quiet in the room, the hum of the fridge, accent our proximity. Our ankles touch, and all of my body—I mean, *all* of it—wakes up.

Linh's taking out a notebook and pen; she's serious about coming up with a plan, and maybe that's the only reason she suggested meeting here. To get something off her checklist. I try to tell myself I'd be okay if all we talked about was the new beat.

Only thing is, I'd be lying.

"I'm nervous."

I glance over at her, but she has her eyes to the table, her fingers playing with the edge of her notebook.

Maybe I should have played it off, thinking about how guys are *supposed* to be cool and charming—like the male leads of so many films: Chris Pine, Will Smith, Henry Golding. In reality I'm more of a Randall Park character. "Me too. I keep thinking someone we know will pop up and see us, and word will get around."

"Like spies wearing sunglasses."

Instantly, the image of my mom popping out from behind the serving counter, in sunglasses and some funny hat, nearly makes me choke on my drink. "I think we're safe."

Linh cups her drink. "Part of me chose this place for that reason." We smile sympathetically at each other. "But if you're having second thoughts, you don't have to do this. Ali can be pushy sometimes, but I can let her know this isn't your thing."

"This could be my *thing*," I joke. "It might even be my favorite thing out of all the things I like."

Linh catches on. "Careful or Ali might volunteer you for other *things*."

I pretend to shudder. "Don't tell her." The tension lets up and I want it to stay that way, so I rush through. "Look, I would honestly not be here if I didn't want to be. But it's sounding like you might be second-guessing all this."

This time, she raises her chin, like she's accepting a challenge. "I'm not. Not anymore." She fiddles with her straw. "Why are *you* here?"

"Because I've been thinking that it's ridiculous we grew up across from each other and never truly met. Because the night we worked together proved that you aren't like what I've been told. Well, at least what I've heard about your family."

"What have you heard about us?"

I hesitate to answer. It might cut this meeting short. "You really want to know?"

Linh nods.

"Gang members."

"*What?* That's what my parents have said about *you*!"

I try to picture my parents as gang members—my mom might actually be a believable leader—but I keep that to myself. "They also said . . . that you drove out Bác Xuân from his place." Linh's mouth drops open at that. She looks truly offended, and I wish I could take it back. "I mean, that's what I've *heard*. I'm not saying I believe it."

"We would never! He was a family friend. I was there the

moment he told my parents that he wanted to retire. That he wanted to spend more time with his grandchildren! Did your mom say that to you?" My face must have given me away. "Honestly, your mom can be brutal."

I bristle. It's never a good feeling to hear someone you know get called out. "You think she's brutal? Haven't you met Nhi Trưng? She's the real leader. *She*'s the worst."

Something we can agree on. A part of me is relieved the attention's off my mom; I'm not sure I want to hear more about what may have been said against us.

"Oh, we know about her," Linh says. "She wanted the restaurant so badly that she wanted to drive us out to get it. I'm sure she's still trying."

I shrug helplessly. I have nothing to use as a counterargument, because it's true.

"Sorry," I manage, worried that I've ruined things before we could even start working together. In my mind, this newspaper project is like an old rickety bridge above a roaring waterfall. One false move and we'll tumble over.

"I'm not mad at you. It's just—" She has a faraway look in her eyes. "I wonder what else we've been told that turns out to have been a simple rumor that grew into something else."

I lean forward. Careful. "We can agree that our parents are both protective of the businesses and maybe that's why they're like this. I know my parents have spent everything on the restaurant. I can't tell you how many times they've worked through nights just to make ends meet."

Linh grimaces. "I know. Nights when they probably left us alone more often than they should have."

"And when we were too young to stay home by ourselves."

"It's one of the best-kept secrets in this community."

The bridge is stable again.

"What was it like for you, growing up in a restaurant?" I ask. "All of my childhood memories seem to have taken place there."

Linh's eyes light up. "Let me guess: It's where you've watched all segments of *Paris by Night*? Played lava across the tiles?"

"Yes! Getting side-eyed by the regular customers whenever I took over a whole booth."

"Did you have a nap room, too?"

"You mean the place where we stored our bags of rice?"

It was really like parallel lives. The storage room, with all the rice and nonperishable foods, was where I napped as a kid, and as weird as it was, it still brought me comfort whenever I walked in to grab something. I remember it now—the hot summers when I wasn't yet in school, sleeping on a small cot while my parents were working in the kitchen. A pink fan near the end of its life jaggedly blowing cool air at me. A tiny dictionary that my parents kept there just in case they needed to look up words from the customers—I'd look through it when I was bored being out in the main room. A small stool for Mẹ to sit on when she fed me lunch, which happened after naptime.

"I guess to answer your question about growing up in the business: It hasn't been completely bad. I mean, sometimes I'd rather be drawing instead of working, but"—Linh shrugs—"it's such a part of my life that I can't separate myself from it . . . as much as I try to."

Underneath Linh's writing notebook, I spot a sketchbook—white with a bunch of doodles on it: her artwork. Ignoring her questioning look, I take it from under her arm, examining the drawing, which is similar in style to her family restaurant's flyer, only this time it's of a couple strolling down a brightly lit boulevard in some city. It feels like I'm there with the couple.

"Nice. It's cool. Looks like New York." I slide the sketchbook back at her.

"I've never been. It's just something I pulled from Google images." She mumbles the last part, as if she's embarrassed.

"Do you want to go to New York?"

"I don't know, really. I feel like that's what real artists are supposed to do, and I can see why. It's probably cool to see all the skyscrapers, stand in Times Square, just seeing all sorts of different people and cultures. But I can't even think about that yet. I first have to figure out a way to tell my parents that I don't want to do engineering."

I make a face. Engineering. It seems too boring for Linh. Where would her colors go?

"So your parents are the typical Asian parents."

She nods almost morosely.

"I think you should be an artist."

A short laugh escapes her and some tension leaves her face. "Okay, sure, that solves *everything*."

"You're really serious about art. Even when I met you that day.

You did some damage to that paper with your crayons."

"You were the kid with the bowl cut and weird Spider-Man obsession," she recalls, the corners of her eyes crinkling. She's smiling.

I raise my hands in defense. "Don't tell me you weren't obsessed with *something* when you were younger. Mine just happened to be Spider-Man. You apparently had something against art supplies. Poor crayons."

"It was a pointillist drawing!"

There's a look that people get when they're excited—a spark, I guess, in their eyes. I see it when Việt's face lights up, talking about the latest *SVU* episode. In Mẹ when she's cooking *bánh xèo*. In Ba whenever good food is involved. Even Allison's focused gleam as we're in the newsroom comes to mind. Here, with Linh, she has that sort of light behind her eyes. Makes me want to know what that's like.

"Can you tell me about it? Your art—like, what it's like when you're working on something?"

Linh sits back, chewing on a boba. "It's like I go away from my body for a second. It's not an out-of-body experience, exactly. Like, I'm not hovering over my body or anything like that. But I guess I'm zoned in. And nothing can distract me. Whenever I'm working on a piece, my mom always complains that I don't hear her when it's time for dinner."

Then the gleam kind of disappears and she has a faraway look in her eyes. She shakes her head, coming back, not telling me where she went, even though I think I know. Her parents probably popped into her mind. "What about you? What do you like?

Are your parents bugging you to do something you don't want to do?"

"I'm basically a failure and they'd be happy if I just found *something* to do." *Let's get right to the truth of it.*

"Oh, c'mon."

"No, really, I'm nothing compared to Linh Mai of the Oh Mai Mai family."

"Be serious."

I shift in my seat. She thinks I'm kidding, but how do I tell her I'm not? "I'm not good at anything. I'm not sure I will ever be."

"There must be something. Cooking?"

"There's a reason why I'm not allowed to stay long in the kitchen."

"Singing?"

"Sure, I can sing a song now, but I wouldn't want to traumatize you."

"Sports?" At my look, Linh stifles a laugh. "Well, who cares if you're *good* at anything? What do you *love*? What can't you live without?"

I shrug and sip my boba loudly. Nothing's coming up. "I'm not bothered by mediocrity."

"You can't be serious."

"Mediocrity has allowed me to float by without too much pressure or judgment. Being mediocre at school is great. No one bothers you! No one even looks at you."

"You're lying. You *so* care," Linh says it matter-of-factly. Her aim is perfect.

"How can you know that?"

"Your voice went up a pitch." That's a very Việt-like observation.

"My voice—"

Linh takes a dainty sip of her tea but humor lights up her eyes. Her very *nice* eyes—I'm getting distracted. "Yup."

I remember the other night at dinner, when my parents believed in me, maybe too much. I haven't done anything so far to give them that much confidence in me. Nothing to make me look good to their customers who always seem to brag about their freakishly talented kids.

So I give in to Linh. Scratching the back of my neck, I admit, "Okay, fine. I'll try to explain. I look at my parents. I know what they've done to get here. It's never been easy. And lately I think I've been failing them. I haven't done completely great in school. And I'm not breaking any records at sports like my friend Việt."

"Cross-country runner?"

That's a shocker. "Yeah, that's him. You follow sports?"

Linh explains after grimacing, "You haven't been forced to listen to Ali reread newspaper articles to you."

"I would rather run a cross-country race," I deadpan. "Anyway, I'm feeling the pressure more than usual. It's our last year and I guess . . ." I breathe out. *How should I say this?* "I feel like I've ignored all the chances around me, and now I don't have much to go on."

"That's not true!" Linh says forcefully, leaning forward. "Ali and I were talking earlier—"

"Hold on, you were talking about me?"

Not gonna lie: My self-esteem shoots up.

"She was deciding whether or not she hates you." She laughs. And my self-esteem plummets. "I'm just joking. She mentioned how you had a good eye for words. Which makes sense, because, you know, not a lot of guys out there say 'copacetic.'"

She tries to mimic my lower voice, and we both know she fails, so we burst out laughing, so loud that we wake the grandpa slumbering in the corner. He glares, then leans his head back again.

"Maybe you just need to find something worth writing about. Something that you're interested in . . . Maybe this"—Linh gestures not to us but to the idea of what we've agreed to do—"is your chance to stand out." The future. What a dampener it can be.

Linh reads the look on my face right away, because she laughs and drops questions about the future.

We finished with our drinks, and the grandpa is actually still awake, now staring at us through suspicious eyes. The place is closing soon. *Okay, I get the hint.* I lift my cup with the remaining boba and ask Linh, "So how much should I pay you for this life coaching?"

Linh gives me *that* smile.

"Free bobas would work just fine."

CHAPTER FOURTEEN

LINH

Once outside, the silence is comforting and warm, like a good bowl of wonton soup on a rainy day. I feel Bảo's heat beside me, my hand a whisper away from his. During the summer, with tourists flooding in, this part of the neighborhood gets packed with squatting old Vietnamese women, dressed in countryside outfits. It's not as heavy as Bolsa Avenue traffic, especially when the night market's up, but it's still a tourist trap. You're likely to get bullied into buying jackfruit in Styrofoam trays, rambutan or longan, or—if the woman's a *really good* seller—durian. Sometimes I wonder if they ever sell all of their items, and when that doesn't happen, where they go.

The sight of Bảo passing under a lamplight stops me. It's as if he's just stepped into a Caravaggio painting. The light throws off shadows, darkening half of his body. The lines of his face seem sharper.

"What?" Bảo brushes his hand through his hair. "Do I have something on my face?"

"Nothing. The lighting. It was just perfect for a second."

"You notice things like that?"

I shrug, embarrassed that I was caught staring this time.

Bảo hops on a nearby cinder block wall, walking down the length before jumping down, back at my side again. "Remember that bowl of phở? How bad it was? It's probably from—"

"Phở Bác Hồ. My parents hated that place."

"Same." At least our parents seem to agree on one thing—a universal distaste for anything that refers to Hồ Chí Minh in name. Reminds them too much of the war. The owners made some poor excuse when they opened—saying they were referring to an elderly relative. But you have to be so ignorant to open something like that here. It closed not long after me and Bảo met.

"But I never got to see you draw Spider-Man, did I?"

"Because of our parents."

Something passes in his eyes that makes me shiver. "Did you ever think about what it would have been like if our restaurants weren't competing against each other?"

It's a loaded question to wrap up our time together, but I answer as honestly as I can.

"I think I thought about the idea of you, if that makes sense. But this is different. I finally get a chance to know you—and you seem nice."

"Don't worry, the nice-guy act disappears once we meet for the fourth time."

"Great. I was really sensing asshole vibes back there."

It feels like an hour before we finally get to Ward Street, where our paths diverge. This is what I'll remember: his bashful wave and the shadows swallowing him up as he heads home.

When I'm inside the house, only Ba is up. Back problems, most likely. I can smell the Bengay emanating from him again. He sits in the dark living room, TV on, but with the cable off. The static from the screen lights up his sleeping face, a hypnotizing pattern.

"Oh, *con về rồi*?" he asks groggily, stating the obvious. "How was studying?"

"*Dạ.* It went well." The lie leaves me a bit too easily, though I feel the weight of it in my stomach. But it has to be done. I take off my shoes, then make my way to my bedroom. "The test will be easy. Now go to sleep."

"Ah." I'll give him two more hours before he drags himself to bed and wakes up early to start his routine again.

My mom's knock wakes me up the next morning. My mouth's parched, and the light almost hurts my eyes. I remember that I didn't drink any water after drinking boba. Is it possible to be hungover from too much boba?

I hear Mẹ lightly pad across my room. Her shampoo—Head & Shoulders, which she shares with Ba—tickles my nose. The bed sags just a bit when she sits by me, patting my side. This was how she'd wake me and Evie up before heading off to a long day at the restaurant.

"*Con, dậy đi. Chín giờ rồi,*" she whispers, her voice as smooth as the glide of a brushstroke across a well-primed canvas.

I twist my head to the right and check the actual time: eight o'clock, instead of an hour later like she just said.

"Five more minutes."

"Mẹ just made *bánh patê sô*. Just hot out of the oven. It's only good when it's eaten hot."

I breathe in hints of her promise. Buttery puff pastry. Tender, flavorful chicken at the center. And then my ultimate favorite: earthy Vietnamese coffee just waiting to be paired off with sweetened condensed milk.

Okay, I'm up.

Mẹ knows she has me. I hear a smile in her voice. "See you soon."

Once in the kitchen, I see that it's not just pastry or coffee that she's made. She must be experimenting with recipes. Several pots are cooking on the stove, and on the outside patio, there are two larger pots, which tells me whatever she's cooking there might stink up the house. Various herbs are soaking in tubs of water. At last five bottles and jars of *gia vị* are opened on the kitchen table. Ever-methodical in the restaurant kitchen, she's the complete opposite in our own kitchen.

Still, I love mornings like this.

The pastry is waiting just for me. I sink my teeth into it, flakes falling into my lap. Mẹ has me taste the coffee and milk level, then pours ice over it. As Mẹ busies herself around the kitchen, I

FaceTime Evie, who complains that while other parents have sent their kids care packages, Mẹ and Ba haven't.

"Care package, what is that?" Mẹ asks—or shouts, as the blender breaks down some spices. Evie quickly explains the concept, to which Mẹ says that Vietnamese food, the good kind, can't ever be mailed.

Meanwhile my hands are getting tired holding the phone so they can see each other.

"What about *bánh tai heo*? I'm craving it." My sister loves eating pig ears. Not real pig ears, but sugary biscuits that are shaped like them.

"Okay, if you want, I will make them."

"Don't do it if you're too busy." She points out that Mẹ shouldn't be cooking on her day off. "Weekends are for fun. For people to do a hobby or something."

"Yeah, like gardening," I say.

"No way. Every time Mẹ tries to grow something, she kills it."

"Something is wrong with our soil," Mẹ protests lightly as she grabs something from the drawer.

Evie and I exchange knowing looks. Makes me feel like she's not hours away. In our small backyard, there's a graveyard of plants Mẹ tried to grow: tomatoes, cucumbers, peppers. The only thing that has survived are herbs, though it's only a small selection.

"Sure, Mẹ. Sure."

Evie says she's going on a run next and would text later. Once she's gone, Mẹ asks me worriedly, "Does she sound happy? Does she look thinner to you? Maybe she doesn't have enough to eat."

When we moved Evie into the dorms, we had more food than anything else for her. Luckily her roommate is Filipino, so she and her parents merely congratulated my parents on their preparedness. Then Ba told them to stop by our restaurant if they were ever in the area. That was when Evie decided it was time to say goodbye.

"Mẹ, she's fine. She seems really happy. Don't worry."

"Mà Mẹ là Mẹ. Mẹ phải lo."

I get up from the table, finished with breakfast. I hug my mom from behind. "Yeah, but Evie's got this. She can take care of herself. You know how she is." At that, Mẹ only sighs deeply, and my body mimics the movement.

"Do you miss her?" she asks me.

"Sometimes." And that's the truth of it. I thought it'd be much weirder to go home to a half-empty bedroom. But over the past few weeks, I've gotten used to it. I think of my aunt and the packages she sends Mẹ. I look at her longingly staring out the window over the sink, the light showing that Mẹ seems to have a few more gray hairs than I remember. "Do you miss Dì Vàng?"

"Sometimes," she says quietly. She doesn't elaborate, and I'm wondering if she's going into one of her moods.

I let go and ask if I can help with anything.

"No, there's too much to do. I should do it myself. Why don't you do your homework and if you have finished, go to your *hobby*," Mẹ says, trying to mimic the way Evie says it, but she ends up sounding nasally.

I bite my tongue, feeling like that's how my parents will always see painting for me.

It's just a suggestion, she probably thinks nothing of it, but the easy dismissal of my hobby makes the taste of *patê sô* linger uncomfortably on my tongue.

"You really should find something else to do, Mẹ. You work too much."

"And work is good. Work makes money." As she opens the blender to peer at its contents, she says, "I haven't had a hobby since I was a teenager. Your age."

"What did you like to do?"

A wistful look passes through her eyes. "Travel. When I wasn't at school or helping out around the house, I'd go around Nha Trang to places I'd never been. I would travel to Saigon and Đà Lạt. Oh, Đà Lạt was so beautiful! So romantic!" She laughs. "And when we escaped, my first wish was that we'd land somewhere in Europe."

"Have you traveled since?"

"No, no. Where was the money? *Đời sống đã rất là khó.* I had to work in factories, the nail salon, wherever I could get work. School wasn't a priority since we needed money. Traveling was a foolish idea. An impossible idea." She shakes her head.

"That is why I'm happy to see Evie find her way. She will live a life that's not *khó*. Unlike I had. Unlike your aunt." Her tone shifts to one of disapproval. "And soon enough you will have a good life too."

A good life. A good life only comes if you have security—that's what my mom's basically saying. Anything beyond that is just a pipe dream.

CHAPTER FIFTEEN

BẢO

My phone buzzes as a text comes in. I lift my head from the pillow, my bleary eyes searching for my alarm clock, which tells me the time is eight thirty. Who's texting me *now*? Despite having the uncanny ability to wake up early—probably drilled in by his parents, who took him on morning delivery routes all his life—Việt's never the one to text first; he only responds to them, three days too late. The only other person who texts me consistently is Mẹ, through Ba, and if she wanted me to actually wake up, she wouldn't be this discreet.

Nothing is more efficient at waking you from a dead sleep—while also drawing out an involuntary, undignified high-pitched scream—than a Vietnamese mother bursting through the door without warning.

I grapple for my phone and squint down at my screen.

hey! it's linh. i got your number from ali.

Linh. Last night's events trickle through my hazy mind. Boba. Our walk. Partners.

I sit up immediately.

sorry to bother you so early.

Should I tell her I don't recall ever giving Ali my phone number—and part of me is perplexed at how she managed that? Another time.

no worries! i'm up anyway.

The bubbles appear. An exclamation point! **are you an early riser, too?**

yeah—I start typing, then change my mind. Why would I want to lie about that? **only when my mom's threatening my life.**

😊

she doesn't knock either?

I grin, leaning against the headboard.

very unfamiliar with the concept . . . are you usually up this early on weekends?

sometimes it's the only chance for me to draw.

wow, that's commitment.

💪

anyways, just wanted to let you know our lovely boss—I laugh at this—**has given us our first restaurant. they responded right away when ali emailed some places. kami, it's a japanese**

restaurant in santa ana. i could do next weekend. i'm not work-
ing. you?

I grow more awake with each word. We're doing this! We're making plans, together!

totally. My thumb hovers over my next sentence. **can't wait!**

Bubbles appear. Those damn bubbles.

☺

Now I can go back to sleep.

It's nearing ten when I finally wake up again. Strangely my mom hasn't barreled in to scream at me. When I go down still in my sweats and T-shirt, I see my parents sitting at the table, like they've convened for a meeting. They're already dressed.

"You're not working?" I ask, fighting past a big yawn.

"We're going in the afternoon. But we thought we'd eat out today."

We never eat out. Which can only mean: We're going on a spying mission.

I don't remember when it started, but this isn't the first time we've gone to a competing restaurant to see if it's really any competition to ours. Only my parents would do this. Really. Because they're weird and obsessed, and they like to bring me into their odd hobbies. And maybe, in an odd way, it's their attempt to compromise. I'd always wanted to eat out: McDonald's. KFC. Red Robin. When I begged and begged, my mom's reply was always the same. That it was a waste of money and—

"I can make that. And I can make it even better!"

So far, my parents have managed not to bicker over the GPS and we haven't gotten lost yet. That tells me Ba probably did advance research.

"Anh, slow down," my mom says. She's in the passenger seat, death-gripping the handlebar just over her head.

I look at the meter. Forty-five miles per hour.

"How'd you hear about the place?" I ask my parents, resigned to my fate.

"One of our customers mentioned it in passing," Mẹ says. "But don't worry: That customer is loyal to us."

Oh, I was so worried.

We pull into the parking lot of a plaza. The restaurant's surrounded by upscale jewelry stores and "elite" nail salons, and that confirms—at least to me—that the restaurant won't be legit. It's all too . . . new. Too shiny. Where are the errant shopping bags rolling along with the breeze? Discarded rinds from clementines or lychees?

This is what happens when we step inside "photastic." Purposely all lowercase.

"*Trời Đất,*" my mom mutters first. Usually it's an "Oh my god," but in this case it means, *What shit is this?*

Everything in the restaurant is white: the walls, the tiles, the tables, and chairs.

Even the host is white, wearing a T-shirt printed with a poorly drawn BÁNH MÌ.

Where's the shrine? What kind of Vietnamese restaurant doesn't have a shrine? Where's the red? And yellow? Fake flowers? The floor that's seen better days?

"*Chao, Bac!*" says the host, missing the tones completely. He has the audacity to bow. "Table for three?"

Dumbstruck, my parents nod. Even though the waiter's annoying me, I almost laugh at my parents being speechless for once.

Not for long, at least.

"A white waiter?" Mẹ hisses after we get our menus. We sit in the center at a round table that Ba moves around to see if it's lopsided. It's not, which, to me, makes this place even more inauthentic. "Speaking horrible Vietnamese, too."

"We can always turn around," I say.

"No," Ba says firmly and calmly, pushing a menu to me and Mẹ. "This is competition."

"Barely!" my mom protests.

He overrides her. "Let's see why that customer is talking to you about this place."

We fall silent when the waiter—John, because of course—returns again. He asks if we're ready to order and Ba *actually* pulls out a list of menu items and reads them off.

See: research.

When the confusion dawns on John's face, my stomach drops.

"I'm sorry, sir. Can you repeat that?" John looks to me, like I'm expected to translate for Ba. I look away from him, wanting to prolong his misery. We get this a lot when we go out to non-Vietnamese places—and maybe this is why we don't go out often. Obviously, my dad's accent gives him away. He wasn't born here like me. But even though I understand him perfectly, sometimes he gets nervous—but doesn't want to say so—and he speaks quickly. When I was a kid—bowl-cut me, let's just say—it was embarrassing. Maybe it was the look others gave him, or the visible discomfort in my parents.

Now I'm just annoyed by people like John.

Ba clears his throat, sits up straighter in his seat. "Coffee. For the three of us." He slows his words as he relays the rest.

"Oh, yes, sorry." The red in the waiter's ears—now he's embarrassed—fades while he jots down the order.

The time waiting for our food consists of my mom and dad's airing their complaints against the place. Seems like we're the only Vietnamese family here. The lights are too bright. They gave us "organic" *cà phê sữa đá* that was already served in a glass with ice. Real Vietnamese restaurants make the customers do their own work. The only concession is good-looking waiters—one, as my mom points out, resembles a K-pop star.

Then the food comes. Turns out, even a kid who didn't grow up in a restaurant could tell this wasn't any legit Vietnamese restaurant. General atmosphere aside, the kitchen was only doing a poor imitation of the Việt food I recognize. The *cơm chiên* doesn't have Chinese sausage—what kind of fried rice dish is this? Other crimes include oversalting the phở and not crisping up the fish enough.

"*Dở ẹc!*" my mother says, a look of disgust on her face as she sorts through the mushy fish. She'd already removed the bones and they slid off suspiciously cleanly. If it were really done well, the bones would refuse to come off, and you'd have no choice but to use a hand and chopstick pair to remove them.

"No doubt, this restaurant will close within a few months," Ba finally says, pushing away his unfinished plate. I repeat: unfinished.

Linh's text about our first assignment comes to mind. I ask my parents if I could duck out of my shift early next week. And then the interrogation happens.

"Why?"

"I have a newspaper assignment."

"Newspaper? When?"

"Just this year. I'm writing food reviews."

"You?" my parents ask, simultaneously stunned and incredulous.

"Yes," I answer exasperatedly. "It's something I started doing."

"You are writing about food?" Ba asks for confirmation.

"He does eat like Ba," Mẹ mutters, still staring at me. "But why?"

Because Linh's going to do it too. Not the best answer to give. "Because it's something to do. I thought you'd be more excited that I'm doing, you know, something." Using my chopsticks, I stuff a bite of white rice in my mouth, trying to act casual. Too *nhão*. Mushy.

"Writing . . . You never said you liked it," my mom says.

"Just because I never talked about it doesn't mean I didn't like it."

"You did like reading dictionaries as a kid," Ba concedes. Turning to my mom, his tone shifts to a joking one. "Maybe he's seeing his girlfriend."

Mẹ catches on, her preoccupation flying away. "Ha! Like that would happen."

"Funny, guys. Funny. Girls like me!" I decide to play along. "There's at least one girl in each class who likes me. Kelly Tran. Fiona Su. Cindy Jackson." The idea of these girls liking me sends my parents laughing. Even I'm joining in. Me and Kelly, the girl who despises me for avoiding VSA duties like the plague?

Later, I won't be able to explain why I said what I said next. Maybe it's a slip of the tongue, or because it's a notion even more ridiculous than Kelly, Fiona, or Cindy having a crush on me. Right after Cindy, Linh's name slips through my lips.

A dark expression crosses my mom's face, like clouds engulfing the sun. "Linh Mai?"

There's a dangerous tone in her question, and I immediately retreat. "Just kidding. I've never talked to her in my life."

"Good."

"I mean, she's, like, really weird. Like, really, *really* weird. No one likes her at school," I say. "And she smells!"

Acting: not my career path. My parents continue glaring at me stonily, the playful mood from before gone. "Seriously, I'm not seeing anyone. I really am on assignment for the newspaper."

This causes my mother to lean back, shoulders relaxing.

A different waiter has come back—mixed, Vietnamese and white, maybe. Her grin falters when she notices my mom's fury.

"Can I get you anything else, cô?"

My mom softens her expression, musters a smile. Maybe she's consoled in seeing another Vietnamese person in the room. "Yes, we're ready." She cracks open the menu again. "Let's try the dessert."

◇ ◇ ◇

All the guys here have perfect hair.

That's my first observation as I walk into the restaurant that Ali had assigned us. The host disarms me with his bright smile as he greets me in Japanese. Average height, he's still made tiny by the large wooden desk that he stands behind. The divider's just low enough to let me see the waiters walking around, their polished hair—many of them with the hair of a Silicon Valley guy post-startup phase. Many immaculate man-buns, which the host also has. I'd look ridiculous if I tried wearing my hair like that.

Linh hasn't arrived yet, and in various hand gestures, I let the host know that I'll wait for a few seconds. Looking up: stalactites— thin wooden structures jutting down from the ceiling, painted to mimic the top parts of northern Japanese hemlocks. Somewhere in my research about this place, I remember seeing that the chef is from Kyushu, specifically Fukuoka. Maybe this art was inspired by his home. I sneak my notepad from my back jeans pocket—Ali forced it on me, saying it'd make me look more "legit."

I turn to the mirrors functioning as walls. Strands of hair still stick out no matter how much gel I use. I'm so preoccupied that I don't notice Linh sneaking up on me.

She arches an eyebrow. "Everything okay?"

"Um . . . hair," I manage to articulate.

Her mouth moves like she's fighting words back. Or a smile. "It looks fine."

We let the host know that we're from La Quinta, and as Ali promised, the restaurant was expecting us. Ken, the host, leads us past the dividers. While the waiting room transports you to a different height, the main dining room brings you back to the ground, literally. The floor takes on the cool colors of a modern city; the walls, the outlines of high-rise buildings, adorned and labeled with the sleekness of kanji. Japanese pop music brings an intimate, personal vibe that calms me immediately. It reminds me of seeing out the last customers for the day, of the feeling right before I throw myself into bed.

The other diners are mostly Asian—a good sign—and aged young. We don't recognize anyone, which makes sense since it's a city away. We get seated, and I sneak a look at Linh smiling and nodding at the waitress who swooped in. Linh asks about the artwork, sparking life into the waitress's eyes. Maybe she's an artist, too. I take down parts of the conversation: her uncle's the chef and yes, he wanted the restaurant decor to be an homage to his home island.

"We were just fixated on the idea that art can say so much about family history."

"I totally understand! I'm working on something similar."

I make a note to ask about that. When the waitress leaves, though, we're alone, forced to look at each other, and suddenly my ability to speak has retreated somewhere else. Our time at the boba shop might as well have been a dream. I resist the urge to straighten the bottle of soy sauce between us, just to do *something*.

"You've been taking notes already?" Linh nods at the notepad next to me. "I brought mine, too."

From her small backpack, she pulls out her sketchbook that I saw in the boba shop. I watch her hands, faint paint still on her fingers.

A trademark. Linh notices, glancing down, and tries to hide it. "Sorry, I was trying to fit in some painting time before and probably should have washed it off better."

"No, it's all good. It's very . . . you. You know, being an artist and all that." I see the same expression from before, like she doesn't quite know how to read me, so I rush to add, "Anyway, yeah, I only took a few notes so far. I had to Google how to write a food review. That's the level of confidence I have right now."

Linh laughs, sitting back. "Here's a tip. I've learned in reading art reviews that the best reviews aren't just about the art or whether it's good or not. It's also how other patrons will react to it. What meaning the art piece might have to others."

"Good to know."

"You won't have any issue at all on the food part, though. I mean, we grew up in the business. We know good food, don't we?"

Her words summon into memory our first meeting—the first time we reviewed something together in a way. I crack a smile, relaxing a bit more. We take a few minutes with the menu before ordering a tempura assortment, shrimp and vegetable, to share, then ordering ramen—*tonkatsu* ramen for me and spicy miso ramen for Linh.

"So," Linh says, stitching together her fingers and leaning forward. "What kind of place is perfect for a date? Maybe it'd help to think about that as you review it."

Of course, to contribute to my under-qualifications—add the fact that I've never been on a date, either. Unless you count one lunch with a girl at Burger King during a sixth-grade field trip.

Which I tell Linh, and she just laughs. She'd probably gone on more dates than me. Most of my classmates probably have, too. So it shocks me when she says, "I've never been a date either. So I guess we're even."

"That's comforting." I pick up my pencil, tapping it against my notebook. "Dates have to be somewhere you can actually get to know someone. Like us right now." I wish I could take the words back. *Does she think that* I *think this is a date?*

But Linh doesn't seem to notice, adding, "The noise level has to be just right so that it's an actual conversation. Like, if someone is speaking quietly, you should still be able to hear that person."

"Dimly lit atmosphere with a noise level that's perfect for conversations and whispers," I say aloud as I write.

I feel like she means it. We go back and forth with other requirements of a "perfect date": a nice seating or standing arrangement; an activity that both people like and could talk about later. The waitress drops by with our appetizer, then disappears again.

"Ultimately, I think both people on the date need to be comfortable, as if you could literally share everything and anything. Which is why the setting matters," Linh says.

Our waitress shows up again with a bowl, her fellow waiter tagging along with another bowl. I make a note about the short waiting time. I start salivating the moment the aroma wafts from my ramen—intense and smoky. It doesn't disappoint. The first spoonful of broth coats my tongue in a silky layer, and the noodles are still firm yet give way easily under my teeth. The egg is sweet and salty, soaked in umami.

"Remind me to thank Ali," Linh says into her spoon. "It's not like most other ramen, which goes overboard with the salt."

"Good ramen doesn't feel like you're drowning in a bowl of salt," I pretend to write. "You want to trade for a second?"

We exchange bowls, keeping our utensils. Linh pauses and blows on her broth. "*Ăn đi, con*," I say, mimicking countless cousins or aunts at family gatherings who are almost always chasing an impossible toddler to feed.

Linh's now midbite but she laughs, then covers her mouth. "Don't! You just made me spit!"

"On a date, it's important not to sit across from anyone who spits," I add to my invisible list.

Linh telepathically lets me know to shut up. Her ramen is pleasantly spicy, the texture of the broth similar to mine, the kind that sits comfortably on the tongue, doesn't attack you.

My earlier nervousness is completely gone now as we alternate the time eating, describing our food, and complaining about school and balancing working at the restaurants. She talks about how her parents set her up with an engineering student they know so she can ask questions. Which is a good idea—and I hope my parents don't think of it. I'm fine with limiting the times I disappoint someone.

Linh takes pictures of her ramen, and she starts with her sketch of the restaurant, outlining the most prominent parts: the walls, tables, and chairs. "For size comparison." Her pencil seems to float above the page instead of touching it and she falls silent now, locked in her world. A world I'm finally getting a look at.

Watching Linh's thoughts play across her face is . . . interesting.

I remember how she looked that night, distress rippling across her face, the indecision as her eyes flitted between me and the restaurant.

For years, my parents' issues with her family were a separate, weird thing that I'd accepted, one of their many oddities—like their near-worship of lottery numbers, their insistence with each wrong number that they were *just* about to give that number. Or Mẹ's tendency to use me or my dad to get a double-tasting of samples at the supermarket.

"How can your parents *not* want you to be an artist?"

I don't mean to disrupt her, but it pulls her out of her head.

"I guess it doesn't feel stable to them. My parents aren't really about making tons of money. It's about making just enough to sustain themselves. They didn't have that when they came over, so they wanted it for me."

"They escaped too?"

"They escaped," she confirms. "By boat."

I spoon some of my remaining broth, watching the surface ripple. All my life, I thought it was normal that my mom and dad had left by sea. They'd known each other growing up and left in the same boat owned by the second cousin of a mutual friend. Their connection to this boat owner might have been loose, but they were past caring. Trustworthiness during this time was a messy ideal anyway. They just had to leave. But after hearing conversations from my mom's friends, conversations with other Việt kids at school, families came another way: through sponsorship, through marriage.

But I feel like it does say something about the type of people my parents are—Linh's parents, too—to put trust in the unknowable sea, in the people who navigated the boats to the ultimate destination. Survivors.

"So you don't tell your parents about wanting to be an artist because they don't see it as a viable career."

Linh nods. "That's why I have to keep it a secret. Some secrets are good. They can be helpful."

"Still, it's hard to keep a secret."

"*You're* keeping a secret. You haven't exactly told your parents that you're working with me on this newspaper assignment."

It's not the same thing, but I can't figure out how to say it.

"Me and my art—I'm not really lying. I'm downplaying it," Linh continues. She fiddles with the end of a chopstick, not looking at me now. Somehow I feel as if I've stepped over an invisible line. "Okay, I guess it's hiding. But it's necessary!" She directs the last line at me, suddenly insistent. "First of all, you're a guy, so you probably get away with a lot of things."

I open my mouth to argue, but I remember a cousin at a gathering complaining that her brother had a later curfew because he was a guy. "Okay, I see that."

"But my parents are pretty much insistent that I do *anything* but be an artist. To do this, I have to lie. There's no other way, really," Linh says, defensiveness seeping in at the edges. "I'm not usually a liar."

"I'm not calling you a—I'm just saying."

It's my fault things went a little sour. Linh's now avoiding further conversation by zoning in on her sketchbook. "It's fine."

Later, our goodbye is less hopeful than our last one the night we had boba.

This isn't a date, so why does it feel like I messed everything up?

CHAPTER SIXTEEN

LINH

It's not that I didn't know I was liar. But to hear someone else agree with that? It's piercing. Especially coming from Bảo, because as much as I dislike the label, I know he's right. Lying to maintain stability. Lying to make sure my parents aren't worrying about me or nagging me because they already have to do that as parents. In a way, isn't this saving my parents from grief? He's doing it, too. That's the only reason why we're able to do this whole food beat.

But it's never going to stop if you go on like this, says a voice unusually like Bảo's.

I yell in frustration, glad to have the house to myself for an hour. My parents are still at the restaurant. My sketch from earlier tonight is beside me, nearly done. I just have to add more depth perception. I run my hand across its rough texture.

Bảo can't know the pressure. From what I can tell, his parents aren't forcing him to be something—they just want him to find his path, which he said he couldn't see, but observing him tonight, writing seems to come naturally to him.

I force down the sudden spike of jealousy; his parents are clearly different from mine.

It felt normal in the beginning. If other people were looking in, we probably seemed like two high school students on a real date. When I'm with Ali, I can talk about a lot of things, but she can't understand being raised the way me and Evie were. We grew up differently.

I smile at the memory of watching him try to tame his hair. He didn't know I was there. I can't be sure, but I feel as if his hair is the type to grow faster than it should. I like it long, better than his bowl cut—for obvious reasons. It's the kind of hair that'd be easy to run through with your hands.

My hand. I glance down.

In my reverie, I was starting to outline the shape of his head. I rub at the image, smudging the lines.

But of course I botched the conversation. I panicked when he pressed me about lying. The moment he mentioned lying, I denied it, but I was denying the truth. I shouldn't have shut down. I wouldn't be surprised if Bảo told Ali the next day that he can't work the beat anymore.

It'd be another lie to say that that wouldn't hurt me.

"How was dinner with Ali?"

Flipping over my sketchbook, even though there's nothing to give me away, I look up. Right: my excuse. Mẹ had come back from work at some point. I hear Ba over in their room, opening and closing drawers, getting ready for bed.

"Good. We ate ramen."

Mẹ makes a face. She's not a huge fan, claiming it's too salty for her taste. As she comes over, I shove the sketchbook under my pillow.

"Mẹ missed a call from Dì Vàng. Let's see why she called." Mẹ sits on my bed, and scoots back so that she's against the wall like me.

After a few rings on Viber, my aunt appears onscreen in all of her familiar late-morning, *I was sculpting all last night for fun* grogginess. Her large black-rimmed glasses sit at the end of her nose. She's still in her pajamas, light green elephants printed on the sleeves. My mom has a similar set; the material is perfect for the heat here, too. Dì Vàng is in her apartment's kitchen, a cup of *cà phê đen* beside her. If I strain enough I might be able to hear the motorcycles outside her window, some neighborhood women laughing, loitering on the sidewalk, or a vendor hawking fish or fresh veggies.

"Did you just wake up?" my mom asks. It's eleven in the morning over there, too late for Mẹ's typical wake-up time at dawn.

"Maybe." *Knew it.* My aunt makes a show of yawning and stretching. "What did you eat for dinner?"

"Leftovers. And you?"

I roll my eyes. They say hi and immediately ask about food? My aunt points the phone downward to show her plate of *ốp la*—fried eggs, the yolk runny once pierced—with *bánh mì*, likely fresh from next door.

"Where's the *xì dầu*?" Mẹ asks almost accusingly.

"Chị trying to diet. Less salt. It's perfectly fine without it."

"You sound Mỹ," Mẹ says. I grin, thinking about how much my mom acts like the older sister even though she isn't. My aunt knows how to take it, though, shooting back playful replies. Oh yes, I can see it.

"So, what's happening? You don't usually call me. It's the other way around."

"Did you get my vase?"

"Yes. You shouldn't have sent it. It costs so much money to ship things over."

"I wanted to give you something nice! But if you're that worried about money, maybe I should just deliver my next one to you myself." Dì Vàng leans closer, grinning now. Her eyes are alive.

Does she mean . . . ?

"Are you coming here?"

"Are you?" I ask, pulling the phone from Mẹ's hand. She snatches it back.

"You're coming here, really?" she asks again.

"Yes, it's been way too long. Twelve, thirteen years?"

"When are you coming?"

"Around Tết."

"You're leaving around Tết? But why? It's the best holiday. Traffic will be horrible."

Dì Vàng laughs. "Of course you're already worrying about the travel schedule! Anyway, I've seen so many Tết; I live here. Plus it's been so long! I want to see you. I want to hug Evie and Linh!"

"That can't be the only reason."

"I also might be visiting some artist friends on the West Coast."

"You have friends here?" I ask, though I shouldn't be surprised. When she visited the last time, she managed to make conversation with everyone on the floor of our old apartment building, people my parents and I never even interacted with. She even met Bác Xuân when he came by, and in no time they were trading hypotheticals on what he would do when he retired and moved closer to his adult children and their families.

"I have friends all over the place. I'm international."

"I can't believe you're coming," I say excitedly. It'll be two artists under one roof. We'll go to museums, I'll show her my work. Someone who will understand my language. And support it.

"Do you have enough money to go traveling?"

Dì Vàng tuts at my mom. "Of course I do. My business is good over here; I wish you believed me." She leans in again, seeing something in my mom's expression that I must have missed. "I am no longer a struggling artist, as you seem to think I will always be."

"You've struggled for a long time, I remember."

"I know; I remember too. But I am fine. You shouldn't worry too much, *em*."

Mẹ holds back whatever thought she has and they move on to talking about old friends, some woman they knew who'd eloped in Hội An, then came back without the husband recently. I sit there, silent, content to listen, eyes tracking the level of my aunt's coffee as she sips away at it. Then Mẹ notices my eyes closing slowly. The ramen is finally kicking in, lulling me to sleep.

"Okay, *cho* Linh *đi ngủ.*" They exchange goodbyes, my aunt saying she'd circle back with more info about her visit next year.

Mẹ only sighs as she maneuvers herself off my bed.

"Be happy, Mẹ!" I say, holding on to my mom's arm before she leaves, trying to get her not to worry already. "Your sister's coming over." I see a hint of a smile blooming on her face, though she stops herself, shooing away my hand.

"I really don't know what she's thinking. She's so unpredictable. And she shouldn't spend her money so freely."

"Was it really that bad? Dì Vàng and her sculpting business."

"She'd just started it when she was seventeen right after leaving school. Then rationings were happening and the government was watching anyone who was against *cộng sản* very closely. They stole part of our land, leaving little to us." My mom fiddles with the back of her phone cover. "Many times Dì Vàng would come home without making any sales."

"So what happened?"

"Luckily, we had older aunts and uncles who would come in and out, making sure we were fed. That is the Vietnamese way. But still, Mẹ *biết nghề nghiệp của* Dì Vàng would not help us. Art was only for fun. And during that time, there was no time for playing.

"At the camps, when Mẹ finally made it—just *mười hai tuổi*—I promised I would work hard. So that we would suffer less. So that Mẹ could help your aunt back home."

My mom was fourteen by the time they left the camps and

were accepted into the United States with her cousins and two other refugees they'd grown close to. But she couldn't depend on her cousins alone—they too were thrust into an unfamiliar place with minimal English—and finding work was hard. So, when she wasn't studying to catch up at school, she was working odd jobs. Some of the money went to their daily expenses. Whatever was left over she'd send back to Vietnam, to help my aunt.

"Ah, *Mẹ nhức đầu*," she says, massaging her temples, worries about my aunt plaguing her mind. Then she's off to the next room, muttering about how much she'll need to clean up to accommodate her sister coming over, despite us having plenty of time to prepare.

I still don't understand. My aunt seems so happy, and she's managed to get this far, and it can't all be because she gets some money now and then from America. She's not struggling like before, so why can't my mom see that it all turned out okay in the end? It's like the memories of my aunt's struggle keep her from seeing the good sides to art.

I pull out my sketchpad from its hiding place and trace over the image of Bảo. I barely remember doing this drawing; I was just lost in the act of doing it. It's a type of forgetting that I love, that I can't get anywhere else. Inside my head, I can just *be*. My aunt must know this too.

I text Evie about our aunt coming over, and she texts back, jokingly, **great, there will be two of you.**

CHAPTER SEVENTEEN

BẢO

It's not really unusual for kids who grew up in restaurants to eat in record time. Mẹ had to feed us before the rush hour or else there wouldn't be another opportunity. And now, working at the restaurant, when noon hits, when customers come flowing in, we need to eat quickly.

"So, what, you think she's mad at you, then?" Việt asks, scraping the last of his egg noodles from his Styrofoam plate. An apple sits on his left, a strawberry yogurt that he won't eat to his right. He hates artificial sugar. I'd told him about the restaurant, how things had started out fine. Fun, even, until Linh shut down on me.

"I guess so. Maybe because I basically called her a liar."

Việt shakes his head, like, *You poor kid.* "I don't know, man. It's hypocritical. I mean, you're lying about where you're going and who you're spending time with, too. And why's that?"

I see his point now. "So my parents don't blow up on me. My mom, especially."

"Exactly," Việt says.

"I didn't mean it like that, though. I was just saying . . . I wish her parents could see what she's doing. Because she's an artist. She can't be anything else."

"And you know this after only a few weeks of talking to her."

Okay, he's looking at me like I'm obsessed with her. "Shut up."

Việt grins in return, biting into an apple. "This is the first time I've heard you talk about a girl, let alone the daughter of your family's worst enemy."

"I didn't think you'd ever give me advice about talking to a girl."

My best friend merely shrugs. "Whenever I take a break from watching *Law & Order* or *Criminal Minds*, I sometimes flip to *The Bachelor*, which tells me exactly what not to do when talking to a girl you like."

Sure, very reliable.

"I don't know, dude. Maybe next time you see her, try to apologize. Let her deal with her parents at her own pace."

When Việt's cross-country friends join our table, our abnormal conversation ends. It's a brief respite since I have my limits with their circular conversations about sprint times, better sprint times, and plans for another pasta party before a meet. And I've never seen anyone eat as many bananas in one sitting as Steve, the team captain. Because of Việt, they tolerate my complete un-athleticism, acknowledge me with a slight nod and a "What's up, man."

"C'mon, how long has it been since you washed your uniform?" Steve asks one of the guys.

His friend, who has a watch tan, shrugs. "I dunno. A week?"

Việt's friends are the definition of riveting.

But as different as Việt is from his teammates, at least from what I can see, it makes sense to see him with them. Việt's always been precise and stuck close to regimens, and I guess that's why he and his teammates hang out outside of practice.

I look around and spot Ali and her Viking braid. She's laughing along with some of her friends—didn't think she was capable of that—but I scan her table and don't find Linh anywhere.

Where's Linh now?

Next time I see her, I'll apologize. I stand up, gathering my things. Việt asks where I'm heading. "Gotta finish some homework." The strawberry yogurt that he set aside conjures the memory of Linh ordering her strawberry-flavored boba tea. And the chocolate milk she slipped into my hand.

"Can I grab this?"

A caution cone blocks off the guys' bathroom, where puddles of water glisten on the floor. Old, torn posters and flyers have fallen from their fastenings. Home Economics is having a bake sale. The Vietnamese Student Association is having a carwash fundraiser in a week.

I have to make sure *not* to be available.

Voices volley off the walls outside the cafeteria, but the hallway itself is silent, absent of rustling clothes and slamming lockers. Where does Linh go during lunch?

Then, of course, I know. The art room. Where else would an artist find refuge? I'm there in a few minutes, standing just by the threshold, where we nearly collided a few weeks back. She's crossing the room to sit on a stool by the window, dressed in paint-splattered overalls that I imagine she'd changed into.

I clear my throat. Linh turns. "Oh, hi. What's up? You're not eating lunch?"

"I already did. You?"

"Yeah, I eat pretty quickly. Habit, I guess."

"Of course. We're restaurant kids."

Taking this as sign to come in, I hide the yogurt behind my back, walk into the room. "What are you working on?" I'm close enough to see the canvas now, with just a few strokes of color, a shape yet to be determined.

"I really don't know. Sometimes I come in, grab some tubes, and start mixing colors just because."

I reach up to touch the canvas, but her hand goes around my wrist.

"No touching." Her voice is threatening, but she's suppressing a smile.

I hold up a hand in surrender. There's a different energy to Linh now. A more protective Linh.

I like it.

"Is this where you always go during lunch? I never see you." Of course, I'm admitting I'm a stalker—a shitty one, since I never *can* find her—so that's great.

But Linh turns back, dipping her brush into a jar of water, before answering: "It's nice down here."

Unable to find other things to say, I hand over the yogurt. Her brow furrows in confusion before she glances up. She accepts it, her fingers lingering against my palm. *Breathe.*

Linh says "Hmmm" before setting it down. "What's this for?"

"To apologize." I seize the moment. "Or try to. Look, when we were at the restaurant, I might have asked some questions that you clearly didn't want to answer. I didn't mean to push you or accuse you. I guess I realized only after that I was being hypocritical too."

"And you think a yogurt's enough to make it up to me?" She faces the canvas again, her tone monotonous.

Oh shit, should I run?

"N-no," I stutter. "It's—well—"

Her laughter splits the air. She faces me again, and her eyes soften. "That's nice of you to say. A part of me knows you're right, and I don't like it either. Lying is not who I am. But—" She shrugs. "I don't see another way to do this without lying."

"We'll be partners *and* liars."

"We're pathetic," Linh groans, laughing into her hands covering her face.

"You just realized that?" I ask. "I meant what I said, though." I pause because, when Linh looks at me suddenly like that, words escape me. So I stare at the floor. "I really wish your parents liked the idea of you as an artist. Your work, it has a way of drawing people in. I'm the least artistic person on earth, and I just wish you could feel freer to do it."

"Thanks."

"Okay, I guess I'll just leave you alone now." I start backing away, even though my legs don't want to move.

"No, you can stay. I don't mind. But only if you're quiet." She gives me a pointed but playful look.

I take the invitation. "I'll be over there." I wince when the stool I pull out squeaks against the floor. My backpack slams against the table. "I need to start on my article anyway." I remember how I shoved my notepad to the bottom of my backpack. I'll need to dig it out.

"You haven't started it yet?" she asks incredulously.

"Um . . . no."

"Use this for inspiration." She's right next to me now, opening up a see-through folder and sliding a page to me. A sketch, all inked up. I know what this is.

"How did you do it so quickly?"

"I just did." She shrugs. Am I cursed to surround myself with casual geniuses? Việt's tolerable, he doesn't rub it in my face that school comes easily to him, and here's Linh basically saying, but not bragging, *I'm just naturally talented.*

"Oh, come on." I glance down at her sketch of the restaurant. It captures the dimness of the room, the structures hanging down from the ceiling, the columns of Japan's cityscapes. It looks print-ready.

"Better get started on your end of the deal," she teases me, right by my ear. "Or else you'll have to answer to Ali."

"Teach me how," I say, boldness coming from nowhere. I stay as still as possible.

"How to what?" she asks, a hint of amusement in her voice. Disappointing me, she takes a step back.

"To get inside my head. Like what happens when you paint."

"Close your eyes, then."

"Are we going to meditate?"

"Just do it."

A few seconds pass and soon I feel her prying my fingers open, placing something wooden in my palm. I feel it: It's long and there's rubber at the end; it's a—

I open my eyes.

Linh's trying to hold back a laugh, looking down at the pencil in my hand. "I can't teach you something like this. You have to do it yourself because writing is personal to you. So"—she gestures with her fingers, her tone becoming stern—"turn around and just do it."

"*Now* I see why you and Ali are friends."

"Thank you," she answers proudly. And she turns to walk back to her easel.

And this is how I spend the rest of my lunch, hidden away, just the two of us.

The cool metal under me, the hum of the air-conditioning. I listen to Linh washing her brush periodically in water, the brush hitting against glass, sending out a ringing sound, the scratch of brush bristles. And the sway of her ponytail when she tilts her head to examine her work.

I zone in on her sketch, the colors perfectly capturing the decor. I can even smell salt in the ramen. I close my eyes, tight. The warm broth layers my tongue in flavor. The chewiness of the noodles. Linh's laugh as she tried mine.

I begin to write.

Barnes & Noble Booksellers #2938
5555 S. Virginia St.
Reno, NV 89502
775-826-8882

STR:2938 REG:002 TRN:8456 CSHR:Taylor B

Pho Love Story
9781534441941   T1   12.99
(1 @ 12.99)
Subtotal   12.99
Sales Tax T1 (8.265%)   1.07
TOTAL   14.06
VISA DEBIT   14.06
Card#: XXXXXXXXXXXXX9813
Application Label: US DEBIT
AID: A0000000980840
PIN Verified
TVR: 8080048000
TSI: 6800

A MEMBER WOULD HAVE SAVED   1.30

056.04B   02/11/2022 02:28PM

CUSTOMER COPY

Returns or exchanges will not be permitted (i) after 30 days or without receipt or (ii) for product not carried by Barnes & Noble.com, (iii) for purchases made with a check less than 7 days prior to the date of return.

icy on receipt may appear in two sections.

Return Policy

th a sales receipt or Barnes & Noble.com packing slip, ull refund in the original form of payment will be issued from y Barnes & Noble Booksellers store for returns of new and read books, and unopened and undamaged music CDs, Ds, vinyl records, electronics, toys/games and audio books ade within 30 days of purchase from a Barnes & Noble oksellers store or Barnes & Noble.com with the below ceptions:

Undamaged NOOKs purchased from any Barnes & Noble Booksellers store or from Barnes & Noble.com may be returned within 14 days when accompanied with a sales receipt or with a Barnes & Noble.com packing slip or may be exchanged within 30 days with a gift receipt.

A store credit for the purchase price will be issued (i) when a gift receipt is presented within 30 days of purchase, (ii) for all textbooks returns and exchanges, or (iii) when the original tender is PayPal.

Items purchased as part of a Buy One Get One or Buy Two, Get Third Free offer are available for exchange only, unless all items purchased as part of the offer are returned, in which case such items are available for a refund (in 30 days). Exchanges of the items sold at no cost are available only for items of equal or lesser value than the original cost of such item.

Opened music CDs, DVDs, vinyl records, electronics, toys/games, and audio books may not be returned, and can be exchanged only for the same product and only if defective. NOOKs purchased from other retailers or sellers are returnable only to the retailer or seller from which they were purchased pursuant to such retailer's or seller's return policy. Magazines, newspapers, eBooks, digital downloads, and used books are not returnable or exchangeable. Defective NOOKs may be exchanged at the store in accordance with the applicable warranty.

Returns or exchanges will not be permitted (i) after 30 days or without receipt or (ii) for product not carried by Barnes & Noble.com, (iii) for purchases made with a check less than 7 days prior to the date of return.

licy on receipt may appear in two sections.

CHAPTER EIGHTEEN

LINH

The next day, Bảo barges into the art room without any announcement, as if he'd always spent his lunches here and he was running just a bit behind. His hair is windswept and fashionable at the same time, like a breeze purposefully styled his hair. But it's his gaze I notice the most. Last year in an art theory lesson, we were taught about the gaze—or "the Gaze," as my art teacher wrote on the board and underlined three times. There are many definitions of a gaze—it could be the spectator or the patron's, or one person in the art piece looking at another person in the same frame, or, more disconcerting, the art looking back at the spectator. It's what's fascinated critics about *Mona Lisa* for centuries—how her outward gaze appears both superior and subdued, defiant and diminutive. That gaze, that look, can carry the whole artwork.

Now, I can only describe Bảo's gaze as shining. Vibrant. Made even more intense since he's looking straight at me. He was looking for me.

I set down my brush and palette when he offers a piece of paper to me. "It's my article," he says in a rush. I wonder how much caffeine he's had. "I worked on it last night. Can you read it?"

"Me?"

"Yes."

Hesitantly, I take his paper, which he really did write. His handwriting is solid and straight, nothing like the chicken scratch I'd seen from other classmates.

"You *actually* hand-wrote this."

"At first I was just jotting random things down, and then, I don't know, it turned into sentences. Didn't even realize how much I was writing." He grins. "I think I actually understand what you meant, when we were talking at 7 Leaves. I was outside my body."

"Ali never lets me read her things," I start saying, though I'm pleased that he remembers what I said. I never have an issue with what Ali writes. I just know she's good. Secretly, maybe she's always wanted a person to challenge her, find the mistakes that she can't spot herself.

Bảo looks so eager that I wouldn't want to turn him down anyway. "That's Ali. This is me. And I want you, specifically, to read this."

"Why?" I say, laughter bubbling in my throat.

"Because I've never written something like this. So I want you to be the first one to read my first article."

"Since I'm not a writer, I'll probably just say it's good. And even if it's bad, I'll probably lie."

"I think I'll know if you don't like it."

"How? I *can* lie." I pretend to think. "Didn't we talk about this before?"

"All right. Let's test it out."

Suddenly, from his seat, he hooks his foot around one leg of my stool, pulls me closer so that our knees touch. His eyes are fixed on me, and I want to look down, but I force my gaze ahead. I won't let him win. His hands loosely hold my wrists.

"Do you like phở?"

I almost burst out in laughter. He's being so ridiculous. "Isn't that an obvious answer?"

"Do you think I'm annoying?"

"Again, obvious."

He glances down. Strands of his hair fall into his eyes as he pauses deep in thought. His knee bumps against mine. "Do you think I'm handsome?"

That came out of nowhere. My eyes widen.

"Oh, I see," he says dramatically, beaming widely. "Your face just told me everything."

My heart is *racing*. "That proved nothing. I wasn't expecting that question. And you were only making broad interpretations anyway. My reaction doesn't mean that I think—"

"So I'm handsome, got it," he says cheekily. He easily ruffles his hair, a direct attack on my nerves right now.

I *have* to look away. I can't deal.

"You want me to read your article or not?" I ask.

Bảo raises both hands in defense.

I shake my head, trying not to smile, before turning my attention to his review.

As a visual person, I like his opening, his descriptive language painting the scene. I remember the wooden stalactites hanging from the ceiling, the intimidating sensation of gazing up at them, only to be transported to the forests they were emulating. I grin when he describes the staff's hair as "perfectly coiffed."

But the food is where I can understand why Ali chose him for this beat. He knows just the right words to describe the ramen and its broth (*full-bodied, tinged with enough salt just for the tip of your tongue*), the spiciness of my ramen (*happy tears, not fiery tears*), and by the end I forget that I've already eaten lunch. I have a craving for Japanese food again.

Bảo's staring intently at me when I look back up.

"Well?" he prompts me.

"It's horrible," I say. But he sees my face—reading it, as he said. And a beautiful smile comes to life.

Ali takes offense when I tell her I let Bảo into the room while I was working on an art piece. It's something I never let Ali do. For a good reason.

I'm in the newspaper room, her domain, waiting for the warning bell to signal me to leave. She has her curly hair tied up high in a messy bun on top of her head, a pen buried in there somewhere. Her feet are on the teacher's desk, and Rowan, entering the room to disappear into his office, points at them, then to the floor. Ali does exactly that . . . until his door closes and her feet are back on his desk.

"You barely tolerate me when I'm in the room," she says with a fake pout.

"Yeah, because you're distracting!" I shoot back. "You can't sit still *and* you won't stop talking. I need to concentrate."

"Oh and Bảo isn't distracting."

"He's not, actually," I quickly say. Then I remember him "reading" me. "He's really . . . considerate."

I thought I wouldn't be able to work with Bảo in the room, conscious of my every movement, the slouch that I've picked up over the years, the mess of my ponytail, how unattractive I must look in my overalls. I felt his gaze on me at times, but when I got the nerve to look around, he was turned away, preoccupied with writing.

Then I forgot about him. I abandoned thoughts about what image I want to make. Yamamoto likes to tell us that it's not always about what we want to put on canvas, that we should let our brushes, pencils, or whatever utensil we use, guide us on unexpected paths. I fool around with colors because most of my memories come up from color. The yogurt that Bảo handed to me brings me back to the first moment I tried strawberry cotton candy at Huntington Beach.

"You like him distracting you," Ali says mischievously. She brings her feet to the floor, scooting closer, but I avoid her comment, pulling out the sketch that I made for her. Really, I was prolonging my time here. I wanted to see her reaction when Bảo handed in his review. I wanted her to say it's as good as I thought it was.

"*Anddd* here's your sketch—"

"Come on, Linh! Tell me more—"

"Oh, perfect, you're here too." Bảo's at the threshold, one backpack strap slung over his shoulder. His hair is messy again; he must have been rushing over. I *have* to stop fixating on his hair. He hands a USB stick to Ali.

"There, my article. *And* it's on time." We share a look, nearly laughing. I guess he took what I said to heart.

"Have you ever heard of e-mail?" Ali mutters.

As Ali turns to her screen, Bảo moves closer to me.

"I've imagined many scenarios of how she'd react if I handed her what I handed you. One: She'll rip my pages to pieces." He pauses. "Actually, that's the only scenario," he admits. He's cute when he worries.

"You'll be fine."

Ali doesn't say anything immediately during her review. It goes on for two more minutes. The dripping sound of the sink from its art room days starts irritating me. Anxiety radiates from Bảo's shifting stance.

"Okay." Ali whirls around, slowly crossing her legs. I envision her as a big-shot editor poised to tear apart some poor journalist's article. "Linh drew this?"

"Yes."

"And you wrote this article."

"Yeah."

She folds her hands together and twiddles her thumbs. Slowly, a smile spreads on her face, one I've never seen directed at Bảo. "This is good. No, this is *great*. You two really did it."

Bảo scratches the back of his neck, a blush rising in his cheeks. "Really?"

"There's this one line about not spitting at the person across from you when you're on a date, but I don't get it, so we'll need to cut that line." I throw Bảo a look—I hadn't read that line, so he must have added it after—and he winks. Winks!

"But we'll run it this issue," Ali finishes.

Fast forward to a week later.

Bảo and I didn't break new ground with our review and sketch. It's not on the front page, either. It's not going to change anything, and no one is treating us differently or even acknowledging us as the writer and artist. But I notice that there are fewer stacks of newspapers around the school.

I'm in the quad packed with students. The temperature's nicer today; people are playing Frisbee, couples are lounging on the grass together, and some dancers are trying out new moves, staying inside their exclusive circle.

"This! Why can't Alex take me to places like this?" says a girl whose name is Lilly. She's on the swim team with her brother Ben.

"Because he thinks getting boba is an adequate date," her friend points out.

Yamamoto was happy to learn I was the artist. Turns out she was planning to use discarded newspaper copies for her paper-mache unit—which I will definitely never tell Ali—then unexpectedly caught my name in the byline.

"I didn't know you were part of the newspaper, too."

"It's a favor for a friend," I said, a bit embarrassed.

"I like it! And the writer. Wow, it's a great pairing. You're full of surprises, Linh."

"Looks like people are *actually* reading the newspaper," Bảo says, now sneaking up behind me. "For once."

"Careful, Ali might be around."

This feeling that I have whenever I'm around him—energy zapping through my veins, the warmth in my cheeks, a never-ending want to watch him without being obvious—doesn't seem to be going away. At the restaurant, I'm glancing more often at the window—not to watch him, like Ba, but just to steal another look at him.

Hidden away in the art room, we're not as jittery. It's our sanctuary. We've fallen into an unspoken pattern, me painting while Bảo works on an assignment for the newspaper or some other homework.

Ali's right. This is becoming something more, but like many things in my life, it can't all happen at once. These feelings, this crush, whatever you call it, they're something to keep to myself. To contain before it gets reckless.

We find Ali eating her own lunch, a neatly cut egg salad sandwich. There's a stack of newspapers next to her. Leave it to her to pass around newspapers during her break.

"Look!" she squeals.

"Yeah, it's great. Just what you hoped for, right?"

"I *knew* the front-page article would be a hit." From what I recall, the front page is about the school's lack of cybersecurity, authored by my indomitably spirited best friend.

Bảo gives me a look before throwing his bag onto the ground. We won't ruin her joy. He stretches onto his back and lies there for a moment, the sun shining strong down on him, highlighting the lines of his face again. What *is* it with his face and light? It's just too perfect. I sit on my hands to stop myself from sketching him . . . again.

Another part of me itches to join him, lie right next to him and take in the sun. I settle for sitting, stretching out my legs so that my shoes are just by his ear. Just one touch away.

Bảo's best friend, Việt, finds us a few moments later, and introduces himself to me and Ali. Ali's already trying to recruit him to be a reviewer after hearing that he's obsessed with dark, gritty television shows.

"Think about it," she says. "If you start now, you can be the next Roger Ebert."

"I'm not really a writer. I can't write like Bảo," Việt answers simply.

Bảo, now sitting, looks genuinely shocked to hear the comment, but Việt doesn't seem to notice. "Thanks, man."

"Knew all those words you collect would pay off someday."

I can tell from Ali's expression that she's not done trying to recruit Việt. She means well; she just wants to leave a mark when she graduates, but some people don't see that as easily and might stay clear of her. A wave of sympathy washes over me until I remember what Bảo said about Việt. He's cool and collected and seems to do his own thing. Maybe he'll be the first one to really handle Ali's assertiveness.

The four of us are a little weird together, but somehow . . . I can't ask for a better group to eat lunch with today.

"Oh, great!" Ali's staring at her phone. "We already have our next restaurant. Are you two ready?"

Instantly, I look to Bảo, and I know his answer, because it's mine, too.

"Ready."

Days later, I get home and see another set of shoes by the door. A guest? It's a weird time, and usually if people come over, they come over at night. I sniff the air, picking up a familiar scent: oil, so food's being fried, and as I follow the scent, it clicks: Mẹ's making egg rolls. As I walk closer, I recognize the guest's voice.

"Mẹ, I don't *need* another set of dishes. Where can I put them? I don't even have a kitchen."

"You have a communal kitchen, don't you?" my mom asks in Vietnamese.

"Yeah, but other people in my dorm are shitty and they'll probably steal all my things."

Mẹ and Evie, wearing a UC Davis hoodie, sit at the round table, spooning meat into defrosted egg roll wrappers while my dad carefully peels each of them away. Seeing me, he beckons me, probably wanting me to take his place, but I ignore him for now—

"Evie!" I squeal, going in for a hug.

My big sister laughs as we nearly fall over. She hugs me without her hands touching me. "Please rescue me. Mẹ's forcing me to take *all* of this back with me." She points to the kitchen counter filled with Costco-size food and pots and pans. Probably from the basement, where she keeps so many on-sale things, saying that one day we'll need them. The Bounty rolls I can understand, but four types of wooden chopping boards?

"I didn't know you were coming home."

"There's only so many text messages from Mẹ that my phone can hold. *Con ăn chưa? Con có muốn về tuần tới không?*" She softens her voice to mimic our mom.

"*Mẹ nhớ con*," our mom says defensively.

"Yes, I know you miss me, but can you miss me less?" my sister says, jokingly rolling her eyes.

"You should have told me, or else I wouldn't have stayed so long at school," I say, taking a seat.

"Linh is always staying late," Ba chimes in. "Too many times, I think, for her art classes. You have to think about school, not art. Good grades will get you into school, not art."

I lean back into my chair, stomach dropping. Not again. Across the table, Evie gives me a sympathetic look. It hits me then how much I miss her. She's usually the one saying, "Art isn't always painting and drawing. It has a lot to do with creative thinking and not a lot of people can think that way, think like Linh." She always had a way of explaining things to make them sound so much easier, sound like it could work in an ideal world.

Like now: "Well, it's cool that Linh does this. And she's good. And there's *tons* of people who do art in college."

"Yes, but have you met one with a job?" Mẹ asks.

"No, but that's because I don't hang out with—"

"See!" Ba interrupts her. "See, artists don't get jobs."

"You *can* get a job," I finally say, my voice loud. "It might take a while, but it's not impossible." My parents glance at me at the same time. Something behind my dad's eyes makes me bite my tongue.

"Art is fun," he says shortly. "But that's just it: It can only be fun. It can never support you. Con, Mẹ and Ba have worked so hard so that you can have a better life." My sister and I exchange suffering looks, knowing where our parents are going. Ba catches the exchange and merely tsks, though it might be because the layer he's trying to peel isn't complying. "Evelyn is on the right track, so we don't have to worry as much about her."

"The texts from Mẹ about my eating habits prove otherwise," Evie mutters.

"Now it's your turn," Ba finishes. He gestures for me to start filling the wrappers. The key is to put a modest spoonful of meat inside, then roll up tight enough and seal it with egg wash so that it doesn't uncurl when the roll hits oil, which happens too many times to mine.

"First batch is out!" Mẹ emerges, shows us a batch of crispy, golden egg rolls in a sieve, layered with a paper towel to catch excess oil. "Try one."

My sister bites into one, then beams at Mẹ. "Just what I needed."

We fall into a familiar pattern as we work together. Evie regales us with tales of college so far. I try not to laugh whenever her recollection gets interrupted by Mẹ and Ba as they ask about her friends, about their nationality, if they're *mập hay ốm*, where they live, what their parents are like. But my sister answers each question patiently, already anticipating their questions. I make a note to do background checks when I get to college.

I stay quiet, still stung by my parents' tone when they said I could never make a living from my art. They don't get it.

That feeling of missing having my sister around? Disappears in not even two hours, especially since Evie's back to sharing a room with me for the weekend. She's already dismayed by how messy I've made it. "If I find one thing missing, I'll kill you," she says casually as she searches her drawer for something. I actually think she's taking inventory until she pulls out Q-tips. She just emerged from the shower and has her long hair wrapped up in a towel turban.

Evie bends over to examine a sketch of mine. "This one's great. Did you just draw it?"

"Yep."

"I don't understand how you can do things like this. See something, then put it on paper. I can barely do stick drawings." She's only teasing me; she's remembering the kitchen table conversation.

"Tell that to Mẹ and Ba."

She sits down on the edge of my bed. "They told me about your interview with that engineer. I almost didn't believe it. How'd it go?"

"Horrible."

"Figured. Engineering's not for you." She says it like an undisputed fact, though I wish it were my parents stating that. "I have tons of friends majoring in engineering. They're logical, *organized*—" I throw my pillow at her, which Evie deftly catches with a grin. "Hey, I'm not finished! What I mean to add is a 'but.' They can't look at a painting and see what you see. And they can't create things like you do. Not instinctively like you do."

Now I want to take back my pillow. She's being nice. She's always nice.

"I think about telling them. But I have this feeling that it won't go well."

In a better reality, Evie would dispute that fact, would tell me to "go for it." But Evie is Evie. She grew up with me. She knows our parents. She knows what they've said about having art as a career. So thoughtful silence is the expected response.

"I lied about it going well," I admit.

"Figured. You know how your face gives you away."

"You're, like, the fourth person to say that about me!"

She lifts her chin, appearing haughty. "I'm your sister, so I know. I always knew whenever you stole one of my shirts."

I roll my eyes. "That only happened twice."

She points at me. "Lie."

I shrug. I might have stolen from her a couple more times, but at least she's older and she won't enact revenge against—"Oof!" The pillow slams in my face.

"Evie!" I protest loudly.

From their bedroom, where Ba was probably trying to fall asleep, he yells for us to quiet down.

We laugh mutedly and fall back into bed. Evie cuddles closer to me, while I pretend to kick her away, telling her to go back to her bed. But we only have a day or two together, and then she'll be back at UC Davis, miles away, living a completely different life from me. I don't mean it. I want her close by.

In one perfect move, Evie launches the pillow at the light switch, and we fall under darkness. We lie in silence. I'm counting each time the ceiling fan makes a complete turn, signaled by a nearly indescribable screech.

"UC Davis is good?"

"It's better than I could have ever imagined, Linh. The campus is beautiful. And the science lab—" She sighs. It sounds like she fell in love with her lab instead of, like, a person.

I envy her. She's where she wanted to be. Where she always dreamed of going. Plus, while she and my parents have disagreed on things—curfew and sleeping over at a friend's house— they've never argued about Evie's future. They never had an issue with it.

"I wish I could like what you like," I whisper in the dark.

Evie's foot touches mine; it's cold and I kick her. I can feel her smile in the dark. "If you liked what I liked, you wouldn't be Linh."

"Life would be so much easier if I liked what you liked, though."

"Easier?" I imagine her lifting herself into a sitting position. "How would that have made it easier?"

"It's something safe. It's something our parents approve of."

"Safe. Huh."

I sense Evie's mood shifting, then I replay what I just said. "I don't mean that in a bad way, Evie. It's just, you're doing something that Mẹ and Ba approve of. Meanwhile, I want to be an artist. Definitely what they wouldn't want me to do."

She doesn't answer right away and it's making me uneasy. I have half a mind to get up from bed and turn on the lights, just so that I can see her expression.

Then she sighs. "It's not easy, Linh. It's never been easy."

She's speaking not at me, but to me. "If I'd ever taken an art class in high school, I'd get an earful. Whenever I asked them to hang out with a friend after school, they'd say no, there were too many things I needed to do. I had to wear them down. But for you, it's different. They treat you differently. They allow you to do more things.

"And there are some moments where I think about how I decided on biology. Am I doing this because Ba and Mẹ pushed me toward it? Or did I always like biology? Where does the line between what I want and what our parents want end?" I had to think, too. I'm not so sure. "See, I don't know. It's different for you, though. Two years makes a whole lot of difference."

"I'm sorry," I say in the dark. "I didn't . . . well, I guess I didn't notice." But I was only younger by two years, and I lived in the same house, so how could I have missed this?

Evie eases back into bed. She throws her leg over mine. "It's generally accepted that in families like ours, the older kids have it way harder. We're the guinea pigs in a real-world lab." Her tone shifts to something more playful. "What did Hasan Minhaj say one time? Older siblings 'go to war' for their younger siblings? Because that's what it was like. That's what I did. So that really means, you owe me everything."

I shove her lightly by the shoulder. "For what it's worth, I think you're made for biology. I don't remember you ever liking anything else."

"That could be." Evie sighs, and yawns.

CHAPTER NINETEEN

BẢO

Slowly, I'm getting used to being on the newspaper, being a part of a team. After the success of my first review, Ali's not so on top of me anymore. In her eyes, I've stepped up; she's still delegating proofreading tasks to me, but she's giving me multiple articles—more than anyone else on the editing team.

My classmates are coming by to talk about their edits, having revised what they wrote and asking me to look them over. One side of me wonders if they ask me because Ali can be a little intense—"passionate" was Linh's word—but I like to think that they truly want my help. Even if my classmates are using me to avoid Ali, it feels good to be approached like this. To have them trust me with their work.

Each writer looks at language so differently. Ali focuses on the message in writing—is the point getting across? Where can the writer be clearer in their intention? Me, I like the writer's style. One person can say something that's been said before but in a way that's completely different; their unique experiences and personality infuse their words, their sentences.

I'm working with Ernie's article summarizing the National Honor Society's induction of new members. Ernie shrinks under attention in person, so whether he knows it or not, he uses a lot of passive voice in his writing. Things are done to the subject; the subject isn't taking action. The budget cut to the arts was cut *by* the budget committee—not the budget committee cut the budget for the arts program. Compared to Ali's writing, which gets straight to the point, Ernie lacks confidence.

"I couldn't get into astronomy; that's the only reason why I'm here," he says glumly, reading my edits.

"I didn't want to take this class either," I say, trying to cheer him up.

"Yeah, but you're good at it. And Ali doesn't go after you." As if she were right behind us, Ernie glances over his shoulder.

Ali's sandwiched between two designers huddling around her. They're going over proofs for the next issue. I might not understand their process, though I don't have to. It's hers, it's theirs, something only they can understand.

Ernie's eyebrows scrunch together like he's reading a different language. I know where he's coming from.

"Journalism might not be for everyone, but you're not bad at all. Maybe you just need to find something you like writing about," I finally say, channeling Linh. "What are you interested in?"

"I dunno. I like skateboarding. Reading comics."

"Anything else?"

"I guess I watch a lot of Netflix. TV stuff."

I remember Ali trying to recruit Việt as a writer. This might be perfect. "Would you want to write about a show? You can ask Ali if you can do it. She's looking for a reviewer."

"Really?" he asks hesitantly. "Do you think she'll let me?"

Looks like I'm not the only person who's intimidated by her. I laugh. "I'll talk to her."

Later, as the dismissal bell rings and students fly out of the class-room, I stop by Ali as she's scrolling through her phone, answering texts. "Oh, hey, Bảo. Did you work through Ernie's article? Thought it needed to be tightened but otherwise it's good to print."

"Yeah, everything worked out. I heard Ernie's into TV shows. Watches a lot of Netflix. Maybe he should try the entertainment section."

"Really? He never told me that."

"He didn't know we had an open spot."

Ali nods, calculating something in her head. "Sure. Why not?" The alarm clock on her phone goes off. "Shit, I'm gonna be late."

"Where are you going?"

"Part-time gig at a local newspaper."

"You work at a school newspaper *and* a real newspaper too?"

"Of course, what else would I do with my time?" she says simply. I pretend not to look so shocked but, first she doesn't use study hall in favor of heading the newspaper here. And now I learned that she also works part-time. She must really love the newspaper.

Imagine my surprise when one of Việt's friends sits down in front of me at lunch. It's miserable and raining outside so most people are in the cafeteria. Việt hasn't even sat yet, but Steve, the banana-eating captain, takes a seat across from me. He's grown out his brown hair, tied it into a little ponytail—to be ironic? In all our time together, we haven't really held a conversation.

"Hey, you busy?"

"Uh, no."

"I wanted to see if you can do something for me."

"You're asking *me*?"

"Yeah, Việt said you're on the newspaper or something. Said you edit shit."

"Uh, yeah, I edit shit."

He digs into his backpack that almost looks Army-issued. Removes his brown-bag lunch. Used tissues. A paperback and dog-eared Carnegie's *How to Win Friends and Influence People.*

My eyebrows go up.

Steve clears his throat. "My mom wanted me to read it," he mumbles.

Fascinating. "Right. Uh, you needed my help on what, exactly?"

Finally, he yanks out a crumpled, lined piece of paper with his chicken scratch all over it. He smooths it out against the table's edge, like you would with dollar bills at a vending machine. "I'm working on my personal statement for some college applications, and I have an essay, but I can't really make the first paragraph stick. My sisters read it and liked the essay in general, but they say the introduction makes me sound like a fifth grader."

"Ouch."

"I know." He grimaces. "But I think they're right. I know we always have to open something with a strong statement, but I can't come up with anything. Can you help?"

If Ali were in my seat, she'd have a few more words to say to Steve, probably things worse than his own sisters. But me, I try to be more sympathetic.

I feel for my red pen in my backpack and blow out some air. "Okay, what are you trying to say here, exactly?"

His essay is about his love of running. How it's not just a physical thing, but a mental thing for him. When he's stressed out or upset about something, he puts on his shoes and just runs, no destination in mind. As I switch between listening to him talk and reading his words, I'm starting to understand what his sisters said about the introduction. It doesn't even sound like him. It sounds mechanical, forced.

"Start with a feeling," I tell Steve finally, circling his paragraph. "I like what you said about letting your mind take you on a trip and how you like being surprised by where the run's taking you." Kind of like how Linh talks about painting. "So why not open with that?"

"Yeah, but shouldn't I write some sort of thesis statement, too?"

"In a way, yeah. But to call it a thesis statement makes it sound like a school paper. You're writing a personal statement, a personal essay, about something personal to you: running."

Steve nods, looking down at his pages.

I add, "So be honest and open with that. Make the readers feel what you feel when you run."

Steve doesn't say anything immediately. I re-cap my pen just so that I can have something to do. Maybe I'm not even helping. Maybe I've made him more confused.

Việt finally arrives, saying something about waiting for more Sloppy Joes. By then, Steve's nodding to himself, reading my edits. When he looks up, he's a bit more reenergized. "Thanks, man." He fist-bumps me before sneaking away to the library to type up his new introduction.

"So, did you help him?" Việt asks through a mouthful of ground beef.

"I think so. Why'd you tell him I was good at editing?"

He shrugs. "Because you are."

"How would you know?"

"Ali."

"You've been talking to Ali?"

"Yeah, she's cool. She keeps trying to recruit me for the entertainment section, and I keep telling her no."

Việt: My best friend with nerves of steel.

"Well, I think we might have someone for that section now and I just told her. Maybe she'll leave you alone."

"It's all good. She doesn't really bother me."

A sense of unease settles inside me. They're talking to each other, which means they must *like* being around each other, which means . . . "What else do you talk about?"

The saying "Waiting for the other shoe to drop" has never felt more pertinent as I lean forward, expecting Việt's admission of feelings for Linh's best friend.

"We talk about when you and Linh are getting together."

That shoe, from who knows where, never falls.

"What?"

Việt grins. "Yup. Ali's saying after the fourth review. I'm saying way before that."

"*Why* are you even making bets?"

"Something to pass the time."

"Who do you think is gonna win?"

"I am, which is why I'm telling you now that this all needs to happen after the second restaurant review. So hurry up."

Việt's more invested than I thought he'd be and—Ali.

Oh God. Has she said anything to Linh?

Before I can even ask these important questions, a plethora of bright colors blocks my field of vision. I look up to see pin-straight bangs against a prominent forehead.

Kelly Tran, president of VSA, the club I've ditched way too many times.

"Bảo. It's been a while."

"Uh-huh." This cold reception is expected, given how I skipped duty on a Saturday because *it was a Saturday.*

Việt quickly excuses himself from the table.

He also skipped along with me.

"You know, I've been meaning to find you. I'm feeling like you're not taking your membership seriously. If you continue to miss more meetings, I'm afraid you can't be in the club anymore." There's a threat to her voice, but it's entirely ineffective since I wasn't even aware I was still a member.

Movement behind Kelly's head brings my focus to Linh, and my heart leaps. An excuse! An escape.

"Oh, hey, Linh. Great, you finally came. I know we have to go to that thing."

"Thing?" Linh asks, an eyebrow quirked. Then with a familiar smile, she says, "Hey, Kelly."

I say, "That thing, yeah."

"Oh." A pause. A side glance at Kelly. "*Oh*. Yeah, totally. Let's go."

Kelly's looking between us, probably wondering how we even know each other. "Wait, since you're both here: How about you join our table at the Thuận Phát next weekend? We're raising money for the club."

Damn it.

"Um," Linh says, hesitating only a little. "Sure, I think I can do it."

"Awesome!" Kelly does a French exit, relieving me of her colors. "Thanks, Linh. Thanks, Bảo!"

"I guess I'll be there, too," I say grudgingly.

"Sorry, I didn't think *you'd* be roped in," Linh says sympathetically.

171

"Yeah. Well, you're too nice. You could have said no to Kelly."

"I like her. We had some classes together and she was always nice. And this club is her baby, so of course I want to help." She bumps shoulders with me. We'd started walking together without thinking. "C'mon, I'll be there. It'll be fun."

"You're forgetting one thing. This is public. Way public. My mom, her friends—hell, everyone who owns a business near us— shop there. Weren't we trying to avoid being seen together?"

"Now you're just trying to get out of volunteering."

Yes and no.

Well, mostly yes.

"Wear a disguise," she says somewhat cheekily. "We'll figure something out."

Baseball cap and sunglasses. That'll be my disguise for today.

"Who are you? Are you trying to be a gangster?" Mẹ asks immediately when I come down from my room in the morning.

"No, I'm protecting myself from the sun."

"Well, you don't look like yourself."

Perfect.

My mom had been happy to hear me mention an effort to volunteer. Maybe it's something to share with her gossip circle. *Bảo is such a good person. He thinks of other people.* Ha.

While clearing the dishes at breakfast, she offers to drive me. Well, have Ba drive me as she rides along. That would meet two of her goals for the weekend: (1) force her son to do something and (2) get some grocery shopping done. Mẹ doesn't go to Thuận Phát too often, maybe every month or so. I guess she hasn't been there in a few weeks.

I immediately object, imagining her seeing Linh at the table outside Thuận Phát. She'd *flip* the table, most likely.

"I'll take the bus. Don't want to bother you—"

"No, it's fine—"

"Really. Anyway, there isn't anything on sale today. I checked." I grasp for an excuse. "But Saigon City Marketplace has sales." I mention the one that's a bit closer, and I must have said the magic words, which land on Ba as he sets down *Người Việt* at the table. What's the point of going when nothing is on sale?

"*Thôi, để nó đi đi,*" he says. "*Mình sẽ đi* Saigon City.*"

My mom relents. "Mẹ *did* want to go to Saigon City to see what herbs are on sale . . . Maybe I will go today."

"Great."

"Don't come back too late. Or eat anything for lunch. I'm making something."

"Got it."

I get on bus sixty-six and it drops me off at McFadden. I walk a few minutes to the supermarket. The parking lot is already packed like sardines, Camrys and Highlanders cruising to find the first open spot. Mothers marching like they're on a mission, their kids dragging their feet. Older shoppers walk with the help of their adult daughter or son and others rely on their canes and walkers.

I see the sign first: HELP VSA, made with enough glitter to stop traffic. Kelly's doing, most likely. Linh sits at the table, glancing around. She's dressed in a simple white tee and jeans, sunglasses on top. I slide into the empty seat next to her.

"Ta-da."

"Bảo?" She laughs and taps on the bill of my ball cap. "Nice disguise."

"Thank you. I think it was your suggestion."

Linh scrutinizes me. "I guess it'll work. I almost didn't recognize you."

"That good, huh?"

"Usually your giveaway is your hair. So yeah."

"How's it going so far? Kelly putting you to work?"

Together we watch Kelly, who has stopped a disheveled-looking man who must have been forced to do a last-minute grocery run by his wife. He attempts to escape, to no avail.

"More like she's doing it herself. Which I think is why not a lot of people want to do this."

"Can I tell you a secret?" I lean in, beckoning her, and she follows with a smile playing on her lips. "I'm glad you're here. Because I wouldn't want to be alone with her; she despises me."

Her laugh catches the other volunteers' attention.

"Why are you laughing? It's true."

"First it's Ali who hates you. Then it's Kelly. Now what did you do to her?"

"I skipped volunteering."

"Okay . . . ?"

"Three times."

"Bảo! No wonder she loathes you."

"Sorry, that was all back when I wasn't as motivated."

"What's motivating you now?"

A couple of shoppers have come by, inquiring about our table, and Linh greets them automatically, putting on a smile like she did this all the time. Her energy is palpable and contagious.

"No one in particular," I answer her question, more to myself than to her.

Meanwhile, Kelly passes down another pile of flyers to replenish our stack. She sips a boba from Boba Corner 2. "What's with the ball cap?"

"Bad haircut."

Time passes slowly, but it's not so bad with Linh next to me. We pass commentary about Kelly's determined efforts to solicit money while we hand out flyers about VSA's upcoming events. I spot faint paint marks on the back of her hand, which weren't there yesterday. She must have fit in some painting time this morning.

"Were you painting?"

"Oh, yeah," she says, sheepish again. "Trying to, at least. I need to submit something to the Gold Key competition. I'm realizing that the deadline is getting closer and closer."

"What are you going to do?"

"I'm working on a few things about memory. Good memories. The kind that last a while and show up unexpectedly."

"Like?"

"A restaurant scene. Just me and my parents as we were closing up in the first year. It was a tough year, that first year. People were hard on them." Linh looks over at me and I know what she's thinking. My mom. The General and the others, the snide remarks they made at the restaurant and also freely in public—

"I'm sorry."

Linh shakes her head. "Anyway, my sister and I never really saw our parents because they were always working. But that night, we finished and it'd gone well, and I remember seeing my parents standing by the front windows, just chatting, saying goodbye to some customers. A totally normal scene."

I'm there with her, can feel the window's smooth glass against my hand and its warmth after facing the sun for the whole day. Linh's tone changes into something like reverence and she lifts her hand, gesturing as if she were smearing paint all over a canvas. "But the sky behind them was swathes of blush red and purple and yellow. It took my breath away. It was really beautiful. So I'm working on a small canvas for that."

"That sounds nice."

"Yeah, it was." She looks over at me. "How about you? Still okay with mediocrity?" she says teasingly, leaning forward. A piece of her hair has caught itself on the neck of her T-shirt and I feel like I want to move it away.

"Hey, I've advanced a little." I copy Linh, moving closer even though there's no reason to. "Someone asked for my help the other day. One of Việt's friends needed help. So I helped."

"Did it go well?"

"Yeah. It doesn't happen often—someone asking me for help. Especially with writing. So I was kind of surprised."

"I'm not." She looks deep in thought. "There are people out

there who don't have the energy to help people get better. They just accept the other person's flaws, and sure, there's less conflict to deal with, but it's almost like living out a lie. *Then* there are people who aren't afraid to point out something's wrong—even something as little as a typo. In the end, you're making *something* better, and that's more than other people are willing to do."

I clear my throat, trying to quell my emotions fighting against one another. "That's about the nicest thing anyone's ever said to me. Isn't that sad?"

"Sad and true for all kids with demanding Asian parents." Warmth spreads through me. Other curious shoppers have come to the table, but, not for the first time, I see only Linh in front of me. Beaming. I have to blink a few times to remember where I am.

CHAPTER TWENTY

LINH

"My middle finger can't be that big."

"It's not big. It's normal size."

"On the page, it's big," Bảo says in protest. "It's offensively big."

I laugh, turning my pencil upside down and erasing the lines of his "offensive finger" until it *looks* thinner—but not true to size. I was using the back of an extra flyer to sketch Bảo's hand. "Better?"

"Yes."

"I didn't know you were so sensitive about your fingers."

It's easy, when you're having fun, to forget about matters that seemed important only an hour ago. Or at least pretend that they don't exist. The canvas of the restaurant—more of a portrait of my parents—drying at home, one of many I need to finish if I want to even have a chance at the competition.

The deadline is coming, and in moments when I imagine I'm keeping that date far away, it creeps up on me. There's so little time.

Great. I promised myself that I would leave some of my worries at home, and now I'm just buried in thoughts.

I glance at Bảo. At least we're having fun together. We're not looking over our shoulders. But that thought doesn't last long.

I'm the one who spots her first.

And by "her," I mean *them*.

Our mothers, walking down separate parking lanes. Mine is looking through her purse. This morning, before heading to the restaurant, she mentioned she might need to run to the market, but I didn't think it'd be this market. She doesn't like Thuận Phát because of the size. Plus they never have enough of the fish she likes to use.

Bảo's mom walks forward, but squints with the sun in her eyes. I nudge Bảo, cutting him off mid-conversation with another class-mate, and in a second, understanding—and panic—manifests in the visible parts of his face.

"Shit."

"Let's go," I say, pulling him along inside, my heart beating madly. Bảo lowers the bill over his eyes.

Through the automatic sliding doors, the market's smells rush at me: fried pork, herbs, and lingering incense from the owner's shrine. I'm brought back to my childhood, when weekends often meant wandering the aisles, riding on abandoned shopping carts, climbing piles of sacks of rice, and begging my parents to buy me strawberry Hello Pandas and Marukawa gum packets.

The two of us dash into one of the aisles—the one with all the dried fruits, seeds, and peanuts. An older woman catches sight of us and narrows her eyes, before wheeling her cart and turning right at the end.

"Out of all the days," Bảo moans. His phone vibrates in his hand. His mom. "Should I answer?"

"Yes, pick up. You don't want her to be suspicious."

"Hi, Mẹ," he answers, forcing cheeriness into his voice. "Yeah, that was me. I was just taking a break." Pause. "Where did I go? I'm in the . . . snacks aisle. You're heading—where? The peanuts aisle?"

An alarm goes off inside me. I make a split-second decision and dash into the aisle to the left, where sriracha and other Asian sauces are stocked. The lady from before huffs in annoyance when I nearly ram in her. She mutters under her breath about teenagers these days being *mất dạy*, yet continues shopping.

Then I hear Bảo's mom. Her voice is loud as she addresses Bảo, jolting me. I don't think I've heard it since that day at the temple. I duck, catching a glimpse of her through the shelves low on stock. "Bảo?"

"Yep," he answers hoarsely before clearing his throat. "It's me."

"Mẹ almost forgot con wore that hat today. Look *kỳ*. Mẹ thought con want snacks."

"Well, I thought I'd just meet you here." He glances at me swiftly, then uses his back to block me—and my line of vision. "You couldn't find anything at Saigon City?"

"No, there was nothing much on sale. But there's plenty of things on sale here."

"Uh, sorry, I guess I read an old flyer."

"Do con want a snack?"

His reply is quick. "Oh, no I think I'm—"

"Con?" I pivot sharply. Mẹ. "What are you doing?"

"Oh, I'm just . . . I'm hungry." Meanwhile, I try to listen to the conversation on the other side, to see if they're moving. Bảo and his mom are walking to the back. Too close. Our mothers can't see each other—who knows what will happen! So I steer my mother the opposite way, into the nuts aisle, moving us like a revolving door would. "But never mind, I figured I would just wait for lunch to eat."

"Mẹ can buy you something if you need it."

"No, no, I think I'll be fine for now—let's just—" Unfathomably, Bảo's mom is walking past our aisle, him trailing behind, probably thinking we'd have moved by then. He freezes, then runs ahead, grabbing a random snack. I hear him ask if he could get this.

Thankful for the distraction, I loop my arm through my mom's. "Actually, can I get an egg tart?" That, on any other occasion, would have been a normal request. It was always a reward for me and Evie for behaving while our mother completed her shopping.

Mẹ smiles slightly, the corners of her eyes wrinkling. "Some things never change."

Even though we're a good distance away from Bảo and his mom, I keep an eye out for them as Mẹ points at the pastries—the guy at the counter only speaks Malaysian. My mom ends up buying enough for the volunteers, and when she finishes checking out her groceries—watching the prices climb closely—she waves good-bye at me and leaves none the wiser.

I run into Bảo around the corner of the exit. He stops me from going further, grabbing my wrist, and I hear his mom complaining to him about the final receipt before telling him she'll see him back at home. "Don't eat too much," she says, though she's shoving another bag of snacks his way. The other volunteers are going to love us.

Then Bảo's mom is gone.

And we're both alive.

Returning to the entrance, Bảo and I plop down at the volunteering table, exhausted. Kelly asks why we just disappeared, but we hold up the box of pastries as an excuse. The volunteers eagerly dig in, and Bảo gladly reaches for an egg tart.

"See?" he says in between bites. "This is why I don't volunteer." A triumphant grin starts forming until he looks down at our knotted hands.

I don't pull away.

He doesn't pull away.

I'm staring at our hands together, trying to pretend that they aren't ours, just like I did to Bảo's hand before. I was studying his fingers objectively, sketching them as nothing more than a prop.

But I can't do that now. Because it *is* our hands, and neither of us is letting go. My heart pounds. Adrenaline from before or now? I'm not sure. His thumb caresses my knuckles in a move that seems natural, like he'd always held my hand like this. I inhale sharply. In different circumstances, this could happen. This is possible in an alternate reality.

My other hand, I realize, is resting on the table, exactly on top of the sketch of his hand.

We don't say anything, and we don't move until someone down the table asks me to hand them extra flyers, so I have to let go, and I do it like I've been scorched. *Don't look at him.*

The rest of volunteering for us is spent in silence, and I'm lost in how to handle this impossible, unsaid thing sitting between us.

CHAPTER TWENTY-ONE

BẢO

I've been thinking about Linh's hand a lot, her paint-marked hand fitting into my palm. I remember it like it was a living heart, pulsing. I've replayed that moment we noticed what was happening and decided not to care, the moment that I knew we'd stepped into a new place without planning to. I wish there was a word stronger than "palpable," but I guess that was sufficient for now.

When she let go, I wanted so badly to snatch her hand back. When she muttered a quick goodbye to me, I wanted to tell her not to leave. We couldn't just ignore what happened.

She didn't pull away. She could have, but she didn't. Does that mean she feels the same way as me?

Việt and Ali had seen it before us, apparently.

The next week, to my disappointment, unfolds like the days before our worlds collided on Phở Day. Our schedule consists of way too many misses. At lunch, when I stop by the art room, I don't find her there. I know for a fact that Linh's avoiding me, because she skipped the next restaurant coverage, mentioning it to Ali, who told me she was overwhelmed by work and painting. There's truth in that, I'm sure, but not completely.

She's scared, and I wish I could tell her that I am, too. That I don't know how things will work. But if we could hold hands a bit longer, maybe we'll figure it out.

I had to go alone to a Malaysian restaurant, while most of the customers enjoyed meals among large families. They must have felt sorry for me, a high school boy, dining out alone. The chef gave me a doggy bag of some kind of cookies that Ba demolished later in the night.

As we sit across the table at 10:00 p.m., feeling Mẹ's absence as she was still at a friend's house for a mani and pedi, I have this ridiculous thought to ask for advice. *Ba is a man. Ba has experienced things like this . . . right?* Then I stop the idea almost immediately. I must be getting desperate if I think it's a good pick to ask my dad, stone-cold Dad, for girl advice when we don't exactly enjoy small talk in general.

Tonight must be different, because Ba starts the small talk anyway. Those cookies must be good.

"We're going to need your help in the next few weeks at the restaurant."

"Oh, okay. What's happening?"

"Your mom and I are planning a *Bánh Xèo* Day to introduce different kinds of *bánh xèo* to the menu. So things will be busy."

Just like Việt had suggested.

"Did Việt mention anything to you?"

"Why would he?"

"Never mind." I think about the special. Linh's family—Linh—are going to see it as a direct response to their Phở Day. Great: One more reason for our parents to despise one another.

"Why now?" I ask warily.

"To make sure our customers don't get tired of our menus."

"Will it work? We don't usually do different kinds of *bánh xèo*."

"We never really know when things will work. We weren't sure a restaurant would work, but here we are. There is no use playing it safe when it comes to our restaurant." Ba gets up and puts on the teakettle. He shuffles to the cabinet where we keep various tins of tea leaves. *"Muốn trà không?"*

I shake my head, thinking tea will only keep me up later than I should.

Playing it safe.

If my dad's willing to do something that might not bring him any sure result, maybe I can do the same.

Later I stared for longer than I'd like to admit at a text to send to Linh. A text asking her to meet again, face-to-face. I wasn't as blunt; I had a good reason to text her, since Ali sent me another restaurant to visit. So I mentioned that to her.

Then her bubbles begin to appear, so I shut down the Messages app, until a ring tells me to read it.

sorry to be MIA. your article on that malaysian place was great.

thanks! do you think you can make the next one?

i think so.

CHAPTER TWENTY-TWO

LINH

I've been thinking about Bảo's hand a lot, his thumb unthinkingly brushing the top of mine. A moment brimming with potential, but neither of us could say a word about it. Because we know. We both know the risks that we were taking, just sitting next to each other. We barely escaped our mothers back then.

"What do you think, con?"

It's after dinner; the dishes have been cleared and a pot of freshly brewed Jasmine tea sits between us. Ba and Mẹ push a large binder of fabric toward me. They're thinking of ordering newer place mats and tablecloths for the restaurant, eager to keep up the momentum from Phở Day. Usually they don't bring me into business decisions about the restaurant, but I've "always been good with colors," Ba said. One of the only occasions he'd acknowledge my art abilities as an asset, like the ad that I'd done for the restaurant.

I touch one that is the lightest green available, which might soften the harsh lights in our restaurant. We can find a light beige place mat to match it. Add a small vase of flowers, and I can see it happening. "This could work."

My parents lift it up, assessing it. There's a glint in my mom's eyes that I've only seen for food. She's having a vision for the restaurant, just like my dad. Things are going so well. They're happy. I'm happy too, even though I have a list of things to do. This . . . thing with Bảo has to be kept safe, confined to what we do in the art room, secreting moments away from everyone's eyes.

I can't do anything to upset the balance.

"Good, con," Ba says in approval. "Good."

I got the text from Bảo asking if I could go to the next restaurant. There's a blank feeling to his message, a straightforward ask, and I wonder if Bảo's determined to pretend that our hand-holding didn't happen, too.

I told everything to Ali, about volunteering, our near escape, our held hands. She said it's like we're in some romantic comedy or something, but also freely expresses how she thinks we're both being ridiculous. In fact, she hasn't shut up about it, even as we're trying to finish some homework at the restaurant. Ba's out running errands, specifically finding a saucepan to replace one of ours with a broken handle. I glance at the tables that used to have our worn white tablecloths, which have now been replaced with the pastel green I liked, the beige place mats to follow soon.

"Linh, is that why you missed out on the Malaysian restaurant the other day?" Ali asks, light bulb turning on. She asked this after Bảo handed in his review and she noticed I hadn't sketched anything. I told her how busy I was, mentioning the Gold Keys, and she understood; now my friend rather than the editor in chief was asking me.

"Yes," I say finally. "But it would have been so awkward."

"So what are you going to say to Bảo's text? No? Then he'll really think something is up. Don't avoid this, Linh." She grabs my hand. "I know you. I know you want to disappear into your paintings." I try pulling away. "I know you want to keep things inside. Bảo seems to want to explore more with you, but if you don't want that, you have to tell him."

I look around to make sure my mom isn't nearby. She's in the kitchen. "That's the problem, Ali. I do want him."

Her expression doesn't change. "Then talk it out, at least."

"But our families—"

"Again, I'm not going to pretend I know everything about your families. But sitting here avoiding him will not help at all."

She reaches for my phone and places it between us. "Call him. Or text him. But silence isn't the answer. It'll make things worse."

"What will make things worse?" Mẹ comes by with two glasses of iced coffee for us. She glances between me and Ali expectantly, but neither of us answers. Wants to answer.

As always, Ali's right. Avoiding Bảo isn't the right way to handle this. And I miss having him in the art room with me.

"If we didn't get our iced coffees, which we seriously need if we want to stay awake. So much homework," Ali says, suddenly perky. She takes a loud sip of her drink. "Tastes great, Mrs. Phạm."

CHAPTER TWENTY-THREE

BẢO

Chơi Ơi is the opposite of a traditional Việt restaurant. The restaurant name itself parodies *"trời ơi,"* an expression my mom likes to use when she's annoyed at me or at my dad. But the name turns the exclamation into something more playful—literally, "Play!"

Inside, the restaurant, located just at the edge of Fountain Valley, has a high-vaulted ceiling and deep red walls brightened by lanterns. Columns are decorated with eye-catching nighttime cityscapes of what looks like Vietnamese cities, rendered from photos.

Linh had arrived a few minutes before me and was inspecting one of the photos. Of course.

"See something interesting?"

Linh jumps, then brushes back her hair sheepishly. The movement brings my attention to her hand, the one that I held.

"Didn't think you'd make it," I say, watching her closely.

We'd almost had to reschedule again, though, because things at work were getting busy for me and Linh. Lisa, the girl who'd seemed too nervous to work at a restaurant, had called out sick, so Linh had to pick up a shift. I also know the deadline for the Gold Keys was drawing closer and closer. In my texts to her, I wasn't sure what to do or say to help—lethologica: the inability to find the right words—but being here seems to bring back some spark in her eyes.

She knows how I feel now. Ball's in her court.

"Figured you needed me," she answers simply. "Unless you already have another artist friend lined up."

As the host shows us to our seats, I'm hoping her emphasis on "friend" isn't purposeful.

I focus on the restaurant instead. According to the existing interviews I'd read online, the owner and executive chef Brian Lê had trained in Paris, then Italy, but as much as he loved European cuisine, he always considered Vietnamese his first love—thanks to his father, who's a retired chef. So he came back to the States and opened up his restaurant, which has been reviewed by the *New York Times* and the *Los Angeles Times*, which praise his specialty: his *bún bò Huế*. Not for the first time, I wonder how Ali managed to be so persuasive that someone with this much notoriety and posh training had agreed to invite two high school students to taste his food.

But the moment Chef Lê bounds out of the kitchen into the dining room, it all makes sense. Maybe in his late thirties, he wears a worn ball cap backward and his chef's jacket is opened to reveal a T-shirt that says, ALLOW ME TO EXPLAIN THROUGH INTERPRETIVE DANCE. And his wide grin—kind of like a kid who was told he could have as much candy as he wanted—coaxes a smile from us.

"What's good, little ones?" He gathers each of us into a bear hug. "Glad you're here. Brian Lê. Or Chef Lê." *Now* he shakes our hands.

"My mom's maiden name is Lê," I say.

"Maybe we were related way back when, who knows." He winks.

I like him. "Thanks for letting us stop by. Just tell us where we should sit. We won't be in anyone's way."

"Sit?"

"Um yeah, we're here to review your menu," Linh says.

"Don't you want a tour, too?"

We didn't get a chance to walk around at any other restaurant. Do reviewers usually get this kind of access?

"Come on, let's take you guys to the back where all the magic happens." Without waiting for us, he turns and we stand helpless for a few beats until we follow him into his labyrinthine kitchen. It's like Mẹ's kitchen, only cleaner and probably more organized. And probably staffed with more people who are less apt to mess up.

So, not like our kitchen.

The cooks give us a quick look before focusing back on their dishes. One cook sprinkles chopped raw green onions over a platter of freshly cooked *cá chiên*, the snapper still sizzling from its quick fry in a sauté pan. Another guy uses a ladle the size of my hand to trans-

194

fer bubbling broth into graphite-colored bowls. Even the cooked rice, which someone's spooning into bowls, looks better than usual, gleaming under the restaurant's expensive lights. I'm glad my parents aren't here to see this.

Another chef yells, "Behind!" before passing us with a large pot smelling of pineapples—*canh chua*, most likely. Meanwhile, Chef Lê points to different cooks and their specialties. Picks up ingredients that he insists are totally "high-grade." Narrowly crashes into his employees as they busily rush around, though it's all done in odd synchronicity like they're used to his chaotic energy.

Chef Lê stops before one large pot in particular. With a flourish, he lifts the lid and beckons us to lean in. "Smell that shit and tell me no one will want to eat it." Seeing his expectant look, we do as we're told.

"That smells—"

"—delicious."

Linh and I lock eyes before releasing immediately.

Bún bò. An earthy, fatty broth, a powerful punch of citrus from lemongrass. It's familiar. It's home in one punch. Chef Lê shoots us a smile, likes seeing us confirm how good it smells and *looks* without us wasting words. Maybe he's a bit smug about it.

"This is just a preview, of course. Wait until you taste everything."

Somehow I wonder if he mistook us for someone else. Linh thinks the same, saying as much to him.

"Nope, I know who you are: Badass high school students." He points to us with both index fingers. Me and Linh share another glance, nearly bursting out laughing. What a weird guy. "I was your age once upon a time. When I was in Paris and in Rome, I made things that cost even more than I could afford. I hated that. And sometimes the food wasn't even good. If I can make any Việt kid your age happy and wanna come to this restaurant, then I guess I did my job." He directs us back to where we came in. "Now that you got the tour, let's get you back and you can taste all the magic that happens here. You and your girlfriend will love this."

"She's not—well—" I know I'm stammering.

"What if he's *my* boyfriend and *he*'s just tagging along?" Linh says.

Chef Lê smiles again. "Oh, touché. She's got some spice!"

"We're partners," I quickly clarify, saying anything so that Chef Lê doesn't get the wrong idea and keep going with the joke, making things even more uncomfortable between me and Linh.

Back at the table in the center of the room—"Newly renovated! So you can experience everything," Chef Lê says—Linh and I sit across from each other, absorbing the flurry around us.

"Settle down and food's going to come out in a sec."

I turn to Linh. "Did we even order?"

"Nope, but I don't think we're going to have a bad meal here," Linh says.

A line of servers brings out the appetizers and immediately our table goes from empty to crowded. A good thing, since it makes me less aware of how I'm sitting, holding myself. How far away my hands are from hers and how weird it'd be if I reached for her again.

Turns out Linh and I have nothing to say to each other. For good reason.

The reason being we're more preoccupied with the food that may or may not be better than my mom's.

"If my parents were here . . . ," Linh begins to say into her bowl of *bún bò Huế*.

"They'd steal this recipe. Mine would do the same."

"Sorry, this recipe is legit sealed," says Chef Lê, who'd come back five minutes ago to check in on us but sat down as if he was part of the party. I guess this isn't unusual for him because the servers set up a plate for him right away. "My dad would chase me out of California if it somehow leaked."

I grin as I write down his quote. I'm already five pages in with my notes—most of the pages filled with details from the kitchen and atmosphere instead of the actual food. Linh has started some sketches of the appetizers and entrees. "Is your dad the cook in the family?"

"Yeah, Poppa Lê had a small place in Santa Monica about half the size of this place. I basically grew up there."

"Our families have restaurants, too," Linh offers.

"No surprise—you two have healthy appetites," Chef Lê teases us.

"Where did the idea of opening up a restaurant come from?" I ask.

"Probably from my dad. Loved what he did with the place. He just wanted to make customers happy." Chef Lê laughs, now with a faraway glint in his eyes. "I was always tagging around at his place and he'd yell at me because there was legit no space. My mom, though, she completely disagreed with me going into a culinary career. Even culinary school! It wasn't exactly . . . stable, you know."

Linh shifts in her seat, catching the message. Seems like a theme with Việt mothers.

"So when I told her I wanted to open a restaurant, she went off on me. I know she was worried then, but we said some stuff to each other. Lot of angry words."

"What happened after?" Linh asks quietly.

"My mom didn't talk to me for two years. But it's not like we weren't a part of each other's lives. They lived just a few minutes away from me. I'd talk to my dad, who always updated me on my mom and what she was doing. *Always*. I mean, I knew what she'd bought for groceries because he'd tell me! It was the same thing for me. I bet my mom knew what I was up to each week."

Chef Lê points at the entrance as if someone would make an appearance. "Then, the day after I got that *Los Angeles Times* review was the day my mom appeared at the door. My dad had dropped her off! He was tired of the fighting and called us the two most stubborn people he'd ever met." He lets out a loud laugh. "And we made up, just like that. After that she was always show-ing up here, playing host but also correcting my chefs' mistakes, correcting *my* recipes."

"Two years," Linh whispers in dismay.

Chef Lê nods knowingly. "We lost some time. I think about that all the time now that she's gone." He pauses. "It's been six and a half months."

That last bit shocks me—I didn't come across that in any of the articles—and I put down my pencil. "I'm sorry," I say, hearing Linh offer the same condolences. The sentence sounds so canned; something I'm not used to saying. I don't know anyone who's actually lost a parent. I've heard about it, but the concept seems so far away. So impossible.

"Do you think about her a lot?" I ask.

"Legit the other day. I was creating a recipe, something that I had as a little kid and only my mom could make it. I just wished I'd asked when she was alive. And then I just had a kid, too, so I'm wondering how to tell him about my mom. There's still so much history that I don't know. My dad casually mentioned the other day that he'd lost a sister when he was six and she was two. Seven siblings I knew about, but not his sister. . . ." Chef Lê trails off, looking back at the kitchen. "History, man. There's a lot hidden." Then he perks up, remembering where he is. "Anyway, I'm still glad we came back into each other's lives. We had a good time together."

A server comes by with a message for Chef Lê from the kitchen. He needs to go back, so he does, leaving me and Linh to ourselves again. A busboy stops by with his bin to clear the plates and we hand them over, too accustomed to doing it ourselves.

"He's nice," I tell Linh as she packs up her things.

"One of a kind." She turns her notebook upside down, showing me her quick sketch of him, ball cap and T-shirt captured perfectly. Much like my notes, her focus is Chef Lê and his dynamic personality. "There's a lot to unpack."

"Right, his mom."

"And going two years because she didn't like what he was doing. That's hard to even imagine." She sighs loudly, shoving her colored pencils into her messenger bag. "That's another reason I don't ever see myself telling my mom the truth."

Now that we don't have any food to distract us, or Chef Lê to dominate the conversation, or anything else between us, the elephant in the room comes back, the reason for how hesitant we seem to be acting toward each other.

"Hey," I say as gently as possible. "Can we talk?"

"We are." All of her emotions have shut off.

"Linh, I mean about the other day."

"I don't think I can stay longer," she says in apology. Her expression is twisted, like it's physically hurting her being here. "Can we talk another time?"

"I know what you're thinking."

"Believe me, you don't know half of it, Bảo," she says firmly.

"Well, you can tell me, then. Because I'm here. I'm all ears. Even if you don't want—" *Us.* My thoughts pause. What if I'd misread everything up until now? What if I thought she liked me because I liked her too much and Linh was being too nice to say something? Like how she was nice to Kelly even though she didn't have time to volunteer? Like now, how she's avoiding it so that she doesn't reject me outright?

She's barely looking at me. Maybe I'm closer to the truth than I thought I'd be.

"I can be here as a friend," I finally say. "Really, no hard feelings."

"Thank you," she says with such relief that it hurts. "I'm sorry." There is a painful pause as Linh pretends to check the table to make sure she hasn't forgotten her belongings. I squeeze the back of my chair, fighting the urge to just say something—anything to make her look at me. Before I can think of anything, Linh says a quiet goodbye and leaves.

I exhale. *So that's it. She doesn't feel what I feel.*

I head to the front, thanking a Black woman with the name tag Saffron—which I had to look at twice; it was too perfect for someone in the business. The way she stands tall reminds me of my mom when she's fired up and of Linh when she's excited about light or some obscure painting that I wouldn't know about unless she told me. I feel like I should fix my hair and anything else on my body that's out of place.

"Brian made the best food for you tonight. Usually it's not this good," she jokes, her French accent apparent.

"Hey, do you want to keep your job?" Chef Lê says, emerging from behind a divider, wiping his hands on a hand towel.

"That's not for you to decide," she retorts, "since I own half the place."

This doesn't faze him and now he merely sports a smile. "Mr. Nguyễn, meet my partner and wife."

"Partner but his boss," she playfully chastises him. "Oh, and also his wife."

"Yeah, yeah. Anyway, Saff, this boy here, he's going to be big one day. I can feel it. He's like Anthony Bourdain, rest in peace."

I blink at his unexpected compliment. This is what it means when someone gushes, I guess. "Thanks."

"You made me think, you know. Not a lot of people know how to do that," Chef Lê says, looking serious.

I brush the back of my neck. "I was just asking questions."

"That's the best type of interview. You gave me room to just talk." He claps me on the shoulder, and I sway from the weight of it. "Come back anytime. You and Linh. I saw some of what she's sketching. She seems great, too."

"She is."

"But she's *really* not your girlfriend?" He makes a show of looking over his shoulder. "Or, I'm sorry, you're not really her boyfriend?"

"No, she isn't."

"Yooo," he says with a slow-forming smirk, "you like her, don't you?"

Saffron elbows him. "Bry! Stop teasing him."

"It's complicated."

Chef Lê just laughs. "Good luck, man."

"Con!" My mom calls for me the moment I step into the house. *"Biểu đây."*

I'm home on time, so that's not why she's calling for me. *Shit, did I leave the toilet seat up again?* I take the steps slowly, trying to figure out what I must have done wrong. Running through me, though, something I can't ignore, is an urge to sit down and just *write*. Because Chef Lê is more interesting than I thought he'd be. Because I'd rather get lost in writing than think about the failed attempt to talk to Linh about us . . . about her rejection.

Mẹ, just showered, stands in front of the bathroom sink. She leans toward the mirror—her mirror counterpart looks at me. A Vietnamese ballad spills out from her bedroom. Ba must be at the restaurant still.

"Here," she says, and hands the tweezers over. "I need you to pull out a white hair."

My mom likes to complain that she has so many because of me. I guess I probably shouldn't tell her it's because she's just old.

Sighing, I take the tweezers from her, agreeing to a task that I've been subjugated to since I was old enough to hold these things and also since my mom spotted her first one back when I was in sixth grade. I'm not the only one, though. Việt's had to do this too.

"Where?"

"*Nè.*" She holds it up and I squint. Got one. "Did you finish your project?"

"Yep."

"Good." I feel her gaze through the mirror. "You are out a lot these days." I accidentally pull out a black hair. "Ah, *mày làm gì vậy?*"

"Sorry." I do it more gently. "The newspaper keeps me busy."

"Con still writing reviews."

"I am, yeah." I'm not sure why but Chef Lê comes into mind again, about his early struggles with his mom. Two years. I wonder if me and my mom can ever stop talking for that long. And who would instigate it? "There's this guy I met on my assignment. Brian Lê."

"Vietnamese. What does he do?" she asks almost immediately.

"He's the executive chef and owner. He's pretty young."

"It is hard," she answers sagely. "But impressive for his age."

"He was talking about his parents and the things he wanted to ask them."

"Oh?"

"His mother died in the past few months."

Mẹ clicks her tongue. *"Tội quá."* Poor guy.

"Yeah, and he mentioned not knowing everything he could have known about her while she was alive." I thread my fingers through her hair, rechecking my work. "Why don't you talk about Vietnam more?"

"I do! I talk about it all the time." She looks at me directly through the mirror.

"Yeah, I know, but more specific things. I know where you lived, what my grandparents did. That you escaped at night. But that's more like an overview. Why don't you tell me the smaller things?"

"Because you don't ask. But the things I do tell you, you always say, 'Oh, I don't want to hear it, I don't have time, Mẹ, I heard you say this already.'" She mimics what she thinks I sound like.

"My voice can't go that high," I say grudgingly. I *have* said those things, though.

"I am your mother, so I don't have to tell you anything most of the time. Some matters are too adult for you," Mẹ starts to say in a familiar *There's no use arguing* voice.

"Okay."

"But, if you do want to know more, Mẹ will try to answer you. But my memory isn't so good anymore and things are just from so long ago. Mẹ wonder if the past should stay in the past."

"Maybe, but maybe not." Silence eases in as I concentrate on her hair.

"All of this writing business is making you different." Our eyes meet in the mirror again. She tilts her head, regarding me like she would with a recipe that was missing one crucial ingredient.

"Good different?"

"Maybe. You seem less weak."

I refrain from rolling my eyes. "Thanks."

"What is making con write?"

I don't expect that kind of question from Mẹ, so I wonder if it's a mistranslation. "Like, why am I writing?"

"Yes."

"I don't know. I'll get a good grade, I guess." Even my answer, said out loud, doesn't sit right in my head. I couldn't care less about the actual journalism class and getting good grades and all that. But I have to admit, I feel more and more solid when I have a pen in hand. When there's an article that needs fixing and it's up to me to make everything sound right. I did that for Steve and Ernie. I did it for myself.

Linh had said I'd find something to be passionate about. What if she's right?

"Who is right?"

Oops, I'd said that last line out loud. My mom gazes expectantly at me.

"Mẹ," I begin. "Weren't you saying earlier in the year that you wanted me to find something? Be more motivated?"

"Con want to be a writer?"

In my mind's eye, far into the future, I'm seeing myself in a newsroom, a big one. In some big city. I see nights working under desk lamps. Ink staining my shirt cuffs, eyes tight and bleary from unrest. I see words flowing from my fingertips.

"I'm thinking about it."

"Writing is hard. Con might not find a job." Mẹ, always blunt.

"I know."

"You might need to live in our basement."

"What—I won't."

"You can if you will need to."

"It's all cement."

"We will work on renovating it. Just for you."

"So much confidence," I mutter.

Mẹ pats my hand, holding the tweezers. "Mẹ saying the basement is yours if you need it. You can stay as long as you want."

I imagine thirty-five-year-old me, journalist, writer, or whatever, living in the dungeons of our basement. Maybe some people would be okay staying with family, but I don't think that's for me. As I look back at my mom, I see her contented smile, and the corners of my mouth tilt up. All that nagging she's done over the years finally paid off, she's likely thinking. And now she can worry less, have less gray hairs.

I wince at the idea of her satisfaction swiftly turning to anger once she realizes who's been a part of this change inside me. Linh's apologetic face appears suddenly. *I'm sorry.*

I say nothing more and continue to scout for the rest of Mẹ's rebellious hair strands.

CHAPTER TWENTY-FOUR

LINH

Two years. Two years that Chef Lê went without speaking to his mom, despite having the bravery that I lack to follow what he wanted. He's made a career of it, yet it took a while for his mother to come back, and that was only by his father's doing.

I'm sitting at my desk, finessing my sketch of Chef Lê, who's now grinning back at me. I'll need to redraw it so that it's publishable. Other pieces of paper are scattered across my desk, some homework sheets and different drafts of the Scholastic Art Award application. The essay still needs filling out, but everything's turning into hieroglyphics and my eyes must be red after me rubbing at them so much. I've been struggling to put words to paper, and now

I think I've highly underestimated what Ali and Bảo do seemingly so easily.

My thoughts turn ugly, too many colors mixed together. *Would it even matter if I ended up getting this award? Would it do anything? Would it change much?* I guess this is what it means to tear your hair out.

I wouldn't know how to stand it—me and my mom not talking, for whatever reason. I've only done this with Evie; growing up we've had a few arguments that all seem childish now, but back then we'd go days without talking. Instead of trading nasty words, we'd fight by turning the bedroom lights on and off at inopportune times, seizing control of the washer and dryer even when a load wasn't finished, and completely ignoring the car-sharing schedule. The longest silence between us had lasted a week, broken only when Ba had done something ridiculous at the restaurant, and me and Evie accidentally met eyes, stifling our laughs.

But a laugh wouldn't solve how much I'd already lied to my parents.

And then there's Bảo and that moment outside the supermarket. His questions while we were at Chơi Ơi.

If I were anyone other than Linh Mai, someone *not* from a family who despises his, I'd be excited. There'd be no hesitation.

But I can't be. Hence why I practically ran away when Bảo broached the topic just as we were leaving.

What am I even doing anymore?

My phone buzzes in my pocket.

"Bảo?"

"Hey, Linh."

He never calls me this late. We've only texted so far. The deep pitch of his voice through the phone sounds more intimate.

"Is everything okay?" I hold my breath. Not the question I want to ask, because obviously, something happened between us. Something I hope he doesn't bring up again, because I can't deal with it right now.

"I wanted to let you know: I'm going to be a writer."

"What?"

"Yeah, I've figured it out. It's what I want to do. And I wanted you to know because you're the one responsible for it."

I lean back in my chair. In the mirror I look at when applying makeup in the morning, I'm smiling. "Bảo, I did nothing. It's all you."

"Lies." He pauses. "I told my mom, too. I can't tell how excited she is, but she's not complaining about it, at least."

"So your mom's accepting?"

"She offered the basement to me in case I can't find work after college, so I guess so."

"Lucky you." I try but I can't keep the bitterness from my tone. Immediately, I feel horrible. "I'm sorry. Imagine me saying that but without the vitriol." He only laughs, clearly in a good mood. "No, seriously. This is great. I'm not surprised. So whatever I did to influence you, I guess I'll take it."

"Ever since we met, you haven't said I can't do it. You've just accepted that I was starting to write, and I think you're the first person in my life to do that."

I turn in my swivel chair, smiling against the mouthpiece.

"What are you doing now?"

I hear Bảo typing away on the other side, and I'm sure he'll hear my eraser squeaking against the desk as I write another grammatically incorrect sentence.

"It's taking me ages to write my statement for the Gold Key application. *How* do you write?"

He snickers. "That's like me asking how you paint."

"Seriously, if there's a secret, tell me. My Gold Key statement still needs to be written."

"Be honest."

Is it a comment, in a not-so-subtle way, on what I haven't been honest about? Annoyance spikes within me. "Bảo—"

"What I mean is, you spend so much time worrying about your parents, how to tell them about the real you, that this is your chance to have a conversation only with the one reading your essay. You don't have to worry about your parents. Or anyone else." *Like you?* I ask silently. "Think about what you want. What you want to make and add to the world." He stops suddenly. "Wow, I sound like Ali, don't I? All of this motivational talk."

I smile, hearing genuine awe in his voice. Ali was my number-one fan before I knew I needed one.

"She'd be honored to hear you say that. You know she likes you now." I don't tell him that if Ali had an issue with him, it wouldn't be so subtle.

"Sure. Deep down."

"Exactly."

"Deep, deep, *deep* down."

I roll my eyes.

"Don't roll your eyes." I hear his smile.

"I'm not!"

"You are. It's not too hard to imagine you right now."

"Oh? And what are you imagining?"

Bảo exhales into the phone. I wait. My pencil hangs loose from my fingers as I rest my elbows on the desk. Outside it's completely dark, save for the streetlamps that've dimmed to save energy; they'll return to full force in a few minutes. Somewhere a dog growls and barks, and on the opposite side, a smaller dog chirps back. Talking to each other with a fence—maybe many—in between them.

"You're at your desk. You have your hair in a ponytail. You're leaning all the way forward in your chair because you're deep into your work. That's how you always are, especially when painting." I exhale a shaky breath. *This guy.* "Whenever you're thinking you rub your thumb on that bump on your middle finger, where your pencil's usually resting. The desk lamp is giving you a warm glow; it's the type of light you like—not too bright, not too dim." Then he lets out a half laugh. "Am I right?"

I hear the creak of his chair as he leans back. Probably looking smug.

"You're wrong."

"Am I?"

"My hair's down, not in a ponytail."

"Sorry for the gross assumption." He lets out a deep sigh. "Sorry, I'm taking up your time. You want me to go?"

I keep drawing. "No, it's fine. You can stay." It's comforting just to have him on the line, made even better by knowing he's not pressing me.

By the time my mom comes in without knocking, Bảo's off the phone, but not before I texted him my sketch of Chef Lê. I cover it up with some loose chemistry notes. Her wet hair is wrapped in a towel and she's already applied her Crabtree & Evelyn body lotion, which signals she's about to turn in. Her eyes sweep the room—the dim lighting, various half-finished homework sheets scattered on my bed, and the rainbow of papers across my writing desk. I shift to the left to hide my Gold Key essay drafts out of sight.

"We're doing another Phở Day."

"When was this decided?"

"A week ago."

"But why?"

Mẹ removes her towel and rubs out the water in her hair. "*That* restaurant is having a *Bánh Xèo* Day, so your father decided we should have our own. So we will need you in a couple of weeks."

I've already cut my time for art in half and am no closer to finishing my pieces for the Gold Keys. And now this. "Mẹ, I can't. I have so much to do."

My mom glances down at the papers across my desk. "You have a lot of homework?"

"Yeah, but it's more homework than usual."

"But you have always managed to do your homework on time. You shouldn't worry—"

"Just because I've managed before doesn't mean I can't be stressed out." I'd cut her off without realizing it, a harsh tone ringing in my ears. I bite my lower lip.

Perhaps she's really tired or just disappointed; she doesn't press me. "We can talk more tomorrow, but *con phải ngủ đi*." Mẹ runs her hand through my hair, telling me to sleep. She runs a hand on my shoulder before leaving the room.

The drive over to the restaurant is silent. My mom must have said something to my dad about my reaction last night, because he's not saying much either. A Vietnamese song plays low in the background, a crooning one that my mom likes to play in the house at nighttime, something like a lullaby. The sun is just peeking out over the arched roofs of restaurants and stores, as if wary of the people below it.

Ba yawns. I yawn back. He switches on the blinker, and we turn onto the street. We pass Bảo's restaurant and it's dark inside, but any minute now, his parents will turn the OPEN plaque around, and Bảo will be there, too. I think he mentioned having to work on Sunday.

"*Sao mà thấy con mặt bực mình vậy?*" Ba asks, his voice still gruff with sleep.

"I'm not angry," I mutter, which, of course, gives me away. "I'm just stressed."

"Schoolwork?" Ba asks.

I nod.

"Why is it stressful now? Last year was more stressful." Which is true, in a way. I was busy worrying about SATs and didn't have much time to work on my paintings then, either, but now . . . everything is happening at once.

I deflect. "Why do we never have enough people at work?"

"Lisa quit. It was unexpected."

"Then hire people who won't quit."

I meet Ba's furious eyes in the rearview mirror. "*Con này*," he starts to say. Mẹ shushes him, probably knowing his anger will not help here. But the tightness of her posture shows that this argument isn't finished.

Mẹ takes the back entrance while I help Ba lift the security grilles up front, walking in once the front door unlocks. The fans begin to turn, working against the heat. But instead of telling me to grab an apron like usual, or delegating tasks to me, like refilling the napkins or getting ice from the freezer or unwrapping the bins of herbs we'll need for the day, my mom nods for me to join her in the kitchen. Ba goes his own way to check last night's sales and the timesheets.

The two of us are in the kitchen, our steps echoing off the walls. I take a stool.

She dons kitchen gloves and pulls out her wooden cutting board, starts slicing onions. Next to her is a vinegar bath that the cooks made, so Mẹ just needs to complete the pickling process. She dips her finger into the vinegar bath, then adds a spoonful of sugar before dumping in the onions. I watch her stir it, then taste it, before she pushes the bowl toward me. My turn to try it.

"Vừa không?"

I ignore her question, staring resolutely at the tabletop. Heaving a sigh, my mom leans forward, resting her elbows on the prep table. Her hair has already loosened from its bun. I see bags under her eyes. The guilt that's become all too familiar nowadays flares up. But I still hate the idea that I'm expected to be the replacement when someone else isn't available. And the last special would have failed if it weren't for Bảo's help—which will not happen again.

So I look away. I hear my mom's lips part, then close. Maybe I've made her angry too. Aside from three or four blowups—including the time when she stumbled across me and Evie drawing pictures with crayons on our old apartment walls—she's been decidedly calmer than Ba.

Instead, her voice takes on its usual soft quality, with an indiscernible tinge. "Con, I know this isn't how you want to spend your time. And Mẹ and Ba hate having to ask you to work.

"But you don't know how hard it was to start up this restaurant. It wasn't about inheriting customers, finding new customers. It was inheriting a whole neighborhood of people who didn't want us." Mẹ's voice cracks. Anguish, that's the note I'd heard. "You don't know how that feels."

"You never told me," I retort, though my intent to sound annoyed is weak. I've never heard Mẹ sound this way. It tugs the same part of my heart storing all the hugs and kisses and laughs she's given me through so many sacrifices.

"Because you shouldn't have to know those things. We wanted to protect you." A spike of anger rushes through me. I'd hate to say it was in response to Bảo's parents, because that would mean I was angry with him, too. Still, it's clear that the cold welcoming had hurt my parents, made them feel less than welcome.

Mẹ shakes her head like she's denying the memories brought up. "The gossip was horrible, not just from that restaurant. Everywhere. But if I addressed it, people would add something else to the mix and there'd be no ending to it. So I ignored it. I put my everything into the food here, to make it speak for itself. Then your dad made friends and we made loyal customers." She gestures to the restaurant. "Phở Day made me so happy because it worked out. And now we're doing well. But it is always a game here. It's always a game to win, to maintain that we belong here."

I wonder if Mẹ means not just this community but in America in general.

I keep my head down. "Will the gossip ever stop? Will we always need to fight B—" I catch myself before saying "Bảo's parents." "—the Nguyễns' restaurant?"

Thankfully, Mẹ doesn't seem to notice. "Gossip and rumors never stop. They always come back in different forms." The knowingness in her voice—and the palpable feeling that there's something more she's holding back—triggers me to glance at her.

"Like when?"

It takes a few beats for Mẹ to make her decision. When she sits down across from me, I lean forward on my stool. "When I was eleven. Back in Vietnam," my mom starts, "Dì Vàng was ready to marry a neighbor who grew up with her. They were always together, and when our families realized what would happen, we began to set up our meetings to talk about expectations and the future for the two of them. The man was smart, nice, and always put the family first."

"Was he an artist too?" I try to picture my aunt with a boyfriend or a husband, but I only see her as I do now: her blurry face enlarged on the computer when we'd speak, her loud, assured voice when she talks about art. That's her true love; I can't imagine someone else in her life.

"Of course not," Mẹ answers quickly. "One of the reasons why your grandparents liked the man, before they passed, was because he was a logical person. He was going to inherit the family business, too. They knew that he would be able to support her when she couldn't do that herself with her art." I hold back from protesting. She said that as if it were a fact. As if my aunt weren't doing well for herself now.

"One day, though, he left, apologizing to everyone through a letter. But oh, the gossip! His family and the whole neighborhood were blaming Dì Vàng, as if she had done something, when it was actually him who'd run away from his promises. His responsibilities."

"What happened then?" I ask. "With the guy and with your sister?"

"I learned that he died." That can mean many things: during a battle, during one of the bombings, or during the escape, the same route that my family miraculously survived. "It is horrible, yes. All of it. He was, at the end of the day, good, and he would have made a good match for my sister." I sit back, cupping my tea for warmth, feeling as if a part of me has turned inside out. Her art. That's why her art always feels so sad. In each artwork she produces, she leaves that melancholic imprint behind.

"Why haven't I heard of this before?"

Mẹ sighs as she pushes back her hair. "There was no reason for it to come up. And it is something of the past—what good will it do to bring it up? Your aunt certainly doesn't mention it. We are in the present now—we look to the future." She takes an apron off the hook and offers me my apron. "We ignore all gossip and do our best.

"Con, I know you are busy. But you did such a good job last time. You can do it again. And you will survive your schoolwork. Because you are my daughter."

I take the apron from Mẹ. She smiles, and it's so grateful and so understanding that I muster up a smile, the weight on my shoulders even more insistent.

CHAPTER TWENTY-FIVE

BẢO

In the newsroom, just as the dismissal bell rings to let out class, the phone rings, too. Shouldering past our classmates flooding out of the room, Ali answers with a brisk tone. I can see her in the future now, poised over the phone, a notepad and pen in hand. She waits for a few minutes until she turns, fixing me with a look. I start walking past her, but she stops me.

"Bảo, it's for you."

That's new. I take the phone as cautiously as if I was just asked to take care of some dangerous creature. "Hello?"

"Yo, *em!*" Chef Lê. I know it immediately from his voice. "It's me: Chef Lê from Chơi Ơi! What's good?"

"Uh, hi. I'm in school right now." Is he calling about the article? It doesn't sound like he's calling to yell about how bad it was. I picture him at the same table, his chef jacket's sleeves rolled up. Maybe with his feet propped on the seat across from him until his wife, Saffron, comes by to smack them off.

"Yeah, sorry, I was looking for a way to contact you and figured this was the best way. I saw the article online. It's legit the best review I've ever gotten. Thank you so much."

"Oh, thanks."

"What, you thought I'd hate it?"

"I had that thought."

"No way, the review is great and I appreciate it, dude. But I'm actually calling because I saw your girlfriend's—"

"She's not my girlfriend—"

"—artwork with the piece," he says over me on purpose. "I dig it and was wondering if she did things like that on the side. Either draw or paint on a large-scale."

"She's actually a painter. That's her main medium."

"Fantastic. So here's the thing: A lot of the decor at my restaurant is pretty modern, but I have this one column in the back of the restaurant that needs some TLC. I was thinking a big-ass mural. You got her number?"

"Uh, sure. Hold on." I pull out my phone and read out the number. "So, you're going to pay her?"

"What, are you an agent now?" He laughs. "Yes, dude, I'll totally pay her. There's no such thing as free labor."

Ali watches me expectantly, arms crossed. I hang up a few seconds later and face Ali, who asks almost immediately, "Are we in trouble?"

Dazed by the quick turn of events—from Chef Lê's praise, which I wish I could have recorded for posterity, and his offer to Linh—I shake my head. "I think Linh just got offered her first gig."

On a Sunday, we drive to the other side of Westminster to celebrate one of my second (or third?) cousins' first birthdays. Walking into the house, we see a layer of shoes swamping the front door: Nikes, Crocs, loafers from various relatives who've flocked there for the celebration. Cousins and nieces and nephews, or second cousins if you want to be technical, dash through the hallways only to stop when my aunt—one of my father's many cousins—emerges from the kitchen with a pair of chopsticks in hand that foretells their fate if they misbehave. A mom chases after her toddler, who dashes around with Usain Bolt–like speed, as if knowing that his mom will give up if she's too tired. I give her maybe fifteen minutes and she'll start bargaining food for her love: *Ăn đi con. Ăn đi con để cho Mẹ thương.*

My mom made *chè Thái* as a sweet treat, a punch-bowl worth that she fretted over last night. But the kitchen table, as we discover, is already covered end to end with food that no one was asked to make but brought anyway. Somehow, with gatherings like this, no one ever brings duplicate items. I see someone already provided the egg rolls: crispy and hot from their oil bath.

Tinfoil trays of *bánh bèo*, disks of rice cakes just small enough to fit your palm, are paired with jugs of fish sauce ranging from mild to burning off your tongue, which is what most of the men here like.

Cậu Trí, who I'm glad I only have to see occasionally, makes a point to serve me the mildest fish sauce. Asshole. After a round of mandatory greetings and pretending to recognize all of the guests, I sit down at the men's table—a bunch of tucked-in polos, belts, and a few Bluetooths glued to their ears. They're red-faced after a few bottles of Heineken and Corona and don't even know I'm there.

So I end up drifting toward the kitchen to grab a drink. Việt's already there, and you'd think I'd be shocked to find him surrounded by women forty years older than him, gossiping and cooking together. Yet, still, it looks like he's been there all along. He stirs vinegar and sugar in a bowl. The conversation sounds heated, and I catch a few harsh words in rapid Vietnamese.

"So how did you get roped into this?" I ask.

He tastes the dressing. "My mom knows one of the other moms or something. One of the delivery customers." Which is the answer you would expect at this type of gathering.

Việt quickly catches me up on the gossip getting swapped around.

Apparently some guy they all knew couldn't find a wife here, so he went back home to Vietnam and miraculously got married. They're due to come back in five weeks, but *where will they stay? What are they going to do?* The wife doesn't speak basic English, from what they're saying. From the snide comments and the tsk-ing, I don't think the new couple's gonna have it easy here.

"C'mon, let's grab something to eat," he says, shaking out his wrists. How long has he been stirring?

We leave the kitchen. I think Việt's mom calls his name, but he doesn't react, so maybe that's my imagination.

Việt and I are relegated to sit at the kids' table. I'm pretty sure I'll be at this table until I'm married, whenever that happens. Việt is across from me, while twelve-year-old twins—maybe directly related to me?—violently elbow each other, then stab each other with chopsticks, until their mother comes over and hisses at them to behave. Another cousin, five years old, stares at me with a mouthful of rice, snot running down her nose. She uses her tongue to wipe some clean, even as her own mother tries to shove another spoonful into her mouth.

Not the best seasoning.

Other kids continue to wreak havoc, seizing an escape from supervision. "He farted!" yells a little girl as she dashes across the living room, earning bemused looks from the adults.

Seconds later: "I didn't địt! I didn't địt!" a boy, maybe her brother, screams, running in the same direction.

"Kids are fascinating," Việt deadpans.

My dad's other cousin comes over, tells us to stand up, that she hasn't seen us for ages. I lean on my toes to look taller than Việt, but he beats me by standing straight, for once. Then the subject, as always, turns to where we're planning to apply to school.

"Your mom tells me you are going for the big schools," she says to Việt, impressed.

He answers dutifully. "Trying for it. I want to major in biology

223

and then become a doctor." But why does he sound so dulled by it?

"Your mom tells me you have the grades for it, too!" Then her eyes slide over to me. "And . . . con?" This aunt knows by now that my chances of going to the same schools as Việt are close to nonexistent.

"I'm still deciding."

Her smile fades. She saves herself by plastering on a fake one. As if my self-esteem weren't already low enough.

Here's Việt, who can probably get in anywhere. And me. Then again, I don't think Việt's ever said if he liked any particular college, let alone the idea of going to med school.

"You serious about majoring in biology?" I ask once the aunt disappears.

Việt shrugs, picks at his papaya salad. "It's an answer that gets them to stop asking."

I'd use that answer if only I knew people wouldn't immediately call me a liar.

"Seriously, what *do* you want to do?"

"Forensic science."

"No surprise there," I joke. He stares at his food, not saying anything for a moment. He's usually not this quiet, not with me. "You okay?"

"Mentioned the idea of it to my parents the other day. They yelled at me for hours. My ears kept ringing after."

Maybe that's why he avoided his mom before. When he talks about his parents, I don't exactly think of the word "empathetic." It's his mother's shrewdness that my mom admires. Việt's father's honesty has earned my paranoid father's trust. But emotionally, they're not the people to rely on. And they're strict when it comes to Việt's studies.

"Exactly," he says, reading my look. "That's just another reason for my parents to fight. They've been doing that for way too long."

"But forensic science is still a type of science. It has a lot to do with biology, right? Shouldn't they be happy? I mean . . . maybe they'll come around to it?" I say unconvincingly. I always assumed Việt's situation was better than mine. But then again, these days, I'm assuming a lot. Especially when it comes to Linh.

Việt smiles. It's the quiet kind. The sad kind. Because he knows that my words can't be much help now, can't change things. "They're never happy these days."

We sit in silence, scraping our paper plates clean. I want to fill it with something, so I tell him, "I kind of told my mom that I wanted to be a writer."

"A writer." Việt stares blankly at me, and I swallow, realizing that he'd just told me how his parents were shutting down his dream. I'm an asshole. This was what Việt was talking about before about me, him, and Linh having different variations of parents. Different circumstances in which we are either allowed to go for our dreams . . . or not.

I breathe easier when a genuine smile blooms across his face. He punches my shoulder. *Fuck.*

"Dude, no way! What did she say?"

I rub my shoulder. "She didn't blow up on me. She said I could use the basement if I didn't get a job." Which isn't so nice when you say it out loud. But Việt knows my mom and her weird sense of humor.

"The fact that she didn't get angry is something big!"

"It's not serious or anything."

"C'mon, you know that's the best you can get from them." He shakes his head at a thought he doesn't voice to me. "Sometimes I can't believe how fast things move.

"It's like this. We were in our own worlds. Me with cross country. You with . . . um. Actually I don't know which world you really belonged to."

"That makes me feel really good about myself."

"Obviously you've found your shit. We're growing up. You're becoming a writer, falling in love—" My heart wheezes at his choice of words. I haven't told him about Linh essentially rejecting me.

I hadn't even had a chance to talk to Linh one-on-one, or mention Chef Lê, who's trying to reach her. Last I heard, she hasn't responded to his calls.

"When are you going to make the Grand Gesture?"

"Grand Gesture?"

"Dude, like on *The Bachelor*. It's the thing you do to signal that you're serious about someone."

"Right. And what does *The Bachelor* do exactly to show that?"

"Helicopter rides. Day trips to a beautiful winery. Farm visits. Which actually doesn't really make sense to me."

Someone please help me.

◇ ◇ ◇

There were many failed attempts at singing karaoke. Plus, the little ones needed to go to sleep soon, including the birthday boy. So, the night ends with a tradition. Twelve items are laid out before him, all of them somehow representing a possible career. Whatever he'd choose would be his profession in the future. I'm sure it's all for fun, but I think the parents are secretly betting everything on the kid's final choice.

My cousin, bib just removed, stares wide-eyed at the crowd around him, mesmerized by the camera lights shining on him. Then he glances at the items: a calculator, a fork, a toy stethoscope, and other random things from around the house. After a few minutes of goading and laughing from his audience, he scrabbles for the stethoscope, causing everyone to cheer. He sucks on the diaphragm.

Mẹ is seated, surrounded by her cousins and friends, also rocking the Asian glow, though I'm sure she's only had one drink. There are traces of laughter on her face.

"Mẹ, what did I choose?"

"Huh, con?"

"When I turned one, what did I choose?"

She has to think about it for a few seconds, and my aunts chime in with answers that are all wrong. An emotion dawns on my mom's face and her answer finally comes, sending my mind reeling—possibilities feeling an inch closer to reality.

"A pencil."

There's a whisper of a word inside my brain as Mẹ reveals this fact, this forgotten memory. Serendipity. It was just a game back then; I was a child who picked the most interesting thing to me. Or something I could bite on.

Now, it's real. The word is "serendipity."

Things are falling into place. The possibility that I can be a writer. My mom's acceptance, or something close to it.

The only other piece is Linh.

It's a reckless idea, me wanting to be with Linh. My mom wouldn't like it as much as she likes the idea of my writing. There's also no way it can ever come true.

So maybe it's okay for me to feel this way. As long as nothing happens. As long as I can still be her friend.

CHAPTER TWENTY-SIX

LINH

Gold Key. Phở Day Part II. Gold Key. Bảo. Gold Key. Bảo. There are so many things competing for purchase in my mind. I want to shut off these rivaling thoughts, but my normal way of coping—painting or sketching—isn't happening as easily. I'm fidgeting, my attention straying. I made the mistake of looking in the mirror this morning and could have sworn that a ghoul was staring back at me.

I'm in the art room during lunch, as usual, feeling Bảo's absence. The window curtains are drawn to block the afternoon light, but not enough to block the rays completely. The room is awash with pale blue and it calms me so much. I'm in the center of the room, earplugs in to try to get myself to focus, though I end up preoccupied by the motes of dust seemingly suspended in the air.

My phone vibrates once. I look over and see that unfamiliar number again. I've gotten it two times already. Probably spam, so I've been ignoring it.

"Hey, Linh."

I pause, wanting to see if I have to turn to greet him. He'll see the ghoul that was me this morning. When I do turn around, his expression doesn't change. "You busy? Need to talk to you—"

I brush back my hair, nervous. "Bảo—"

He holds up a hand. A sheepish smile is on his face. "Not about *that*. It's actually something that Chef Lê mentioned to me. Did he call you?"

"Chef Lê?" Now I'm confused.

"Yeah—" His eyes catch on something to his right. He laughs.

"What?"

He points to his hair, then to mine. I mimic the gesture and thread my fingers through mine, feeling something wet—it's *paint*.

"Oh, shoot." I whirl around, trying to spot the roll of Bounty that I always keep around, but I can't find it. Embarrassment flushes my face. *Great.*

When I turn back, Bảo is there, gently grabbing the wet piece of hair and dabbing it with a paper towel. I hold my breath, relishing the feel of him close to me, the feel of his eyes on me. His touch. Tender.

"There," he whispers. "All better."

He steps away and I feel my shoulders fall. My heart pumps at an indecent pace.

Bảo realizes what he's done and he drops the towel on the nearest stool. "Um, anyway. Chef Lê's been trying to reach you."

"Oh!" I glance at my phone. The strange number. "What does he want?"

His smile looks strained. "Give him a call back. He'll explain. But I think it'll be good news. It might actually be fun, you know. It's perfect for you."

He stands, shoulders slightly hunched, unsure. Before, he would have made himself comfortable at his own table. Might have even hovered nearby to peek at my work.

I hate that I did this. The stilted conversation, the pauses. It'd been easy before. Now everything's changed because of these feelings—because of all that's working against us.

"I guess . . . I guess I'll see you later, Linh," Bảo finally says.

The room is awash in more shadows than I realized.

If I looked tired earlier, I can only imagine how I look now, even more so with the mystery of Chef Lê's message weighing heavily in my mind. My parents aren't as tactful about my appearance when I come to work. Ba's straightening the tablecloths that just came in. I was right. It made the light inside less piercing to the eyes. It's almost like spring has come to the restaurant. The fake daisies that we bought complete the picture.

My dad stares at me a little longer. *"Con bệnh hả?"* He uses the back of his hand to feel my forehead, checking if I'm sick.

"*Mẹ sẽ* make ginger tea," Mẹ says, standing up from her booth, where she was eating an early dinner.

"*Ngồi xuống đi*," Ba suggests to me.

"Ba, Mẹ, I'm fine." I brush away his hand. "I just . . . didn't put on makeup this morning." *And I also have too much to worry about.* But the closeness allows me to see the bags under his eyes. He must be worried about Phở Day again. We're all worrying, them more than me. My issues pale by comparison to theirs.

"You look worse than that." Ba turns to Mẹ. "Perhaps she should go home and sleep."

"No, I'm okay," I grumble, even as the thought of bed is enticing. A chance to be alone and recharge.

"Right, she should sleep."

Ba says firmly, having Mẹ's agreement, "Sleep. We want you to be rested for Phở Day."

But I don't go home, not right away, at least. Instead, I'm sitting in my car outside Chơi Ơi. After leaving my parents' restaurant, I drove around mindlessly, taking the longer route home, an excuse to clear my mind. But then I remembered the missed calls from Chef Lê's number. I shoved my phone away in hopes that I wouldn't need to think about it. Or think about Bảo. Before I knew it, though, I reached down for it, and started driving.

The parking lot is relatively bare, but I expect it to fill up around dinnertime, which is within an hour.

Why does he want to see me?

I meet Saffron, his wife, at the front. "My husband was raving about your sketch!"

"Oh, thank you, I'm glad he liked it." My voice comes out flat. *Did I sound like this the whole day?*

Her smile falters by a fraction. "Are you okay?"

I sidestep the question. "Um, is Chef Lê around?"

"Oh! He'll be happy to see you. The column's been something of a sore spot for us, and he couldn't figure out what to do until he saw your work. He knew you'd be the right person to dress it up."

Column? It hits me then, that I hadn't even thought to listen to his voicemail. But now it all connects.

At her words, the first spark of warmth comes back to me. Chef Lê actually wants to hire me? A high school student?

"Go ahead, you can find him in the back."

I'm heading in that direction until I see the tape cutting off a section of the restaurant, a curtain shrouding that part in mystery, keeping it out of sight from wandering customers. Curiosity getting the best of me, I cross the room and part the curtains to face the white column. It's a good size, with a lot of space to work with. Done right, it could make a nice splash.

"Miss Mai!" Chef Lê says, dropping a towel that he was using to wipe his hands. "Glad you got my message."

"Is this—"

He nods, slapping the column. "Yep, the real estate."

A vision of what it could be surges forward in my mind. This column is in the center of the room, so it should naturally draw the eye. It needs bold colors, ones that won't clash with the rest of the walls, but complement them. Mostly, the decor already shows off landscapes. What we need now are people. Faces as vivid as the discerning ones who will come to dine here.

Emerging from my thoughts, I almost miss the amount he's offering to pay me. I ask him to repeat himself. "If you're gonna try to say that's too much, I'm not going to listen," he says good-humoredly. He reminds me of my parents, how they don't let anyone refuse payment.

"Why me?" I manage to ask.

Chef Lê tips his head back and his laugh bounces off the walls.

"Like I told Bảo, I know talent. You're talented, Linh."

Talent.

A wave of sadness catches me off guard. It travels up inside me, splitting into tendrils. There are people who have faith in me, and they shouldn't. I'm not the person they need. I'm always second-guessing myself, running away scared.

I touch the column with my fingertips; it's damp and newly painted with base coat. I spot the tarp and drops of white, and I see a pair of Converse. Red.

Bảo. Saffron appears right behind him, carrying some towels. "Chef Lê, where do you want—Linh?"

I look closer. The edges of his sleeves appear as if they'd been dipped in white as well. Some specks are on his jeans.

Did Bảo do this? Was Bảo actually painting?

"Right over there's good. You came just in time. I'm trying to strike a deal with Linh."

"Oh." Bảo stays put, glancing between the column and me.

"You're supposed to paint the column, not yourself," I say, fighting back a smile. He offers an uncertain one in return. Another pause, one that Saffron appears to notice, because she sets down the towels, then coughs delicately.

"Bry, I need to talk to you for a sec. Over there?" She's already walking back out toward the curtains.

"What, now?"

"Yup." She disappears outside.

Chef Lê follows half in, half out. "But, Saff—" There's some whispering, growing more insistent. "What do you mean, leave them alone? We're just—" A hand grabs his collar, yanking him through the curtains, out of view. I look over at Bảo, who's watching in bewildered amusement. He catches me peeking and normally we'd laugh together, but he sobers up immediately.

He examines his sleeves. "Shouldn't you be at work?"

"My parents sent me home. They think I might be getting sick."

He frowns in worry, and walks closer, less hesitantly then he had before. My heart leaps when he touches me on the forehead. That doesn't help things. "I knew you looked off before. Shouldn't you be in bed, then?"

"I'm not sick. I'm just tired."

"You have a lot going on," he murmurs. His hand curves around my jaw, his thumb lingering on my cheek. He stays like this longer than I think he realizes.

And when he does, he takes a wide step back. "Sorry."

"No, it's—" Again, the air between us tightens. "Why are you here, Bảo?"

"I had a day off. So I decided to stop by and give a hard copy of my piece to Chef Lê. And then we just got to talking and he wanted to get the column ready." He quickly rushes to add, "But I told him you didn't say yes yet. He just got excited and pulled out all of this and before I knew it—" He gestures to the mess on his clothes. "When Chef Lê wants something, he just does it, apparently."

I circle the column, my fingers tracing the parts that are relatively dry. Bảo follows close behind like there's a string loosely connecting us.

"A small part of me, I guess, was still hoping you'd show up."

"But you couldn't have known I'd come here."

Still, he came. "I know." The earnestness of his statement moves the ground beneath me.

The column. Big and vast. There are so many designs it can take. So many possibilities in every way. I can paint another cityscape. I can paint the people that Chef Lê holds closest to him: his wife, his dad, his late mom. I can make the colors as bright as they can be—I can use normal colors; I can mix my own. I can make something beautiful out of this.

Inside, the tendrils of anxiety settle down. I take a deep breath.

Bảo's offering these options to me. Just like the night he stepped over enemy lines to help me. He always wants to help me. I'm always the one to turn him away, always having a reason to keep a distance. This understanding touches me in a way I can't voice with words, and God, I wish I could paint my feelings right here for him.

Yet, words—my inadequate words—are all I have in this moment. So I choose.

"Hypothetically, if I accept Chef Lê's offer, it'd take a lot of work to get this mural done."

A handsome smile graces his face. "You could do this. I've seen your work."

"It'd be hard, too. I probably won't know what to do with it half the time."

"That's fine. Inspiration doesn't come that easily."

"It's something just for me."

Bảo nods again. "After all the things you're doing, you deserve a break sometimes."

"Even though I still wouldn't know what to do about our families."

"It's oka—" He levels his gaze at me. "Linh?"

"Thank you," I say in a rush, before tackling him with a side-hug that coaxes a short laugh from him. After hesitating for a millisecond, his arms come around me, and we lean into each other.

When I paint, there's always a moment where I *just know* that I'm finally finished. The colors and textures come together to depict a feeling of *rightness*.

Us, here, is that rightness.

I breathe him in. I nestle my head into the crook of his neck, fitting myself into him like a piece of puzzle.

Yes, I want him. I want us.

Him loosening his hold on me and the sharp catch in his breath tell me he finally gets it. Still, he leans back to confirm the answer. A hand that circled my waist slides up my arm. The other gently, so gently, remains on my hip. A fine shiver passes through me and I hold my breath, but my heart hiccups. He cups my cheek with a hand and his face inches forward.

"Can I?" he asks.

I meet him there.

Ecstatic colors surround us, the happiest of colors, yellow, orange, pink swirling. Blooming. Like we're in Monet's *Water Lilies*.

No. This is all mine. This is *my painting*. I want to memorize this feeling and make my own masterpiece.

I press my lips against his more insistently. He makes a small noise of surprise, but I feel his smile. It's surreal, us kissing here. I've tried to tamp down all of these feelings for the wrong reason, but now I can show them. This, *this* feels so right: the quiet smack of lips parting before coming together, the exhaling out of noses, and his hand light against my neck, keeping me in place—not that I ever, ever want to move away. All I care about right now is his arms around me, his lips on mine, and the utter freedom I feel to slide my hands through his hair. Finally.

CHAPTER TWENTY-SEVEN

BẢO

I'd showed up here without any expectations and just started painting. Everything was already there; Chef Lê had already bought everything Linh would need, so sure that she'd answer his call and accept the offer. I didn't have the heart to tell him that Linh was already busy, and this was the last thing she needed to add to her pile.

Then she appeared. The white of the column glowed under the light and she was entranced. I was entranced by her. But I tried to hide it. Act like we're just friends because that's what we are. Just friends.

Is it possible to be this happy?

Our kiss steals the air from my lungs, and that's the only reason I eventually pull away from Linh. I rest my forehead against hers, disoriented. I never thought I'd ever feel weak-kneed—that was for damsels in distress or elderly people with low blood pressure—but I guess it's the same for first kisses.

Linh's eyes are hazy when I look into them, then I watch them clear up, reality rushing back with a vengeance. I read all of this easily because I know her worries. Some of them are mine exactly. She opens her mouth. "Just pause," I say, desperate to keep the moment to ourselves. Her mouth closes. "We can delay it for a few more minutes."

"You're acting like me," she says, half teasingly. "But once we step outside, nothing's changed. We'll still be Bảo Nguyễn and Linh Mai, whose families hate each other."

"But here," I counter, arms going around her waist, "even if it's just for a little while, we're Bảo Nguyễn and Linh Mai, food reviewer and artist. And we've made it work for the past few months," I try saying.

Linh smiles sadly because she knows I'm stalling. Her hand goes back into my hair, and if I could ever pick a moment to freeze, it'd be now, with that tender look in her eyes. Tired, yet hopeful. Indulgent. Actually, just one adjective wouldn't be enough to explain it.

"Hey." I touch her chin, marveling that I'm allowed to do this. How easily it comes to me. "We'll figure it out. One step at a time."

"Okay," she says before kissing me. "What's the next step?"

I try to think of lighter things that don't have to do with our families, a breach we'll need to figure out how to navigate.

"I'm your boyfriend."

"I would think that was obvious."

"I guess Ali and Việt saw this coming before us. We'll need to let them know."

"What do you mean? Ali knew how I felt, but Việt did, too?"

"Apparently they talk to each other. About us."

"Oh God." Linh rests her forehead against my chest. She mumbles something that I can't hear.

"What's that?"

"Romeo and Juliet. Ali's not going to shut up about us being Romeo and Juliet now."

"We kind of are," I say. "Our parents hate each other. Our secret meetings. This column looks like it'd even fit the time period."

"Are you saying you're going to poison yourself? Will I need to find a dagger somewhere?"

"And a tomb. We need to be prepared."

She laughs, but doesn't say anything. Just lets me hold her. Or she's holding me. It's all the same at this point.

From behind the curtain, I hear Chef Lê and Saffron whisper-arguing. "So should I knock, then?"

"Bry, baby, it's a curtain. You can't knock."

After letting Chef Lê bear-hug us—Saffron shaking her head all the while—and tell us how he "knew it," we talk about the column and his initial vision. He wants it to complement the red wall yet act like a statement piece—something to lure people when they come into the dining room. He hands Linh a couple of photos of his family—many of them of his mother from throughout her life. They remind me of the black-and-white photos on our wall and our family altars. When my relatives were posing for those portraits, I wonder if they knew what they'd be used for, if their sober stares were made on purpose.

Ultimately, Chef Lê says, he's leaving other elements up to Linh but he'd like to have his family incorporated somehow.

"I have a few ideas," Linh says, holding the photo while doing another walk around the column, taking in how much space she has to work with. She's very much an artist at work, not some high school student playing around.

And she's my girlfriend. *Girlfriend.* I beam at her, even if she's not paying me any attention. I think about the kiss. I think about her worries. And of course, thoughts of my mom and dad seep in, threatening to taint these new feelings, but I hold on to the memory of our kiss.

Chef Lê spreads out the photos, moving them around like puzzle pieces. He's explaining what he knows about them so that Linh can decide which ones to work with.

When we first met him, he talked about the questions he had that will never be answered. He talked about discovering parts of his past in innocuous, unexpected ways.

If I look into my family's past, could I find an answer that would explain today?

Linh is arranging times to start on the mural and unexpectedly throws a question my way. "Are you free for the next couple of Thursdays? Chef Lê says that works for him."

"Do you want me here too?"

"Of course I want you here."

"Like . . . paint?" I gesture to my clothing. Linh's face twists. Ah. That's an obvious answer.

Saffron steps in smoothly. "You're welcome to just hang around. Do homework and the like. Bry will try not to bother you too much."

"Always trying to insult me, isn't she?"

"Really?" I ask, ignoring Chef Lê. Linh squeezes my arm excitedly. "Sure, I can do that."

In an irreverent move that only Chef Lê could manage, he finger-guns me. And I guess we have a deal.

CHAPTER TWENTY-EIGHT

LINH

The next morning, my alarm clock doesn't wake me. No, it's someone tickling me awake, pulling me out of pleasant dreams. I was stuck in a painting of my own, but I was happy. I could paint with my hands, no brush needed, and everything I touched took on color. I walked into a little cabin at the end of a long rainbow road, and opened the door, and I think it might have been Bảo standing with his back to me. I reached out to tap his shoulder, but a pair of hands got me from behind—

I jerk out of bed and flip the light switch on.

Evie.

"What are you doing here so early?" I exclaim, launching myself at her as she catches me, laughing. She smells like a brand-new car.

Ba was supposed to leave in an hour to drive her here. "I rented a car to drive in myself. Didn't think Ba needed to be up this early," she says. That explains the smell. "But here you are, sleeping in. How lazy."

I glance at the alarm clock. Seven in the morning. "Hardly." I push back my hair, mussed from sleep, and focus on her. She's wearing her UC Davis sweatshirt again, the hood covering her hair. Her eyes are alive, probably hyped from the coffee she must have guzzled down during the long trip. "I'm glad you're here."

"I couldn't leave you three to fend for yourselves."

I hug her again, the strength of it surprising me and her. But she doesn't say anything else.

I'd been so mad for the past few weeks, busy with the Gold Key submissions, my feelings for Bảo—just having so many thoughts weigh me down. I know it was selfish. I know I could have handled it all better. If Evie were in my place, she would have handled it differently for sure.

But now that I was honest with Bảo, that's one thing off my chest. As for the other things?

"Ouch, Linh. You're hugging me way too tightly!"

It's rare for me to wake up before my parents, but it's all worth it, watching Evie tiptoe into their bedroom down the hall, leaning down close and blowing air into Ba's left ear. He lets out a snort, lurches over. His arm swings up until he realizes who's right beside him. "Con!"

"*Gì?*" Mẹ says blearily. Then she's instantly awake.

Mẹ playfully slaps my sister's arm, scolding her for driving all night and not letting any of us know. What could have happened on the road? And she was alone! But her wide smile undercuts her rebuke; she's happy to see Evie here. I'm reminded of past Sundays when my sister and I would sneak into their bed, crawling like toddlers until we could sandwich Mẹ and nearly knock Ba off his side. We're older now, all grown up.

We could still knock Ba over, if we really wanted to.

After showering, I walk down to the kitchen. Mẹ makes a feast for breakfast like she's preparing soldiers for battle: cooking eggs *ốp la*, *cà phê sữa đá*, and some leftover *bánh ướt* from the restaurant. They're talking about Bảo's restaurant, especially their plans for later tonight.

"*Bánh Xèo* Day," Ba remarks. "Why didn't we ever think of that?"

"Making *bánh xèo* was never my strong suit," Mẹ says.

"Maybe you should practice," Ba replies.

"Maybe *you* should," she retorts, before turning her attention to the sauté pan, where another serving of over easy eggs is ready to be flipped. Evie and I grin at each other.

I look down, realizing that my mom had set before me a bowl of *cháo gà*, warm rice porridge with chicken meat, freshly chopped parsley, and a few turns of ground pepper. My mom must have made it late last night at some point. A rush of warmth washes over me, and I haven't even taken a bite.

She settles into her seat to my left. Ba's at my right, and Evie's across from me. The seating that we'd had as we shared countless dinners. "Let's hope today goes off as well as last time," Mẹ says.

I thread my fingers through hers. I hope so too, but I also would hate that to mean that Bảo's family somehow fails, and maybe that makes me a traitor. I brush aside the thought, focusing on my mom and the rest of my family.

"We'll be fine."

CHAPTER TWENTY-NINE

BẢO

The weather is dreary and gray, but it bodes well for tonight, my mom proclaims. It means rain is coming—the perfect excuse for *bánh xèo*.

At home in our kitchen, my mom woke up early to prep. I shuffle into the kitchen in my sweats, trying to compute what my eyes are seeing. On every surface available—the table, the counters, the top of our rice cooker—sit metal food buckets, each holding the food items that would go in each batch of *bánh xèo*: shrimp, pork belly, bean sprouts, and more. I see another batter that's not as yellow; it might be the desserts she's trying out, something that resembles a crepe, ready for fixings of strawberry, Nutella, and banana.

Mẹ comes in from outside, raincoat on, her pj's underneath. She shakes out her wet hair. From her morning shower or from outside, I'm not sure. Behind her on the outside stove, whatever's inside the pan sizzles and pops.

"Need help?"

"No touching," Mẹ answers tersely. She tries to clean but all she's really doing is moving from one bucket to the next. I haven't seen her fretting like this since she found out about the Mais' first Phở Day. And it all makes sense.

"Mẹ, are you nervous?"

"Nervous? Mẹ not nervous."

"What's the Vietnamese word for 'nervous'?"

"*Lo lắng*, but Mẹ not *lo lắng*," my mom counters. "*Chết cha.*" She does a double take toward the outdoor stove, cursing when she sees something I can't. I watch from inside as she scoops the batter from the pan and dumps it onto a plate—with other failed attempts, I guess.

"Mẹ," I say firmly once she gets back in. "What can I do?"

Mẹ sighs and glances down at her bowl half full of batter. "I've done a couple of batters. But something is not right. I'm about to put in another layer right now. Here, let's use another pan. Everything else is almost cooked."

She lets the pan sit for a few seconds over the fire before instructing me to douse it with two bottle-squirts of oil. She adds shrimp and pork belly. After waiting a couple more beats, using her chopsticks to mix the batter, she deftly pours in a thin layer and it slides into the pan with a satisfying sizzle.

"It's tricky, getting the layer just right," Mẹ says, adding in bean sprouts. "Too much and it won't be crispy. *Không giòn.*"

"How do you know when it's crispy?"

"The edges look as if they want to peel off." Seconds pass and she has her spatula ready. She folds the pancake in half, the other side golden brown. I grin. If she were in Chef Lê's kitchen, he'd probably be praising her. *This is the shit*, he'd say.

The *bánh xèo* slides off easily onto the plate that I'm holding. The rain has let up, but water from the gutter drips by my feet. I'm about to head inside again to actually get a raincoat, when I hear Mẹ speaking.

"I used to love *bánh xèo* as a child. During the monsoon seasons. Your uncle and I would eat this up whenever our parents made them," she says. "We would leave the door open and watch the rain from the kitchen."

"Cậu Cam?" The uncle who I resembled. The one who didn't make it.

"When I cook things like this, I remember him. I'm sure he'd be surprised by how good of a cook I've become. He was always so critical of my skills," she says fondly.

After a moment, realizing that's all she's going to say, I mention, "*Everyone* says your *bánh xèo* is the best one, you know."

Mẹ tsks, pretending to shun the idea. "I wish people will say that to my face." But she smiles at me, her hood covering most of her face. I know her, though; I know she likes to hear praise like this. She glances up at the sky, watching for something I can't see. "I'm hoping the rain doesn't make everyone stay inside. If so, both restaurants might lose, which can't be helped. But until then, we think this deal will get a lot of customers. Even more than *that* restaurant."

Later at the restaurant, Linh texts me.

how are you doing?

you spying on us?

why do you think I kissed you?

i knew it

thinking about you

I look over my shoulder. My mom's busy cleaning up.

me too

also you're going down tonight

oh, it's going to be like that?

game on

After a few hours of prepping, service is about to begin. The line doesn't compare to Linh's, not at this hour, but still, there are people waiting outside the restaurant, umbrellas up. So far, no one looks upset that they're in the rain. Ba walks down the line, handing out menus for consideration and even some samples of *bánh xèo*. One guy takes a bite and says, "*Dude*. This is the best thing I've ever tasted. Even my mom doesn't make it this good."

I only saw the back of my dad's head, so I have to imagine his reaction to being called a "*dude*."

"Game on, man," Việt says, standing right next to me as he ties his apron strings behind his back. He was here earlier with us, his parents tagging along as they dropped off a fresh batch of shrimp for tonight's service.

In the flurry of everything, I remember that Việt doesn't know about me and Linh yet.

"How's the bet with Ali going?"

"No changes from last time."

"I don't think it's necessary anymore." After making sure no one's nearby, I tell Việt everything about my visit to Linh in the art room, my note to her, and then our meetup at Chef Lê's place and our decision to test out our relationship.

Clearly, I catch him off guard; he blinks but doesn't say anything for a few beats. Suddenly, he's thumping me on the back—channeling Chef Lê's strength—congratulating me.

"And there's no better way to test a relationship than competition."

"Thanks for the reminder, Việt."

"Personally, I don't think anyone can really win. Both restaurants are doing different specials, so it's going to draw different people. Don't tell your mom I said this, though. She wouldn't like it."

"Who wouldn't like what?" Mẹ asks, appearing behind us as she dons a pair of kitchen gloves. "Why are you talking instead of working?"

"Nothing, we're just wondering if anyone's ever going to make *bánh xèo* the way you do. What if the other restaurant tries to copy us?" Việt answers, so sweetly that Mẹ might see through him.

Mẹ doesn't even bat an eyelash as she says, "They're no good at making *bánh xèo*."

"You've had theirs before or something?" I ask, surprised that she would know how it tasted. Or at least it sounds like it. She used to call their other foods bland, especially the phở, and I always thought it was an assumption on her part. A way to mock them.

Mẹ waves her hand. "I just know it."

"Oh." Her quick answer bothers me, though. It's more of a feeling than anything. But there isn't time to think about it more, because Ba is shouting for us to get into formation up front and seat everyone he's about to let in.

The deal started out as a combination special—phở plus a free mini pancake. It was going fine until the first ticket for one complete order of *bánh xèo* emerges, and then another, and then another. Soon enough, we find tables ordering *only* pancakes and not phở.

The customers are mostly Việt, with a few stragglers who probably spotted a flyer at a Vietnamese market.

One woman—strikingly blond—with a hint of some European accent asks me to describe *bánh xèo* to her. She's in charge of ordering for her family of five who look the most out of place in the restaurant—and I'm guessing Bolsa in general.

"Have you ever had a crepe?"

"Yes."

"Well this is kind of a like a crepe, except it's mostly savory. Think about the crispiest thing you've ever eaten. Got it?" The customer nods, looking like she's hanging on to my every word. I feel suddenly powerful, and I go with this feeling.

"You're sitting outside under a storefront's umbrella. It's raining, but not pouring, and you can smell soil, gasoline from a motorbike just passing through. Someone places this bright yellow pancake in front of you. It has turmeric, juicy pork belly, soft prawns, and crunchy bean sprouts tucked inside, and you drizzle salty and spicy fish sauce all over it. One bite . . . and you're gone."

The customer blinks twice and sits back. "You sold me. One for everyone at the table."

"You won't regret it."

Back in the kitchen, I hand over my slip to Mẹ, who does a double take. "Five?"

"Five," I repeat with a wide grin.

"Did you tell them we put gold in it or something?" she mutters. I catch a hint of a smile as she turns back toward the kitchen line to bark an order.

Over the years, my parents have had to deal with various levels of nasty customers. Abhorrent. Unconscionable. Sometimes, the criticism comes from other Vietnamese people. The broth's too bland or the egg rolls haven't been cooked enough or the *nước mắm* doesn't have enough lime. Mẹ's quick to have a word with them, her voice turning firm when she's speaking in her language. By the end, they always agree to disagree about the recipes.

"Every Vietnamese person is different. Our family may be different according to region."

But some customers are on a different level. Like today.

Around four in the afternoon, Việt comes up to me by the service window looking, for once, concerned.

"What's up with you?"

"Dude, it's ridiculous. Some guy's saying we haven't given him enough egg rolls."

"How many did he order?"

"One side."

"And we gave him two?" At Việt's nod, I ask, "So what's the deal?"

"He doesn't believe me, thinks we're scamming him. He wants to speak to the manager." I hesitate then. That would be my mom. It's fine for my mom to berate Vietnamese customers—somehow she manages to win them over by cracking a joke or two, then she gives them an extra side of something. But in English, she's different. I can see it in her face when she struggles to find the right word, the right retort. It's one of her biggest insecurities. Then she loses her cool, getting angry mostly at herself.

I search the room and find the trouble immediately. His face is sunburned and he has his sunglasses on top of his head. His hair's all spiked up. While he waits for attention, he leans back, arms crossed, fingers tapping away his impatience. It looks like he's with his wife or girlfriend and their kids. The woman's leaning in, whispering something, but he just stares straight ahead, jaw clenched. I wonder how the kids must be feeling.

Mẹ makes her way from the front desk to the table—and steps back when the man rises slowly. He towers over her in a way that reminds me that my mom's actually under five feet. It's always her voice and manner that make her seem taller than she is.

"Shit. I have a bad feeling about this." Việt and I get closer to the table.

"—if you're dissatisfied with the taste of it, we will happily make another order for you."

"Jared," the woman next to him whispers. "Let's just have our meal. It's fine."

"It's *not* fine, Beth." He looks down at my mom. "I wanna know why you're scamming us."

"A scam?" Mẹ asks.

"What, that word not clicking for you? Do you even know English?"

"What the fuck, man," Việt whispers to me.

"Mister," Mẹ starts over, regulating her voice. She speaks slowly, but clearly, "We always serve two egg rolls for each order. Look around at the other tables."

She gestures to other tables, where customers have stopped eating or are trying not to look interested in the drama. The man can't help but look around too, and he lets his arms fall loose. From my place, I breathe out. There. It's just a misunderstanding. He's going to apologize soon, and then everything will go okay.

But that doesn't happen.

"This place is shit. Shitty food. Shitty owners who can't even speak fucking English." His voice is booming and if the customers weren't listening before, they're listening now. "I'm not paying for this," Jared declares.

"What—" My mom's sputtering now, shocked by his declaration. As am I.

Before another word can be said, the guy forcefully pushes his chair in and barks at his children to get up too, which they do, eyes on the ground. Embarrassed, maybe. I would be. The little girl looks close to tears, even. "Hey," I jump in. "That's not cool, man. You already ate, like, everything." Which is true. The phở, the *bánh xèo*—save for the side order of egg rolls—are all cleared. But my protest goes unheard. Beth scrabbles for her purse hanging on her chair and almost hesitates to follow Jared. Mouth opening, then closing, she finally heads toward the door.

I'm the first to move. "What the hell!" I try moving past my mom, planning on calling the police on them, or *something* that would make them pay, but Mẹ quickly catches me by the wrist.

"Con, it's not worth it."

I'm shaking with anger. "But—"

"We have to get back to work." Mẹ gives me a hard look. "There are other customers to take care of. This family won't make a difference." To the remaining customers, she turns and smiles diplomatically. "Please, return to your meals. Sorry for the disturbance." She repeats it in Vietnamese.

My mom saves her complaints about Jared and his family for the kitchen. I'm sure this has happened before but it was the first time I'd seen it in person. I grew up here, living around people who looked like me. We belonged to the same temple, our parents knew each other. I didn't expect to see someone from the outside look so sure of themselves as they spouted hate.

I lean forward, elbows on a prep table, and say, "Do you think that guy's going to come back?"

"No, I won't let him."

"Shouldn't you report him?"

"There's many men like him. Are we going to report all of them?"

"Yeah, but . . ." I trail off; I don't have a real solution. I guess I just don't like the feeling of some guy treating my parents—and other owners in the area—like this. It was more painful than hearing the waiter at photastic ask my dad to repeat himself. This guy basically attacked them. "I don't know, it just seems wrong."

"We are not new to this," Ba says shortly. "We have lived in other places before Little Saigon. There are much worse people."

"He won't come back, con. *Đồ quỷ*." Somehow she makes swear words sound like a natural part of our language.

"He's an asshole," I agree. Now she scolds me for using a bad word, but I press on.

"Let's get back to work."

CHAPTER THIRTY

LINH

My phone chirps. A text from Bảo. My parents are finally sitting down with friends who'd stopped by at the tail end of service hours. The men brought out Heineken, signaling that it'll be a bit longer until we get to leave the restaurant. Evie is busy with cleanup tasks, though from what I can see, she's catching up with the line cooks who looked after us when we were younger, and the less senior servers are taking care of clearing the tables. I sneak out, promising myself ten minutes of my own time.

The air is cool enough for me to wear my jacket outside. I use the lamplights to guide me away from the restaurant, to the small park usually populated by skateboarders and people exercising outside. Bảo's there, sitting on a graffiti-ridden bench. He sets a Styrofoam container on the bench and stands when he sees me. His smile is weary, a perfect reflection of mine. He kisses me.

"Peace offering," he says, handing me a container. I laugh and hand him my own, which I had hidden behind my back. Inside Bảo's box, he'd packed away a small slice of *bánh xèo,* while I gave him egg rolls nicked from the kitchen. We sit there, eating food cooked by our family's respective enemy. I wish I could say I understood why their food is considered a threat, a reason for my dad's competitiveness when it comes to them, but I can't really taste the difference, even if the *bánh xèo* is good.

"Do you think it's possible that our parents actually know each other?" Bảo asks. "Like, actually interacted with each other? Maybe way before us. Vietnam, or sometime after their escapes?"

"Wouldn't they have said something, though?"

"Come on, it wouldn't be unusual for them to hold back a few things from us."

I think about the comments my mom and dad have made about his family. *Have I missed signs?*

"What makes you say that?" I ask.

"My mom mentioned something about your mom's cooking. About her *bánh xèo* not being good, but she sounded like she *knew.* Like she's had it before."

"Okay . . . ?"

"How much do we really know? Like Chef Lê said, there's stuff that they don't tell us because it isn't relevant to us."

"So, what, you want to ask your parents about us?"

"Nothing too direct. Nothing to raise suspicion. You okay?" Hands together, he runs his thumb over my hand. I wonder if he knows what he's doing. "It's a lot, I know."

I don't want to run away again.

"For now," I say.

"My mom just texted. She's wondering where I've gone off to; they're heading home."

"I know," I sigh. I hate thinking that the moments we spend together are only temporary. That, when we get back to our separate restaurants, we'll need to pretend that our lives have no bearing on each other. When it's the opposite.

He takes my hand and we start walking back. I imagine a time when we don't have to hold hands in the dark, when we can visit each other on lunch breaks without having to find a secluded park.

"We'll find another moment," Bảo says, reading my expression. "We still haven't had a first date yet."

"If you think about it, haven't we've gone on many dates already—between the restaurants that we went to and our meetings in the art room?" I say, even though the word "date" causes my stomach to tumble.

We stand at the intersection between Larkin and Sylvester, knowing we'll need to let go. By day, the plaza is packed with cars, but the parking lot is empty now. A neon sign saying CLOSED burns brightly in the dark, casting a metallic sheen against Bảo's face. It's silent save for grasshoppers hiding in nearby bushes.

"This is going to be different. Let's go somewhere where I can hold your hand like this." He squeezes my hand. "Brush aside your hair when it falls in front of your eyes." Like now. "Kiss you." He leans in, capturing my lips.

"Our first date will be ours alone," he declares.

On a Saturday, my parents and I attend a two-part wedding: the traditional Vietnamese ceremony and the American reception—all in one day. The bride, Fay, is the oldest granddaughter of Bác Xuân. I've talked to Fay a couple of times, our circles of family and friends overlapping because of our business, and liked her. Rather than being involved in the food business, she went to dental school and later opened up her own practice in southern California. Her partner is her soon-to-be husband.

Attending a wedding ceremony means I'll need to squeeze into my *áo dài*, which grows tighter each passing year. It means seeing strangers who know everything about me through information shared over various phone calls, store errands, and house get-togethers. It also means there's a high possibility of me sitting at the kids' tables at the reception—with the actual ages ranging from two to college students. Since Evie's back at college, I'll be the only teenager at the table, but for the first time ever, it won't matter.

This wedding is an opportunity.

My mind latched on to Bảo's suggestion as I fell asleep last night. Is it possible that there's more to our families' feud besides our competitive restaurants? Is there something else that might have driven them apart and made our families this way?

I can't ask my parents outright; I'm not even sure there's a way to ask them subtly.

But, as all Vietnamese know, information gets around. At least one person has to know the truth. In my parents' network, there's only one viable person who might know more about my family—and Bảo's. The best connection that we have so far is Bác Xuân, Fay's grandfather, who gave my mom a chance with the restaurant. And who helped most of the businesses around here, including Bảo's family restaurant.

Mẹ and I are getting ready in her bedroom. She's just put on her *áo dài*, a yellow-and-white floral pattern adorning it from top to bottom. She needs me to hook together the sides so that skin there doesn't show.

Apparently Fay and her husband are not going to last, my mom confides in me. They'd picked the wrong dates, didn't consult the right calendar, or something like that. I don't think those things actually have a real bearing on the outcome of their marriage, but my mom—and her friends—certainly do.

The ceremony at Fay's house proceeds smoothly. First the men and the women from each side of the family exchange gifts in red tin baskets covered by red velvet. It's a way of the husband asking permission from the bride's family to see her. Both families line up at the shrine, also decorated in red. Fay, radiant in her traditional red *áo dài*, emerges from upstairs, her arm looped through her already crying mother's. When she joins her soon-to-be husband, Dũng, who's wearing the traditional blue *áo dài* for men, the image of them is striking. They're the most colorful people in the room, and their happiness only makes them glow brighter.

I imagine the murmurs from the crowd fade when Fay and Dũng face each other to exchange vows. Dũng, so nervous, bumbles his way through his speech, his words earnest and sincere, and Fay reaches out for his hand when he pauses, holding back tears. We're all smiling by the end of the ceremony.

Later, the wedding transitions into a modern American wedding. The *áo dài* disappear—though Fay's mom opts out of changing—and we move for the American ceremony to a Catholic church, the reception to follow in its courtyard right after. I've changed into a periwinkle dress that stops above my knees.

I do my best to avoid the women in Fay's family. They like to tease. They think, *Well, there's one Vietnamese woman off the market! Let's see who else has potential,* so they crowd the young ones and joke about their boyfriends. I can just imagine the fury on my parents' faces if I were to ever answer the question honestly. That me and Bảo are finally together.

I try to fight back my smile when I get the question for the fourth time tonight. I guess it feels less tedious when you actually have a perfect answer.

Fay and her husband, Dũng, couldn't look any happier. Probably both from the relief of finally seeing their wedding go off without a hitch and from the actual idea that they're just starting a new life together.

By now, food and lots of alcohol have sated the guests. The elderly ones sit clumped off, chattering away about past and present grievances. My parents are sitting with Fay's parents, chatting.

The younger generation are tearing up the floor, moving along to the American music blasting from the speakers. They're heedless of the expressions of shock, and some amusement, from their parents and family members watching. But there's also a few braver older Vietnamese guests who've joined the floor, and I think I can pass the night away just watching it happen. The strobe lights are blinding, disorienting. I almost forget about Bác Xuân, until I see him a couple tables away, seated in a wheelchair on the edge of the dance floor. My heart wrings at the sight of him; it's been so many years since I've seen him in person.

I escape the flailing elbow of a seven-year-old to my right and make my way over. "*Thưa*, Bác Xuân."

Bác Xuân looks up slowly and reveals a nearly toothless smile. "Ah, *cháu*."

"Do you remember me?" I ask cautiously in Vietnamese.

"Of course. Liên Phạm's daughter," he replies. "You look just like her now. What a beautiful young woman you've become."

I laugh, sitting down across from him. Age spots outline his cheek. His hands sandwich mine, trembling faintly. There's a glossiness in his eyes that I mostly see in my family's elderly customers. They're past the point of worrying, their lives already fulfilled. I think it's a look of satisfaction, or I hope it is.

"How are you doing? What are you doing in school? And where is your sister—you have a sister, don't you? I remember she was very smart. And you still draw?" He seems happy to talk to someone, finally. I smile with relief, just glad that he remembers me.

"Evie's away at UC Davis, studying biology."

"Ah!"

"And I still draw. I'm a painter, in fact."

"So I can see." He gestures to my hands. I really thought I washed them well, but I missed a spot on my pinkie finger. *"Giống y hệt dì của cháu,"* he mutters, amused.

"My aunt?" I ask in English, jostled by the comparison. Then I remember she visited him when she was over here. "Dì Vàng, you mean."

"Of course. Ever since she was little, she would have her hands in something messy. Mud. Then clay. Sculpting was her true passion."

The disorientation comes back and now it has nothing to do with the lights. "You knew my mom and aunt back in Vietnam?"

"I lived just a few houses down from them. In Nha Trang."

I lean back into my seat. That's why my aunt had been so familiar with him on her last visit. They weren't just meeting; they were *reuniting*. I glance past Bác Xuân, feeling as if the ground shifted underneath me.

Back in Nha Trang. *Before me.*

Bảo's right. There's more to the story than we've been given.

"Oh, your mother and your aunt! They were inseparable, especially after your grandparents passed. It was always interesting seeing your mother act like the older sister." Bác Xuân shifts in his wheelchair, his pillow slipping sideways. I get up and fix it quickly, earning a pat on the shoulder. "Thank you. The community, just like here, was important in our neighborhood. Individually we didn't have much, but together, we had everything we would need, even as the *Cộng sản* were starting to take everything we had. We looked out for each other. Mẹ, your mother and aunt, the Lês, especially after the fall of Saigon." He pauses.

"Ah, forgive me. She's no longer a Lê; she's now a Nguyễn."

Nguyễn.

"It was a miracle that we all found each other again when we made it over here. It took longer than we all imagined."

Nguyễn as in Bảo Nguyễn?

"Bác Xuân," I say, interrupting him midsentence, "by Nguyễn and by 'she,' do you mean the woman who owns the restaurant across from ours?"

"Of course, who else? She runs her restaurant like a true entrepreneur. Just like her own mother. I thought that by encouraging her and your mother to see each other again—the restaurants facing each other—they would be able to move on from the past." He shakes his head. "Ah, terrible what happened."

"What happened?" I ask immediately, though I wish I hadn't, because it signals a change in Bác's expression. He actually looks uncomfortable now.

"You don't know?"

I shake my head.

"Ah, well. It is not my story to tell. If my wife were here"—Bác Xuân's wife had passed before I remember meeting him—"she would tell you everything, but I don't think I can. I don't think I have any right to."

"I won't tell my parents, I swear. I've been wondering about the other family, why they've never spoken to each other. Why they seem to hate each other." I place a hand on his arm, but he only pats it again, this time with sympathy.

He chews on his lip, deep in conflict. "We went through many things to get here, *cháu*. Things that we do not speak of because it might pain us too much. Show some respect. It will all come out in due time." He nods to another person over my shoulder, then wheels himself away, oblivious to the thoughts roiling inside me.

I stalk the room, deep in thought, the wedding fading in the background. My mom and Ba have now included Bác in their conversation with Fay's parents. Mẹ is smiling and Ba throws back his head, laughing. They're both red from the wine at the table. Looking at the group, I wouldn't have been able to see the shared history with Bác; I always assumed they'd met in California. But there's a story between them—and between my mom and Bảo's mom.

The bride and groom do their rounds around the room, trailed by a red-eyed, pale photographer who looks like he doesn't know what sleeping means. When they get to my table, where I'm now sitting, the kids all hold up their fourth glasses of soda that their parents, under the dim lighting, and amid the noise of celebration, don't know they're having.

Fay spots me and gives me a quick hug. I push the revelation from Bác Xuân to the back of my mind. She introduces me to Dũng. Up close, dressed in a chic white dress and crisp black-and-white suit, they really do look like models.

"How'd you guys meet?" I ask.

At my question, Fay and Dũng exchange one look and a small

smile, full of meaning, full of secrets only the two of them can know. "Well, we were in college and in the library cramming like usual."

"It was the first time I stepped into the library, actually," Dũng jokes.

"We checked out books at the same time. Mine was a chemistry book."

Dũng glances down in mock shame. "And mine was a manga book."

"Something I'll never stop teasing you about." Her husband pulls her close, planting a quick kiss on her forehead.

"Our first date, because we were poor college students, was actually on campus."

First date. Bảo said we'd have one soon, but will that all change when I tell him what I've found out? That the history between our families goes even further back than we realized, to a time that neither of us belonged to?

Turns out Dũng had been the one to ask her out first. "We had a picnic on the quad, then walked around campus, ended up at the library, where I made dinner in one of the study rooms."

Fay gazes up at Dũng with a soft smile, so tender I feel like I'm intruding. "And did your parents approve of you two?" Then, the DJ decides to turn up the music, drowning out most, if not all, of my question. In Vietnamese, he asks if everyone is having fun.

Fay leans over, asking me to repeat myself. The photographer snaps a photo of us. I shake my head.

"This wedding is so much fun. Congrats!"

CHAPTER THIRTY-ONE

BẢO

I die. Again and again and again.

"Damn it," I say, throwing Việt's console to the ground. I've played *Apex* before, but not as badly, but I guess that's what happens when my mind isn't on the game. Instead, it's on a certain painter, and that date I was so confident to suggest.

We're at Việt's house on our day off from work. Việt is ensconced in his beanbag chair, looking like he was browsing the Internet rather than systematically destroying me and my team. "You suck more than usual," he says oh-so-observantly.

"Thanks. Sorry, let's try it again."

"Okay, whatever you say."

I haven't had a chance to see Linh, only text her. She said the wedding had gone okay, and that she needed to tell me something, though it might be important since she didn't text me what the thing was, just that she'd see me soon. A small part of me wonders if she's regretting everything that happened—if I'm putting more hope into a relationship that can't work out. But that kiss Linh had given me, the texts since then—and the promise that we would see each other—made it sound like she was in this, all the way. What did she need to talk to me about?

When I think of romance and dating, my mind plays out the South Korean dramas that get Mẹ giddy: You know, the kind with the impossibly good-looking guy and the impossibly good-looking girl who's disguised as an awkward person. Cue scenes with intermittent slow-motion physical contact, gauzy romantic music. Then they somehow end up trapped in an elevator and fall asleep slumped together. These things don't happen in real life.

I never thought that I'd be staying up late reading *Seventeen* and *Marie Claire* articles on first date ideas. I never thought I'd be reading those magazines, period. So far, the options are boring and generic, but I keep trying because my other option is to ask the person who knows Linh best for ideas and that's Ali, and I don't want to go there.

One thing that's consistent in the articles is that dates should be activities that two people would want to do together. We've done the restaurant thing. Movies could work, but we've already had six years of silence, once I think about it, so that's off the list. I thought of Phước Lộc Thọ, but a local mall crawling with people who know either set of parents would make us paranoid the whole time.

I am so desperate for an idea that I consult Việt in between games. All I get is a blank stare.

"But you watch *The Bachelor*!"

"I do. But his dates actually suck!"

Not helpful.

The next day, I resolve to find another source: Chef Lê's place, which is just starting to switch from late afternoon to dinner service. It works out well, since it's the same day Linh has resolved to submit her paintings to the Gold Keys; she just needs to choose between her final pieces.

Linh disappears into the back to grab a fresh paint mixer, and that's when I bring up the whole date issue.

"First date?" Chef Lê shouts across the room at Saffron. "Babe, they're going on their first date!"

"I heard you; you don't need to shout," she sings back to him, joining us at the center with a sparkling water with lemon in hand.

"So what, Bảo, you need some tips?"

"Yeah, kind of."

Saffron says, "Any date you think of will be fine. As long as you don't do what Bry did."

His head swivels in her direction. "What do you mean by that? Mine was the pinnacle of romantic dates."

"You took me to the Eiffel Tower."

Ohhhh. But Chef Lê is less than quick to get it, apparently. "Yeah, it's beautiful."

"Honey, I'm French. Seeing the Tower is like Americans visiting Washington, DC."

Chef Lê leans forward now, elbows on the table. "So what made you want to go out with me again?"

Amused, Saffron takes a sip of her sparkling water. "I guess it was the day we went shopping. Which we didn't really call a date, but it was one."

"To buy the floor lamp for your apartment? Going *shopping* was what convinced you?"

"I thought it was sweet that you decided to go somewhere that you had zero interest in just because I said I wanted to go. I'm not about big gestures. So when you volunteered to come with me, I loved you even more."

"So if I took you to the bridge with all those locks, we wouldn't have ended up together?"

"I would have left you right away."

"Regular comedian today, aren't you," Chef Lê grumbles before disappearing into the kitchen.

Saffron winks at me and with laughter still in her voice, says, "It was actually three dates before I decided I liked him. But don't let him know."

I grin, thinking back to what Saffron just said. It wasn't the date's destination that really mattered to her; it was the gesture. She seemed to appreciate something less extravagant, as long as it felt real.

At that exact moment, Linh comes back, mixer in hand. "Don't let him know what?"

"Nothing," Saffron and I pipe back.

◇ ◇ ◇

An hour later, an idea catches on. I'm sitting down, my back pressed against the heaters emitting air that's neither hot nor cold. Seeing that I had nothing to do, Chef Lê asked if I could look over his brief speech. As comfortable as I've grown with writing, it's still a shock that someone would trust me with their writing like this.

Hell, I still can't believe *Ali* put some semblance of trust in me.

After journalism class today, Ali updated me about Ernie, who handed over his first television review about a *Black Mirror* episode. It was like another person had penned it. The writing was strong, energetic, and went deeper into the narrative than I'd ever be capable of doing.

Now, Linh is just a few feet away, wearing her usual paint gear, nestled comfortably on the top of a ladder as she outlines parts of the mural with chalk.

She has a sketch clipped to her mini canvas and every minute or so, she squints at it, then stares hard at the mural. As if she's imprinting the image with her mind. Not for the first time, I'm not in her orbit anymore.

If I walk out, will she even notice?

I set down my laptop and stand, fighting back a smile.

"You'll go blind if you squint that much."

"You sound like my mom."

"I'm channeling mine." I grin once I'm by the mural.

"*Shut up,*" Linh answers, refusing to look at me.

I wish I could lean up, steal a kiss. It's been a few minutes since our last.

"Bảo," she says, still focused on her design. "I can feel you. You're hovering."

"Just . . . making sure the ladder's secure."

Linh rolls her eyes at me, then shakes her head so that her ponytail slides off her shoulder, back to a free hang.

"What photo do you have?"

"It's called a reference photo. Chef Lê gave it to me."

"Oh."

I know I should let her concentrate. And that she needs to get this mural done. But I also can't wait to ask my question.

I clear my throat. "So are you—"

"I haven't figured out a way—"

We stare at each other, laughing nervously as we talk over each other's sentences.

"No, you go. You haven't figured out a way to . . . what?"

"At the wedding, I ran into Bác Xuân, who gave us the restaurant. And he actually knew my mom before they ever lived here. He knew her back in Vietnam."

I blink at her sudden statement.

Linh blows out air. "*And* that's not the only person he knows." She gazes down at me. "He also knows your mom from Vietnam."

"Whoa," I say. I sit down by the foot of the ladder. Linh eventually comes down, gesturing for me to scoot over as she sits right next to me. I think the air circulation has somehow gotten cut off, because suddenly I'm dizzy and barely feel the surface beneath me.

Linh goes on, maybe too lost in her own thoughts to notice my reaction. "So I'm starting to think that this feud goes way back—

before we were alive. It happened back *there*, and it must have been bad if our moms aren't talking to this day."

"That's—"

"Exactly."

"And you don't know what caused it?"

Linh nods and shrugs at the same time. "Bác Xuân wouldn't say another word. He said it's not his story to tell."

Linh tells me what Bác said about their neighborhood being close, how they all helped each other in need. Almost as if they'd become a family. So whatever happened between them had to be capable of breaking apart a family. Based on gossip from my mom's circle, that could be anything. They'd mentioned a family whose youngest son had gotten into drugs, which got him banned from ever entering his childhood home. A man who was sixty years old went back to Vietnam to find a wife half his age, leaving his ex-wife and two kids to basically fend for themselves. The wrongs done to the family seemed limitless.

"Okay, we're getting somewhere," I say numbly. We are, but what if we eventually find something that's bigger than we ever imagined? What if it turns out it's nothing we can ever fix? What would that do to our families? To me and Linh?

Linh slips her hand into mine. "I'm still here, you know. Nothing's changing the way I feel about you. Whatever we find out, we'll find out together."

CHAPTER THIRTY-TWO

LINH

Bảo kisses my hand, making me blush. Obviously the fact that our parents had known each other in Vietnam scared him, just as it scared me, and yet he's still here. Holding my hand. Our break is interrupted by Chef Lê. He's been so grateful that I'm taking on his mural, that in addition to paying me commission later on, he's been feeding us whenever we come by. He's also calling me "Miss Mai"—and Bảo likes it so much that he teases me whenever we're alone.

"Yo, you two are like an old married couple," Chef Lê's voice booms across the room. He's carrying two plates of *bánh cam* over to us, a towel slung over one shoulder. Even if I didn't see him walk over, I would have smelled it: thick, glutinous rice balls fried till crispy, with sugary mung bean nested within—a soft surprise once you bite through the outside.

Chef Lê has a big, smug grin plastered on his face. "Time for a break."

I try to turn it down; it's the polite way as my parents taught me. "No, I have to finish this sketch for the mural."

"The mural can wait a few minutes. I'm not going to have someone faint on the job. Come here." Bảo shoots me a grin and heaves himself off the floor, going to reach for one sesame ball.

His phone, though, rings at the wrong moment. He grimaces at me. "My mom."

"Better pick that up before your mom calls again," Chef Lê says seriously, perhaps remembering his own experience with his parents at our age.

Bảo presses Accept. "Hi, Mẹ . . . Uh, yeah, I'm with Việt, just shopping." Which is half true. Việt's out shopping, just with his track friends, I'm told. Bảo glances at me before turning away, still talking to his mom. Apparently he needs to run to the store to get something.

"Are you two not supposed to be here?" Chef Lê asks.

"Kind of. I'm not supposed to be here with *him*."

"What'd he do?"

"Nothing. It's just . . . complicated. Our families hate each other. Restaurant rivalry." At one point, that had been accurate. But now . . .

"No shit. That's rough. So I don't imagine you have a lot of chances to hang out."

"We've been finding time to steal. Sometimes at school and after school. And here. And we're going on a date soon, I think."

Or I know, since Ali texted me earlier saying that she had a "talk" with Việt, who apparently told Ali that Bảo was doing research.

"First date, that's big. But he hasn't asked yet?"

"I think he was about to."

"I can remind him." Chef Lê nudges me by the shoulder. If I had a brother, I think he'd be like him.

"What are you going on about?" Bảo asks, pocketing his phone.

"Oh, you know. Deep emotional stuff," Chef Lê says casually.

A harried line cook surfaces from the kitchen, yelling Chef Lê's name with equal parts annoyance and authority. Her hair has reached maximum frizz capacity. It's obvious this isn't a new thing—Chef Lê wandering during duty when he's really supposed to be manning the kitchen. He wouldn't last a day in my mom's kitchen.

"Oops, I guess I have to go back there." He heaves himself to his feet and slings the towel back onto his shoulder. "Now eat before the sesame balls get cold."

"Here you go, Miss Mai," Bảo says, handing me one. It's still warm.

"Thank you, Mr. Nguyễn."

I grin, loving his sudden shyness. For a wordsmith, he clearly doesn't have the right ones lined up now. So I answer for him, put him out of his misery.

"Let's go on a date."

"Good, because I have an idea."

In a modern art class in freshman or sophomore year, we looked at a Van Gogh painting from his time spent at Arles. He was always a tragic figure, someone who went through so much difficulty, only to receive fame years after his death.

He'd capture a simple rendition of his room: his bed, two empty chairs, portraits of unnamed subjects that seemed to stare right at the bed where he would usually go to sleep. As if his world had turned inward. As if there was nothing outside for him.

Van Gogh's room is my mom's kitchen.

After my shift, right before we start to lock down, I find my mom alone in the kitchen, stirring a ladle in a large pot. She's not committed to it, just turning the spoon, slowly and slowly. Something must be bothering her, just as Bác Xuân's statement has been bothering me.

I don't know how to bring it up. How can I even start a conversation and transition it smoothly over to the past—a past that my mom seems to volunteer to talk about less and less? What right do I have to bring something up that may be painful to her?

Let it go. It will all come out in due time, Bác Xuân said.

Will it be too late then?

Mẹ comes back to life; she picks up her stirring, then takes a sip. After adding a handful of sugar, she turns, jumping at the sight of me.

"You scared me, con."

"Sorry," I finally said. "What were you thinking about?"

"Dì Vàng. She's coming very soon. I wonder if I'll have everything ready by then."

"Are you excited?"

"Of course. She's my sister. It's been far too long."

This is an opening. I should ask, shouldn't I? But perhaps it's my mom's mood, perhaps it's the feeling that I'm trespassing somewhere, but I keep the question to myself. I'll ask next time.

I will.

I'm in the art room after school the next day. I don't have to work today, so I'm taking the extra time to just paint. Paint without needing to worry about what to submit since I did it right after stopping at Chef Lê's. I know I chose the right paintings in the end, the ones that mattered the most to me and best represented the theme I was capturing: memories. Memories about my parents and growing up. About my journey as an artist. About Bảo and the discoveries I'm making as we have more time to ourselves.

I only stop painting when Yamamoto comes in, announcing her appearance with a dumbfounded, "Huh." I turn on my stool, facing Yamamoto, who's behind me, and wait for an explanation.

But it doesn't come, not right away.

"What are you thinking about?"

"I'm not sure. Your colors are the same, but something about this is . . . lighter." Yamamoto regards my canvas, tilting her head.

Lighter? I try looking at the canvas the way she is. But it doesn't seem out of the norm of what I usually paint.

"Like, what gives?"

I bite my lip. "I *might* be seeing someone."

"You're kidding me!" She smiles, pulls up a stool beside me. "Wait, let me guess. Tall, lanky kid? Kind of good-looking? Who conveniently comes into the art room at lunch, but someone I've never had in art class before?"

I smile at the thought of Bảo hearing how he was described . . . until her words catch up with me. I nearly drop my paint brush, but Yamamoto only laughs. "Saw him the other day. It's fine, of course. I remember being your age. And from what I can tell"—she gestures to the canvas, still seeing what I can't—"spending time with him is making you happy. And your art's never been better. At the same time, I'm still supposed to be your teacher. So if it happens again, you'll get sent to the principal's office." The threat's diminished by her subsequent wink.

Yamamoto turns to leave, throwing me another grin that makes her look years younger. "This is the type of thing they like to see."

"Who?"

"Scholastic. Gold Key."

"Thanks," I say, blushing.

"I know it's going to be a long time until you find out the results. So, to hold you over, I'm giving you an early holiday gift."

Now I'm dubious. "You've never given me a gift before."

"I will now." She beams. "Guess who I want to spotlight at the end of the year Art Fair?"

So caught in more looming deadlines—and crises—I'd forgotten about the Art Fair. Only one person gets spotlighted in their own exhibition. And all previous artists who were lucky enough to get picked had also won various Scholastic awards. Yamamoto has said again and again that this was just a coincidence and that what happened at school had no bearing on Scholastic results. But the myth is there, and in the past I'd even believed it.

I just never believed it could happen to me.

As if the world is conspiring to help us make up for lost time, Bảo and I get a day to ourselves one Sunday. Mẹ left early to visit a friend's house to cut herbs and bring home fruit, which translated to a daylong affair of gossiping and catching up about their families. Mẹ will drop Evie's name a few times, I'm sure of it. That also meant Dad would want to make his own outing to visit friends at their restaurants and cafés.

I'd always imagined going on a first date would be the most nerve-racking thing, an event that would set my stomach alight with butterflies. A time for two people who like each other to be alone. But for me and Bảo, we've only known *how* to be alone. So as I'm walking toward our meeting spot, I feel no different from when I'm with him in the art room.

Until I see him: standing in the middle of the park, fresh from the shower since his hair is still wet. He's wearing a button-up red-and-black plaid shirt and loose jeans, and smiles cheekily once he's spotted me. The butterflies kick up in flight.

He points to my camera. "I wasn't aware you wanted to

document this. Should I sign a form of consent?" he teases me.

"I capture memories, remember?" I snap a photo of him—he covers his eyes. "And it's been ages since I've used it."

He poses, lifting his chin up. "I guess I'll volunteer to be your model. I'm a great model."

"Says who?"

"No one." Bảo grins. "Absolutely no one."

"Yeah, that's what I thought."

Laughter and movement from behind catches my eye.

Perfect.

"Hold still," I whisper.

"What?" I laugh as his eyes widen.

A family celebrating a birthday has taken over a table, filling it with mouthwatering food and presents. Some brought balloons of all colors, weighing them with a rock. Cerulean, canary yellow, and cherry red bump and bob next to each other. But from where Bảo is standing, it's almost as if the balloons are sprouting from his head. Smiling, I look through my camera. *Click*.

Then Bảo is free to move, whirling around. "If it's a bee, I'll run."

"No, look." I move closer to him and he dips his head down to see my camera screen. He smells as fresh and clean as cotton.

"Nice." Our eyes meet—an indescribable *whoosh* passes between us, so strong I feel the need to look away.

"So where to?" I ask.

We pass a squad of elderly Asian women, coordinated by their visors, oversize sunglasses, and faces whitened with 80 SPF sunscreen. They're windmilling their arms. They look at us as if we're in the way—and for one small moment, I wonder if any of them have come to either of our restaurants or know our parents—and imagine how quickly this would travel.

And how possible it'd be for everything to unravel in an instant.

"Judging by your look," Bảo says, interrupting my spiral of thoughts, "you're thinking that we probably shouldn't have our first date so close to home."

"Spies."

"Exactly what Việt said. So, I have a place in mind that I think you'll like. Do you trust me?"

I thread my fingers through his.

"Let's go."

CHAPTER THIRTY-THREE

BẢO

As I'm driving, doubt creeps in. Did I really pick the right place to go on a date? An ad for Ellen's Studio appeared during a search—as if the universe was taking pity on me as I considered different date ideas. It was far away enough that no one would know us. And it was something creative, perfect for Linh.

Confidence in my plan dimmed when I made the mistake of telling Việt about it. He replied with a straight face, "Aren't you supposed to impress your date? Not embarrass yourself?" We were in the kitchen then, so the line cooks and other servers—Eddie and Trần included—then offered their own dating advice that seemed borderline illegal and might have been fun, I don't know, back in the nineties.

I sneak a look at Linh. She's wearing a jean skirt and a white flowy blouse, a part of it tucked in. A picture of comfort. She catches me looking and I will myself to stay put and not look away like I would've months ago. A bright smile graces her face like we haven't seen each other in days. A thrill shudders through me.

Once we stop at the plaza, Linh leans her head out the window and makes a noise of surprise at the storefront. "Pottery?"

She unbuckles her seat belt and slips out. I follow her, watching with some hesitation. Her eyes go soft and she slips her arms around my middle, almost mirroring her impromptu hug that day we decided to start all of this. "Where did you find out about this place?"

"Oh, I heard it was good. I love . . . er, ceramics."

"Liar," she whispers, before fitting her hand into mine, leading me inside. I'm content to follow her. Inside, my veins are like highways and all cells rushing through me like high-speed cars.

"Wheel-throwing," that's what it's called, the instructor tells us, but we can't throw the wheel? Her voice, melodious and deep, demands our attention, and for a few minutes Linh and I watch as she demonstrates how to handle the clay and gently shape it. The wheel should be at a medium pace, and she makes us practice. But I might be doing it wrong, because the clay wobbles unevenly. Laughter sounds from next to me.

Linh's been watching me, but now she's purposefully focusing on the teacher. Her lips twitch.

"Oh, shut up."

"I didn't say anything."

"Your face says it all."

I stop pretending to be mad when Linh has her turn at the wheel. Her hands merely guide the clay into the shape it's meant to be—no frantic movements to force it one way or another. "Of course you're good at this."

"I'm really not. I'm just okay. My aunt, though, does this for a living."

"The one in Vietnam."

"Yeah, I haven't seen her in ages. But she's coming over because some of her international friends are displaying their work around the country." You had to be pretty smart to navigate a foreign country like that. "My mom's already worried about her. She's acting like the older sister and all that."

The mention of her mom prompts my question. "So do you think your aunt knows what happened between our families?"

"Oh, that's nice!" the instructor interjects. At Linh or someone else; we're not paying attention.

"I don't think it's possible that she wouldn't. I mean, if my mom and your mom were actually friends, surely they would have known each other. Hung out together."

"Do you think you'll get a chance to talk to her about it? When she's here?"

"Still figuring out how to approach that. But yeah." Linh gets tired of her hair falling into her face and hurriedly brushes it away with the back of her hand. In her rush, clay that caught on her wrist swipes across her cheek. I wait a few seconds. She still doesn't notice. Of course.

Our instructor stops by, examining Linh's work: a small teacup. Mine's just a cylinder, like the cardboard that's left over when toilet paper runs out.

"My, you've done this before, haven't you?"

Linh smiles politely. "A few times."

The instructor nods her head in approval and her eyes slide over to mine.

"And yours . . ." She quickly assesses it and takes a breath. "Well, I'm glad you could come by today."

She walks away, leaving Linh in a fit of laughter and me trying to hold my dignity intact.

"I tried."

"Oh, you did." She shakes her head. "Though this is fun for me, you must be bored out of your mind. We could have done something else, you know."

"But I chose this place because I thought you'd like it. Also, I'd never use the word 'boring' to describe what it's like being around you."

"Oh? And what words would you use instead, Mr. Wordsmith?"

"Honestly, my vocabulary isn't big enough for what you're asking."

I won't tire from that look in her eyes. Soft amusement, a moment where the worries slide from her mind. Her hand rests on mine. "Thanks. I'm having fun. But it's because I'm with you. Next time, we'll go where you want."

Next time.

I refuse to let go of her hand until the instructor tells us to place our ceramics on a shelf.

"Let's trade," Linh says suddenly. "Mine for yours."

"Really?"

"Yes."

"But then you're stuck with mine."

"I don't care. It's one of a kind. It's something that you made." She tilts her head, sending me a dazzling smile. "So I like it."

"Okay, one more thing, then. Need to mark it with something."

On the bottom of each ceramic—the teacup and the whatever-the-hell-it-is—I etch our initials: *BN + LM*.

I get a kiss for that.

CHAPTER THIRTY-FOUR

LINH

One of the places I'd pick to represent California, the real California, where people grew up their whole lives, planted their roots, and left things behind for their family to take over, would be Huntington Beach. People know colors here, with their skateboards, parasailers, and sunglasses screaming out their personality. Hip-hop beats from boomboxes and live musicians, mostly guitarists, clash in the air. Everything is alive here.

When we were kids, Evie and I could have spent all day here if it weren't for my parents, who were wary of too much time in the sun. Never mind that they always slathered the both of us in too much sunscreen. Never mind that we were mostly sitting under umbrellas. We'd beg them to buy us cotton candy, but would get a lecture about cavities and bad teeth. I'm glad I'm getting the chance to enjoy things now.

Bảo offers me his hand, and I take it.

"I like your face today."

I laugh. "I believe you'd call that a *non sequitur*."

"You're speaking my language." Bảo pulls me in by the waist. He doesn't explain right away, just holds me close. "I meant that I like how calm you look right now. You're not worried. The thing between your eyebrows"—he pokes me at that spot—"isn't there."

"The wrinkle's not always there."

"Not always, but I notice it when it appears." He swings our arms.

"Well, I have one less thing to worry about—my application's sent off. So I guess it *is* better than before. But that's been replaced now by something else to worry about, right?"

"Our moms, yeah. And however your aunt might fit in."

I nod. "I know we have to ask. I know. But a part of me doesn't want to. To find out something that might change everything."

"It's scary. I think we have to ask the question eventually. If we really want this"—he holds up our clasped hands—"to work. I hate hiding. I hate not being able to kiss you before we go to work, right across from each other. I hate not being able to walk in the park near our homes, just because I might be seen with you."

"I hate that too," I say. The feeling of lying has become all too familiar. It's not the nervousness of hiding something now—it's the shame that weighs me down, more and more. "But you know how our parents are with the past. What if, by asking questions, we make things worse? With our parents? With us?"

"But if we don't start asking these questions . . ." He shakes his head. "Remember what Chef Lê said? About having these questions he wants to ask his mom but knowing he can't because she's gone?"

"How it's too late?"

"That could be us one day. One day, they're not going to be around as much. That's what's happening next year—we're going to college and they'll be living out their lives—and in no time, it'll happen. The chance to ask will pass."

On our way back, dusk is our cover. Me and Bảo hold hands—his clean, mine still stained with paint no matter how clean I tried to make them. I mention that to Bảo, but he only shrugs. "Feels like a hand. Feels like mine." He reaches our clasped hands up, kissing mine, then smiling, knowing I was watching, probably blushing. "Plus, you wouldn't be you without it."

Together we walk into the ocean and take in the waters that stretch ahead of us.

"What?" I ask, looking up at him.

"Nothing. Just . . ." He trails off as he leans forward, and our lips touch again. I slip my fingers into his hair. My heart beats double-time, and the way he's looking at me sends a rush of heat through me.

I meet him there when he ducks his head to kiss me. It's him making a strange sound when I stand up so that I'm flush against him. I can feel all of him, him me. A small wave crashes against us and I stumble until he catches me at just the right time. We laugh together, our sound mingling with nearby notes of happiness: kids shrieking as they splash up a storm, squawking seagulls flying and dipping into the ocean, lazy guitar music tickling our ears. The most perfect day.

A phone call wakes me up. I hear murmuring from down the hall, until I hear an exclamation. I stop mid-stretch, waiting to hear more, but the whispers return and then nothing. *Am I dreaming?* It happens sometimes, whenever I shut off my iPhone alarm, feeling a false confidence that I'll get up, and I descend into a dream where I do just that: wake up, eat breakfast, go to school, as if everything was normal.

I drift above myself until the cabinet door slamming shut wakes me up completely. I'm still in bed.

This time, I walk to the kitchen, clearing away the gunk from my eyes. Mẹ is washing dishes, her shoulders tense.

"You're up early."

I look to my dad for an explanation of her mood, but Ba is determinedly concentrating on his issue of *Người Việt*. It all feels . . . off, wrong . . . angry. What did she find out just now?

"What is it?" I ask hesitantly.

Mẹ twists the water handle closed. "I got a call. Someone is spreading bad rumors about us."

"Rumors?" I sit down, nerves on edge. "What kind of rumors?"

"*Con chuột,*" Ba answers shortly. Then, making me jump, "*Rats!*"

"What?" I yelp. "We don't have rats in our restaurant."

"That horrible restaurant. That *woman,*" Ba mutters, directing his rant at Mẹ. Ba ignores me, his newspaper forgotten, and punches in some numbers on his cell phone. He disappears from the room; I can sense his anger but I can't hear it.

He mentioned a woman. Only one person can get Ba this riled up. But rats—is Bảo's mom truly capable of spreading this damaging rumor? The rumors before had been trivial—easily dismissible— aside from the one about Bác Xuân. But rats . . .

"Apparently *someone* noticed that we'd changed our tablecloths and place mats and *somehow* that led to the idea of us having rats. A customer called me and said so. Said she was trying to warn us. She said it was the Nguyễns spreading this rumor."

"But that's not true," I say. "It can't be."

"You know how rumors go. We've discussed this."

"No, I mean about the rats. Will people really fall for it?"

Mẹ turns, her mouth set in a thin line. "It will be hard to convince people that it's all lies."

"So what are you going to do?"

My mom merely shakes her head. "Go to school. This is not your issue."

"Will everything be okay?" I ask.

"Ba is talking to the Health Department. They've already called us wanting to schedule an inspection, but we are trying to clear things up. . . ."

"Will everything be okay?" I repeat. She doesn't answer, only leans against the counter, waiting for Ba to get off the phone with whomever he's speaking to.

CHAPTER THIRTY-FIVE

BẢO

In the morning, a half hour before classes start, I head to the art room, where Linh texted me to meet her. The lights are on low, the sun straining for passage through the blinders. Long shadows cast against the floor. Motes of dust drift lazily across the room. At first I can't find Linh, but she's there, on the center stool, facing a blank canvas. She sits empty-handed.

"Why's it so dark in here?" I ask, approaching her. I lean down, aiming for a kiss, but her lips are stiff against mine. I tilt my head in question. "Everything okay?" A sense of foreboding washes over me.

"Your parents spread a rumor about our restaurant."

"What rumor?"

She gnaws on her bottom lip. "Rats."

"*What?*"

"They said rats are in our restaurant."

"And you think my parents did it." The fact that she doesn't answer right away tells me. A spark of annoyance flares up inside me. "They *wouldn't*, though. No way. Linh, they might be harsh sometimes, but to spread a rumor like that . . . that's *just*—"

They're my parents. This rumor . . . it's beyond my mom. She isn't cruel. They wouldn't jeopardize Linh's family restaurant just because of the feud—or whatever happened in the past—would they?

"A customer told my parents they heard it from you."

Some of the hot air leaves Linh and she leans against me. "I'm only telling you what my parents told me. And they're pissed, Bảo. I don't know what to believe. This is serious."

"She wouldn't do it," I answer tersely.

"I'm sorry." Her apology sounds hollow to me. How would she feel if I came out attacking her mother? "I'm only saying what my mom says. And I can't help but wonder—about the time we took over the restaurant, if—"

"*I'll talk to them,*" I say, cutting her off. Angry at the accusation. Angry at how possible might it be, given the past offenses my mom had against Oh Mai Mai. "I'll just ask them."

She folds into me, apologizing again. "I'm sorry, I really don't want to believe it. I'm just so, so confused. And angry. And—" I instantly wrap my arms around her waist, trying to calm us both down. "I'm just *so* tired of this, Bảo," she mumbles into my chest. "How is this ever going to work?"

I'd like to think my parents are good people. They've gotten us this far. They have friends, a network of people. They can't go so far as to create this rumor to destroy competition. They wouldn't . . . would they?

"I'll talk to them," I repeat, wanting to make it sound like that will solve everything.

School passes in a blur, my thoughts occupied by Linh, by the rats, by my parents' potential hand in it. Even Ali, perhaps after texting or talking with Linh, leaves me relatively alone in journalism class. And then I get a text from Linh saying they need to close down the restaurant for a day. The inspector is still coming by, regardless of her parents' efforts to dispel the rumor.

One day gone; one day of potential profits gone.

When I get to the restaurant, Mẹ's circle is there at the usual booth. Ba is elsewhere; he might have gone to visit his friends—the husbands of the very wives his own wife befriended. Friends. Followers. Whatever they call themselves. As annoying as their laughs were before, it's even more grating today, since I know what they may be laughing about. They're celebrating. Hyenas laughing.

"Mẹ, can I see you for a second?"

"Oh, hi, con. Are you hungry? I just made a new batch of phở and can get it ready for you."

"Not hungry." Not while Linh's—or her mother's—accusation clings to me like a cloying cologne. I sense the General's eyes on me, as well as the other women's. "Can we go to the back?"

In the kitchen, alone with me, my mom moves around as if nothing is wrong. She flicks on the stovetop, reheating a stock pot of broth, seemingly ignoring what I said before about not being hungry.

"I heard there's rats going around. Not here but at the restaurant across the street. Have you heard anything like that?"

Something passes over my mom's face, too quickly for me to catch. But her tone, as she answers, is even and as hard as flint. "Yes, I think I heard that too."

"But they don't have rats."

"How do you know?"

I sag against the counter behind me. I hear the challenge in her voice and it confirms it all. I wanted Linh to be wrong. So badly. But this is a deflection. My mom's purposefully not answering my question, which can only mean . . .

The rumors. My mom *did* spread them.

The headache from earlier today comes back full force. Maybe that's why my next questions come out louder than I expected, louder than I'd ever spoken—dared to speak—to my mom. "Why is it always *them*, Mẹ? Why are you always trying to ruin *them*? What, like they're not people, too? They're like you, Mẹ. They have this job, it's what they do to put food on the table, pay for their oldest daughter's tuition. Linh's graduating soon, too. This rumor could really ruin things for them."

Mẹ's mouth falls open. Then closes. Opens again. Stunned. "How do you know all of this?"

"Know *what*?"

"Linh. It sounds like you know her."

This is it. Maybe if she accused me of this earlier in the year, before I knew how I really felt about Linh, I'd waver and deny being close to Linh. I remember Linh in my arms, trembling from anger and worry.

"I know Linh because I'm friends with her. Been friends with her for a few months now." *And we're more than that now.*

"*Gì?*" she asks me to repeat myself.

A river of laughter from her circle reaches the edges of our space, but it dies down, engulfed by the tension between me and my mom.

"We were partnered up for an assignment," I continue, watching her expression. "The newspaper. And I've been spending time with her. The articles I've been writing—the one about the Vietnamese chef, and other places—I've been going with her and she's been making the sketches. We're partners."

"How's that possible?" she asks almost in wonder, before her tone switches up, reprimanding me. "I told you never to talk to them. Never to interact with them."

"Which never made sense to me. It's impossible to avoid them."

"Yes, it is possible if you make it so. If you listen to what I told you."

"Well, I'm sorry, I didn't listen to you," I say, my voice gathering strength. I've gone this far, and I don't see a way back. "But I like Linh, Mẹ. I realize she's just like me. With a family just like ours. She's one of the nicest people you've ever met. And I don't know what you have against her family—"

"What has she said? About our family?"

Her question throws me off. I cross my arms, suspicious. Instead of chewing me out for admitting that I was friends with her, she asks *that* question? "Why does she have to say anything about us?"

Mẹ closes her mouth. "Never mind." She swiftly turns. A line cook steps into the kitchen, AirPods in. She barks at him, bringing him out of his musical reverie, to clean up the prep table a bit more. I could feel her anger, even if it were miles away. Most of the time I keep it separate, observing it from afar. Sometimes my dad and I can laugh it off. Simply steer clear. But now, the anger is like tar. I'm a part of it. I'm the reason for it. I feel what she feels.

"What *do* they know about us? What aren't you telling me?"

"Nothing for you to worry about." She turns her back, busying herself with moving around pots and pans. The line cook, sensing the mood of the room, quickly departs, leaving me to ask:

"Mẹ, is this about what happened in Vietnam? What Bác Xuân knows?"

She slams an empty pot against the stovetop before whirling around. Before I know it, she's around the table, yanking me toward the back entrance to our alley, until we're both outside, standing between a heap of black trash bags and broken-down cardboard boxes. "How did you—*why* are you asking these questions?"

"Because I'm trying to figure all of this shit out!" I yell freely. "All of the secrets. The way you're acting. Why I can't even mention Linh and her family's name without getting this kind of reaction from you! Or maybe it's because I don't want to think that you, Mẹ, could do this to another family. This can't be you, Mẹ. I didn't think you could be this cruel."

"Cruel?" My mom sucks in a breath. A movement catches my attention, rendering me speechless.

Tears.

Falling like snowy specks.

I look to the side, hating to see them. My body screams at me, my heart thudding at the idea of betraying her—*you made her cry; you did this!* But another voice inside me protests: *She is crying because she's guilty.*

"It wasn't me who said it," she finally whispers. "It was Dì Nhi. It was said inside this restaurant; I didn't think anyone would take it seriously. It wasn't meant to leave here. I'll talk to her."

The admission doesn't help. Not one bit. "That won't help. This is Dì Nhi we're talking about. Everything she says takes on a life of its own. And you should have stopped her. And now their restaurant's in danger."

"Con being dramatic. It will go away. Like all rumors. So Mẹ not sure why con being so—"

"Linh told me a health inspector's coming by. Making them close down for the whole day. Imagine if you had to do that, Mẹ." I turn my back on her. "Linh's just like me. And she's scared of what's going to happen to *her* parents, to *their* restaurant. It's their only means of living."

I can't be near her, not right now. I almost turn to go back into the restaurant, when suddenly her voice stops me.

"Your uncle died because of that girl's family. My brother died . . . because of *them*. They are murderers." Her voice cracks at the very end.

I pivot, reaching for the words to lead me back to my mother, who brushes past me, escaping into the depths of the kitchen. In my imagination, her words keep echoing back at me.

What the hell?

What the hell is going on?

CHAPTER THIRTY-SIX

LINH

It's crushing to see my parents look scared. Because when they're frightened they're no longer the people who raised me to be strong, but strangers who look older than they really are.

The inspector came by. He's Vietnamese as well. He gave my parents a brisk handshake, clipboard under his armpit, but before stepping into the dining area, he gave a good sweep of the room, eyes calculating. I wondered if he was judging us, how we lived. I wanted to yell that this was all a cruel joke. It was embarrassing to have him rummaging through the kitchen cabinets, bending over and checking under the tables, feeling along the walls for cracks and damages.

Despite the Health Department clearing us, I see how the rumor has done damage afterward—small, but damage nonetheless. Customers who'd visited us daily dropped off until Ba, turning on his charisma, appealed to them, explained the situation, offered them discounts on future meals. The favors that my parents were so reluctant to ask for are used now to recoup whatever unquantifiable loss the rumor had cost us. Luckily, it seems like the stream of new customers hasn't been affected.

There's no way to tell if Bảo's talk with his mom helped in that matter, but the next time I saw him, he said his mother promised to have a word with Nhi Trưng, the real culprit. He doesn't say much more, though. Sometimes I catch him spacing out, eyebrows furrowed. I'm prone to daydreams, but not Bảo. So he must be bothered by something.

I would hate it if his relationship with his mother was tainted by this. Even if she did play a part in spreading the rumor—even if—I don't want to demonize her. Just like I wouldn't want Bảo to demonize my own parents for their prejudice.

He feels maybe more unreachable, even as we spend most of our free time at Chef Lê's restaurant, finishing up the mural. I like painting from this height; I'm untouchable, unreachable, too . . . and everything below is smaller. Issues farther away.

That same distance seems to overtake my parents. I rarely see them in the morning, and when I work after school, they're preoccupied at the restaurant. Dì Vàng's visit is only a few days away, too. It'd be impossible to bring up what I heard from Bác Xuân.

Lately, Bảo doesn't seem as intent on finding out more about our families' shared past.

I feel, somehow, that me and Bảo are running out of time. That the both of us are being pushed toward an edge, but we won't know if we'll go over until the very moment it happens.

CHAPTER THIRTY-SEVEN

BẢO

In the next two weeks, my mom makes herself scarce. She talks to me, but pretends that she didn't drop a bomb on me about Linh's family being possible murderers. We don't even discuss my friendship with Linh, and I don't know if she really thinks I'll follow her request to not see Linh. At this point, I can't. I won't.

I don't tell Linh, either, secure in the knowledge that Mẹ wouldn't want to tell anyone. Even her gossip group. They still come in, and when they see me, they still treat me with the same level of disinterest. Their laughter is the same as I retreat to the back.

When I'm not at work or at home, conscious of this weird shift in my relationship with my mom, I find refuge at Chef Lê's. I watch as Linh's mural blooms to life. At her request, we're not letting Chef Lê past the curtains anymore; she wants to surprise him with a reveal. Saffron's gotten a peek at it, though.

She'd carried her ten-month-old son Philippe against her hip. He was yanking at the handkerchief wrapped snug around her neck, but she paid him no mind, taking in Linh's work of art. Beaming. "He'll love it. He'll absolutely love it."

In exchange, Chef Lê said he wants to invite a few friends over for the reveal and close down the restaurant for the night. It'll be small, he said, and it'll be a chance to "debut Miss Mai" and "share her talents with the world." Well, Fountain Valley, at least. Linh tried to protest but she was up against four people—Chef Lê counts as two. She really had no choice.

CHAPTER THIRTY-EIGHT

LINH

Soon enough, it comes time for Chef Lê to reveal his mural to his friends and family. His missive to me and Bảo, as well as Việt and Ali, is to dress "fancy." I'm not sure what that means coming from a man who wears T-shirts underneath his chef's jacket.

I'm not expected to work tonight and Mẹ and Ba are already at the restaurant. *It'll be a late night. Food is in the fridge*, reads the sticky note in my mom's neat cursive.

I'm about leave for Chơi Ơi, finally settling on a strapless black dress paired with an old burgundy shawl I found my in my mom's closet.

As I'm in the closet, curious, I see old boxes of photos. My parents always tell me they'll put these photos into neat scrapbooks. First it was planned for the weekend, then during the holidays when things died down, and now they've pushed it to retirement age. But my dad, in his defense, did start the project.

Not in his defense, he got tired by the time the photos started showing Evie at age four and me age three.

My parents keep the photos in bulging shoeboxes from Payless, Ann Taylor, and Adidas. But the sepia photos from Vietnam are stored in pocketbooks, underneath crinkling plastic. There are a lot of beach photos—a given, since Nha Trang's known for its beaches.

In one photo, my mom lounges on the beach in a one-piece, sunglasses tangled up in her hair. Behind her is my aunt, who might have just pushed her from behind—their smiles are identical, even with five years in between them. It seems impossible to think that outside the frame of this photo, the country they knew was changing rapidly. And yet here they were: joyful. The next photo appears to be from the same day, only now they're standing. Same with the next handful of photos. I've never seen my mom smile so much.

And I stop.

Bảo is in this photo, still at the beach, standing right next to my aunt. But that can't be. I was just thinking of Bảo right this second; that's why my mind brought him to mind. That must be why, as I come across this photo, his face appears on the photo.

It's him.

And yet it's not. Of course. This was before he was born. The man's hair is far longer than Bảo's has ever been.

I find the answer on the other side of not-Bảo. I've seen her only in glimpses—coincidental looks as she leaves the restaurant for some reason or another—including that time at the Vietnamese supermarket.

Bảo's mother is in this photo, indisputably confirming what Bác Xuân shared with me.

Two women, who supposedly hated each other, and did everything to avoid each other, are embracing like they're sisters. So that must be Bảo's uncle, the one who died at sea.

Back before the second Phở Day happened, Mẹ mentioned my aunt had a fiancé, didn't she? Someone who died.

Of course.

It's *him*.

My aunt and his uncle had been together. Until . . . what was it? He left, causing his family to lash out and blame my family. What did they say in their defense?

And how the hell did all of that bring us here?

I take the bus instead of driving, not trusting myself to navigate in this confused, somewhat dizzying state. I bring the photo along, tucked inside one of my dress's pockets. It crinkles as I walk a certain way, reminding me of its existence.

Our parents knew each other back then—or at least our mothers. And, even though it would have seemed impossible before this photo—they were good friends. My aunt was in the group as well. Does my aunt know about the Nguyễns' restaurant too? Know that they now hate each other?

Bảo and I were wrong, absolutely wrong. It was something

entirely bigger than just the businesses. And far bigger than we'd feared.

I stop. Bảo. *What am I going to say to Bảo? With everything going on!*

The dining room is closed for the public tonight, and one of the waiters standing at the door grins when I tell him my name, playfully gesturing me forward. Inside, the room is awash in soft lighting. Jazzy music plays in the background. Ali is dressed up in all black with red shiny-but-sensible heels that still make a statement, and she waves excitedly. Việt stands next to her, his excitement level less obvious, of course, but he still gives me a small wave, one hand in his pocket. And Bảo . . .

Now I know what books and old movies mean by *dapper*. Like Ali, he's dressed in black. He looks far older, and for a moment, a vision of an older Bảo—someone like his uncle in the photo—supplants itself over my vision. One blink and it's the Bảo I know again. Once I'm close enough, he hugs me, lifting me off my feet. I laugh as his kiss meets my crown.

"You're way more excited than you should be," I mumble as I retighten my ponytail.

"How can I *not* be? You have a mural. This is *your* reveal."

"I'm nervous."

He brushes my cheek. "Don't be."

Putting aside the last few weeks, I want to tell him about the photo, but the way he's looking around the room, pointing out the size of it—the way he just looks so *proud* of me makes my throat tighten up. I ignore the photo for a moment.

"Local genius displays award-winning art," Ali says with her Banner Move, which I approve only in this instance. "Linh, this is . . . I don't know, I'm out of words."

"For once," Việt quips. But he's grinning and adds his own congratulations. "You think they can tell we're all, like, two decades younger?"

Focused on finding my friends, I forgot to really look around. The other guests must be Chef Lê's friends—people in the restaurant circuit. A couple are dressed in bright colors—artists? Fashion designers? The idea of Chef Lê having all sorts of friends from different crowds feels right.

"Miss Mai!" Chef Lê shouts, barreling through the crowd like an overgrown puppy. He gives me his signature bear hug, and I feel a wave of affection wash over me. "You ready for this?"

"Did you have to invite this many people?"

"*This many people.* This is the smallest gathering I've ever had. Didn't want to overwhelm you." He playfully pushes me by the shoulder, crashing me into Bảo, who catches me and grins. "C'mon, the mural's so great. Everyone in Orange County has to see it." And with that, he pulls me by the elbow into the center of the crowd. My friends laugh, trailing behind.

"Friends, you know this place is my baby and I love showing it off. I want everyone to be reminded of why they're here. For me, it's a reminder of why I'm here, how I'm the chef right now. It's a reminder of everything that my parents have done. Especially my mom." He clears his throat as a somber look passes over him. His father, or who I assume to be his father, clasps him on the shoulder, showing his support. "I wish Mẹ could have been here to see what the restaurant's become, and I hope to God that she knows she doesn't have to worry about little me anymore."

A respectful silence settles in the room. A few people clap in encouragement.

"Well, not *little* me, because, you know." The mood shifts again—laughter. "Anyway, I'm intentional in everything that goes into this restaurant. It's Vietnamese, one hundred percent, and I like to think the decorations are reflective of that. But this column"—he points—"I couldn't figure it out. I needed something." He pauses dramatically.

"That's why I was so excited to meet a special artist who came in here with a young man. Before they met me, believe it or not, they were *just friends*, but you know how I like to meddle—"

Bảo clears his throat. "Um, Chef Lê—"

"Okay, okay. Long story short: I'm the only reason they got together and they should thank me," he adds in a rush, despite Bảo's suggestion. The crowd laughs and I glance in mock suffering at Bảo, but instead of embarrassment, the look in his eyes is soft like the warm glow of the light above us. "All I want to say is I told you so. Anyway, they wrote this bomb piece for their school newspaper but it was better than anything I've ever read. And it led me to discover the extraordinary talent that is Linh."

He gestures for me to stand next to him and I'm emboldened by the applause. "Is everyone ready?"

The wrap falls with a *whoosh*. A flash blinds me for a split second. I haven't seen the mural from afar in this kind of lighting. I'd only been up close, using the smallest brushes imaginable, observing for all kinds of imperfections, and so I rarely stood aside to see what I was building layer by layer, color by color. The crowd eases forward, murmuring to one another. Bảo slips his hand into mine, squeezing, and a few feet away, Chef Lê is pointing out details of the mural to the friends closest to him.

It's a collage of him and his mother, based on photos that he gave me: her hugging him on his first day of school, him standing on a stool to help his parents roll out *bánh bao* doughs, all the way up to a scene from last year, of them together in the kitchen. It's celebrating her and everything she gave him—and more.

A round of guests come by to congratulate me.

"A high school student did this?"

"Is she available for other work?"

I duck my head at some of the praise, but I can't deny how they make me warm all over. "Beautiful," Bảo says, kissing my temple and hugging me from behind. I lean back against him, my mind running on imagination. Somewhere, far into the future, people might come to my exhibition and feel the same amount of awe that I've had toward other artists growing up.

I want to stay like this forever.

"If this writing thing doesn't work out, I'll be your manager."

"Sorry, Ali's going to be my manager."

"PR, then. I'll write the best PR," Bảo says as he pulls up a few houses away from mine.

I laugh. "You don't know a thing about art."

"But I know a few things about you," he returns cheekily. He leans in as smoothly as he can with his seat belt keeping him back and kisses me twice. He doesn't pull away, his eyes roving over my face. Looking for something. "I'll let you go—you're probably tired from the all-star treatment that you got."

A satisfied laugh bubbles in my throat, and I want to protest, but he's right. We can't push it. I slide out of the passenger seat, careful not to close the door too loudly. The movement reminds me of the photo in my pocket, which slips out, catching Bảo's attention. I grab it, wanting to keep it out of sight, out of mind, just for tonight.

"What's that?" he asks, resting a hand on the steering wheel.

"Look closer."

He squints and leans forward, assesses the man's head full of hair, his lean frame, his smile—and disbelief dawns on his face. "That's my uncle."

"Yes."

"How . . . ? Isn't that . . . ?"

"My mom and my aunt." I exhale. "Bảo, there is more to the story. First it was my mom and your mom. Then there was the question about my aunt, but here it is. Proof. My aunt and your uncle were together at some point."

Bảo releases his hold on the steering wheel, dragging both hands through his hair.

"What do you know about him?"

"He died," he says, staring straight ahead. "He tried to escape by boat first, but he died. And my mom doesn't talk about him much. Hurts too much, I think."

"Of course. It was her brother." I try to think, try to connect the dots between my mom, my aunt, his mom, and his uncle, and I know there *is* something, but everything feels unfocused. Just out of reach. "I think he was the one my aunt almost married. But he left. For some reason he left."

Bảo is tight-lipped. I feel his mind working itself into a frenzy.

"I told my mom about you."

"What?"

"I told her how we became friends, how we worked together. I didn't mention *what* we are, but I think she knows. But she didn't really blow up about that. It was what she said after, and I didn't tell you right away because I didn't want to ruin things. I didn't want there to be another reason for us not to be together."

"Bảo?" I slip my hand back into his. "It's okay. You can tell me." I don't care that he didn't tell me right away; I tried hiding the picture from him. We both didn't want to ruin things. Now, even if we don't have all the pieces, we're gravitating closer to the truth.

"My mom said that it's your family's fault that my uncle died." He turns his head, meeting my eyes. "She called your family murderers."

I suck in sharply. Moths dance around one of my neighbor's porch lights. Behind shaded windows, multicolored lights from their television pulse. My gaze falls on my house, dark save for the light from the back of the kitchen, shining half its usual luminosity.

"Murderers," I whisper. What a horrible word. An impossible reality.

What does this all mean? How could my mom, my aunt—or both—have played a hand in his uncle's death? Had they gone with him? Did he drown, then? And where was Bảo's mother in all of this? "They couldn't have—" Killed. Murdered. Done whatever they were rumored to have done.

"Linh, I have no clue what that means. I'm just saying what she said, but . . . fuck, this is all messed up." The desperation in his voice pulls me back into the car, and I reach for his hand. "I really don't know what to think."

"I don't know either, Bảo. I really don't."

"We have to talk to them. At least we have something tangible in front of us. They can't deny it now."

"I can only nod.

Tomorrow. The truth will come out tomorrow.

Bảo kisses me goodbye. We linger, noses touching, breathing in and out again. Then, he gives me one last kiss. He backs up and drives off, leaving me wondering how I'll be able to go to sleep tonight.

But then my living room lights snap on, the curtains part sharply, and two silhouettes appear, facing me.

My parents are home.

The exaltation from tonight's showing, the peace that I felt being with Bảo—it all gradually disappeared as details of the photo came out and Bảo told me what his mother said. Any good feeling that was left bursts into nonexistence the moment I step into the house.

My parents' shoes are by the front door, neatly against the wall as always. The room feels colder than usual, but maybe it's me, shivering at the prospect of my parents, who'd come home early to find an empty house, when I said I'd be home.

I hear them exchange sharp whispers, and they stop when I get to the kitchen threshold. My mom's at the kitchen sink, washing dishes. Ba sits at the table, mandarin peels sitting in front of him. Neither looks at me.

"I'm sorry. I realized that I needed to finish up a project. And I sort of lost track of time." I force out the lie, instantly hating myself. "I'm really sorry."

My mother still doesn't turn around. Ba's focused on something on his phone.

"I'm really sorry," I say again, hating how stale it sounds.

"We don't care that you're late. Not now," my mom says. Her voice sounds clogged, like she'd just been crying a few minutes before.

Ba abruptly pushes away his chair, as if ready to storm from the kitchen. But he doesn't; he just paces, his steps heavy. "Are you going to tell us where you really were for the past hour? Or will you lie again?"

Oh no.

Ba turns his phone, slides it toward me. His Messages app is open, showing a photo that was received a half hour ago.

The photo is of me and Bảo. At the mural reveal, the moment the curtains had fallen. I remember there'd been a flash, and I guess whoever had taken the picture had sent it his way. "The person who puts our ads in the newsletters. She was there and told us how proud we should be. To have our talented daughter showcase her first mural!" Ba shakes his head. "I should have answered, 'What daughter?' After all, what daughter hides this from us?"

I feel cold all over. I swallow hard, trying to summon the right words to explain everything. I know I have many things to defend; I don't even know where to start. How can I explain meeting Bảo? Wanting to do art, not engineering? Being at the reveal, rather than at home? Words are out before I know what to say. "Mẹ, I know I'm not supposed to talk to the Nguyễns—"

"Bảo, you know him," Ba says.

"We're friends. Good friends. I didn't expect it to—"

"This isn't just about the boy or his family. *Con này nói láo từ hồi nào tới giờ*," my mother interjects, directing her anger at Ba. She twists the water off, wrenches her gloves from her hands. They smack against the sink. Her sharp voice stuns me, jumps out into the space between us like a flame on the stove turned up too high.

"It's the lies. All of them. How long were you seeing this boy? How long have you been doing this painting for that restaurant? How long were you lying to us about *everything*? *Tại sao mày dám làm như vậy tới cha mẹ.*"

How dare you.

How dare you do this to us, your parents.

"I didn't know how to tell you," I say weakly. About everything. "Ba, Mẹ, I've always wanted to be an artist. But I couldn't tell you that because you were always saying things about Dì Vàng, about how that kind of life will be hard. You'd never approve.

"And with Bảo . . . I didn't know what to think at first, but I got to know him and he's nothing like I always thought he'd be. He's a friend—a great friend—and as much as his family has gone out of its way to hurt us—he's not them.

"By the time I was getting further along with my work, by the time I . . . spent more time with Bảo, I couldn't explain it."

"So you thought you'd go on like this. Never telling us about *any* of this," Ba finishes.

"No!" I quickly reply. I shake my head. That's not it. But what do I want to say? What can I say? "I didn't want to do this forever. I was *just* starting to find a way—"

Mẹ overrides me. "So you didn't trust us. Your parents."

I'm so tired. "That's not it. It's not that."

"You lied about the boy."

"Yes."

"You lied about your painting job."

"Yes."

"You were elsewhere today."

So many lies. I pinch my eyes closed. "Yes."

"I wanted you to have a good life. A safe life. A happy life, by raising you the right way."

It's confusing—her words, how suddenly they come, how sad my mom sounds.

"But we hardly know you anymore," Mẹ says. "And you never thought of us as you were making these lies."

"That's not true, Mẹ."

"Tomorrow," Ba adds, ignoring me. "You will go home right

after school. No more staying after school to paint. No more seeing *thằng đó*."

"I can't—"

"*Cha mẹ nói sao, con phải làm*," Ba says with finality.

"I don't understand!" I shout, finally, hating that I'm beginning to cry. I sound like a baby. I sound like a kid. "I'm not the only one lying, am I? You're lying too, aren't you?" I shakily reach for the photo that I found in the shoeboxes. "What's this, then? Why didn't you tell me you knew the Nguyễns? That you were close with them, too?" I smack the photo against the center of the table. "And why they're saying you're murderers."

My mom barely glances at it. "I don't have to tell you anything," Mẹ finally snaps at me. "There are things that only adults know. This is one of them. You are a child, con. *Nhiều thứ con không cần biết*. The pain that will happen to you. Everything I've done in America, I have done for you. To give you a good life. To raise you well so that one day, you will not need us anymore." Mẹ angrily wipes away a lone tear running down her cheek. "*Ba mẹ nói thì con phải nghe*. Art will get you nowhere, con, because I've seen it for my sister, your aunt. *Nó sẽ làm cuộc đời của con rất là khổ*. And I can't let that happen to you Not after everything Mẹ—*my family*—has gone through."

The sight of her tears makes my heart feel as if it's being gnawed on from the inside. I want to tell her to listen to me, listen to what I'm saying. But she's shaking with anger. Her hair has fallen loose from her clip. And her eyes . . . I look down. I think this is the first time she's doubted that I love her.

My mom storms out of the kitchen and a few seconds later, her bedroom door thuds against its frame.

I brace myself, wait for my dad to scream as well. His gaze is on me. Yet, he's calm. I think I want him to yell now, because it'll show he's feeling *something* toward me. But the quiet between us is cold and cut off. Like I'm beyond reproach, like I'm worthless.

He snatches up the photo I showed Mẹ. He turns his back on me. "If you don't honor your parents and listen to us—after all that we have done for you—then we have failed. We have failed as your parents."

"I didn't mean to lie so much," I say weakly.

Ba doesn't say more. He walks away from me.

The next morning, I wake to an empty house. My cheeks are dry and tight from crying. In the kitchen, I splash cold water on my face. My parents have already left for the restaurant. No note or anything, no breakfast Saran-wrapped in the fridge. I wonder what hurt more: the yelling match we had last night or the resulting silence. Disquieting. Unforgiving.

My walk to school is slow and painful, as if my body is also hurting. I keep my head down too, because if I pass someone I know, the polite thing to do is smile, but it's not something I can muster. Neither does sitting in class interest me.

Bảo's at my locker, holding on to his backpack by one strap. I see the worry on his face, then his eyes rove over me, and his eyebrows quickly furrow. Of course I know why; I saw my face in the mirror. It's blotchy, my eyes are swollen, and the bags underneath

323

create the illusion that I smeared gray paint below them.

"What happened?"

His look of concern hurts rather than helps. "I can't. Not right now," I say. I put in my combination.

I don't comprehend right away why my touch is slippery, why my vision starts blurring. Then Bảo's arms are around me, and he's mumbling "What's wrong?" again and I'm saying things into his chest and he can't hear me.

Soon enough I'm half walking, half leaning on Bảo as he moves us into an empty classroom. Empty for how long, we're not sure. I hate how I'm a cliché, crying in the middle of the hallway. People are probably thinking we broke up. They're going to go to class and gossip. Roll their eyes, but then forget about it next period.

I tell Bảo everything as I nestle against him, last night's ugly words between me and my mom flowing out of me in a furious, murky stream. If I could take back last night, I would. If I could go back to the beginning of this year—before *everything*—I would.

Even if it means never meeting Bảo?

CHAPTER THIRTY-NINE

BẢO

I don't know what else to do but hold Linh. Drop a kiss on her head now and then. And just hold her more. She's trembling, her voice breaks, and I don't have anything to give her but physical comfort. Still, it feels empty, temporary, and Linh needs more than that.

"I mean, I've never seen them look at me that way. Especially my mother. It looked like I broke her heart." Linh sniffs. "And maybe I was too honest toward the end. Throwing that photo in their faces only complicated things more."

"Don't think that. You got it out there. All the things you were holding back for months. It's there." I wouldn't say that telling my mom about Linh made things better—but it didn't make things worse. Just uncomfortable. I'm more disturbed that she pretends as if we never had that conversation, as if she hopes I'll forget about it.

"But now everything's a mess!" Linh gestures to the ground, as if the argument with her parents were physical things just scattered below our feet. "It's all out there, but tangled up, messy, and—"

"*It's out there,*" I try saying. "You don't have to lie anymore."

That's not the right thing to say. I can tell by her face falling, her voice turning dull. "I guess that was the actual problem for them. Lying. Me, lying. You saw it from the beginning."

"Hey, don't go there," I counter as gently as possible. "If you're a liar, I am too. And parents blow up. They say things in the heat of the moment. I've argued before with my parents. You have too, probably."

"Not like this, Bảo. Never like this." She slides off the desk, sniffing and wiping back stray tears, looking so defeated.

"It hurts, Linh. I know it does. But there's always a way out."

"How?" Linh asks, an edge to her voice. "Tell me how. Because I don't think I can keep doing this, Bảo. Trying to defend what I've been doing. And what we were about to do, digging into the past." I read between the lines. Does she want to give up?

"Don't you want to know?" I ask, reaching for her hands. "Don't you want us?"

She doesn't move.

"Oh." I never thought a nonresponse could hurt me so much. Not a word, but that look on her face. Empty.

"I don't think I can keep doing this, Bảo."

"You're scared, Linh. I know you are."

"Ever since we started *this* . . . no, even met, I think, my life has been about putting one fire out after the next."

"So, what? You think it'd be better if we'd never met? Never spoke to each other again?"

The bell ringing to announce first period cuts through our silence.

"Maybe, Bảo. Maybe."

CHAPTER FORTY

LINH

Everyone is just about settled in class and any minute now a school aide will start her rounds, trying to catch kids playing hooky from class. The noise in each classroom—chattering, laughing, the droning of a documentary—reaches me. I'm not sure where I'm going until I stop by rote.

Ali, to no surprise, sits at the front of her AP History class. She sees me through the door window, a smile ready on her face. She stops mid-wave. Then her hand shoots straight up.

"Mrs. DuBois?" she says, the sound muffled.

"Yes, Allison."

"Can I go to the bathroom?"

"Why didn't you go before? We're just about to—"

"Thanks!" Ali bolts from her chair, swiping the bathroom pass from the whiteboard's frame.

Out in the hall, she pulls me aside and lays her hands on my shoulders. "Linh?"

And I just cry.

CHAPTER FORTY-ONE

BẢO

I'm not sure how long I stay seated in the classroom, but the period bell ringing makes me stand. I don't feel like myself as I walk out, the teacher looking curiously after me.

Linh doesn't want us.

Somehow I make it to another classroom, and only when Việt arrives do I realize it's Forensic Science today. He offers a packet of Orbit gum. When I don't take it, that somehow draws his concern. He waves his hand and I'm forced to look at him, really look at him.

"What's with you?"

I might have spoken in sentence fragments. Or rambled on and on. Or shouted. Not so sure, but Việt listens the whole time. Today our teacher's routine lateness is to our advantage, and our class-mates are clumped together to one side, watching a YouTube video or something that makes them snicker now and again.

"Do you think she means it?" I ask.

Việt chews his gum slowly. He plays with the corner of his worksheet, which was filled out—reminding me that I left mine at home. Great.

It's not like I haven't been rejected before. It's not like I haven't disappointed my parents in some ways—and will continue to do so—for a lifetime. But I guess it fucking sucks when I hear it from Linh.

I thought she saw something in me. And I wanted to believe in whatever she saw. I thought we would figure out the truth of us together.

Mr. Lynch enters the room, hungover by the looks of his mussed hair and wrinkled polo. He yawns a "Good morning" while the other students snicker knowingly. I don't care about that.

I put my head down, feeling just exhausted.

I don't care about anything.

CHAPTER FORTY-TWO

LINH

Doing as I was told, I skip work and head home, lying in bed, facedown, pillow over my head. I try to drown out my thoughts, my worries, scenes from last night and today pounding inside my mind. I would have tried to take a nap, but my phone rings. Someone's calling on Viber.

"Oh, Linh," Dì Vàng says when the visual stabilizes, sounding like I was the one to call. She's at an airport, sitting in a packed waiting area. Beside her is a nosy grandmother who stares suspiciously at my aunt, then looks away. "Five more hours until I land in Cali!"

I summon all of my energy into a smile and tell her how excited I am to finally see her. I must look like something's wrong because the next moment she leans in, squinting, and asks, "What's wrong? Were you crying?"

What a way to welcome my aunt to the States after seven years.

Before I know it, I'm telling her everything that's happened in the past few months. It pours out of me. Maybe a screen separating us makes it easier for me to speak freely. Or maybe because Dì Vàng looks a bit like my mom now, and I wish I could explain this all to her. I start from the beginning—and for me, the real beginning was when Bảo crossed the street because he saw I needed comfort. I start with *him*, not mentioning him as the son of my parents' nemeses or as the nephew of her former fiancé, but the boy who offered to help when he didn't have to. I tell her about him and his writing and my painting—how our relationship had formed and blossomed along with the art I'm finally making.

I tell my aunt about our meetups, and then our dates. About that happiness that came in revealing my mural—that initial silence, then uproarious applause from strangers who loved what I'd put out there. And then I tell her about the moment things went wrong with my parents, everything that I had hidden from them coming out and me having no real way to explain myself.

I should have known where I would end up. I knew that lying was wrong, but I'd thought it was the only way to do the things that I wanted. Wasn't it? I finish my story with that question, one that my aunt needs to look away to ponder.

Then she sighs and sips her coffee, which she got from Auntie Anne's. "This doesn't sound good, Linh."

"I know," I say miserably.

"It's a lot to take apart, but I think it's the act of lying that hurt my sister the most. She loves you, Linh. And I don't think she feels great about being left out of your life."

"I didn't mean to do that."

"Oh, I know you didn't," she says sympathetically.

"I'm sorry, I don't mean to unload on you right before you even land here."

"I can think about it on the plane ride over." She leans back in her seat. "So this boy," she says almost wistfully. "I remember being your age—what that was like." She smiles quickly before it disappears. "From what it sounds like, this boy seems very *đàng hoàng*."

I inhale. I'm on the precipice here, and once I say this, once I hear her reaction, I really can't go back. "That's something else I need to tell you. You know Bảo, kind of. Because you know his parents, or his mother. And his uncle. The one who died."

Her lips part, the sun from the far-left window, facing the planes, touches her face, obscuring her expression from me. *"Trời ơi."*

She knows. She remembers.

The kiosk attendant starts calling people to board.

"Dì Vàng—" I start to apologize, knowing that this thought will occupy her mind over the plane ride, and there won't be anything she can do to stop it.

So in shock, she only manages a goodbye before telling me she needs to step in line. "It's been so long. But I guess we all have to face this, once and for all. I will see you soon."

◇ ◇ ◇

The drive is excruciating. A song plays in the background, the kind to lull me and Evie asleep during rare road trips. This was before Mẹ and Ba opened the restaurant, when their work hours were slightly more forgivable. We'd drive within California—to a park or to visit a relative. In intermittent moments, my mom would reach her hand back and my sister or I, giggling, would put our hand in, asking her to guess whose it was.

"Tay của ai vậy?"

Mẹ would pretend to think, squeezing the hand, fingers, guessing whose hand she's holding. Of course, my mom had the rearview mirror and could easily see who, but I thought it was just a superpower she had because she was a mom.

In the arrivals wing, my parents and I sit with three seats in between us. Every few minutes, Ba gets up to stretch his legs, then stand by the window, hands clasped, to observe the planes taking off. The area is alive with vibrant clothing and languages mingling and flying right over my head. The walls are wide and white, and tired passengers flow from the customs gate, their dull faces turning into laughter, surprise, eagerness as they reunite with their families. Then the most colorful person emerges—a woman with her hair piled atop her head, for convenience, rather than looks. Her neck scarf, blouse, and pants show a bizarre spectrum of shades of green, pink, and yellow, though they all seem to mesh. She's here.

My aunt shrieks, causing the other off-loading passengers to look back at her, some with shock, some with amusement. Leaving her bag there momentarily—a woven bag that's seen better days—

she and my mom, who's suddenly come to life, embrace. Her hug is strong and tight. I feel it myself.

"You look so skinny!" my aunt exclaims, squeezing my mom's cheeks, shoulders, hips, but she bats her hands away.

"What are you wearing?" my mom asks dubiously, in the same way my sister asks when something doesn't compute with her right away.

"The latest Vietnamese fashion," she retorts pompously. "I bought you the same scarf."

"You shouldn't have."

"Fine. I'll give it to Linh." She turns to me, opens up her arms. "Look at you, all grown up! You're so beautiful." I stay there for a moment and I hear Mẹ tell Ba to pick up the bag Dì Vàng left behind.

I don't know why, but I start crying. Maybe I was exhausted by this energy in the house, by what I did to get us here, or that I didn't expect my aunt to hold me for this long. Or that it would make me miss the way Mẹ used to hug me. My aunt's arms tighten around me.

CHAPTER FORTY-THREE

BẢO

I'm glad that Việt is not someone to press me. He knows what's happening with Linh, but he doesn't force me to explain. Doesn't tell me to stop moping. Just lets me deal with this my own way. At work, he keeps chattering on about his TV shows, not caring that I'm not listening to half the words. At school, in Forensic Science, he does most of the work, telling me to write this and that down.

But one morning, I think he may have had enough. He's calling my name as I'm zoning out, and when I don't answer him right away, he punches me in the shoulder—the pain jerking me awake from my daze.

"Look. Someone screenshotted these Yelp reviews."

I pull his laptop closer. It turns out Jared, the guy who accused my mom of scamming him, had been making rounds, based on these online Yelp profiles all under different names. He was hitting several businesses with the same message:

> *Fucking FOBS—if they're going to open businesses here, they should speak in English, since they can't even do that, they should go back to where they belong.*

I click on my parents' restaurant. Similar message.

My first thought? *Run-on sentence.* Then I hear Jared's self-righteous voice. It may or may not be him, but since he was the most recent person to say things like this, my mind uses him as the person sitting in front of a PC, trolling because he doesn't have better things to do with his life. I see his wife hovering over his shoulder in their home somewhere, pleading for him not to hit that Post button, then walking away, shaking her head, when he fully ignores her.

Go back where? Where else would Linh's parents go? My parents? By now, half of their lives have been spent here. The country they remember is not the one that exists today. So why should they go when they so clearly belong here?

This guy doesn't know shit.

"He's everywhere," Việt says. He clicks through other names from our neighborhood shops. Nail salons, *bánh mì* places. Jared, or whoever it is, has really been hitting up every prominent Vietnamese place nearby.

"Do you think a lot of people have seen this?"

Việt just shrugs. "For this douche's sake, let's hope not."

The community did see it. Not through electronic means, but something more reliable for our parents: word of mouth. And who hears it first? Mẹ's group. Her circle, including Nhi Trưng, convened in their booth, bickering quietly among themselves, printed pages of those reviews spread out across the table. Mẹ examines one of them, her glasses at the bridge of her nose. She doesn't look happy.

"So you guys saw it too?"

"Bảo?"

"The reviews."

Mẹ purses her lips, answering my question. "They're ridiculous. Racists."

Leaving the group, she strides to the back where Eddie, Trần, and others are goofing around again. I don't see Ba, until I realize he's in the restaurant too, with the husbands. They've come here about the review as well. In the kitchen, one of the line cooks wordlessly slides down a tin of Café du Monde and Mẹ receives it smoothly, spooning it into a single-cup filter.

"Con muốn cà phê không?" she asks breezily, and starts making one for me before I can answer. I realize that this is the first real one-on-one since our argument a few weeks ago about Linh. We're exactly where we were before. This time, I round the prep table, try to reason with her.

"Are we going to do anything about the review?"

My mom doesn't answer me right away. Instead, she busies

herself with the filter, fiddling with the dripper, twisting it so that the drips run at the right pace.

"Do what?"

My parents have never been the type to make a fuss. They save their comments for the kitchen after hours or the safety of our home. If their opinions are to be shared, they do it with others like them—Vietnamese who've fled home for the same reasons, who read the same newspapers about the home they once knew. I wonder if it's because of what they've gone through; how easily they could have been punished for speaking a word against the communist government. How they saw their friends and families punished for doing exactly that.

It could all be that. But it's not like they'll ever tell me.

I try again. "This review is ridiculous."

"So?"

"It's basically talking shit about every business in our community! We need to do something."

"Why do you keep bothering? What can we do? Hm?"

Her anger rises like a quick flame, knocking me off guard. And also because I don't have an answer. How can we fight someone who's anonymous? Or the lies that they spread online about us?

"What is it that Americans say? It's not your battle."

I shake my head. An antithesis to basically everything she's said to me my whole life. It's always about us. Not one person—us. Together. And I'm not going to let her start saying things like that now.

"These words," I slowly say. "They have consequences. Yeah,

A PHỞ LOVE STORY

sometimes, you don't think they will do much, especially when they're said among friends—within the safety of one place." Her face shifts; she remembers our argument. "But some words, like this, sometimes they win. We can't let that happen. We can't let anyone just see these words on our page and not defend ourselves."

Now my mom just looks tired, decades older than she really is.

"I'm not going to let this person get away with saying things like that. I'm not."

I'm tired.

Of all of it. Of all this useless gossip that never dies, only comes back in different forms. Causes people to hide certain things, then when it comes out it hurts all of us at once.

Someone needs to finally say something in our defense. Even if it hurts.

Later that night, instead of sleeping, I'm up with the lamp on, my computer in front of me. Considering the blinking cursor for a few minutes, I place my fingers on the keyboard, and before I know it, words and sentences fly from my mind to the keys. With each word I type I'm hoping to erase the vile reviews that those shitheads left on our pages. I'm writing this for not just my family, but other restaurants—and I pause—and the Mais' restaurant. As much as our restaurants have clashed, as much as their weird battle has gone on, we still live in the same place. And hasn't Linh always encouraged me to write what I feel? What I'm passionate about?

I sit up straight, stretching my back and arms. A look at the clock shows that I've been typing for an hour. It's the first long piece I've written that wasn't an assignment. It's me on the page, and looking at it, I almost feel lighter.

The first person I want to share it with is Linh, but at the memory of our last talk, seeing her at her breaking point, my energy stills for a moment. That's not an option, so I go to the next person I can trust.

I almost hesitate to show Ali the next day. Who knows what she's thinking about what happened between me and Linh, whether she'll take Linh's side and cold-shoulder me, too, because that's where her loyalty should be. But when I text her for help on the article during lunch, she sends back a quick "yeah, sure," telling me to find her now in the newsroom like usual.

I pack my things from the lunch table and Việt sends me a quick nod. He's been my friend for so long that he knows when to shut up. I haven't heard *SVU* recaps from him in what seems like ages and I've got to give his cross-country friends credit for following his lead, their conversation a little less boring than usual.

Then, because I can't help it, I seek Linh out, wondering if she'll be here or in her art room, cooped up as usual. But she's here, eating lunch with some friends. I stare harder at her, willing her to turn around, to see me, but she doesn't notice.

Swallowing hard, I leave.

"It's not bad?"

"Not bad so far."

"Really?"

"Hey, I said 'so far.' Your next sentence is probably going to be shitty."

We're quiet as she keeps reading as promised. I scroll through Twitter on the computer. She marks up some words and nods sometimes.

"So Linh told me what happened. Well, kind of. Not the whole story. But she did tell me what happened."

My hand freezes on the mouse, but I keep quiet.

"She's been really stressed. I mean, you know she probably didn't mean any of it?"

Ali sits next to me, looking unusually somber. "See, the thing with Linh is that she was alone for a while. Not physically, but alone inside her head. I'm a journalist and she's a painter and though they're both creative things, she never really had someone on that level with her. But you, Bảo, you made her open up a little. Her art has changed. It's transformed. It's been freed." Ali pauses. "I've never seen her that happy, and it's because you walked into her life. I'm grateful for that."

Words are stuck in my throat. This wasn't what I expected when I came to Ali for help.

"I'm not just talking about Linh who's changed. You've become the writer you're meant to be." She nods, like she's confirming the fact to herself.

"Despite what's happening, Linh's just scared. Because it *is* scary. Her world—both of your worlds—have been upturned." Ali shrugs. "Let it settle a little. And don't doubt what she feels for you. Or what you feel for her."

After a few beats, Ali stiffens her back, morphing into the journalist I know and am terrified of.

"You won't ever repeat that to anyone," she says, in her signature *I will cut you* voice. Right after, she smiles. A genuine smile that she'd share only with Linh. "This is great. I actually think it's your best."

"Really?" I say again, like a broken record.

"So good," she says, pushing herself off the counter, "that I think you should try for something bigger than just our newspaper. Because it's not really about the school. It's about the community. Your community. Your home. And if you need help with that, I have the right contacts."

Hearing the word "contacts" come from her mouth still sounds ominous, but out of everyone, she's the best person to help me.

And she does.

WE ARE HOME

To the man posting anonymous flame reviews of several Little Saigon restaurants, to the same man who came into my parents' restaurant insulting everything they stand for:

Didn't you hear your children begging you to stop? Didn't you notice how embarrassed your wife was? Didn't you see the stunned look of everyone around you as you left in a fit of rage, without paying?

There's a lot I can break down here. There are many assumptions I can make about you and where you come from.

But I won't state them here because I don't want to be like you.

Here's a fact, though:

You clearly don't know us.

So let me teach you something.

In Bolsa, everyone you've brushed shoulders with— the very people you dismissed—probably knows more suffering than you will fortunately ever know. They saw their beloved country destroyed by colonialism, then civil war. They left everything they knew for the unknown. They left for a chance at freedom, a chance for their family and their future.

One hand would never be sufficient to count their losses.

But this loss, I think, has made them the fiercest, strongest people I will ever know.

It saddens me that you don't recognize this. It's an unfortunate reminder that as much as my community represents the true American Dream—building a foundation out of uncertain hopes and dreams—people like you would rather be ignorant or spread hate than accept this reality.

But your racism has no power here. Your words mean nothing in Little Saigon. So whatever you hoped to accomplish—in person and online—you have failed.

A person close to me—one of the most passionate, talented people I'm proud to know—once told me that I needed to write about what I really care about. It goes without saying that it's this community. It's my home. It's my family. So it's not cool what you're doing.

I would like to think that you will learn from this and become a better person.

But again, I can't make assumptions.

Thank you,

Bảo Nguyễn
Proud son of Vietnamese immigrants

◇ ◇ ◇

I don't think it hits me what exactly I did by writing the op-ed, until the first customer this morning walks in with her husband. She looks vaguely familiar; maybe she doesn't come here with her husband but with other friends.

"Your son is Bảo, yes?" she asks in Vietnamese.

Mẹ and I stand at the front desk, going over reservations for lunch. Hearing my name, she squints at me, as if to ask, *What did you do?* Her attention turns to the woman, who slides a folded newspaper her way, a perfectly manicured finger pointing at something.

My name.

My *byline*.

Turns out it's in the *Người Việt* morning edition with a translated version.

"When I read what happened, about that awful review, and then this beautiful response, I had to come over first thing. You must be so proud of your son."

My heart leaps at the praise. A stranger, complimenting me? "Thank you." Mẹ pauses, still hesitant.

"It was really touching. Those reviews were vile. I've been here so many times and I've never had a bad meal. So whatever happens, you have my full support."

After getting the woman settled into a booth, my mom takes the newspaper with her to the back, bringing along her grocery-store glasses. I wait tables all the while, my focus split between the back and the customers—many of whom have actually come by because of my article, to my shock.

An hour later, Mẹ emerges from wherever she was, her glasses hanging by her shirt collar. She brings the newspaper back with her, but she doesn't look for me. She takes her spot by the front desk, straight-backed, busying herself with the cash register. And I thought that this was it. The article was written. It's out there.

Then she stops. I approach her, not sure how she'll react, what she'll say about what I wrote. Before I can get a word out, she speaks.

"You wrote this?"

"Dạ."

"By yourself?"

"Yes."

"Are you lying?"

Okay, really? Have some faith in me.

"That's my name, isn't it," I answer, measured.

Mẹ nods. "I didn't know that you would feel this way. Especially about the gossip."

"I only hate the gossip when it's bad. When it really hurts someone else."

"You mean the Mai family." Her voice isn't angry. It's curious.

I shake my head. "I meant what I wrote. This wasn't just about the Mais. It's really about all of us. I didn't like that we were just going to let some guy on the Internet win."

"The article was good. Very good." Reaching out, she cups my cheek. *"Giỏi, con."*

A few minutes later, after getting back to work, I look back and see Mẹ holding up the newspaper against the wall, like she's checking to see how it'll look.

The next day, there *is* a framed picture of my article hanging on our wall of fame: articles about the restaurant when it first opened, the great reviews that have come in. My mom probably pulled in a favor with friends to get it made so quickly.

According to Ali, the article has gone viral, shared by local news sites. She had that gleam in her eyes when she explained: "They love underdog stories, you know. People fighting back against assholes like this guy." And because of the reach, we're getting more and more customers, even from outside Bolsa.

There's a small collective of people in our community taking it upon themselves to look out for future racist incidents—online and in real time. Walking into work one day, I see my mom's friends crowded around someone's laptop, systematically scrolling through old reviews to report them. The General, ironically, might have established herself as the leader.

I can't be sure that this will help stop the gossip wars, but it's still a welcome change. And it was one article that started it. Mine.

At school only the kids whose parents run businesses in the area paid attention to the news—and I didn't realize that it was actually a lot of people. Some classmates came by to high-five me or say "Nice article" and things like that. Lunchtime surprised me too:

Apparently Việt looped in some of his cross-country friends into the whole deal, and they were nice about it, joking around about me being famous now. Even Steve was so curious that he forgot about his banana.

I tried to look for Linh. Not that I would know what to say, but I wanted to know if she read what I wrote. If she knew that I, in my own way, was reaching out.

There are flyers now showcasing the upcoming Art Fair, so Linh's picture is verywhere that's eye level. I want to tell her how happy I am for her, really. Even though she doesn't seem to want to talk to me anymore.

Ali's become my pseudo-publicist, in a way. When a local station wanted to interview me on camera for a brief segment, she demanded that they send her the questions for approval. I'm 100 percent sure that she added some questions that would involve me mentioning the school newspaper and my role in it.

And that's what's happening now as I'm in front of the restaurant, fiddling with the collar of my dress shirt that my mom forced me to wear. "*Đẹp trai*," she said this morning when inspecting me, ultimately approving the look. My dad let me borrow his belt for my pants.

The female news anchor prepping me reminds me not to move so much because the microphone is sensitive and will pick up extraneous noise.

"You have to zoom out," I hear Ali telling Tim, the cameraman. A professional. "Just like—yeah, there it is. Perfect."

"Kid, I know."

After the countdown, I can't even hear myself talking. I just see the host nodding intently, and her mouth forming words, then she addresses my parents directly. They keep shifting behind me, uncomfortable, fidgeting in the spotlight.

"You must be so proud of your son," the reporter finally says.

I almost chime in, wanting to tell her, "Well, that might be a stretch." But my mother answers first. She looks directly at me and nods silently, seriously. It makes me stand straighter.

"Of course I am proud. All of this makes me wonder how he turned out like this."

"It was all because of me," Dad says from the other side. His joking side has come out, though the reporter looks confused, not sure if he's serious, so she just laughs nervously.

Finally, she signs off and the record light dims. I guess I *did* do okay—or maybe my eyes are screaming *I SUCK!* and she just feels bad for me—because the interviewer shakes my hand, telling me, "Good job," before telling her coworkers to pack up.

Later, when all the cameras have gone and customers have dwindled enough that everyone can catch their breath, I spy my dad Windexing my framed article, even though I'm sure it's already spotless. He steps back to inspect his work.

Ba notices me a beat later. *"Gì?"*

"Nothing." I fight back a smile.

"Okay," Ba says. "Get back to work. Stop being so lazy."

I happen to look up, out to the Mais' restaurant. It looks as busy as it was when I first crossed the street, first had the courage to speak to Linh. It's busy, too, perhaps because of the article, but that's not what caught my eye.

I saw a movement from behind the window.

A flash of long dark brown hair.

I miss her.

CHAPTER FORTY-FOUR

LINH

I miss him. There are so many things I want to tell Bảo after reading his letter. I'm so proud of him.

I wish I could be like you.

You're speaking the truth, without worrying about consequences.

But I'm ashamed of how I ran away—not just from our last conversation, but before. It was him always having to pull afloat, reminding me that I can't hide from problems. Because it'll build up and bury me until I can't breathe.

The house is made less tense with Dì Vàng's arrival. The past few nights have been light and fun, full of laughter. It was almost as if the argument in the kitchen never happened. But take her presence away and we're back to square one between my parents and me. Terse. Cold. Punishing. Dì Vàng has been visiting friends in Washington—perhaps even Bác Xuân—and she comes home late, or not at all, staying at her friends' places. She'll have to leave again and miss my exhibition at the Art Fair in a couple of days.

But the one night Dì Vàng does stay, she comes to me to talk. She's just showered and is dressed in pale green pajamas. My drawers are packed with similar clothing, gifts from her across the years. Her long hair rests on her left shoulder in a beautiful clean braid and she's peering closely at the artwork above my desk. Her eyes linger on Bảo's sculpture of whatever from our first date and she tilts her head in puzzlement before moving on. It was shipped here a couple of days ago.

"You are just as talented as your mom always tells me."

"Thank you," I say quietly, suddenly nervous. I'm still adjusting to seeing her in person—unpixelated and in real time.

"I'm not lying. Your mom's so proud of you. Your dad is, too, but you know how it is; he says it from the background." She throws a grin over her shoulder as she pulls back the bedcovers and slips in, looking right at home. Far from sleeping, my aunt props her head up. "Is everything okay now? Since we last spoke."

I pause. "There's been no change."

She stretches her hand toward me and I reach for her, the space between us only an illusion. "I'm sorry."

"Has Mẹ said anything to you?" I ask hopefully. She shakes her head.

I stare at the ceiling for a moment, listening to the low hum of the air conditioner turning on, the hush of sprinklers in our lawn. A car passes by, headlights shining into the room before disappearing. I want to ask about Bảo's uncle, but she's not offering to tell me herself. Does she want to ignore it too?

"I will tell you everything, Linh," she says.

I look at her in surprise. She must have read my mind.

"I will, I promise. But I have to sort things out, too. My sister doesn't even know that I know, so just give me some time. It'll all come out."

Bác Xuân had said the same thing.

"Mẹ always talked about you like you're some sort of tragedy. Like your art was a punishment."

"I was in a bad way after all that happened. But what my sister doesn't understand . . ." Dì Vàng pauses. "Or maybe, one day, what you can *help* her understand, is that for people like us, sadness is part of our inspiration. Others might bottle up their sadness and pour it out on certain occasions, but we let it pour from us and into our medium. It's the same for most emotions, and we do it so that we can make room for more."

I nod, remembering how my art was the only thing to calm me when things with my parents and Bảo were collapsing.

She then adds softly, "We all lost something precious during that time."

I think Ba has grown tired of the tension between me and my mom, despite Dì Vàng being there to cut through it all. Now she's off visiting a friend in San Francisco, scheduled to come back later this week. Ba's kind of annoyance takes only a day or two, much like when he sprained his back. But whether it's the food, or the silence, or being in-between, I won't ever figure out why Ba shows up outside my bedroom as I type out the captions to my Art Fair display. Just a few more days to go. Ba doesn't come in, like my mom; instead he hovers, like he's waiting for my permission to enter.

"Homework?"

"Kind of." A half-truth, not a full lie. His attention is on the paper in front me, the scraps on the floor as well.

"Come eat. I made soup. *Canh sườn bí.*"

His signature, bland dish.

"Mẹ's not coming home?"

"Working late," he says.

I guess even if he were mad, he wouldn't starve me. Without another word, Ba turns left, back toward the kitchen, where he's already set the table. Two bowls are stacked on top of each other by the rice cooker. He fluffs the rice with chopsticks, but doesn't fill the bowls. I sit down, sensing he doesn't want me here just to eat. Maybe he wants to tell me again how disappointed he is, and I feel my stomach drop.

Ba settles in his usual seat. One of the light bulbs above us is dead, washing the top of Ba's head in a dim glow. It highlights his white hairs—he has so many these days. And it doesn't look like he's shaved, the hair on his chin appearing as if it's just sponged-on black paint.

"Mẹ and Ba are disappointed, con," he starts. "We didn't think we would raise a daughter who would lie to us so much. Lie and think we wouldn't figure it out."

I bite my lip, thinking of how I tried to argue with Mẹ and how poorly that turned out.

"It is not just that: disappointment. You hurt us." I shift in my seat now, unaccustomed to hearing that word from him. Come to think of it, I'm not sure I've ever heard it said here. The concept is unfathomable—how could Ba be hurt? He's always so forceful, so set in his ways. One of those Roman marble sculptures that miraculously never chip.

I whisper at his pause. "I'm sorry." I repeat it in Vietnamese, though it doesn't seem to register with him because he says right away:

"But a part of me wonders. Ba and Mẹ should have noticed more why you were acting strangely. Noticed that you looked . . . sadder than we are used to. I noticed that right here, in this kitchen that night." He gestures to the spot where I'd been. He leans forward. "*Ba không muốn con be sad.*"

I don't want you to be sad.

"But you are happy here." It's then that I notice Ba had something in his other hand. A clipping of a newsletter, the kind that businesses pass around door to door, and it had the photo of me and Bảo that someone had texted. Was that only two weeks ago? The Linh there is proud, proud of herself, and also happy in Bảo's arms as they look on at the mural, her work, her art. Ba's right. I was happy.

But why is he showing this to me now? Will he say something

about Bảo? There's no denying what we are in this pic. Instead, he seems to be ignoring him, literally putting him out of the picture.

"We want you to be happy, but we don't want you to suffer."

"Like Dì Vàng," I whisper, recalling my mom's words repeated over and over.

He shakes his head. "Like we did. *Khi Ba tới nước này,*" he starts, before switching to English. "When I came here, my English was not good. Still isn't good. But back in Vietnam, I could stand in front of a classroom and speak without fear. My teachers told me I would be a great businessman. That I would make everyone broke because everyone would want to buy whatever I sold!" He smiles at the memory, proud. "After escaping, after coming here, I wanted to try that. I wanted to try marketing and advertising because it was something I loved to do, and before you were born, I went to school for it."

A thought tickles my brain, and I go searching for it, finding it in a few seconds. In the box of photos, there was one showing Ba in a classroom. Maybe it was from that time? I knew Ba didn't have a degree, but I didn't know that he tried for it.

"But because of my English, I sounded unpolished in presentations. I couldn't speak to even my classmates. It was hard, and I started to hate it. I started to hate doing what I loved to do, which I never thought would happen.

"I know other people could have moved on despite this. Your mother is someone who would, because she is strong. I wasn't. And then Evelyn was born. And then you were born, and there was no more time for school. We had too much to worry about. We had to survive."

I reach for his hand. A strange sense of understanding comes over me. He went after what he loved to do and couldn't do it, or finish it, as hard as he tried. But that didn't mean he was a failure.

"You can go back to school. There's time."

Ba waves away the suggestion. "I am happy at the restaurant now. In a way, I still do marketing and advertising." Like the phở specials and how every time a new customer comes in he flashes his smile, his charisma. "But I am scared for you, con." Another word I don't often hear from Ba. "Art will be a hard life."

I hold my breath.

Will. He might not know the significance—maybe he *does*—but this is the first time I heard it as a possibility.

I grab on to it, squeezing his hand. "Ba, I know it will always be hard. But I *can* do this. I *am* doing this, now." I remember his words before, about how other people might have continued, unlike him. "Don't you think I'm *strong enough*?"

"Of course con strong. You are Linh Mai," he answers quickly.

I smile faintly. "I want to do this. I *can* do this. I know I can. Because I have you and . . . Mẹ. You guys did the surviving for me and Evie," I say, bringing up his words from before. I wonder if Mẹ feels this way as well, and maybe that is why she's never seen art as a path for me. She is scared, too, her own history tinged with so many struggles in Vietnam and after. It might be with her forever.

I know if I close my eyes now, I will see Mẹ, in this kitchen, tears in her eyes. I see her at my age, when she came here, when she didn't have what I have now, which is opportunity. All because of them.

"Ba, all the struggles that you went through. You've surpassed them. Now you just deserve to live."

Ba glances at the table, blinking. Holding back tears. I've never seen him cry, and I don't think I will, but to see him this close unleashes my tears. I fall apart; I understand, now, just a bit more of what he's gone through, mourning his life that he never got to really have. He's tired. We sit there, hand in hand for a few minutes, until I feel Ba's squeeze.

"Does it really make you happy? Painting?"

"Yes."

"Are you *sure* you don't want to do engineering?" he asks.

I laugh now, shaking my head so that my tears fall to the table. "Definitely sure."

"*Thôi,*" he says after clearing his throat. His voice is gruff. "*Đừng khóc nữa. Rửa mặt đi, xong xuống ăn cơm.*"

I laugh. *Wash your face.* The Vietnamese dismissal that I got as a child whenever I'd cry after getting yelled at. I rush down the hall to the bathroom, splash cold water on my face, and glance into the mirror. The redness is still there, but I feel different.

For the first time in weeks, I'm a bit lighter.

I return to the kitchen to a bowl now full with fluffy rice, *nước mắm,* and a bowl of *canh bí* between us. I scoop a spoonful, tasting it. "No salt."

Ba tsks his tongue. "You try cooking it, and we'll see how well you do."

Our chopsticks hit the insides of our bowls, us eating our meal quietly, comfortably, even. When Ba finishes his first bowl, he sets it down.

"That boy across the street from us. The one who wrote the article that everyone is talking about." Ba points to the photo with his chopsticks. "So you do know him."

I take a large gulp, hoping that we're not going to head into another argument, because that would break me. I nod.

"Is he your friend?"

Another nod.

"Bạn trai?"

Boyfriend. Not anymore. I'd hurt him. The urge to cry comes back, the corners of my eyes prickling. It's not only Mom I'll need to apologize to, but also Bảo. "We . . . we haven't seen each other in a while. And I'm not sure if we will again."

"Okay," he answers simply. Perhaps remembering that it is Mẹ I would talk to more often than Ba, he merely returns to his meal. A part of me wonders if he's realized that he's never showed me this much emotion, so he may be reaching his limit in one night.

I still miss him.

As mean as I was to him, as hurtful as my words were—even if I didn't mean it—he still wrote that article defending us, our community, including my family.

Linh, you really messed things up.

Things at home are not much better, but not worse. A plan came just at dawn, at breakfast, watching my mom cut coupons and my dad read the crime section of the paper. Ba has been trying to cool Mẹ down, smooth things over between us, but my mom's stubborn.

Every cold shoulder, every glance past me, hurts me more than I realize. Maybe I can't fix that right away. I did lie to her. But there's something else I can try fixing now, and maybe some good will come out of it.

I stop just before the front facade of Bảo's restaurant. Suddenly the alley door opens; a mop of black hair appears—and it's Việt. I freeze in my steps, and he does the same. Unsure of his reaction—if he'll just ignore me—I feel relief coursing through me when Việt speaks to me.

"You saw the article?"

"I did. It was great. I'm really proud of him."

"Does he know that?"

Both of us know that we haven't spoken since that day in the art room.

"I'm gonna be blunt, Linh. You're a friend now, you know." How matter-of-factly he says this, and I almost start crying. Unbelievably, Bảo's weird best friend has also become someone I can trust, too. And he's still speaking to me. "So I'm saying this as a friend to a friend. If you don't really like Bảo anymore and you don't want to date him, I'm okay with what you did." Every bit of me wants to scream *NO*. "But if you did it because you're scared or something . . . don't you think Bảo's feeling the same way? I mean, he knows that everything is stacked against you two."

"I'm sorry."

"You know he did all of this for you." In typical Việt fashion, he only shrugs. "Ultimately, it's between you and him. If you choose to end the relationship, just do it the right way."

He expects me to agree, to let him go.

"Is that what you want?"

I don't move. That's the last thing I want to do, but I don't say that. Instead, I ask, "Is Bảo's mom inside?"

Something lets up in his eyes. And he nods, as if saying, *Good choice.*

I wince at the jolting ring of the front door bell. The sun hits the wall differently, revealing even more of its imperfections—cracks in certain places, discoloration under constant sunlight. Bảo has said that wall was always an eyesore. My eyes drift from the wall to the front desk, where Bảo's mother stands and stares at me, her glasses at the end of her nose. It isn't as severe as I expected, but I still take a deep breath.

Her reaction is strange, like she's seeing something I can't. Maybe there was something else there, but it disappears in a moment and she's emerging from behind the front desk. Will she make me leave?

"You're one of their daughters. You're a Mai."

"Dạ, chào cô. Tên con là Linh." I figure answering in Vietnamese might be polite. I suppose it works, since she just nods. Waits for me to take the lead.

I switch to English. "I saw what Bảo wrote in the paper." I point to the frame on the wall. "It was really nice of him to defend our community."

"It was good, yes."

"He's so good at writing. I'm sure you're proud of him."

"And you know he writes?"

"We're friends. We'd never spoken to each other before until this year and we've become . . . close."

"Friends." Her eyes widen like someone learning what it means for the first time.

"Yes." *There, that's out in the open.*

"Anyway, what he did meant a lot. That he'd write something nice about our family. I don't . . . pretend to know what happened. To make you hate us"—I rush through my words when I see her open her mouth—"and I know I'm not a part of it, and that's fine and all. I don't think my parents would even want me here."

I breathe out. "But they were glad to have someone defend them. It meant a lot. So . . . thank you." I take a step forward, but Bảo's mother doesn't back away or anything. I unroll the paper I'd worked on, slowly. I feel her gaze on me, taking stock of me, unsure why I'm even here. "It was so nice of Bảo, especially since . . ." I gulp—no need to give her another reason to kick me out.

It feels like a weird dream being here. It's just me and her. Like me and Bảo, we've existed in the same place, a few feet away, and now we're here in front of each other.

I glance at the wall that Bảo had brought up in some of our conversations. "I want to do something for you. You see, I'm a painter."

"An artist?" she asks numbly.

I tilt my head, not expecting that reaction. It sounds like she's in disbelief. "Yes, that's kind of how me and Bảo first started working together. And I had a vision for this wall. It's beautiful as it is, with all the photos, but I wonder—" I bite my lip before unfurling the paper fully.

Essentially it's a mural I'm proposing. One of Nha Trang from a bird's-eye view. The waters, the streets crowded with motorcycles. An ode to where they'd come from. They'd keep the picture frames, but it'd be like the faces in the landscape. A nice reminder of the past—even though it wasn't all that nice. As I gesture to different parts of the mural, I'm hyperaware of her hands, slightly pink like they were just washed under warm water.

"I'd like to do it for you one day."

"Why?" she asks, incredulous.

"Bảo told me the next thing you wanted for the restaurant was a new wall." My voice trembles. "He really loves you. You're his mom." Now I'm just babbling, so I summon my remaining courage. "I want to apologize to Bảo, but I don't know how. He's the most honest person out there, more honest than me. Because he cares. Because he's special. He means a lot to me." I break off before I start to get too emotional. I put on a brave face, starting to back away. "Anyway, thank you for your time. And please let me know if I can help in the future."

"Why don't you tell him all of this yourself?"

I smile sadly. "Because he was right: I'm still scared."

CHAPTER FORTY-FIVE

BẢO

The door rings in the next customer and I say hello without looking, counting a customer's change before handing it over. "Thanks for coming by." Plastering another smile on my face, I focus on the newcomer, only to realize it's not a regular customer.

It's Linh's father. Years of spotting him by the window looking out at us, of his profile just before disappearing into his store, tells me it's him. He stands with his arms crossed behind his back—Vietnamese style. I instantly sense disapproval from him—as if Vietnamese fathers underwent the same aura training before having children—but it's more of a gut reaction than anything else.

"*Tên con là Bảo?*"

"Dạ. Chào, Bác."

He nods. Probably noticing how atrocious my Vietnamese is but accepting my attempt, at least. His eyes sweep the room, and my mom's panicked voice sounds choked up inside my brain, *Why is he here?!*

He switches over to English. "Your article is very good." He holds out the latest edition of *Người Việt* where it's folded to show my op-ed. "And you defended us well."

Us.

"Are you a writer?" he asks.

If I answered *I think so*, he'd probably think even less of me. "Yes, I am. I'm thinking of doing it in college."

He shakes the newspaper at me—not in a threatening way, thank God. "I think it would be very good for you."

"Th-thank you," I manage to get out.

Again the silence falls heavily and I try not to squirm under his scrutiny. I wonder if he knows I was seeing Linh before everything blew up.

"You are Linh's friend."

It's not going to stop just because of the argument. At least, I hope. "I am . . . Do you want to talk to my parents or . . ."

His face changes. "No, no." He shakes his head. "Don't let them know I was here." A corner of his lips turns up. "I'll get in trouble."

Ah, the terror of Vietnamese wives. I just nod and wave as Linh's father backs out, hurrying across the street so quickly that I must have hallucinated his entire visit. I don't know how long I stand there, watching the restaurant across from us, mirroring my dad's own surveillance stance. Is it possible that my article managed to bridge some gap? Can forgiveness be born from this?

I dip my hand into my back pocket, brushing up against the folded-up flyer for the Art Fair. I hold on to it as I cross the street.

CHAPTER FORTY-SIX

LINH

I snuck out for the Art Fair. No, that wasn't exactly it. My parents had to have known I was leaving. I made noise walking down the hallway, made sure my keys jangled loud enough, before shutting the door. All done to see if they would say anything. But there was nothing. Them not monitoring where I'm going is so much worse.

The auditorium isn't filled to capacity like it is for sports events, but when I walk in, I'm surprised by the number of people here for the Art Fair. But farther in the back, ribboned off—dramatic!— is my display. I see some other classmates, like Eric and Spencer, exhibiting their art.

Spending so much time nose-to-canvas, obsessing over the littlest details, I forget to see the whole picture. I forget what everything looks like when it's all put together. And now, easel set up like this, I feel like I can see a story.

I did all of this. Everything here I can call mine. Despite being alone tonight, I'm latching on to this.

I don't think I've ever smiled so much. As I wait for people to come by, I reread my statement. I had Ali look at it, but what I really wanted was for Bảo to see it. He was always good at things like that. But it's my fault that I can't, I know that. I pushed him away, hurt him. And now I'm paying for it.

The compliments are nice and heart-warming, but temporary. My smile fades once each exhibitor leaves my display. I watch a classmate and his parents pose for some pictures. His dads look so proud of him. I turn around, fighting back a burning sensation in the back of my eyes. I wish Mẹ and Ba could be here, but I couldn't bring myself to mention the fair, even if Ba is starting to come around to my art. I wish I could have told the truth from the very beginning. Maybe then they'd be proud enough to be here, just this one time, for me.

Soon enough, the Art Fair crowd has dwindled, people are leaving, and some other artists are already taking down their canvases, to store here or bring home.

"Linh!" I see Ali's curly hair before her face. She squeezes me to death, rambling about how proud she is of me. "Total masterpieces! How are you feeling?"

She'll be worried if I answer honestly: that I feel alone and I can't seem to stop it, even if everyone's responding well to my artwork. The people whose opinions matter the most . . . just aren't here.

Offering me some comfort, whether she knows it or not, Yamamoto quickly passes by, squeezing me tight, whispering about how proud she is of me. That if I don't get the Gold Key scholarship, she'll visit their headquarters, wherever they are, and protest.

I force a smile, which fades as I spot *him*.

I think I say hello or some version of it, right as he does the same. He's stumbling over his words now before he finally stops himself, fixated on the floor. Will it be like this from now on?

"You look nice. Professional," I offer.

"I needed to impress someone." A smile plays on his lips. My heart leaps at his answer but I try not to show it, waiting. Then I notice the bouquet that he's offering me sheepishly. "I heard about your mural idea. My mom told me."

I accept the flowers. "She was really shocked when I came by."

"She could barely speak. That's not a common thing." He pauses before turning to my paintings. "So, tell me about them."

He's not walking away. He's here and his presence gives me a small semblance of hope. In this moment, it's enough. I slip my hand into his, relishing in his warmth, and pull him toward my work. The earliest of them depicts a common scene from my childhood, me waiting for my parents to finish prepping for the next day. I painted my ten-year-old self into a booth, preoccupied with blowing bubbles into my water. Mẹ has popped her head out from the serving window and is likely trying to talk to Ba, who's at the front desk.

I show them my family restaurant's facade, that night Phở Day ended with a success. I tried to infuse the contentment I felt at seeing Mẹ's face through the yellow haze of the streetlights shining down, the glistening of puddles left from the storm.

I lead Bảo to my painting of the art room the first time he visited me. An idyllic scene, the afternoon light streaming from the window, touching the desks and stools, and my back as I faced the canvas. I painted in Bảo's backpack and a hint of his shoes peeking out as one table blocked the view of his body.

These memories grew out of me over time and in the last few weeks. The act of painting them is now a blur; I was so focused on my canvas that I barely kept track of time. Maybe because I'd never desired more to escape. Seeing my paintings now, displayed like this, is somewhat of an out-of-body experience, but it's also hollow. I wish my parents could see them, too, see how much my art and my life with them, here, are so deeply intertwined that it's no longer about trying to undo these ties.

The concept of me being an artist *without* them doesn't exist.

I peek at Bảo's reaction as he leans forward to study the details of the art room. He still hasn't let go. I realize that my hands, despite the hard scrubbing, still show residues of paint. But the sight of it against his clean skin is comforting. Normal.

"I thought I knew what you were capable of, but this is beyond that. I don't think I can pick a favorite. I love all of it." He's looking at me now, and perhaps it's foolish hope that makes me spot a familiar wistful gleam in his eyes. The kind he'd send me before bringing me in for a kiss, before brushing aside a strand of my hair.

And I know I should just say it. "I'm sorry, Bảo. More sorry than I can ever express. The mural was just one attempt to try to make up for what I said."

"Linh, you don't have to—"

"Your article was honest—the exact opposite of the way I'd been acting. I was scared of telling my parents the truth. So I lied, and those lies just kept piling up. I hurt you. I hurt them, and now—this, while it's all that I can ever dream of—it just feels empty." I gesture to the paintings behind me, with colors and emotions that were painted, in a way, for them. "I can't really celebrate because I hurt so many people to get here."

He stops trying to protest, bringing his arms around me. I don't understand how much I needed his full touch until my nose is pressed up against his shoulders and comforted by his familiar scent. "I was hurting. I didn't know how to deal with all the secrets coming up. But I lied to you, Bảo. I want us. I've always wanted us."

"I think I knew that. At least, I hoped what I was thinking was right." He leans back slightly to catch my eye, his thumb caressing my cheek.

"Thank you for being brave, Bảo Nguyễn."

"Ahem."

Ali, surprising me, hugs the two of us from behind. "Finally, Romeo and Juliet are back together. I thought you'd be mad at me for letting him see you."

"Letting me?" Bảo asks, but Ali ignores him.

"But I have to admit, these past few weeks have brought me and this guy closer. If we paired together, we could really change the newspaper-making business."

I hold back a laugh at Bảo's grimace, which Ali can't see since she's facing away from him. Yet that laughter turns into confusion when she asks him, "Are they outside?"

"I was getting there." He's almost . . . shy? "Linh, I know there are important people you want to be here, who are missing here. But they're not, not right now." Bảo tilts his head, gestures to the exit. "They're outside."

"What—" *They?*

Who . . . ?

I leave a trail of flower petals as I dash out of the auditorium, down the long streak of hallway with loitering parents and younger siblings amusing themselves with whatever they can touch. I find my aunt at the very end of it, alone. She welcomes me with a smile.

"Dì Vàng!" I fly into her arms and she returns my hug with a deep chuckle. Her shoulder purse slides off and falls to the ground.

"Surprised?"

"Shocked. How—"

"Well, I was always planning to come. The thing about visiting a friend—that was a lie. I wanted to surprise you." She looks at a point over my shoulder. When I follow her gaze, I don't see anyone. I pivot, confused. "That was him, wasn't it?"

Not finding the right words, I merely nod.

"He's the spitting image of his uncle." She says this lightly, but there's a whole story behind her eyes. What she'd already told me was likely only half of it.

She shakes the look away and pushes me gently out of her arms. She steers me to face the exit. "What—"

"Go. Some important people are waiting just outside for you. I'll meet you back inside. Apparently there's a superstar who's displayed her work here. Be the brave, honest person that I know you are."

My steps outside are far more hesitant. The scent of cigarettes clings to the cool air. They've dressed up. My dad with his polo neatly tucked into his belted dress pants. He stands with his back to me, arms crossed behind him, head tipped back like he's watching for a sign from the sky. Next to him is my mom, always favoring softer floral patterns, in a red-and-white knee-length dress that I've never seen her wear.

It's possible that she bought it just for tonight's exhibition— and the thought makes me hopeful.

"Ba. Mẹ." I clutch the flowers to my chest. They're ruined by now. "I didn't think you'd come." My steps toward them seem unusually disruptive and it's only because my parents are so quiet and still. Such lifelike statues.

"We didn't know this was happening until today. Con didn't say anything directly." Accusation rings clear in her voice.

"So how did you know to be here?"

"Someone slipped a flyer under our door," Ba explains evenly.

Someone. "Ali?"

"Maybe," Ba says. He stares unblinkingly, but doesn't say anything. Now's the time he's going to try for subtle? What could he . . . ?

Bảo.

So that's what his smile was for.

"After what happened, I knew you wouldn't want to come."

"Con knew? How could con know that?" Mẹ fires back. The red in her dress seems to take on a life of its own, a fire in the night. Ba interrupts her, telling her in Vietnamese to lower her voice. He's playing the opposite role today; his eyes beseech me, reminding me of when I cried and cried. He's on my side, but he can't do much if I don't explain myself.

If I don't finally tell the truth about myself.

"Mẹ, I don't want to lie to you anymore. And I know I've lied. About what I wanted. About my art. About Bảo, too, and our . . . friendship. At the time, I thought all of this was necessary."

My voice cracks. "I'm a painter. And I really love what I do. Nothing makes me happier. When everything in the world seems tough and harsh, painting's where I go. It's like you and your cooking, Mẹ. Don't you ever feel like you can disappear in it?"

Mẹ folds her arms, and keeps her eyes fixed to the ground.

"I still wanted to make you proud and show that everything I was doing was *because* of you, not despite you."

"There are other ways to make Ba Mẹ proud. Above everything, you should not lie to us."

"But I didn't mean it like that. Mẹ, please. I draw *because* of you. Because you've always tried your best to raise me right. Because you work so hard, never find time for yourself, so I'm doing this for you, for both of you. Everything you're doing has allowed me to be happy. I wish you had that when you were younger. You worked so hard, you gave everything of yourself away just so that I could have a good life. And I believe that. I have a good life. I have a happy one."

"Please. I want to show you what I mean. Can I show you?" I hold her hand. The fact that she doesn't pull away encourages me.

I lead her back into the school like I did at Huntington Beach, that time we saw my first real artist. It wasn't just because I wanted to see; it was because I wanted my mom to see it too.

Distantly, I hear Yamamoto greeting my parents. I don't eavesdrop, but I stand aside and observe their faces. A bit of confusion. A bit of disbelief. They must be overwhelmed because it's not just Yamamoto gravitating toward them; it's other parents whose kids also displayed their work.

What surprises me more, though, is the quiet awe burgeoning in their eyes, a reaction they would have to my pieces from elementary school art classes.

Taking my mom's hand again, I point to a scene that I hadn't shown Bảo yet, hadn't gotten to. I painted it because I was remembering how much simpler life was a few months ago.

It's a nine-by-eleven-inch piece depicting the hours following our first special: the three of us celebrating in the kitchen. It might have been dark outside, but inside the kitchen, under the bright ceiling lights, we were exhausted and hopeful. My mom bends closer to the canvas. I hope she sees the look in her eyes that I tried to capture, that tired contentedness. I hope she sees me leaning against her, shoulder to shoulder. And I hope she sees my dad and how tall he sits. Most of all, I want her to see how the three of us are together, a family. We are strongest only together.

"I really love this one," Yamamoto remarks, standing just behind me. I spot my mom squinting at the tattoos along her arms, more curious than horrified.

"Why?" my dad finally asks.

"Because I've come to know Linh over the years, Mr. Mai and Mrs. Phạm. I've seen how much she cares about what you think. But I've also seen how present and alive she is through her art— probably more than she realizes. And just a few minutes ago, watching you walk into the auditorium, I saw how Linh lights up knowing that you're here to support her." Bảo's right; my expressions give me away. "All of this"—she gestures to the paintings—"this is Linh and what she values the most. In one exhibition."

"Being an artist . . . it's hard," Mẹ says slowly. I wonder if she's cautious to voice this opinion in front of a teacher.

"Oh, it is. You know it is. And from my brief conversation with your sister"—Yamamoto tips her head at my aunt, who's mingling with people at the opposite side of the room—"she knows, too. But in anything you love, isn't there always some bit of sadness, some essence of suffering? That, to me, is what makes art worth it. Suffer through it—mine the emotions you keep inside yourself, face whatever's emotionally burdensome, take control of it—then emerge reborn in the end."

She speaks directly to me. "This is what Linh is doing. It's such an honor to be her teacher. I hope you know that Linh's one of a kind."

◇ ◇ ◇

Yamamoto squeezes my arm, before drifting back into the crowd, like a kind spirit. Other classmates and their parents surround me and for the first time tonight, I bask in their warm glow. I keep an eye on my parents simultaneously. They're walking around, peering at other artwork. My aunt soon joins them and points at certain canvases and sculptures, perhaps explaining the different media. Ali's been going around the room interviewing other artists, explaining that she couldn't show bias in her reporting. Bảo, though, seems to have disappeared, understanding that I needed more time with my parents.

The auditorium clears out and only five or six families linger. My parents rejoin me along with my aunt, and all I can do is follow them as they wordlessly head back out into the hallway. Our footsteps squeak and echo into the empty space. I'm sandwiched between my aunt and my mom. I'm struck by the need to clutch Mẹ's hand again.

Mẹ's voice startles me from my thoughts. "From now on, con can't tell more lies. *Đừng nói láo nữa nghe không?*"

I nod, promising that there won't be any more lies between us.

"Art is what you want? It makes you happy?"

Ba had asked the same question.

"The happiest, Mẹ."

We walk some more, now standing in the parking lot. The faint smell of grass, barbeque smoke, and asphalt surrounds us. "Mẹ *còn* mad at you," Mẹ answers calmly.

"I know. But I promise, I won't—"

379

In a split second, I'm crushed against my mother. Her arms leave no room for escape. "You know you are my life, con," Mẹ whispers fiercely into my hair.

I blink away tears, my head buried in her shoulder. I feel Ba patting my back, and my mind flashes back to a younger me, a sleepy me, who's carried up to bed by my parents.

"Don't cry," Dì Vàng says, happiness pure in her voice.

I'm not sure which one of us she is talking to.

In the car, as we're pulling out of the lot, Mẹ reaches back with her hand. I grasp, asking whose hand it is.

"What a silly game," my aunt mutters with a smile. My mom and I grin at each other through the mirror.

My family spends the rest of the ride bashing other artists, even though I think they're all great. Dad called them "*dở quá.*"

"So how much better am I as an artist?" I tease Ba.

And his answer surprises me in the best way possible, as he sends me a big, fat smile in the rearview mirror.

"*Một trăm* percent."

CHAPTER FORTY-SEVEN

BẢO

Tết in Little Saigon means tons of road closures. The few police officers who didn't grow up around here look befuddled by our penchant for bouncy music, performances from dojos, and bedazzled floats filled with flowers—lots of them. The American flag and South Vietnamese flag hang along light poles.

The air is filled with the smell of fried sweets—bananas, I think—and the crowd ranges from young to old. Little kids run along, some struggling in their bright silky *áo dài*, followed by a parent looking stressed out and clutching their child's mini *khăn đóng*. But the hate of hats is universal in kids their age. Old dads try locating their wives, who've abandoned them for friends; today's their day off. I sputter when some stray balloons collide with my face. A sunshine-y version of "*Xuân đã về*," celebrating the arrival of spring, blasts from a float made out of straw. Miss Teen Vietnam, California, sits perched at the front, waving prettily from it. People holler from the crowd.

"Look at how skinny she is," Mom mutters, clutching her purse to herself. She then nastily eyes a pack of girls who inadvertently pushed her to take pictures of the passing float. As much as she hates crowds, she always makes a point of attending the celebrations. I think it reminds her of her childhood. And she always manages to run into some Vietnamese friends.

The cash prize is the other draw, ranging from five hundred to five grand. "How else will we pay for college?" Ba replied when I asked why we entered with little chance to win.

Scarily, there was no joke in his tone whatsoever.

The usual float from Vietnam America TV 57.3 passes. Another float comes by, some local florist shop, and they're launching bouquets into the crowds. Mẹ smacks my dad on the shoulder. "Look at the flowers!"

Lo and behold, she isn't the only middle-aged Asian oohing and ahhing at the flowers being thrown to the crowd. With swiftness that surprises me, my mom jumps to grab a bunch, holding them over her head victoriously. Ba makes some joke, though I can tell he's proud of her.

Just then, I see the familiar swish of hair across the street, standing behind the fence. Linh. She leans over, peering for the next float to come by, and she's smiling. That's my girlfriend across the street.

A real girlfriend. *As opposed to . . .?* says a voice strangely like Việt's in my head.

Could she be more beautiful? This time, she's tied her hair in a side braid and is clapping along to the music.

Linh is with her parents and another woman who must be her aunt. She has long hair just like Linh. She mentioned she was visiting. I push my way up to the front, earning some elbow jabs along the way, but I can't help but feel as if something is pulling me toward her. I wave my arms wide, yell out her name.

She notices.

What are you doing? her panicked eyes seem to say.

There's nothing to be scared of anymore! Our parents know we're seeing each other, I say back with my eyes. When nothing changes in her expression, I realize that we haven't mastered telepathy just yet. Behind me, I hear my parents calling my name, confused.

The crowd is so ferocious that it crushes me against the fence. Linh still looks scared. At this point, neither her parents or her aunt have noticed me . . . but then she does. The aunt, at least. Her face goes slack, stopping me in my tracks. I've never seen anyone turn white that quickly, but why at me? But her eyes don't lock on me; they slide right past me . . . zooming in on my parents, who, I turn and realize, froze in the middle as well.

It's like the meeting at the Buddha temple again.

Then something weird happens. Linh's aunt turns . . .

And runs.

CHAPTER FORTY-EIGHT

LINH

I never expected Bảo to be at my doorstep.

Or that he'd be able to come into the house at all. But that's what's happening now. He's sitting next to me in the living room, as if we do this every week.

"You okay?" he asks, tucking a hair strand behind my ear, which makes me panic. My eyes go to my dad, who's sitting in his usual chair; he keeps shooting us inquisitive glances, but if he disapproves of our proximity, he doesn't say much. My mother, who let Bảo inside in the first place, is more preoccupied with my aunt, who, upon returning from the parade, walked straight into the master bedroom, locking the door. Not answering anyone, even my mother as she pleads for her to come out.

"What's happening? Are you okay?" she asks through the door.

The bedroom door creeps open and we all stand when my aunt appears, red-eyed but otherwise composed.

"Sorry, I needed to collect myself." Her eyes sweep the room before landing on Bảo, the only one who doesn't belong. Seconds pass, the silence grows disconcerting. "I saw you at the fair, but to see you in the daylight like that . . . you really do look like your uncle."

"So I've been told."

"How much do you know?"

I speak for myself and Bảo, explaining how Bác had told me about our families knowing each other back in Vietnam. About the photo I found, which was when Bảo sheepishly recounted his story about what his mother said—not the accusation—but the distress that she expressed when she found out we knew each other.

Mẹ sits silently, nervously, as Ba stands by the living room window, watching us.

My aunt turns back to Mẹ. "I already knew they were here."

"How?"

"Does it matter?" my aunt counters. "Now why didn't you tell me all of this?"

"I didn't want to hurt you again. I didn't want to bring up memories that were meant to be forgotten."

Dì Vàng shakes her head. "That was a long time ago. I'm an adult now."

"You were in love with him," Mẹ says. "And he left you without a thought. That was his fault. And his family's. And it was all unforgivable."

"Do you know why he left?" my aunt asks sharply. "He was to inherit the family business."

"That's a reason to celebrate, not abandon you. He should have been taking care of you."

Dì Vàng scoffs, throwing her hands up. "Of course! Because I was destined to be poor just because I'm an artist."

"We all know the struggle. You couldn't just ignore it. It was the reality." My mother looks to me now, only this isn't about me. "Our parents were just doing their part and looking out for you."

"But I'm here. And I'm fine, you didn't need to protect me. You don't have to."

"You're lying to yourself. I knew you were sad after he left. And I could barely speak to his family after that. How could I? When they were the ones who drove him away, convinced him of a better match."

"They're not to blame at all," Dì Vàng says.

"How? How do you know?" Mẹ demands. My dad mutters something; I suspect it's to tell her to calm down, but he's silenced with a withering glance.

"Because I was the one to tell him to leave."

The puzzle dislodges again, my understanding of this very weird situation disappearing in a millisecond. My eyes move between my mom and Dì Vàng, a staring contest in play, both willing the other to speak first. Ba sits silently, arms crossed, his expression emotionless.

"What?" my mom whispers.

"What no one knows, no one but me and Bảo's uncle, is that we were never together."

"*Gì? Nói lại,*" my mother says, confused.

"We were a distraction. He liked Huyền."

"Huyền?" Mẹ looked away, a hardened version scoffing at the name. Now I wonder what that woman did to get on my mother's bad side.

"Yes, Huyền."

"Who was she?" I ask.

"Neighborhood girl," Dì Vàng explains quickly. "But her family was poorer than both of ours and Cam's family would have never approved of the match."

"Hmm," my mom mutters dismissively. "Because they were prejudiced." Bảo stiffens beside me. First time over and he's indirectly insulted by my mother.

"I could say the same about ours," my aunt retorts, her tone severe enough to rival my mom's. "Financial security, wasn't it? Ultimately that's why our parents approved of us so much.

"But Cam was my best friend. And he loved my other friend, so I pretended that I was seeing him whenever we left the neighborhood, but I was really bringing him to see Huyền." Once the last words leave her, her secret finally released, she sits down. She touches her necklace in thought. "Then the whole engagement happened and we were swept up with family expectations, trying to make things work out.

"Remember, Huyền had to leave because her parents fled first. And then he was so sad. I couldn't get a word out of him. I couldn't make him happy, even as his best friend. So I told him to go after her. Life was already miserable back home because of Viet Cong, you know that. Having a broken heart as well?" My aunt shakes her head. "So I told him to go. Find her wherever she is and tell her the truth. Start a new life together."

She exhales shakily. "I didn't think he would lose his life along the way."

I look over at Bảo, his mouth slightly opened at the revelations emerging in our living room. He'd been in the dark just like I was, and now things are just beginning to make sense. These decades of blame from our families manifesting in what we thought was just a silly competition.

"That can't be true," Mẹ says.

"It is."

"Why didn't you say anything?"

"How would I even *begin* to explain myself? It was, to everyone, a perfect match. Mẹ and Ba"—hearing my aunt mention her parents makes her sound young again—"it was something they were happy about too."

"But Cam's family—they blame you. Don't you remember how angry you were at each other? The yelling that happened. His sister said horrible things."

"She'd lost her brother."

"Still! They shouldn't have said you were heartless. Worthless."

Is that when things went sour? I remember my mom's reaction when she saw the picture of me and Bảo. Her anger overpowered me, overpowered any logic. I can only imagine the ugly words that flew between our families.

"My family doesn't know the truth, do they?" Bảo asks. Mẹ's eyes fly to him, widening before narrowing, as if she's just realized who she actually let in. "That's why they're still angry at your family."

"The things that were said were hurtful. But they didn't hurt me. *They* were hurt. They'd just lost a son. A brother." She turns to my parents. "If you lost me, wouldn't you react the same way, look for someone to blame?

"There's only so much anger you can hold. But I'm hopeful, because here are Linh and Bảo, willing to move past this."

"Bảo's great," I say. "And his family cares about him just as much as you care about me."

He squeezes my hand, a smile playing on his lips. This time I don't blush; I'm bolstered by his silent agreement. "When a bunch of racists hounded our place and nearly everywhere else in Bolsa, he wrote an article, for all of us. Because it's right."

My aunt appraises him and, based on her smile, seems to think more of him. "He wrote what he thought was best. He didn't let a little history get in the way of what's right."

Bảo shifts in his seat. "What if you spoke to my family?"

My mom sits up straight. "What? No, no, no, it's too much. I don't want to see them. It's . . . too much has happened."

"All because I held back the truth for years. And now look at what happened. I have to take the blame for that. We're going," my aunt says.

"But—"

My aunt turns to me, then brings her gaze up to Bảo. "Call your parents."

Even though he suggested it, his Adam's apple nervously bobs as he nods.

CHAPTER FORTY-NINE

BẢO

My mom paces the restaurant, nervously smoothing out her dress, the same one she wore for our on-camera interview. She's pretending to mutter to herself—meaning, very out loud at me and Ba—about how Linh's family has the nerve to come over uninvited, like uncultured swine.

Never mind the fact that Linh's family called to explain their visit.

Or that I told them Linh's aunt would be here too.

Or that the time was one that my mom decided.

Not knowing what to do with myself, I join my father in the kitchen, where he uses a ladle to pour *chanh muối*—salty limeade—

from a large jar into six drinking glasses. Limes are packed tightly for months, then finished off with a bit of sugar, water, and ice. I find myself salivating; I haven't had it since I was little.

Ba looks up briefly, finishing the last glass. "They made the best lemon tea. Linh's grandmother. After school, we would all go to her grandmother's house for a glass. It was refreshing."

"Oh," I say, unsure how to respond to the comment, a memory about the other family, whom they'd hated for so long, shared so willingly. I'm saved from answering as he gestures for me to bring the glasses out and place them on the table.

The light falls on our family's black-and-white photos, which have watched over me as long as memory serves me. The sight of them sends me some hope. Whatever happens today, they will be our witnesses.

As I wait at the front desk, tuning out my mother's dark thoughts, eager for a glimpse of movement outside the windows, I can't help but feel a strange sort of calm, too. An inevitability that started the moment my mother let Linh into the restaurant, despite her family and who she is.

I hold on to the feeling when I see Linh leading her family over. "They're coming."

"So what!" my mom calls out, but she leaves the kitchen, starts fretting with the dishware and silverware.

"How are things over here?" Linh murmurs once inside. We stay back as our families file into the dining room.

"Frickin' weird." I don't take my eyes off our families, together in one place. It's like I'm watching my favorite television show live for the first time: familiar players but unknown outcomes. "I checked my mom for weapons and she's clean."

Linh stifles a laugh, then squeezes my hand before letting go too early. I run my hand down her back in a fleeting gesture of comfort—for the both of us—before focusing on our respective parents in the dining area. My mom saw this interaction, brief shock sparking in her eyes, but says nothing.

She stands stiffly next to Ba

"It's been a while," Linh's mother says.

"It has." My mom nods at Linh's aunt. "I didn't know you were visiting." Her familiar brisk tone has given way to a different sound. I realize then that her voice is wavering.

At Ba's gesture, we all sit at once: three on each side of the booth, with Linh's aunt pulling up a chair at the head. I can't remember how to move my hands, where to put them. Linh throws me a hesitant smile across the table. Her ankle brushes up against mine.

"Are you staying in America for long?" Mẹ asks.

"Yes, only a few weeks. I've been planning on visiting for a while. So far things have been exciting." Linh's aunt keeps her tone light and airy; she's treating this like a regular occurrence.

"And what do you do now over in Vietnam?"

"I'm still an artist. I sculpt. I make jewelry and vases." She reaches into her bag and places down a figurine—a red dragon with yellow spots along its body. My mom doesn't touch it. Ba's the one to take it in hand.

He nods solemnly. "A beautiful dragon." Still he pushes it an inch back to Linh's aunt.

"Don't you know why it's a dragon?"

Here I'm lost and fascinated at once—nameless emotions cloud, then disappear from my mom's face.

Dì Vàng's smile is wry. "Year of the Dragon. Cam's year."

My mom glances down once at the dragon before clearing her throat. "Why is it that you're here?"

"I was surprised to see you at the parade. Linh had mentioned you, but seeing you so abruptly, I ran. I remembered our last encounter. I remembered what we said. And now I think it's time we put this all to bed."

"What is there to say?"

Linh's aunt inhales. "I know you blame me and my family for your brother's death. That you think I somehow hurt him and made him leave the country, and that's how he died. And what I want to say is that I am guilty. But not in the way you think."

My mom leans forward, the chair creaking.

"Before he left, Cam wasn't in love with me. He was in love with someone else."

"Are you saying he was unfaithful?" My mom starts rising from her seat, ready to defend her brother's honor, yet Linh's aunt remains seated, shoulders squared—just like Linh when she has her mind set. Even though we've barely spoken to each other, I'm beginning to like her. This is someone who, long ago, knew how to stand her ground against my mom, a force of nature even though she was younger.

"I'm telling you the truth. My truth. And his."

"It's not his truth, since he is not here."

"He was in love with Huyền. Remember her? The grand-daughter of the woman who always sold fish to the neighborhood on Saturday mornings? The freshest kind! Didn't we all used to admire how neatly she was able to braid her hair?"

My mom's brow is creased. "She told us her grandfather would braid it. Because her grandmother's hands always smelled of fish." She sounds far away, her mind's eye sifting through memories.

"Yes! Huyền. She was a lovely girl. So smart. So beautiful." Linh's aunt pauses. "The only strike against her was that she was poor and her parents had abandoned her.

"Cam and I were close, so I knew of his feelings. I always knew. The whole time, I was the one orchestrating their visits, giving them time to spend with each other while you all thought we were together."

"Why?" my mom breathes.

"Because I did love him. And because I knew he was happy with her."

"But the engagement—why . . . how?" Ba asks.

"Like I told my sister, we were just swept away by it. We couldn't get out of it. I saw that Cam was miserable. But everyone was so stuck in their ways. And so Cam resigned himself to it."

"If he was so resigned—you would have been married," my mom says harshly.

"I told him to go. You know how vocal he was? How miserable he would have been in that country? Even if she hadn't gone, he would have eventually left."

"And he died."

"And that's something I'll never forget. But then I think of it:

Who controls the storm? How can anyone divine the seas?

"Don't you know that I feel the same way? That if I could *make* him love me that would be enough? But that's impossible. You can't control who you love, any more than anyone can control the seas that took him from you. From me." Her voice cracks. "From all of us."

Linh looks at me.

I hold Linh's gaze.

"*Không bao giờ em không nhớ* Cam."

There's not a day that goes by that I don't remember him.

A pause so long that we can hear the kitchen fan rumble and the clock in the back of the room tick away. The air returns, allowing us to move. In this moment, we're all standing on a precipice.

I hold my breath as Linh's aunt reaches over, clasping my mom's hand. She doesn't pull away. "Cam is gone." But she gestures to everyone. "And don't you think he would be even more upset to see how our families turned out in the end? We were once so close.

"We were like family. We suffered together. We celebrated together. To hear what has happened all these years in between— which I only found out because Linh told me—it's just wrong. This . . . rivalry."

My mom raises her chin. "It's natural for restaurants to compete against each other."

"Ours was not natural," Linh's mom interjects.

"What did you expect? Your mother was always the better chef and she was the one to teach you how to cook. Of course I felt intimidated when you arrived on the scene." Never in a million years did I think my mom would admit her recipe was inferior.

"We didn't know you were across from us when we agreed to buy the restaurant from Bác Xuân. We never meant to compete; it was a way to provide for our daughters."

"Who turned out brilliantly," Linh's aunt adds, throwing a proud look at Linh, who tucks a strand of hair behind her ear. I'm briefly distracted by the blush on her cheeks. "And it seems like your son has grown up admirably because of your hard work, too." I scratch the back of my head as Linh playfully kicks me under the table. "We can all agree on that."

She softens her tone. "But isn't always competing with each other tiring? At what point will you have won? Either of you?"

I'm not sure if my parents have ever asked themselves that question. But I know the answer. There is no point to it. There's no winning if all this competition has been masking a war on matters unrelated to the number of customers that come in, the number of bowls sold each day.

By the way my mom sags into her seat, she's probably just reached the same conclusion. Her eyes skirt over to our wall. She might be looking at her brother, having a silent conversation with him.

"Bác Xuân . . . By selling the restaurant to you, I sense he was trying to get us to forgive each other."

"Very unsuccessful," Linh's mom says.

"He was always nosy."

"So nosy."

"*Ông tò mò*," Linh's aunt says, and she turns to her sister. "Wasn't that what our mother always called him?"

"My parents called him much worse names." *Wait. Is my mom hiding a smile? It can't be.* I turn to Linh, who appears just as shocked by what's unfolding now.

"*Thôi, không nói nữa,*" my dad says, his bones creaking as he rolls back his hunched shoulders.

"*Mình làm gì được bây giờ?*" her dad mutters in agreement. *What can we do now?*

Our dads arrive at an agreement first and now it's up to our mothers.

Our parents glance down at the plates, pushing around their food, running out of words.

Dì Vàng takes a sip and winces. "*Chua quá, chị.*" Too sour.

I gulp. This is it. Everything will be derailed.

Then, unbelievably, a full-blown smile appears on her face. "Some things really don't change."

Instead, my mom sniffs in a way that tells me she's not really mad. "Blame your mother. She never wanted to give me her recipe."

Our families have a lot of catching up to do. Their reminiscences continue, pushing me and Linh out of the conversation. But it's fine, because at least everything is out there, finally out there. Sharing one look, we rise from the table, and me and Linh head outside. We find a spot by the curb and sit down—right across from the very spot where we shared our very first laugh.

Linh rests her head on my shoulder. "Is this a dream?"

I laugh before dropping a kiss on her crown. "If it is, let's stay inside it for just a little while longer."

"Do you think everything's going to be okay?"

Linh turns her head to look back at our families and says, "They can't really forget the past, though. With one like theirs it's too impossible. But will they be able to move forward now?" Her gaze lands on me again. "I think so."

I squeeze her hand in agreement.

CHAPTER FIFTY

LINH

The Mais and the Nguyễns will never be the best of friends they once were decades ago. Too much history clouds the waters we share. But at least there are fewer words left unsaid. In a spirit of forgiveness, the Lunar New Year passed with ease.

My mom and Bảo's mom have taken to sharing their home-style recipes, updating each other with each culinary treat they make at home. Sometimes they visit each other at their respective restaurants. My dad and his dad mesh well; if anyone looks closer, it would seem that they were brothers. My aunt now calls Bảo's mom—whether she wants to hear from her or not. Bảo's still trying to figure that out.

I know things will be all right. Because each visit, each moment spent together, each laugh shared repairs what's been broken, like a brush of gesso gently rejuvenating something precious from long ago.

I don't think Chef Lê understood what he was getting into when he invited me and Bảo *and* our families to his restaurant. He apologized profusely, saying he meant to do it right after my mural was unveiled, but his son, Philippe, had gotten sick and there wasn't enough time.

Faced with two strong women with strong opinions on cooking, I almost expect Chef Lê to melt under their interrogation. But of course, he had his own Vietnamese mother to contend with growing up, and he easily deflects the heat. I would even say they are impressed by the kitchen workflow and some of his dishes—maybe even curious to get their hands on his recipes.

In the dining room, I glance across the table, watching Bảo try to fend off his mother's insistence that he needs to eat more rice. My own mother warns me to watch for bones from one of the plates of *cá chiên* sitting at the center of the table, even though I've eaten this kind of fish my entire life. Meanwhile, our respective fathers sit across from each other in companionable silence, preoccupied by their own bowls of rice.

Bảo's hair is still slightly wet. Seeing Chef Lê and Saffron's son across from him, he tries to make the poor kid laugh, but Philippe is completely unamused. Once in a while, from his position on his father's lap, he glances confusedly for help from his mother. He only smiles when Saffron mutters an endearment in French, then crawls into her arms.

Ali had jokingly said that this was the dinner of the century, and I'm sure if I told her where I was going, she'd probably follow. Lately, she's had this ridiculous idea that she'll write a novel about two warring Vietnamese families whose respective son and daughter fall in love. I don't know how she'll do it, but I guess Ali can do anything once she puts her mind to it.

Under the table, I feel Bảo squeeze my hand. We don't quite hide it from our families—us dating, even though "no dating until you're married" is a common refrain from our parents. And when I do leave the house or take a break to visit Bảo at his restaurant, my dad's always saying, "Ah, her *bạn*." Her "friend."

We'll get there . . . like everything else.

Our dinner finally ends and the laughter in our throats—courtesy of Chef Lê's comedic timing—finally settles. Toothpicks are distributed and there is momentary silence as each adult digs into their teeth.

A server sidles up to the table, setting down the bill.

A quiet "Oh shit" slips out from Chef Lê's lips as he remembers *exactly* who's at the table and the accompanying struggle of Vietnamese families fighting over the bill. He mutters about checking on the kitchen and scurries away. Saffron and Philippe soon join him.

"Let me get this," my mom says first, using the tone that commands the line cooks and servers.

A glint appears in Bảo's mom's eyes. "Oh no, let me."

"*Thôi, được rồi*. Please, let me."

Who will win?

I jump when Bảo whispers in my left ear, "Let's get out of here? Before they really kill each other?"

I nod and leave the table. So focused on the bill, our parents don't notice our departure.

Outside, we find ourselves in an alley, a familiar meeting spot for us, I suppose.

"Last time we were in an alley, you almost turned me away," Bảo says.

"Oh really?" I arch an eyebrow.

"Are you going to turn me away again?"

Grinning mischievously, I press him against the wall and plant a loud smack on his lips. We burst out laughing the moment we part. "Smooth." The grin stays on his face. "Linh?"

I sigh, content. "Hmm?"

"You have paint in your hair again."

I really did try to stay clean. I shrug. "So?" I say, challenging him.

He gives no response, a glint appearing in his eyes, and he reaches for me, pulling me to him by the loops of my jeans. His thumb caresses my cheek, and his eyes are soft.

Now we kiss for real.

ACKNOWLEDGMENTS

I have so many people to thank. Ba, I am thankful for your quiet love, comfort, and encouragement. I will always remember your patience as I scoured the bookshelves at the Cheshire Public Library—and later earned too many fines. Mẹ, you are the strongest person I know and I would be lost without you. I've grown to understand your strength and sacrifices more and more. I think my love of storytelling started with you—those nights when you'd tell stories about your childhood, squished between me and Chị An after we'd pushed our beds together.

Ba, Mẹ, I love you, I love you, I love you. I can't imagine not being your daughter. I don't think either of you ever tried stopping me from reading and writing, and I am glad for that.

An, our lives take us on different trajectories—*very* different, lol. Your brilliance, your strength, and your love have gotten me through so many things. You are truly my big sister. I love you, and I want the best for you. I'm glad to be your sister-in-law, Kevin, and I can't think of a better life partner for An! I am also proud to be Calhoun's aunt.

Dan, you are a rare human in every way possible and I do love you.

ACKNOWLEDGMENTS

I'd like to thank my extended family as well because when I was really young, we lived or were always together. Now we're scattered across America and Vietnam. I don't take their struggles, unseen and unsaid, lightly: Dì Chín, Anh Bé, Chị Ty, Chị Quỳnh, Anh Sơn, Chị Như, Chị Nhi, Bon Bon, Tin Tin, Gigi, Anh Thông, Ben, Lilly, Eric, Ý Vy, Chị Huyền, Anh Thiện, Jasmine. Dì 10 Lớn, Cậu Đức, Chị By, Anh Hoàng, David, Noah, Sam, and Hannah. Even though we've only seen each other a handful of times, I want to send love to the West Coast fam (it's definitely been more than seven years), and to my family in Vietnam.

Jen Ung, this book literally wouldn't have existed without you. I admire you as an editor and I admire you for being my editor. Thank you for bearing with my lateness, for your insightful notes, for your enthusiasm. I have learned so much from you; you are beloved. Jim McCarthy, you're such an astounding agent, and I'm forever thankful for the support you've shown me from the very beginning. You're the best in the business. To the publishing team behind me, thank you: Mara Anastas, Liesa Abrams, Laura Eckes, Elizabeth Mims, Sara Berko, Brenna Franzitta, Mandy Veloso, Kathleen Smith, Caitlin Sweeny, Lisa Quach, Savannah Breckenridge, Nicole Russo, Lauren Carr, Jenny Lu, Lauren Hoffman, Anna Jarzab, Christina Pecorale, Victor Iannone, Emily Hutton, Michelle Leo, and Stephanie Voros.

I don't think I have enough space to thank everyone in my life, and I'm actually afraid of forgetting people. Please don't be offended if you're not here. Some may know their impact and some may not (surprise!), but I wanted to thank you regardless because you've enriched my life as a person, as a writer, and as an editor: Ali Famigletti—not the Ali in this book—I'm glad to have found a soul sister in you. From the moment we bonded over *Fringe*, from that snowy day in Fairfield, I knew we'd be friends for a long time. Eric Lynch, Spencer Colpitts, and Clara de Frutos—Look at us! We are all so different from each other, and we've done a lot of growing up. I love you. Love and hugs to the Tran family, Mariah Stovall (Beans!), Stephanie Jimenez (Beans!), Luigi DiMeglio, Melissa Bendixen, Lara Jones, Melanie Igelias Pérez, Wendolyne Sabrozo, Chelcee Johns, my Atria colleagues, Fiora Elbers-Tibbitts, Sean deLone, Nick Ciani, Daniella Wexler, Rakesh Satyal, Jhanteigh Kupihea, Amar Doel, Lindsay Sagnette, Libby McGuire, Dr. Tommy Xie, Gretchen and Jeff Messer, Kelly and Stephen Barry, Rebecca Faith Heyman, Bryan Crandall, Caitlyn Cardetti, Steve Breslin, and BTS (sorry, I had to).

Thank you to The Hastings—my MFA "sisters": Ellyn Gelman, Stacey Holmes, Sam Keller, Kerry McKay, Alix Purcell, Sam Sullivan, and Jessica Tumio. I'm eternally grateful to the Fairfield University English Department and the Fairfield MFA faculty who taught there during my time: Elizabeth Hastings, Hollis Seamon, Eugenia Kim, Al Davis, Rachel Basch, Karen Osborn, Sonya Huber, Elizabeth Hastings, Carol Ann Davis, Baron Wormser, Susan Darraj Maddaj, Michael White, and Bill Patrick.

Friends and teachers from Cheshire: I think you know who you are. We may not be in each other's lives anymore, but I see you

ACKNOWLEDGMENTS

and I'm proud of you. Ms. Yamamoto, you left the world as I was writing this manuscript. I was imagining the day I visited CHS and dropped off a copy in your office—the same office where our class, even after we were done, shared more Occasional Papers and proudly hung up our college acceptances. I just want to thank you for inspiring me, for being so kind to many, many, many people.

Thank you,

Loan

RIVETED

BY *simon* teen ♥

BELIEVE IN YOUR SHELF

Visit RivetedLit.com & connect with us on social to:

DISCOVER NEW YA READS

READ BOOKS FOR FREE

DISCUSS YOUR FAVORITES

SHARE YOUR IDEAS

ENTER SWEEPSTAKES FOR THE CHANCE TO WIN BOOKS

Follow @SimonTeen on

to stay up to date with all things Riveted!

Can you fall in love with someone without the humiliating weirdness of having to actually see them? Ask Sam and Penny.

PAST
WATCHFUL
DRAGONS

Madge Anderson Kemp Hooper

CONTENTS

PREFACE

In 1967 Professor Charles A. Huttar of Hope College, Michigan, was compiling a volume of various essays. And so it was at his request that I wrote a piece on C. S. Lewis. Indeed, it was a fine opportunity, for there were two good reasons that I should take as a subject the Chronicles of Narnia. First of these was that I love the books perhaps more than any other writings of Lewis's, itself a good enough reason. Secondly, I was worried that those who talked about "teaching" the stories as Christian "theology" might by such efforts frustrate the spell of Lewis's clearly worked illusion. As he himself explained:

I thought I saw how stories of this kind could steal past a certain inhibition which had paralysed much of my own religion in childhood. Why did one find it so hard to feel as one was told one ought to feel about God or about the sufferings of Christ? I thought the chief reason was that one was told one ought to. An obligation to feel can freeze feelings. And reverence itself did harm. The whole subject was associated with lowered voices; almost as if it were something medical. But supposing that by casting all these things into an imaginary world, stripping them of their stained-glass and Sunday school associations, one could make them for the first time appear in their real potency? Could one not thus steal past those watchful dragons? I thought one could.

Believing, as I still do, that it is possible to endanger the success of the Narnian stories by rousing those "watchful dragons," I set out to explain how I thought such damage might be avoided. However, much as I admire brevity in others, I soon discovered that I have not much talent for it myself. And so, while I began with the near certainty that I should never be able to extend what I wanted to say to the usual span, I was well into this work but not halfway through the task. And yet, as Professor Huttar seemed pleased with things, there was encouragement for the whole project to be concluded. The idea of calling my contribution an "essay" caused my friend Owen Barfield to remark with justifiable humour that, considered as an *essay* "the chief trouble about *Past Watchful Dragons* is that, like a real dragon, it is too long." Anyway, *Past Watchful Dragons* was, despite its length, accepted by Professor Huttar and published by Wm. B. Eerdmans Publishing Co. in a book entitled *Imagination and the Spirit* (1971). This work has since gone out of print.

I wouldn't usually quibble with Mr. Barfield's criticism, but I felt that to the seventh and final Narnian story, *The Last Battle*, I hadn't said all that was needed. Then, when Dr. Francelia Butler asked me a few years later to write a general essay on the Narnian tales for *Children's Literature*, Vol. III (1974), I saw for once that these previous discrepancies could be made complete. That essay was published under the title "Narnia: The Author, the Critics, and the Tale," and has since been reprinted in *The Longing for a Form: Essays on the Fiction of C. S. Lewis*, edited by Peter J. Schakel (Kent State University Press, 1977).

Now we are at the essay's maturity. We should be grateful to Henry William Griffin, senior editor of Macmillan Publishing Co., who was pleased to reprint the original work with whatever additions I should care to make. The new material included will be of interest to all Lewis admirers.

This new material in fact has to do with the time when Lewis gave me his "Outline of Narnian history so far as it is known," and, again, afterward when his brother, Major W. H. Lewis, gave me the few surviving manuscripts of Narnia. I published the "Outline" and quotations from some of the other Narnian fragments in the original essay, but two of them were too long to quote in full. On the other hand, they do not seem a word too long to quote in this book, so regardless of the quality of my own work, I am pleased that I have been able to include in this book Lewis's Narnian fragments in their entirety.

I am grateful to Professor Huttar, Dr. Peter J. Schakel and Kent State University Press for permission to revise and reprint the two essays which form the basis of this book. Only Owen Barfield and I know how much I have benefitted from his comments about my revised *Dragons*. I am further indebted to Mr. Barfield, my fellow Trustee of the C. S. Lewis Estate, for permitting me to quote the unpublished manuscripts of C. S. Lewis here.

W.H.

Oxford
12 December 1978

PAST
WATCHFUL
DRAGONS

1

The Inconsolable
Longing

"WHEN I was ten," said C. S. Lewis, "I read fairy tales in secret and would have been ashamed if I had been found doing so. Now [that was in 1952] that I am fifty, I read them openly. When I became a man I put away childish things, including the fear of childishness and the desire to be very grown up."[1]

Readers of Lewis's fairy tales are not likely to understand simply from reading his Chronicles of Narnia, how deeply his imagination slept as a boy, or how momentous was his escape in losing "the desire to be very grown up." His boyhood was, nevertheless, a period of great fecundity: he wrote many stories about his invented world of Animal-Land at the time, and was, without knowing it, training himself to be the future chronicler of Narnia. Yet grown-up matters, which were all-in-all to Lewis when he wrote about Animal-Land, find no mention whatsoever in the Narnian books.

In Lewis's autobiography, *Surprised by Joy*,[2] we get the impression of two lives—the "outer" and the "inner," the life of the intellect and the life of the imagination—being lived over against each

1. C. S. Lewis, "On Three Ways of Writing for Children," *Of Other Words: Essays and Stories*, ed. Walter Hooper (London, 1966; New York, 1967), p. 25.
2. *Surprised by Joy: The Shape of My Early Life* (London, 1955; New York, 1956).

1

other, albeit at the same time. The "outer" life is chiefly concerned with those things which he spoke and wrote about openly: namely, Animal-Land. The "inner" life—and this is what *Surprised by Joy* is mainly about—is essentially the story of Joy (i.e., intense longing) working on his imagination. Narnia would never have come into existence had Lewis not come to understand the meaning and purpose of Joy.

What drove Lewis to write was his extreme manual clumsiness from which he always suffered: he had only one joint in his thumb. This disability kept him from taking up the hobbies and sports that interest most young boys. (I have seen him try to remove the cellophane wrapping from a pork pie, first with his fingers, then with a knife, then with a fork, then with both, until he finally handed it over for me to unwrap.) When his family moved into their new house, "Little Lea," on the outskirts of Belfast, in 1905, he staked out a claim to one of the attics and there he wrote his first stories, stories that combined his chief literary pleasures—"dressed animals" and "knights in armour." He was, from the first, a systematizer: a characteristic that caused him eventually to become a historiographer of his invented world of Animal-Land. When his brother Warren was home from his school in England it was necessary that it become a country shared with him. "India" (his brother's contribution) was lifted out of its real place in the world and became geographically related to Animal-Land. In time they became the single state of Boxen.

The earliest piece of juvenilia, *The King's Ring*, is about the theft of the crown jewels of Animal-Land in the reign of Benjamin I. This is very early Boxoniana indeed, for Benjamin I succeeded

Bublish I in 1331 and the last Boxen stories take us down to 1903 (Boxen time). When these as yet unpublished stories come out the year 1856 will give Boxonologists occasion for much celebration: Lord Big is born in that year. He is that frog of powerful personality who as Little-Master (i.e., the Prime Minister) carries on his shoulders not only great matters of state, but responsibility for the young kings, Benjamin VI and Hawki IV.

Some of the Boxen stories are very good and one cannot help boggling at the sheer invention and patience that went into the creation of seven hundred years of Boxoniana. Yet, contrary to what readers of Lewis's Narnian Chronicles might expect, the juvenilia are surprisingly prosaic. There is not the slightest hint of faerie or other worlds. The dominant theme is politics: to get into the "Clique" is the ambition of almost every character. Yet none of the characters, to say nothing of the author, seems to have a clear idea of what the "Clique" is. Ambitions run high and are almost solely concerned with money and political power. The daily newspaper is of major interest.

When you consider that romances and fairy tales were the young Lewis's favourite reading, it seems odd that so much interest and energy went into stories about matters that Lewis was later to detest. Yet politics and money, Lewis told me, were the chief topics of conversation among Lewis's father and his friends. Doubtless, the young Lewis wanted his stories to reflect as nearly as possible the words that fell from the lips of grown-ups and the things that to them seemed important.

I think I can best illustrate this by quoting a passage from a "novel" entitled *The Locked Door*. It is rather late Boxoniana—written, it is my guess, when Lewis was about twelve. Although there are obvious traces of grown-up conversation and nights out at parties and the hippodrome, it illustrates the ease and pleasure he found in writing. James Bar, a "hock-brown" bear, and Captain Samuel Macgoullah, a horse, are on their way to a ball given by Their Majesties, Benjamin VII and Hawki V (both rabbits). I have retained Lewis's spelling and punctuation:

Great was the preparation of Bar and Macgoullah when the eventful evening arrived. Bar had hired a handsome to be ready for them both outside the 'Schooner' where they had arranged to meet.

As they drew near the palace, Regency Street became a mass of moving lights dancing to the music of horses' hoofs and the powerful purr of motors: and it was not without difficulty that the hireling Jehu navigated them to the portals of Regency St. Palace. Stepping out they were conducted by suave domestics to the cloak room, which, as is usually the case on these occasions, was crowded with knots of whispering guests fiddling with their gloves. There of course is Puddiphat immaculately clad; there is Reginald Pig the Shipowner dressed in solid and plain evening dress; there is Quicksteppe looking finer than ever as the electric light catches his glossy curling locks; there is Colonel Chutney, formerly head of the war office, but now removed to give place to Fortescue who is also present. After some time of nervous fumbling and hushing, Pig, the most couragious person present, led a sort of forlorn hope to the salon where their Majesties were recieving their guests and where stout domestics dispensed tea etc. The two kings were throwing all their histrionic powers into an imitation of enjoyment, and behind them stood the Little-Master looking rather worried. The boys kept up a continual flow of conversation:—

"Good evening, My dear Pig! How are the ships? Ah, Viscount Puddiphat, very glad you came."

"Good evening Your Majesties. Ah my dear Little-Master I see you've been having busy times in the Clique"

"Yes" said Big drily

The Duchess of Penzly came up, a heavy woman whom they all abominated.

"Good evening Duchess. Hasn't Miss Penzley—oh! Influenza? I am very sorry to hear that" The Duchess passed on to Big.

"Ah, Lord Big, this is a pleasure. How delighted I was to hear you had had some excitement in politics, it does liven things up so, doesn't it?"

"It certainly does", responded the frog brusquely, and engaged a dance.

By way of contrast, it is important at this point to say something about Joy. In his autobiography Lewis defines Joy by first recording three experiences from his early childhood. While standing by a flowering currant bush on a summer day there arose in him the memory of a yet earlier morning in which his brother had brought into the nursery a toy garden. The memory of this memory caused a sensation of desire to break over him. Before he could know *what* he desired, the desire itself was gone and he was left with a "longing for the longing that had just ceased" (*Surprised by Joy*, ch. I). The second glimpse of Joy came through Beatrix Potter's *Squirrel Nutkin*. This little book troubled him with the "Idea of Autumn" (ibid.), and again he was plunged into the experience of intense desire. The third glimpse came to him while reading

Longfellow's translation of *Tegner's Drapa*. When he read

> I heard a voice that cried,
> Balder the beautiful
> Is dead, is dead—

his mind was uplifted into huge regions of northern sky. At the very moment he was stabbed by desire, he felt himself falling out of that desire and wishing he were back in it.

Lewis tells us that Joy, the quality common to these three experiences, is an unsatisfied longing which is itself more desirable than any other satisfaction. The authentic Joy vanished when he was sent to Wynyard School in Watford, Hertfordshire. A few years later he was a pupil at Cherbourg School in Malvern, Worcestershire. It was there, while glancing through the Christmas number of *The Bookman* for 1911, that his eyes fell on the words *Siegfried and the Twilight of the Gods* and one of Arthur Rackham's illustrations to the book, and it returned. In a single moment he was plunged back into the past of Balder and sunward sailing cranes, and felt the old inconsolable longing. The memory of his own past Joy and the Twilight of the Gods "flowed together," he said, "into a single, unendurable sense of desire and loss, which . . . had eluded me at the very moment when I could first say *It is*."[3]

The young Lewis made many mistakes in his pursuit of Joy. As the old thrill became less and less frequent, he attempted most desperately to "have it again." In his impatience to snare it, to tear the

3. *Ibid.*, ch. V.

veil, and be in on the secrets of the universe, he turned from one medium of Joy to another, hoping always to find permanent satisfaction. He shifted from Northerness (a frequent and early transmitter of Joy) to erotic pleasure, only to find that the hounds had (again) changed scent and that though "Joy is not a substitute for sex, sex is very often a substitute for Joy."[4]

Lewis lost his virginity while a pupil at Cherbourg House, but it was the "potent, ubiquitous, and unabashed"[5] eroticism of William Morris's romances which chiefly persuaded him that sex might be the substance of Joy. Interestingly enough, it was a romance of a very different sort that served as a check for this mistake. Almost everyone knows the book I refer to: George MacDonald's *Phantastes: a faerie Romance*, which he bought at Leatherhead station when he was the pupil of William T. Kirkpatrick at Little Bookham in Surrey. Lewis was as smitten by MacDonald as many people are by Lewis. Hitherto, each visitation of Joy had momentarily left the common world a desert. But from the pages of *Phantastes* there emerged a "bright shadow" (later known to be holiness) that transformed all common things—the bread on the table and the coals in the grate—without itself becoming changed. His imagination was, he said, "baptised," and he was carried one step closer to that which he had so long desired.

At about the same time that Lewis was beginning to understand the nature of Joy, he was losing interest in his political stories of Boxen. His inter-

4. *Ibid.*, ch. XI.
5. C. S. Lewis, "William Morris," *Selected Literary Essays*, ed. Walter Hooper (Cambridge, 1969), p. 222.

ests were now mainly poetical. Before going to Little Bookham he began writing *Loki Bound*, a pessimistic Norse tragedy. Commenting later on the contradictions in this poem, he said: "I maintained that God did not exist. I was also very angry with God for not existing. I was equally angry with Him for creating a world."[6] It is perhaps a bit surprising that he failed to notice the contradictions at the time, for he was even then quick to spot illogicalities. Still, one meets people every day who, though they have no actual knowledge of Christianity, are nevertheless convinced that whatever they say about God *must* be true. Lewis may have been enjoying the mood, if not the fact, of infallibility.

It was while Lewis was at Little Bookham—the village adjoining Great Bookham—that he began a weekly correspondence with Arthur Greeves, his Belfast friend. Though very different in many ways, both were enthusiastic letter-writers and each was anxious to share with the other the discoveries he was making. One of their first quarrels was about Christianity. Lewis did not like to talk about this but Greeves forced him to state his position. Writing on 12 October 1916, Lewis said:

You know, I think, that I believe in no religion. There is absolutely no proof for any of them, and from a philosophical standpoint Christianity is not even the best. All religions, that is, all mythologies to give them their proper name, are merely man's own invention—Christ as much as Loki. Primitive man found himself surrounded by all sorts of terrible things he didn't understand . . . Thus religion, that is to say mythology grew

6. *Surprised by Joy*, ch. VII.

up. Often, too, great men were regarded as gods after their death—such as Heracles or Odin: thus after the death of a Hebrew philosopher Yeshua (whose name we have corrupted into Jesus) he became regarded as a god, a cult sprang up, which was afterwards connected with the ancient Hebrew Jahweh-worship, and so Christianity came into being—one mythology among many . . . Of course, mind you, I am not laying down as a certainty that there is nothing outside the material world: considering the discoveries that are always being made, this would be foolish. Anything MAY exist.[7]

In truth, between Lewis's imaginative life and that of his intellect—what I term his "inner" and "outer" life—there yawned a great chasm. And there did not appear to be any way of bridging the two. His imagination, over which brooded his "immortal longings," was peopled with gods, nymphs, fauns, satyrs, giants, paradises. His intellect —and especially now that Boxen with its friendly "dressed animals" had dropped out—was stark and practical. As he himself described it: "The two hemispheres of my mind were in the sharpest contrast. On the one side a many-islanded sea of poetry and myth; on the other a glib and shallow 'rationalism.' Nearly all that I loved I believed to be imaginary; nearly all that I believed to be real I thought grim and meaningless."[8]

When he went up to Oxford after serving in the trenches during World War I, Lewis was determined

7. *They Stand Together: The Letters of C. S. Lewis to Arthur Greeves (1914–1963)*, ed. Walter Hooper (London; New York, 1979).

8. *Surprised by Joy*, ch. XI.

that there were to be no flirtations with the idea of the supernatural. All the images he associated with Joy were, he concluded, sheer fantasies. He had at last "seen through" them. The important thing was to get ahead with the "good life" without the Christian "mythology." But he could not be left alone. In almost every book, in nearly every conversation, a chance reference to Christianity threatened to unsettle his solid philosophical position. Early in 1926, when he was the Fellow of English Language and Literature in Magdalen College, he entertained in his rooms a man whom he considered the "hardest boiled of all the atheists." He was thus amazed when the atheist remarked on what surprisingly good evidence there was for the historicity of the Gospels. He was shattered when the man went on to say, "Rum thing. All that stuff of Frazer's about the Dying God. Rum thing. It almost looks as if it really happened once."[9]

It is not necessary to recount here how, one by one, Lewis's reservations about accepting the Christian faith were swept away (it is all in *Surprised by Joy*). But so they were. After long searching, yet with much reluctance, he was brought to his knees in the summer of 1929 and forced to admit that God was God. He who is the Joy of all men's desiring came upon him and compelled him by divine mercy to surrender a long-besieged fortress. His surrender, however, was to what seemed at the time a purely nonhuman God. He became a Theist. The next step occurred in 1931 while Lewis was riding to Whipsnade Zoo in the sidecar of his brother's motorcycle. When they left Oxford he did not believe that Jesus was the Son of God; when they

9. *Ibid.*, ch. XIV.

reached the zoo he did. After that, the old bitter-sweet stabs of Joy continued as before. But he could not now give them the same importance they once had. That would have been impossible: he knew to what—or, rather, to *Whom*—they pointed.

⁂ II ⁂

The Parts Come Together

Now, what is the relevance of all this to the Chronicles of Narnia? In order to understand them better it was important to consider those things—"dressed animals," mythology, Joy—which played an especially significant part in C. S. Lewis's youth and which, in various ways and degrees, contributed to his conversion to Christianity. There was, however, a stretch of a good many years between his conversion and his writing of the Narnian stories. So, before jumping prematurely into a discussion of the fairy tales, I think it right to show how Lewis's conversion led him to reconsider these same elements before they appear transformed and regenerate in the world of Narnia.

During the writing of the Animal-Land stories, Lewis seemed to have had little understanding of the true nature of beasts. This may not have been so much his failure to observe as the general ignorance or unconcern of some of the writers whose stories he read. When he wrote about Animal-Land, the only animals with which he had any real intimacy were a pet mouse, Peter, and his dog Tim. If one were not told in advance, I wonder how many of us would have guessed that it is animals and not just ordinary human beings who are speaking in the passage quoted from *The Locked Door*? I have read Lewis's juvenilia, but even then my knowledge of who is what is partly derived from the pictures Lewis drew to illustrate his Boxen stories.

His old childhood fear of pain and his later, more astute observations of wild and domestic animals led Lewis to devote a chapter to "Animal Pain" in his book *The Problem of Pain*. His thoughts on the matter are these:[1] As beasts are incapable of either sin or virtue, they can, therefore, neither deserve nor be improved by pain. On the other hand, we must not allow the problem of animal suffering to become the centre of the problem of pain because God has not given us data about the suffering of beasts. As animals presumably preceded man in the order of creation, Satan should be thought to have corrupted the brutes first. After man's own creation, it may have been one of his functions to restore peace to the animal world. This he might have done to an almost unimaginable extent had he himself not joined the enemy and, in his fall, furthered Satan's malice towards the animal kingdom. Lewis believed that animals have consciousness, though not as we know it in ourselves; and this leads to the question of whether they are, like men, immortal creatures. The answer in a nutshell is: "We don't know." As the doctrine of *human* immortality comes late in the history of Judaism, it seems unlikely from what we can discern of God's method of revelation that He would have revealed whether animals are, or are not, immortal.

The greatest difficulty about supposing all animals to be immortal, Lewis went on to say, is that im-

1. *The Problem of Pain* (London, 1940; New York, 1943), ch. IX. See also the essays on "Vivisection" and "The Pains of Animals" in Lewis's *God in the Dock*, ed. Walter Hooper (Grand Rapids, 1970). This last title was published in London as *Undeceptions* (1971).

mortality has almost no meaning for a creature that has no unity of consciousness. If, for instance, the life of a newt is no more than a succession of sensations, it is anyone's guess whether the newt that died today would, if it were recalled to life by God, recognise itself as the same newt. Lewis believed that there is no question of immortality for creatures like newts that are merely sentient. The survival of higher animals he felt to be a more open question.

He believed that the beasts are to be understood only in their relation to man and, through man, to God. As man is appointed by God to have dominion over the beasts, those animals that man *tames* become the only "natural" animals—that is, the only ones that occupy the place God intended for them if men and animals had not fallen. If a tame animal has any real self or personality, Lewis believed that it owes this almost entirely to its master. If it is raised to life eternal, its identity will reside in its relation to the master or to the whole of humanity of which it was a member. That is, as the personality of the tame animal is largely the gift of man, then their mere sentience would be reborn to soulhood in *us* as our mere soulhood is reborn to spirituality in Christ.

One of the most interesting speculations in the chapter on "Animal Pain" is that which seems to anticipate the character of Aslan, King of Narnia. Lewis thought that creatures so remote from us as wild beasts may have no separate selves or sufferings but that each species may have a corporate self. He uses the lion as an example.

Lewis by no means always thought of the animal kingdom as a whole collectively. He had an uncanny eye for their specific traits. In his poem "Impenitence," he speaks of the

cool primness of cats, or coney's
Half indignant stare of amazement, mouse's
Twinkling adroitness,
Tipsy bear's rotundity, toad's complacence . . .[2]

His eyes were also open to those physical similarities that men and beasts have in common. This is why he felt that Kenneth Grahame in *The Wind in the Willows* made the right choice when he gave his principal character the form of a toad.[3] The toad's face, with its fixed "grin," bears such a striking resemblance to a certain kind of human face that no other animal would have suited the part so well. Lewis saw these physical similarities as extending even further: some animals can be most interestingly used in pictures and literature as representing the actual archetypes of some human and animal characteristics. If they do not rise to the archetypal level, many at least, as he says in the poem quoted above,

cry out to be used as symbols,
Masks for Man, cartoons, parodies by Nature
Formed to reveal us.

To correct the possible impression that Lewis was drily intellectual about animals I offer this small digression about his relation to his own pets. When I was living at the Kilns (his home in Oxford), Lewis was affectionately termed "The Boss" by everyone there: his brother (temporarily absent at this time), his two stepsons, secretary (myself), housekeeper, and gardener. Yet I never remember

2. C. S. Lewis, *Poems*, ed. Walter Hooper (London, 1964; New York, 1965), p. 2.
3. "On Stories," *Of Other Worlds*, pp. 13–14.

him speaking a sharp word or giving an order. It was his house, but he was "Boss" by virtue of his unfailing kindness and courtesy. The Kilns "family" also included two cats, an old ginger Tom (a mighty hunter of mice when he was young, but then living on a pension of fish) and Snip (a Siamese which Lewis inherited from his wife and referred to as his "step-cat"). There was also a young boxer pup named Ricky.

They recognised Lewis as the undisputed head of the house, but he never made an elaborate fuss over them. He greeted Tom in the morning, stroked Snip when she jumped in his lap, and passed the time of day with Ricky. Live and let live; just what they wanted. If the door to his study was open, they knew they were welcome within: otherwise not. One summer morning when Lewis was writing at his desk by the open window, Snip took a great spring and shot through the window. She landed with a great thump on top of his desk, scattering papers in all directions, and skidded into his lap. He looked at her in amazement. She looked at him in amazement. "Perhaps," he said to me, "my step-cat, having finished her acrobatics, would enjoy a saucer of milk in the kitchen." I opened the door for poor Snip and she walked slowly out, embarrassed, but with the best grace she could manage.

In one of Lewis's many notebooks, which his brother later gave to me, I found this definition of myth: "A *Myth* is the description of a state, an event, or a series of events, involving superhuman personages, possessing unity, not truly implying a particular time or place, and dependent for its contents not on motives developed in the course of action but on the immutable relations of the personages." Stories such as those of Balder, Osiris, and Orpheus are examples of what he means. They are not dependent on fine details, or eloquent language, although they usually reach us in story form. In enjoying great myths, Lewis believed we come nearest to experiencing as a concrete what could otherwise only be understood as an abstraction. For example, when we read or hear the myth of Osiris, we have a concrete experience. In other words, concrete reality flows into us as we listen to the myth—rather like the passing of food from the mouth of a mother bird to its chick. When we attempt to "taste" it—to know the meaning of it— what we taste turns out to be truths, or universal principles. Or put another way, myth is a mountain from whence streams flow down into the valley. What reaches us down here in the valley is truth.[4]

I have already quoted Lewis's early letter to Arthur Greeves in which he equates Christ with other gods such as Odin and his own Loki. He then believed that Christianity was only one of many mythologies—a belief he held up to the time of his conversion. How on earth, he wondered, have Christians the cheek to claim their mythology true and the others false? In *The Pilgrim's Regress* he attempted to explain not only why the Pagan mythologies are not (totally) false, but how the truths in all of them *cohere*. History (an allegorical character) explains to the Pilgrim that God sent "pictures" which stir up "sweet desire" to both the ancient Jews and Pagans. The Jews were given not only pictures but Rules (the Law of Moses) as well. Both the Jews' and the Pagans' pictures contained the divine call, but the Pagans made up untrue

4. C. S. Lewis, "Myth Became Fact," *God in the Dock.*

stories about the pictures. They sought the end of "sweet desire" (i.e., Lewis's Joy) in one thing after another, trying to believe that what they found was what they wanted. There was no absurdity that they did not commit. And just when their own stories seemed to have overgrown the original message, God would send a new message and their fanciful stories would look stale. If they grew contented with lust and "mystery-mongering," a new message would arrive and the old desire would sting them again. They were, as it were, attempting eloquence before they had learned grammar.

The Jews, on the other hand, were too narrow. Of course the thing they had charge of was narrow: the Road. Once they found it, they kept it clear and repaired and signposted: but they did not follow it. The Jew was only half a man, and the Pagan was only half a man, so that neither was well without the other, nor could either be healed until Christ came into the world.[5]

It was, then, no longer a matter of finding the one true religion among many, but rather finding where religion had reached its true maturity. "Paganism," he saw, "had been only the childhood of religion, or only a prophetic dream. Where was the thing full grown? or where was the awaking?"[6] The whole matter is summed up in an invaluable footnote in Lewis's book on Miracles:

As, on the factual side, a long preparation culminates in God's becoming incarnate as Man, so, on the documentary side, the truth first appears in *mythical* form and

5. *The Pilgrim's Regress: An Allegorical Apology for Christianity, Reason and Romanticism*, 3rd ed. (London, 1943; New York, 1944), Bk. VIII, ch. viii.
6. *Surprised by Joy*, ch. XV.

then by a long process of condensing or focusing finally becomes incarnate as History. This involves the belief that Myth ... is ... as its best, a real though unfocused gleam of divine truth falling on human imagination. The Hebrews, like other people, had mythology: but as they were the chosen people so their mythology was the chosen mythology—the mythology chosen by God to be the vehicle of the earliest sacred truths, the first step in that process which ends in the New Testament where truth has become completely historical.[7]

Although the Gospels have what has been called the mythic "taste," they are themselves History. They are the end of the focusing. As myth transcends thought, so Incarnation transcends myth. We pass, thus, from a Balder and an Osiris, dying we know not when or where, to the great myth becoming Fact when the Virgin conceived.

I believe there is an important connection between Lewis's personal experience of intense longing and the Narnian Chronicles. *Surprised by Joy* is the story of how this longing led to Lewis's conversion. But one of his reasons for writing the book is that he felt it to be a *common* experience, easily misunderstood, difficult to bring to the forefront of consciousness—and of immense importance. *The Pilgrim's Regress*, which is partly autobiographical, is the story of the Pilgrim's quest for a far-off island, the vision of which has stung him with sweet desire. When Lewis realised that the word *Romanticism* in the subtitle was misunderstood, he wrote a preface to the third edition (1943) explaining the meaning he gave the word. It means Joy—as in

7. *Miracles: A Preliminary Study* (London; New York, 1947), ch. XV.

Surprised by Joy. Indeed, the same Joy, or longing, that you and I feel for our own far-off country: "the secret we cannot hide and cannot tell."[8] A longing which, though painful, is felt to be somehow a delight. A hunger more satisfying than any other fullness; a poverty better than all other wealth. A desiring which, if long absent, is itself desired so much that the new desiring becomes an instance of the original one.

A peculiar mystery hangs over the *object* of this desire. We feel we know what it is we desire, but in the final achievement of that desire—when it is actually in our hands—we know the real object of our desire has moved farther afield, eluding us like the cuckoo's voice or the rainbow's end. *All* I want, someone will say, is a university degree, or a happy marriage, or a steady job, or to get the book that has been in my head for years onto paper. But when he is married or settled into the right job, or gets whatever it is he wants, it proves itself to be a cheat. It is not *enough*. It is not what he is actually looking for.

Lewis reasoned that we are not born with desires unless satisfaction for those desires exists. And if we find in ourselves a desire that no experience in this world can satisfy, the most probable explanation is that we were made for a different world. A happy marriage, a successful career—these things were never intended to satisfy our desire for the far-off country: more likely they were meant to arouse it, to suggest the real thing. That far-off country is of

---

8. C. S. Lewis, "The Weight of Glory," *Transposition and Other Addresses* (London, 1949), p. 23. This same book was published in New York as *The Weight of Glory and Other Addresses* (1949), p. 4.

course Heaven. Not indeed that our desire for Heaven proves that you or I shall enjoy it—we can of our own free wills reject it—but it is a good indication that it *exists* and that nothing other than God can be our ultimate bliss.

A Defence of the Fairy Tale

As has been suggested, there is, I believe, a connection between our longing for Heaven and fairy tales such as those of Lewis. At the same time, I am aware that it is difficult, and becoming more so, for the ordinary person to recognise in himself a desire for Heaven. I think this is mainly because most people nowadays are very badly educated theologically and thus have very vague notions as to what Heaven—or indeed life—is all about. Almost every aspect of modern life fixes our minds on this world, and the desire for Heaven has got jumbled up with and camouflaged by such things as "social consciousness" and the like. We are encouraged to seek all our good in "this dim spot." While the tide appears to be turning from the so-called realistic literature, so prized in the 1950s and 1960s, to more imaginative works, we are not yet out of the swamp of deceptive and hideous "realism." To bring up the subjects of Heaven and fairy tales in some quarters is to be howled down as nostalgic, romantic, sentimental, or adolescent—all meant in a contemptuous sense. In short, those still enamoured of the "swamp" accuse those of us not in it of being obsessed with Pie-in-the-sky-by-and-by and they usually equate fantastic literature with "escapism" and wishful thinking. It is clear that our critics see—but without fully understanding it—a connection between our desire for the far-off country and fantastic literature. I am convinced they are right. I think there is one.

Lewis said that marvellous literature evoked his desire for Heaven; but at the same time he believed that no literature is less likely to give a person a false impression of the world than are fairy tales. His thoughts on the subject are clearly expressed in his essay "On Three Ways of Writing for Children." In it he first of all draws our attention to a point made earlier by his friend Professor J. R. R. Tolkien[1] that fairy tales were not originally written for children, but gravitated to the nursery when they became unfashionable in literary circles. Some children *and* adults like them; some children *and* adults do not. So-called realistic stories, Lewis maintained, are far more likely to deceive than are fairy tales because, though the adventures and successes in them are possible (e.g., they do not break the laws of nature), they are almost infinitely improbable. It is possible to become a duke or a millionaire with a yacht and rooms in a posh hotel, or to be the idol of irresistible beauties— anything is possible—but things of that sort are for most of us improbable. On the other hand, no one expects the real world to be like that of the fairy tales.

As for the popular charge of escapism and wish-fulfillment, school stories and fairy tales both arouse and imaginatively satisfy wishes. In one we long to go through the looking glass and reach fairyland (or through the wardrobe to Narnia?). In the other we long to be a rich, popular, successful schoolboy

1. In "On Fairy-Stories," *Essays Presented to Charles Williams*, ed. C. S. Lewis (Oxford, 1947). The essay is reprinted in Tolkien's *Tree and Leaf* (London, 1964; Boston, 1965).

who discovers the spy's plot or rides the horse that none of the cowboys can manage. The two longings are, however, very different. The one directed on something so close as school life is, Lewis argued, ravenous and deadly serious. On the level of imagination it is compensatory and we run to it from the disappointments and humiliations of the real world: and we return to the real world "undivinely discontented," for it is all flattery to the ego. One has been, all along, picturing oneself as the object of admiration. The longing for fairyland is a different sort of longing, for it cannot be supposed that the boy who longs for fairyland really longs for the dangers and discomforts of a fairy tale. "It would be much truer," wrote Lewis,

to say that fairyland arouses a longing for he knows not what. It stirs and troubles him (to his life-long enrichment) with the dim sense of something beyond his reach and, far from dulling or emptying the actual world, gives it a new dimension of depth. He does not despise real woods because he has read of enchanted woods: the reading makes all real woods a little enchanted. This is a special kind of longing.[2]

I have before me one of Lewis's notebooks containing a fragment of a story about a boy who, in his garden, has been having an imaginary joust in the "uncharted forests of Logres." It was written, I believe, before Lewis's conversion, and is a good illustration of the point made above: fairyland, even when it has no conscious connection with Heaven, throws a little enchantment upon the

2. "On Three Ways of Writing for Children," *Of Other Worlds*, pp. 29–30.

present, actual world. The joust ended, the boy is returning home:

> To remember suddenly that this was all a game was like hearing the voice of a friend: all the details of that "real" world that lay behind the game—the holidays just begun, the lighted, carpeted rooms, and, presently, the sound of teacups . . . It was the strangest systole and diastole—no sooner was home regained, than that other world of desert hills and distant, ominous castles enisled in haunted woods, rose up, clothed in its turn with all the alluring colours of the long-lost. And so one swung backwards and forwards. Each world was best just as you left it for the other, as if to blow out these cloudy worlds and then to suck them in again were as functional as the rising and falling of the breast in sleep.

But to return to Lewis's defence of the fairy tale—it is perhaps inevitable that stories so very popular as Lewis's will find objectors, and they have. As far as I can tell, most adverse criticism of the Narnian stories has been the work of schoolmistresses and professional educators for whom the delicate unreality which they call the "whole child" seems to bear little resemblance to the children most of us meet. They claim that the Narnian battles and wicked characters frighten children and give them nightmares. I believe there is no better answer to these charges than that given by Lewis himself in the essay "On Three Ways of Writing for Children." While agreeing that we must not do anything (1) "likely to give the child those haunting, disabling, pathological fears against which ordinary courage is helpless," he was strongly opposed to the notion that we must keep out of the child's mind

(2) "the knowledge that he is born into a world of death, violence, wounds, adventure, heroism and cowardice, good and evil":

The second would indeed be to give children a false impression and feed them on escapism in the bad sense. There is something ludicrous in the idea of so educating a generation which is born to the Ogpu and the atomic bomb. Since it is so likely that they will meet cruel enemies, let them at least have heard of brave knights and heroic courage. Otherwise you are making their destiny not brighter but darker. Nor do most of us find that violence and bloodshed, in a story, produce any haunting dread in the minds of children. As far as that goes, I side impenitently with the human race against the modern reformer. Let there be wicked kings and beheadings, battles and dungeons, giants and dragons, and let villains be soundly killed at the end of the book. Nothing will persuade me that this causes an ordinary child any kind or degree of fear beyond what it wants, and needs, to feel. For, of course, it wants to be a little frightened. (p. 31)

The most hostile piece of criticism which I have seen—attacking the Narnian stories from a completely different angle—is an article entitled "The Problem of C. S. Lewis" and found in *Children's Literature in Education*, No. 10 (March 1973), pp. 3–25. I withhold the name of the author as I cannot bear that it should appear on the same page with that of C. S. Lewis. The article has convinced me that while there is a problem, it is most certainly not Lewis's. It is perhaps enough to say that the author is an educator who is active in some anti-pornography campaign, but who, by the imagined use of Freudian symbolism, has created a hideous sexual phantasy where he meant to warn us against one.

Lewis, of course, never read the article, but I recall a conversation we had about the same kind of thing. The difficulty, he said, about arguing with such Freud-ridden sheep is that *whatever* you say to the contrary, no matter how clear and obvious to a sensible man, the Freudian uses it to support what he's already decided to believe. Or, as Lewis says elsewhere, they argue in the same manner as a man who should say, "If there were an invisible cat in the chair, the chair would look empty; but the chair does look empty; therefore there is an invisible cat in it."[3] It may be a very unorthodox approach to literary criticism, but if the author would accept my challenge of undergoing a lie-detector test to discover whether or not *he* believes what he has written, I am sure that it will be found that he doesn't.

Happily, children are for the most part oblivious to literary criticism of any sort, and I can say with certainty that, while I have met some adults who consider Lewis's fairy tales too "violent" for children, I have never met a child who did not love the Narnias intensely. Further, the children I have met or heard from have, on an average, read the stories six or seven times over. During his lifetime Lewis received thousands of fan letters from children, and it is perhaps of some historical interest to record that even now—fifteen years after the author's death —it is my responsibility to answer the numerous fan letters which children from all over the world

3. *The Four Loves* (London; New York, 1960), ch. IV.

continue to address to Lewis. Recently I answered a flood of letters from children in Australia telling Lewis that they had elected him, on the strength of his Narnian tales, their "favourite Australian writer." And so it continues.

IV

Watchful Dragons

ASKED how he came to write the first Chronicle of Narnia—*The Lion, the Witch and the Wardrobe*—Lewis said: "All my seven Narnian books, and my three science fiction books, began with seeing pictures in my head. At first they were not a story, just pictures. The *Lion* all began with a picture of a Faun carrying an umbrella and parcels in a snowy wood. This picture had been in my mind since I was about sixteen. Then one day, when I was about forty, I said to myself: 'Let's try to make a story about it.' "[1]

Though Lewis had probably forgotten it, there is some evidence which would seem to indicate that the initial impetus behind his Narnian stories came from real children.

At the outbreak of World War II in 1939 four schoolgirls were evacuated from London to Lewis's home on the outskirts of Oxford. It was his adopted "mother," Mrs. Moore, who mainly looked after the evacuees, but Lewis shared the responsibility of entertaining the young visitors. On the back of another book he was writing at the time, I found what I believe to be the germinal passage of the first story of Narnia. It says:

This book is about four children whose names were Ann, Martin, Rose, and Peter. But it is most about Peter who

1. "It All Began with a Picture," *Of Other Worlds*, p. 42.

was the youngest. They all had to go away from London suddenly because of the Air Raids, and because Father, who was in the army, had gone off to the War and Mother was doing some kind of war work. They were sent to stay with a relation of Mother's who was a very old Professor who lived by himself in the country.

I have talked with a neighbour of Lewis's who remembers seeing the schoolgirls, but *which* ones she didn't know as the original children were after some months replaced by others, so that there were perhaps a dozen evacuees emcamped at the Kilns during the first year of the war.

With so little evidence, I have not been able to discover whether Lewis wrote any more of the story at that time. I do not think he did. The next we hear of it is from Chad Walsh who says that, when he visited Lewis in the summer of 1948, he talked "vaguely of completing a children's book which he [had] begun 'in the tradition of E. Nesbit.' "[2] Then, on 10 March 1949, Lewis read the first two chapters of *The Lion, the Witch and the Wardrobe* to his friend, Roger Lancelyn Green, who was the only person to read all seven stories in manuscript. Spurred on by Lancelyn Green's encouragement, *The Lion* was completed by the end of the month. More "pictures" or mental images—which Lewis said were his only means of inspiration—began forming in his head and the next two stories, *Prince Caspian* and *The Voyage of the "Dawn Treader,"* were completed by the end of February 1950. Before the year was out he had written *The Silver Chair* and *The Horse and His Boy* and made a start on

2. Chad Walsh, *C. S. Lewis: Apostle to the Skeptics* (New York, 1949), p. 10.

The Magician's Nephew. The final instalment, *The Last Battle*, was written two years later.

It would, perhaps, have been an intelligent guess to suppose that Lewis began with things he wanted to say about Christianity and other interests and then fixed on the fairy tale as a way of saying them. But that is not what happened. Lewis said he could not and would not write in that way; that he never exactly "made" a story. It all began with seeing "pictures": a faun carrying an umbrella, a queen on a sledge, a magnificent lion. It was, he remembered, more like "bird-watching" than talking or building. Sometimes a whole set of pictures would join themselves together, but it was necessary to do some "deliberate inventing," contrive reasons as to why characters should be in various places doing various things. Lewis maintained that at first there was nothing specifically Christian about the pictures he was seeing in his head, but that *that* element— as with Aslan—pushed its way in of its own accord.[3]

In another essay touching directly on the Narnian stories, "Sometimes Fairy Stories May Say Best What's to be Said," Lewis said that he chose the fairy tale as the form for his stories because of its "brevity, its severe restraints on description, its flexible traditionalism, its inflexible hostility to all analysis, digression, reflections and 'gas.' "[4] It is a form he had long been in love with, and when the time came he felt he would burst if he did not write one. Choosing the *form*, he was to say, was allowing the Author in him to have its say. But then the Man in him began to have his turn.

Of very great significance, he thought he saw how

3. *Of Other Worlds*, pp. 32, 36.
4. *Ibid.*, pp. 36–37.

stories such as he had in mind could steal past
certain inhibitions that had paralysed much of the
religion he had had in childhood. He believed that
the reason we find it so hard to feel as we are told
we ought to about God and the sufferings of Christ
is because an *obligation* to do so freezes feelings.
"The whole subject," he found, "was associated
with lowered voices; almost as if it were something
medical. But supposing that by casting all these
things into an imaginary world, stripping them of
their stained-glass and Sunday school associations,
one could make them for the first time appear in
their real potency? Could one not thus steal past
those watchful dragons? I thought one could."[5]

Lewis had not drawn out a scheme for the whole
Narnian series before writing *The Lion, the Witch
and the Wardrobe*, although he wrote "An Outline
of Narnian history so far as it is known" after all
the books had been written. Because there was no
definite scheme from the beginning, there are a few
inconsistencies in the stories. Like many others,
I read the stories in the order in which I could get
them from the bookshop. It is, however, best to read
them in their proper chronological sequence although experience seems to suggest that, with the
exception of *The Last Battle*, they can be enjoyed
in any order. However, the right sequence as Lewis
caused me to copy it down is this: *The Magician's
Nephew* (1955), *The Lion, the Witch and the
Wardrobe* (1950), *The Horse and His Boy* (1954),
Prince Caspian (1951), *The Voyage of the "Dawn
Treader"* (1952), *The Silver Chair* (1953), and *The
Last Battle* (1956).

For the purpose of following, as it were, the

5. *Ibid.*, p. 37.

mental processes of the author, I have chosen to summarize the books in the order in which they were written.

In *The Lion, the Witch and the Wardrobe* the four Pevensie children, Peter, Susan, Edmund, and Lucy, are sent out of London during the war to visit old Professor Kirke who lives in a large country house. While there, Lucy hides in the wardrobe in the spare room and discovers it to be an entrance into the world of Narnia. She meets there a faun, Mr. Tumnus, from whom she learns that Narnia is ruled by the White Witch, who has cast the country into perpetual winter. Later Edmund goes through the wardrobe into Narnia and meets the White Witch who promises that, if he will bring his brother and sisters to her, she will make him a Prince and feed him on Turkish Delight every day. Following this, all four children find their way into Narnia and meet the Beavers, from whom they learn that Aslan, the great Lion and Lord of Narnia, is on the move, and that the White Witch will be overthrown when four "sons of Adam and daughters of Eve" are enthroned at the castle of Cair Paravel. While they are talking, Edmund slips away in order to betray them to the White Witch. When his absence is marked, the others flee to the Stone Table where they are to meet Aslan. Edmund, on reaching the house of the Witch, learns her true nature. The Witch, with Edmund and her followers, hastens toward the Stone Table, hoping to catch the other children. But Spring begins to melt the ice and snow, thus forecasting her doom. The White Witch then prepares to kill Edmund in order that the prophecy of the thrones shall not be fulfilled. Aslan, however, offers his life for Edmund's, thus satisfying the Magic which the Emperor-Over-Sea put into Narnia at the beginning: that every traitor belongs to the White Witch and that for every treachery she has a right to kill. In Edmund's stead, Aslan is slain with the Stone Knife on the Stone Table. Lucy and Susan witness his vicarious death, but while they are sorrowing the Table is cracked and Aslan, resurrected from the dead, returns to them. He explains to them the "Deeper Magic from before the dawn of Time": If a willing victim who had committed no treachery were killed in a traitor's place, the Table would crack and Death itself would start working backwards. Aslan and those loyal to him then defeat the Witch and the four children are crowned Kings and Queens of Narnia. They reign for many years until one day while following the White Stag (who would give you wishes if you caught him) they chase him into the thicket past the Lamp Post, and—come tumbling out of the wardrobe into the spare room.

Prince Caspian: The Return to Narnia opens with the four Pevensie children waiting on a station platform one year after their earlier adventure. They are suddenly drawn back into Narnia and find themselves in the ruins of Cair Paravel. After rescuing Trumpkin, the Dwarf, they are led by Aslan to the mound, Aslan's How, which covers the ancient Stone Table. Centuries have passed and the human descendants of some Earthly pirates (now called Telmarines) rule Narnia. The original Narnians have been driven into hiding by the usurper king, Miraz. The rightful heir, Prince Caspian (who has blown the Magic Horn and thereby drawn the children into Narnia), joins the old Narnians and, with the help of Aslan and the English children, conquers Miraz's army and brings order and peace to the country. He is then crowned King Caspian X by Aslan.

In the third book, *The Voyage of the "Dawn Treader,"* Lewis introduces a new character from our world—"a boy called Eustace Clarence Scrubb, and he almost deserved it" (ch. I). Eustace and his cousins, Edmund and Lucy Pevensie, are drawn into Narnia through a picture of an ancient ship and sail with Caspian X in search of the seven Narnian lords whom the wicked Miraz sent to explore the unknown Eastern Seas beyond the Lone Islands. Reepicheep, the valiant Mouse, hopes that by sailing to the eastern end of the world they will find Aslan's own country. On one island the selfish Eustace is turned into a dragon. Only after he has learned humility does Aslan restore him to human form. They go on to discover the island of the invisible Monopods and Lucy helps them regain their visibility by daring the adventure of the Magician's Book. By a hair's-breadth they miss landing on the Dark Island where dreams come true. At last they come to "The Beginning of the End of the World" where they discover the last three Narnian lords for whom they have been searching, in an enchanted sleep at the mystic table on which is lying the Stone Knife with which Aslan was slain by the White Witch. As they approach the End of the World, Reepicheep and the three children go forward, although only Reepicheep is allowed to enter Aslan's Country. The children meet Aslan who tells them, before sending them home, that though Edmund and Lucy will never come back to Narnia they shall thereafter know him better under a different name in their own world.

Seventy Narnian years pass, but only a few

months to Eustace, before he and Jill Pole are
called away from their horrible coeducational school
into Narnia. In *The Silver Chair* Aslan sends
Eustace and Jill with instructions as to how they
are to find Caspian's only son, Prince Rilian. They
bungle the first step by Eustace's failure to recognise
the now aged Caspian. One of Lewis's most delightful creations, the marsh-wiggle Puddleglum, leads
Eustace and Jill into giants' country in search of
the Prince. They are waylaid in the giants' city, but
eventually discover Underland where a Witch, who
has the Prince under her power, is preparing to
invade Narnia with her army of Earthmen. Before
they can escape, the Witch, by the use of enchantment, brings them to a state in which they are
almost ready to disbelieve Aslan's existence. By a
great effort of the will, and faith in Aslan, Puddleglum breaks the enchantment. Rilian kills the
Witch (now in serpent form) and they escape to
Narnia—just in time for the Prince to bid farewell
to Caspian before the old king dies. Eustace and
Jill are taken to the Mountains of Aslan overlook-
ing Narnia where they witness the resurrection of
Caspian by the blood of Aslan. Caspian is allowed
to step into this world for a few minutes in order
that he and the children may give the bullies at the
coeducational school a sound thrashing before he
is recalled to Aslan's Country.

The Horse and His Boy is set in the reign of
Peter, Edmund, Susan, and Lucy, as described in
the end of *The Lion, the Witch and the Wardrobe*.
It is, then, a story *within* a story and tells how the
boy Shasta of Calormen runs away to avoid being
sold as a slave. He takes with him—or, more cor-
rectly, is taken *by*—Bree, a Talking Horse of
Narnia. Spurred on by Aslan, who appears in

various guises, he reaches Archenland in time to warn King Lune of the plot by Prince Rabadash of Calormen to kidnap Queen Susan. Rabadash is defeated and Shasta discovers that he is one of the twin sons of King Lune of Archenland.

In the penultimate volume, *The Magician's Nephew*, Lewis turns back to seek the origin of all the other stories. Digory Kirke (who grows up to become Professor Kirke) and Polly Plummer are carried by magic rings into the dying world of Charn. Digory gives way to temptation there which results in their taking Queen Jadis of Charn (later the White Witch) and Uncle Andrew (the Magician) with them to Narnia. They arrive in time to see Aslan creating it. Digory brings back the Magic Apple from whose seeds grow the tree out of which the Wardrobe is made.

The Last Battle recounts the end of Narnia, many centuries after Aslan was last seen moving visibly through the world. Shift the Ape dresses the simple ass, Puzzle, in the skin of a lion and deceives the Talking Beasts and Dwarfs into thinking that it is Aslan himself. By that deception the Calormenes who worship the devil Tash are enabled to overrun the country. Tirian, the last king of Narnia, prays to Aslan for help and is rescued from the Calormenes by Eustace and Jill, who are mysteriously pulled into Narnia from a moving train. They steal Puzzle from the stable, and the Calormenes discover in that same stable the odious Tash (in whom they have lost faith) who carries off the Calormene leader and Shift. Tirian and the remnant of the faithful Narnians are either slain or make their way into the stable. Those who live to go in find it to be the door into Aslan's Country and meet there all the kings and queens of the former stories, with the exception of Susan, who is no longer a friend of Narnia. Aslan comes to the door and holds his Last Judgement. Those who are worthy pass in, while those who are not pass into darkness. Narnia is then destroyed by water and fire and the stable door is closed upon it forever. Those within discover themselves in the *real* Narnia of which the other had only been a copy. Aslan leads them to the Garden of Paradise, where they are united with their friends and see from that great height all that was worth saving from all worlds joined onto Aslan's Country.

V

Inspiration and Invention

IN the preceding chapter it was mentioned that after Lewis had written all seven Chronicles of Narnia he drew up an "Outline" of the history of that world. He gave the Outline to me, and I shall reproduce it here after pointing out a peculiarity of Narnian time and the interesting use Lewis made of it in his stories. All told, there are 2555 Narnian years between its Creation and its End: only fifty-two Earthly years pass during those 2555 Narnian ones. But there is no exact Narnian equivalent of an Earthly year. As will be seen, between 1940 and 1941 of our time 1303 Narnian years go by: between 1941 and 1942 (our time) only three Narnian years.

Lewis knew very well what he was doing as he had long entertained the thought that other worlds might enjoy qualities such as, say, thicknesses and thinnesses. A fine example of this is found in his *Letters to Malcolm* where it is suggested that the blessed dead in Purgatory might experience just such a thing:

The dead might experience a time which was not quite so linear as ours—it might, so to speak, have thickness as well as length. Already in this life we get some thickness whenever we learn to attend to more than one thing at once. One can suppose this increased to any extent, so that though, for them as for us, the present is always becoming the past, yet each present contains unimaginably more than ours.[1]

The "thickness" of Narnian time not only provided the children with more interesting and varied adventures than they might otherwise have had, but Lewis found in it, I believe, a means of pointing out a great truth to his characters—and, through them, his readers. When the four Pevensie children left Narnia the first time, the White Witch was dead and everything appeared to be "settled." If Peter, back in this world, had written of the adventures he had there, he might have been tempted to say "And all the Narnians lived happily ever after." But they did not. And a second adventure helped him to see how ignorant he might have been of the health and future of Narnia and (it is hoped) of this world as well. The point Lewis is trying to drive home is that, as we do not know what stage in the history of the world we are in at the moment, we cannot possibly see the meaning of the whole thing. Are we at the beginning? the middle? or the end? We cannot know until it is over; and we have no way of knowing when *that* will be. To use Lewis's favourite analogy: "We do not know the play. We do not even know whether we are in Act I or Act V. We do not know who are the major and who are the minor characters. The Author knows."[2]

The reader should remember that, while Lewis had entertained various notions of time before writing any of the Chronicles, he had not worked

1. *Letters to Malcolm: Chiefly on Prayer* (London; New York, 1964), ch. XX.
2. C. S. Lewis, "The World's Last Night," *The World's Last Night and Other Essays* (New York, 1960), p. 105. The essay can also be found in the Fontana paperback *Fern-seed and Elephants*, ed. Walter Hooper (London, 1975).

out anything like a "scheme" of Narnia-Earth equivalents beforehand. Having written the books, he *then* found out what they were by compiling the table given below:

Outline of Narnian history so far as it is known

NARNIA	ENGLAND
Narnian years	*English years*
	1888 Digory Kirke born.
	1889 Polly Plummer born.
1 Creation of Narnia. The Beasts made able to talk. Digory plants the Tree of Protection. The White Witch Jadis enters Narnia but flies into the far North. Frank I becomes King of Narnia.	1900 Polly and Digory carried into Narnia by magic Rings.
180 Prince Col, younger son of K. Frank V of Narnia, leads certain followers into Archenland (not then inhabited) and becomes first King of that country.	
204 Certain outlaws from Archenland fly across the Southern desert and set up the new kingdom of Calormen.	1927 Peter Pevensie born. 1928 Susan Pevensie born.
300 The empire of Calormen spreads mightily. Calormenes colonise the land of Telmar to the West of Narnia.	1930 Edmund Pevensie born.

NARNIA	ENGLAND
Narnian years	*English years*
	1932 Lucy Pevensie born.
302 The Calormenes in Telmar behave very wickedly and Aslan turns them into dumb beasts. The country lies waste. K. Gale of Narnia delivers the Lone Islands from a dragon and is made Emperor by their grateful inhabitants.	1933 Eustace Scrubb and Jill Pole born.
407 Olvin of Archenland kills the Giant Pire.	
460 Pirates from our world take possession of Telmar.	
570 About this time lived Moonwood the Hare.	
898 The White Witch Jadis returns into Narnia out of the far North.	
900 The Long Winter begins.	
1000 The Pevensies arrive in Narnia. The treachery of Edmund. The sacrifice of Aslan. The White Witch defeated and the Long Winter ended. Peter becomes High King of Narnia.	1940 The Pevensies, staying with Digory (now Professor) Kirke, reach Narnia through the Magic Wardrobe.
1014 K. Peter carries out a successful raid on the Northern Giants. Q. Susan and K. Edmund	

NARNIA   ENGLAND

Narnian   *English*
years   *years*

visit the Court of
Calormen. K. Lune of
Archenland discovers
his long-lost son
Prince Cor and de-
feats a treacherous
attack by Prince
Rabadash of
Calormen.

1015 The Pevensies hunt
the White Stag and
vanish out of Narnia.

1050 Ram the Great suc-
ceeds Cor as K. of
Archenland.

1502 About this time lived
Q. Swanwhite of
Narnia.

1998 The Telmarines in-
vade and conquer
Narnia. Caspian I
becomes King of
Narnia.

2290 Prince Caspian, son of
Caspian IX, born.
Caspian IX murdered
by his brother Miraz
who usurps the
throne.

2303 Prince Caspian es-   1941 The Pevensies again
capes from his uncle   caught into Narnia by
Miraz. Civil War in   the blast of the Magic
Narnia. By the aid of   Horn.
Aslan and of the
Pevensies, whom
Caspian summons
with Q. Susan's magic
Horn, Miraz is de-

NARNIA	ENGLAND
Narnian years	*English years*

Narnian years	NARNIA	English years	ENGLAND
	feated and killed. Caspian becomes King Caspian X of Narnia.		
2304	Caspian X defeats the Northern Giants.		
2306–7	Caspian X's great voyage to the end of the World.	1942	Edmund, Lucy, and Eustace reach Narnia again and take part in Caspian's voyage.
2310	Caspian X marries Ramandu's daughter.		
2325	Prince Rilian born.		
2345	The Queen killed by a Serpent. Rilian disappears.		
2356	Eustace and Jill appear in Narnia and rescue Prince Rilian. Death of Caspian X.	1942	Eustace and Jill, from Experiment House, are carried away into Narnia.
2534	Outbreak of outlaws in Lantern Waste. Towers built to guard that region.		
2555	Rebellion of Shift the Ape. King Tirian rescued by Eustace and Jill. Narnia in the hands of the Calormenes. The last battle. End of Narnia. End of the World.	1949	Serious accident on British Railways.

There are, doubtless, many like myself who wish Lewis had written stories based on the episodes hinted at in the "Outline." We are, of course, free to state our preferences, but I imagine that, given a choice, it would have satisfied everyone if the

Chronicler of Narnia had given us at least two more stories of the same sort as *The Horse and His Boy*. That is, adventures of specifically Narnian heroes such as Prince Cor who became the second king of Archenland, or the story of how King Gale delivered the Lone Islands from a dragon and was made Emperor by the islanders. If Lewis ever did see "pictures" in his mind of King Gale's adventures, he apparently did not find them interesting enough to make a story, for it will be recalled that in *The Voyage of the "Dawn Treader"* Prince Caspian and the others wonder how the Lone Islands ever came to belong to Narnia. Lewis seems to have at least considered a possible answer for he throws out the tantalising comment: "By the way, I have never yet heard how these remote islands became attached to the crown of Narnia; if I ever do, and if the story is at all interesting, I may put it in some other book" (ch. III). When I did, in fact, ask for more stories about Narnia, Lewis's answer was much the same as he gave to others. "There are only two times," he said, "at which you can stop a thing. One is before everyone is tired of it—and the other is *after*!"

Unfortunately, Lewis almost always destroyed the manuscripts of his published writings. This, as far as I know, is true of all the manuscripts of the Narnian stories, with the exception of a few bits scribbled in his notebooks. Though they don't tell us very much, there is nevertheless sufficient to give us an idea of the "deliberate inventing" that was sometimes necessary when his mental "pictures" did not group themselves into a complete tale. It is also obvious that his first pictures were sometimes supplanted by others, and that pictures that were not used in one story often found a place in some other. In one of Lewis's notebooks the following piece is written in what looks like a very hurried hand, as if it were dashed off the moment it came into his head:

PLOTS

SHIP. Two children somehow got on board a ship of ancient build. Discover presently that they are sailing in time (backwards): the captain will bring them to islands that have not existed for millennia. Approach islands. Attack by enemies. Children captured. Discover that the first captain was really taking them because his sick king needs blood of a boy in the far future. *Nevertheless* prefer the Capt. and his side to their *soi-disant* rescuers. Escape and return to their first hosts. The blood giving, not fatal, and happy ending. Various islands (of Odyssey and St.-Brendan) can be thrown in. Beauty of the ship the initial spell. To be a v. green and pearly story.

PICTURE. A magic picture. One of the children gets thro ' the frame into the picture and one of the creatures gets out of the picture into our world.

INVERTED. Ordinary fairy-tale K., Q. and court, *into* wh erupts a child from our world.

SEQUEL TO L.W.W. The present tyrants to be Men. Intervening history of Narnia told nominally by the Dwarf but really an abstract of his story wh. amounts to telling it in my own person.

What we have here is quite obviously a very rough sketch of *The Voyage of the "Dawn Treader"* which was, when this was written, meant to be the sequel to *The Lion, the Witch and the Wardrobe*. The "intervening history of Narnia told nominally by the Dwarf" comes, not in the *Dawn Treader*, but in *Prince Caspian*, which was, as pointed out earlier, the second story to be written. After telling us in Chapter III of *Prince Caspian* how the Pevensie children rescue Trumpkin the Dwarf, Lewis goes on to say: "So the Dwarf settled down and told his tale. I shall not give it to you in his words . . . But the gist of the story, as they knew it in the end, was as follows." In Chapters IV–VII Lewis tells us what Trumpkin said.

I have a few scraps of the galley proofs of one fairy tale from which we learn a little. It is of no great importance, but the title of this story was, as printed on the proofs, *The Wild Waste Lands.* This was amended to read *Night Under Narnia*, and finally *The Silver Chair*.[3] In Chapter V of *The Silver Chair* the very sleepy Jill is riding on an owl's back. According to the proofs, Lewis wrote:

Jill was once more pinching herself to keep awake—for she knew that if she dosed on Glimfeather's back she would probably fall off—long before the two owls ended their flight. She tumbled off and found herself on flat ground.

It sounds, of course, as if Jill did in fact fall off the owl's back, and so was amended to read in the printed text:

Jill had to pinch herself to keep awake, for she knew that if she dozed on Glimfeather's back she would

3. While Lewis wrote with great ease, he often had trouble settling on what one feels are the "right" titles for his books. For further details about the difficulties involved in deciding on the titles for the Narnian books, see Chapter X of *C. S. Lewis: A Biography* (1974) by Roger Lancelyn Green and Walter Hooper.

probably fall off. When at last the two owls ended their flight, she climbed stiffly off Glimfeather and found herself on flat ground.

By a most fortuitous case of survival, there is in one of Lewis's notebooks a long fragment which appears to be an early version of *The Magician's Nephew* even though it does not contain a blend of magician and nephew as we know them in the book by that title. It may seem disproportionately long to quote in a book of this size, but because it is the only substantial Narnian manuscript there is I have decided to give it in full:

Once there was a boy called Digory who lived with his Aunt because his father and mother were both dead. His Aunt, whose name was Gertrude, was not at all a nice person. Years ago she had been a schoolmistress and bullied the girls. Then she became a headmistress and bullied the mistresses. Then she became an inspector and bullied headmistresses. Then she went into Parliament and became a Minister of something and bullied everybody.

It might have been expected that Digory who had to live with this Aunt would have led a very unhappy life. But there were two things that very nearly made up for it. One was that his Aunt was very seldom at home, and even when she was she got up late and went out in the afternoon and usually did not come back till long after Digory's bed-time. People in Parliament are often like this. And when Aunt Gertrude was away Digory did not have a bad time. The only other people in the house were a secretary called Miss Spink whom he had nothing to do with and Cook. Cook was as nice as Aunt was nasty. She was rather old and had been cook in Grandmother's house long ago when Digory's mother and his

Aunt had been girls together. Aunt did not approve of Cook, but she knew that no one else would stay with her, so she had to keep her.

That was one piece of good fortune for Digory. His other piece of good fortune was of a stranger and more exciting kind. By the time you have read a few pages you will see what it was.

This story begins on a day in Autumn when Digory was not at school because he had been having flu' and was supposed not to be quite well yet. Aunt Gertrude had left at two o'clock with strict instructions that Cook was not to give him Bits, that he was not to Hang About the kitchen, and that he must not go beyond the garden. She may have said this because it looked like rain. She may have said it because she had found out that Digory wanted to go out and meet a school friend. Anyway, she said it.

But this bothered Digory very little, and as soon as the front door had shut behind Aunt he went running and skipping down the garden as if he hadn't a care in the world. It was a nice garden with a grove of trees at the bottom which Digory called "the Wood". Aunt G. thought that trees were unhealthy and said, whenever she thought about it, "I must see about having those trees cut down"; but fortunately she was always too busy and forgot to have it done.

Digory went straight up to the big Oak and said, "Hullo, Oak." And immediately the Oak, with a creaking, oaken kind of voice, replied "Hullo, Digory."

If an oak said anything to you or me we should be very surprised; in fact we should either feel rather frightened or think we were dreaming. But Digory was not surprised at all, for it had been happening to him all his life. That was his second piece—or part of his second piece—of good fortune. Ever since he could remember he had had the gift of being able to understand the trees and flowers. When he was very small he had supposed that everybody could do the same; later on, he found out that no-one but himself could do it, and soon he stopped talking about it for fear of being laughed at. Nobody knew about it except his great school-friend—the one he had wanted to go and see that day—and even he didn't always quite believe it. That was why Digory was not at all surprised when the Oak spoke to him.

"We haven't seen you for a long time", said the Oak.

"No", said Digory. "I've been ill."

"You humans are always getting something wrong with you", said the Oak. "You're as bad as elms. Are you better now?"

"Yes thanks", said Digory.

"Like to come up?", said the Oak.

"Yes please", said Digory.

The Oak lowered one of its branches and Digory stepped onto it as easily as if it were the first step on a stair. Then the Oak raised that branch and lowered the next so that Digory could step one higher, and so on till Digory got into his old comfortable seat in the main fork of the tree. Almost before he had settled down a shrill little voice from somewhere below him said, "May I come up too?"

"Huh!", said the Oak. "It would be a lot of use warning *you* off, Mr. Impudence! On you come, though. I can carry plenty of your size"

"Why, its old Pattertwig!", said Digory gazing down through the leaves to where the newcomer was balancing himself on a dangerous-looking branch of the Silver Birch. Pattertwig was a red Squirrel. And the second part of Digory's second piece of good fortune was that he could understand all beasts.

"Hullo, Digory", said Pattertwig. "Where have you been for ever so long?"

"I've been ill", said Digory.

"You humans are always being ill", said the squirrel, "You're as bad as the cattle. Would you like a nut?"

"Are you sure you can spare it, Pattertwig?", said Digory, "Now that the winter's coming on and all?"

"P-r-r-r", chattered the squirrel contemptuously, "What do you take me for? A nice sort of squirrel I should be if I hadn't got a pile big enough to share a nut to a friend without missing it"

"But you were saying last time we met how hard times were getting", protested Digory. Pattertwig, however, made no answer for he had already jumped from the Oak to the Birch and from the Birch to the Fir and was off to fetch the nut. Digory at once looked the other way: it is considered very [bad] manners among squirrels to watch anyone going to his hoard. To ask where it is would be simply outrageous.

"Aren't you going to talk to me", said the Birch in its silvery, showery, rustling voice.

"Of course I am", replied Digory. "In fact I was coming down to have a dance with you in a moment."

"No good to-day", said the Birch. "I can't dance when there's no wind"

"And when there is", said the Fir in its thick, husky voice, "you dance a great deal too much and slap everyone in the face"

Before the Birch could reply Pattertwig came bounding back holding the nut and running on only two feet. Although he could easily have reached Digory by a shorter way he ran right up the Birch and out along a branch at the top which looked much too small to bear his weight: from that he jumped onto the highest and smallest branch he could find on the Oak. He did all this partly because he was in good spirits, but partly because squirrels like showing off.

"There you are!", he said holding up a fine walnut and sitting up on Digory's bare knee

"Thank you very much", said Digory. "It is kind of you."

"Like me to crack it for you?", asked Pattertwig. "You humans aren't much good at that"

"Please", said Digory.

"When I said times were getting very hard", continued Pattertwig while Digory munched the nut, "I wasn't thinking about nuts. I was thinking about these Grey Squirrels. They're real ogres, if you like. One of those chaps would kill you as soon as look at you, and every year there are more and more of them. I don't know where they come from."

"There were none of them when I was an acorn", said the Oak, "Nor yet when I was in my prime. It's your people, your humans, Digory, that brought them in. They don't belong to this country at all"

"If it was no offence to the present company", said Pattertwig, who had been busily washing his beautiful white chest, "I'd like to ask what Humans are there for at all. I never could see what they did except killing animals or putting them in cages or cutting down trees. No offence, Digory: we all know you're different."

"I'm sure I heard something about that question long ago", said the Oak, "So long ago that I can't exactly remember it. They were put there for something, you may depend on it. I used to know what it was; but I'm getting old."

"Whatever it was", said the Fir, "They've forgotten it too. I mean, they can't be doing whatever they were meant to do *now*."

"And they begin so young", sighed the Birch. "Look at that one on the other side of the wall. It's no older than our own Digory, and there it is doing something horrid with bits of dead trees."

"Is there a—a human, in the next garden", asked Digory.

"Go down this next branch of mine and you'll see it", said the Oak.

Digory set himself astride the next branch, which overhung the next door garden, and worked his way along till he was above the wall. What he saw surprised him very much, for the house next door had been empty ever since he came to live with Aunt G. Apparently it had been taken while he was ill. There were curtains in the windows, the back door was open, and just beneath Digory's dangling feet a girl of about his own age was busily engaged in doing something with planks and sticks and string and nails and a hammer.

You may think that if, like Digory, you could talk to the trees and the animals, you would be far more interested in them than in the boy or girl next door. But then Digory had been talking to trees and animals all his life. He liked it very much, but there was for him nothing new or exciting about it. Indeed he did not realise how much he liked it or how unhappy he would be if the gift were ever taken away from him; just as you and I do not realise till we have toothache how very nice it is not to have toothache. At the moment Digory felt very interested in the girl next door and forgot all about Oak and Birch and Fir and Pattertwig. He looked down between the dry, autumn leaves and said "Hullo!"; and that is what started the whole story you are going to hear.

"Hullo!", said the girl, looking up.

"What's your name?", said Digory.

"Polly", said the girl. "What's yours?"

"Digory", said Digory.

"What a funny name!", said Polly.

"It's no funnier than Polly", said Digory.

"Yes it is", said she.

" 'Tisn't", said he.

" 'Tis", said she, and went on with her work. But presently she looked up again and said "Who were you talking to just now?"

"You, of course", said Digory

"I mean before that, silly", said Polly.

This question put Digory in a terrible fix. "If I say I was talking to the trees", he thought, "she'll think I'm mad. And if I say I was only pretending she'll think I'm a kid." Then he said out loud,

"I was talking to a squirrel."

At this Polly became interested and stopped her work with the bits of wood. "I say", she said. "Have you got a squirrel—I mean, a tame one?"

"It's almost tame", said Digory.

"P-r-r-rl", chattered Pattertwig in his angriest voice. "Tame, indeed! What do you mean by calling me tame? Eh? And why did you want to go mentioning me to that human at all? P-r-r-r!". That was what Digory heard him saying; but Polly heard only the sound of a chattering squirrel. Next moment she cried, "Oh look! Look! There he goes. A red one too. What a beauty!", for Pattertwig was already making off, bounding from the Oak to the birch and out of sight behind the laurels.

"There's nothing very tame about him that I can see", said Polly in rather a scornful tone.

"He was sitting on my knee a moment ago", said Digory.

"Was he really? Honest Indian?" asked Polly.

"Honestly", said Digory.

"Look here", grumbled the Oak. "Look here, that's not the sort of thing at all, you know, not at all. You've no need to go telling her things like that. That was a secret." But Polly heard only a rustling of leaves.

"I say", she said, "I wonder if we could catch him. I read in a book how to make a trap for squirrels"

"There you are", said the Oak, "That's what comes of

chattering to humans. I knew she'd be wanting to eat him or skin him or shut him up."

"What are you making?", said Digory to Polly, not so much because he wanted to know as because he wanted to change the subject.

"I'm making a raft", replied Polly.

"Where are you going to launch it?", asked Digory.

"Didn't you know there was a stream at the bottom of our garden?", said Polly.

"Of course I did", answered Digory, "I've been over in your garden dozens of times. But I shouldn't think it was much good for sailing on. It just goes under a kind of tunnel in the wall on the other side of your garden, and I know it doesn't come up again in the garden beyond, because—"

"No", interrupted Polly, "That's why I want to explore it. I want to sail into the tunnel and find where it goes to"

"It's awfully low", said Digory, "There'd be nothing like room to stand up or even to sit."

"Of course not. That's why I shall be lying flat, paddling with my feet and holding my torch in one hand and my pistol in the other. It might go anywhere. Perhaps it leads down into the bowels of the earth."

Digory could not deny, even in his own mind, that this was a magnificent plan, and he felt rather ashamed that he had never thought of it himself. He had an uncomfortable idea, too, that Polly might think he had thought of it but been afraid to do it.

"There'd better be two on an expedition like that", he said.

"There'd have to be two rafts, then", said Polly.

"I suppose if we can make one we can make two", said Digory.

"It's going to be hard enough making one", said Polly. "Hadn't you better come over and look"

"Alright", said Digory. He swung himself off the branch onto the top of the wall and jumped down into the next door garden. The raft was made out of boards which had once been the sides of packing cases. At least these were the deck of the raft. They were fastened onto crosspieces which were round, being in fact very small logs. There was one at the end and one in the middle, but none yet at the other end.

"Where's the third crosspiece?", asked Digory.

"That's just the trouble", said Polly. "I was going to use this" (she pointed to two bits on the grass) "but it's rotten and broke as soon as I tried to nail it. And these three are the only long bits in the wood shed."

"Even the two you've got are quite different sizes", said Digory. "And that means the raft will be heavier at one end."

"Yes, and you lie with your head at the other."

"Is one's head heavier than one's feet?", asked Digory.

"If there's anything inside it, it is", said Polly.

"And better still if it's solid all through, I suppose", said Digory. Polly, however, had been thinking of something else and hardly noticed this remark.

"I say", she burst out, "I've an idea. Do you see that branch—the little one—on that big tree in your garden. It's almost straight for a bit, or straight enough. Why couldn't we cut that off? It would do splendidly for the third cross-piece."

The Big Tree that Polly meant was the Oak himself. Digory felt terribly uncomfortable. He got red in the face and began talking very quickly.

"Aren't we going ahead too fast", he said, "I mean, this raft needs much more thinking out. Those bits of packing cases don't really join, they won't be watertight, it will go under at once, and anyway what about provisions?"

"Who's going too fast now?", said Polly. "Of course we'll cork the seams—with putty, you know—and then we'll paint her. And we can think about provisions any time. But we can't do anything till we've got a third crosspiece"

Digory didn't know what to do. He felt at once that it would be no good saying "The Oak is one of my oldest and best friends and I'd sooner do anything than cut a branch off him." Yet nothing else seemed to be of much use.

"Let's do it now", said Polly. "There's a saw in the shed"

"I—I—I don't think we can do that", stammered Digory.

"Why not?", asked Polly. "Afraid of your grown-ups?"

"It isn't that", said he, "And I haven't got any grown-ups except Aunt who'd rather see all trees cut down than not"

"Then why on earth not cut a branch when we want one?", said Polly. Then, when Digory made no answer, she added "I'll cut it if you don't know how to use a saw."

"Don't mind betting I can saw better than you", said Digory

"So you say", replied Polly.

"There's no good losing your temper about it," said Digory.

"You're enough to make anyone lose their temper", said Polly. "I never saw such a person! You say you're not afraid, but you won't do it. You say you can saw, but you won't do it. What's the matter with you?"

"I don't know that I'm so keen about that raft of yours", said Digory. "It's all rot about the beastly stream going down to the bowels of the earth. Most likely it's only a drain and there'll be nothing but rats"

Polly, however, hadn't waited to hear him say this and when he had finished he found that she was already coming back from the shed with the saw in her hand.

"Look here", she said, "Even if you daren't do it, or can't do it, yourself, I suppose you're not going to go running to your aunt and telling if I do it"

"I've told you already there's nothing to be afraid of", said Digory. "And any fool can saw. It isn't that at all"

"So you keep on saying", said Polly. "But you don't tell me what it *is*"

"I hate messing trees—living trees—about", said Digory at last.

"Oh, really!", said Polly. "This is too silly. If you don't want to go on with the raft, why can't you say so and have done with it, instead of making such crazy excuses. I believe you *are* afraid after all. Why, you look as if you were going to blub this minute"

"I tell you I'm no more afraid than you are", shouted Digory, now very angry.

"Then I dare you to do it", said Polly.

"Give me your beastly saw, then", said Digory furiously, snatching it out of her hand. A moment later he was up on the top of the wall. He leaned towards the Oak and said in a low voice, "I say, Oak, do you mind very much? It's such a little branch." But Oak said nothing, and as Digory laid hold of the branch he meant to cut, another branch somehow slapped him in the face so hard that it drew blood on his forehead and brought the tears into his eyes in good earnest. He began sawing.

Squeak—squeak went the saw (which was a wretched, blunt thing) and suddenly from overhead there came a great clap of thunder.

"Come down", shouted Polly. "There's going to be a storm."

Digory glanced down and saw that her face had turned quite white. He couldn't help feeling pleased at this and called down to her, without turning round, and sawing on all the time.

"Who's afraid of a bit of thunder."

"I hate it", said Polly. "And it's dangerous to be under trees—and you're using steel—and look! There's a flash of lightning. Do come down. Please. It's not safe." Her voice rose almost to a scream.

It wasn't particularly safe and if Digory had been alone he would have thrown away the saw and taken to his heels. But he was on his metal now and took no notice of Polly's entreaties until at last he had got through the branch.

"There you are", he said in a superior voice as he threw it down to her. "And now perhaps we *had* better go. Here comes the rain"

It did, in torrents. Digory was wet through before he got to the back door, but Cook saw to all that and had his clothes dry and him in bed and asleep hours before Aunt G. came home.

"It's extremely inconvenient for *me*", said Aunt Gertrude at breakfast next day. "But Mrs. Lefay says she is coming to see me—and you, of course—this afternoon"

"Who is Mrs. Lefay, Aunt," asked Digory.

"There is no need to speak with your mouth full, Digory", replied Aunt G. "Mrs. Lefay is your Godmother."

"What's she like?", asked Digory.

"My whole aim in your education", said Aunt G. "is not to put opinions into your head but to encourage you to form opinions of your own. That is why—but I see you are not attending"

"Sorry, Aunt", said Digory who had in fact stopped listening as soon as his Aunt began talking about aims and education, because he had heard it all very often before. "Do go on about my Godmother"

"As I was going to say when you interrupted me", continued his Aunt, "The last thing I would wish to do is to influence your opinions about Mrs. Lefay or about anyone else. I, personally, may not think her either a very useful citizen or a very enlightened woman. I may even consider her manners impertinent and her habits unhygienic. I may wonder what induced your father and mother to select such a person. I may be unable to see that the whole institution of God-parents fulfills any useful function. But I don't want you to take any of these opinions ready-made. You must meet her with an open mind."

Digory began to think that his Godmother might be rather nice

"Fortunately, or unfortunately for *me*", said Aunt Gertrude "I shall not have to go to the House this afternoon, so I shall have to see the woman. You will please to be ready at four o'clock precisely, properly dressed and with your hair brushed and your face washed. Do not forget your nails. The visit will probably not be repeated. Meanwhile, as it is fine this morning, you must go out. I have some messages for you to do. But you will have to wear your raincoat"

"But, Aunt", said Digory, "I'm simply Boiling already"

"That will do, Digory", said Aunt G.

Digory would not so much have minded having his whole morning filled up with messages if they had been messages that really wanted doing; but he knew very well that she had thought them all up for the purpose, as she would say, "Of giving him something to do." She often said boys were happier if they had Something to Do. She loved telling other people what made them happy.

As a result of his wasted morning it was not till after lunch that Digory had a chance to go down to the Wood at the end of the garden. As he got near it he felt rather nervous.

"Oak", he said, laying his hand on the trunk of his old friend, "I'm most awfully sorry about yesterday. You did understand, didn't you? You know I wouldn't for myself steal even one leaf of yours, but how could I go on being dared and told I was a coward and told I couldn't saw—and by a girl too? You did understand, didn't you?"

But the Oak answered not a word. Nor did the other trees when Digory appealed to them. It was the first time in his life that such a thing had ever happened to him. He went on trying to make the trees see reason, but there was no answer. He begged and implored and apologised and then grew angry and said "Alright! Sulky things. Losing that branch was no more to Oak than having my nails cut would be to me. I don't know what you're all making such a fuss about. Oak cut my face yesterday and made it bleed and I'm not sulking about that. Have it your own way."

He turned miserably to go back to the house. At that moment two grubby and quarrelsome London sparrows alighted on the roller. Digory, who had been understanding birds' voices all his life, at once listened to hear what they were arguing about. He had often been able to settle bird-quarrels and send both parties away content. This time, he found to his horror that he could not make out what they were saying. It was just meaningless chatter to him as it would be to you or me. Then a terrible thought struck him. Up till now he had taken it for granted that he was the same as he had always been but that the Trees had changed and become angry. But supposing it wasn't that? Supposing the Trees and beasts and birds were still the same and that the change was in him, that he had lost his gift and become like everyone else? This thought was almost more than Digory could bear. The only life he had ever known was a life in which you could talk to animals and trees. If that was to come to an end the world would be so different for him that he would be a complete stranger in it. He felt as you or I would feel if one day all the grass disappeared and the whole country turned into grey dust: almost as we should feel if all the people in the world went suddenly dumb. Nothing that had ever happened to him was quite so bad as this. Then Aunt G. rapped on a window and told him to come in and get himself dressed and washed.

He could hear the visitor arriving downstairs long before he was ready. This was not surprising, for he had not begun dressing at once when he went to his room. He had sat on the edge of the bed for a long time staring at the carpet and doing nothing. He could not fully take in what had happened to him. Sometimes he tried to believe it hadn't happened: but deep down inside him he felt that he had really lost his wonderful gift and that nothing in the world—no books, or games, or friends, or holidays abroad, or motor-bikes, or cars, or a yacht—could ever make up for it. "What a fool I've been—oh *what* a fool!" said Digory.

At last he got dressed and came slowly downstairs, very slowly, not because he was shy—he no longer cared twopence about his Godmother one way or the other—but because he was so wretched. He went into the drawing room. And the first thing he heard was his Aunt's voice saying "always felt the boy needs taking out of himself."

Another voice, a deep, dry voice that sounded more like a man's than a woman's, replied

"Taking out of himself, eh? How do you do that? by skinning 'em?"

And of course Digory knew they were talking about him. Then he came out into the middle of the room.

The visitor was the shortest and fattest woman he had ever seen. When you saw her face from in front it looked almost square, and very big. When you saw it from the side the long nose and the long chin stuck out so that they almost met. She was dressed in black and her chest seemed to be all covered with some kind of yellow dust.

"Don't be afraid you're going to have to kiss me", said the old woman staring at Digory with very keen eyes under very fierce grey eyebrows. "I'm too ugly for that and ten to one you don't like snuff. I do, though"—and she took out a little gold box and took a big pinch of snuff up one of her wide nostrils and then another big pinch up the other.

"How do you do, Godmother?", said Digory politely.

"I won't ask how *you* do", said Mrs. Lefay "Because I see you do very badly."

"He is just getting over influenza", said Aunt G. "We are quite satisfied—"

"I dare say you are", said Mrs. Lefay "And I wasn't talking about that"

"I thought", said Aunt G., with her lips getting thinner and whiter as they always did when she was angry, "That if you were interested in the boy you might like to hear—"

"Well, I wouldn't", said Digory's Godmother. "Of course he'll get over influenza. They all do except the ones that die, and I can see he didn't."

"I will leave you together for a little while", said Aunt G. with her iciest voice, getting up, and leaving the room.

Digory was standing all this time in front of his Godmother and staring at the large black bag which hung over her arm. Two long biscuit-coloured objects projected from it. He thought he had seen something very like them before but he could not imagine where. One of them seemed to twitch as if it were alive, but that might only be because the bag shook when the old lady moved her arm.

"Well!", said Mrs. Lefay, "*She's* gone. Now for you. I'm not going to ask what's wrong with you—"

"But there's nothing wrong, Godmother", said Digory.

"That's a good lie", said Mrs. Lefay (not in a scolding voice but rather as you might say, "That's a heavy shower") "And you needn't tell any more because, as I said, I'm asking no questions. But I'll tell you how you look. You look exactly like what Adam must have looked five minutes after he'd been turned out of the Garden of Eden. And you needn't pretend you don't understand. And—drat the boy, what do you keep staring at?"

"Its—its your bag, Godmother"

"Oh *him*", said Mrs. Lefay. "Well you can see him, but Hands Off." She loosened the mouth of the bag and out popped the head of a live rabbit: it was his ears, projecting from the bag, that had so puzzled Digory.

"That's Coiny, that is", said Mrs. Lefay, "Out for his afternoon ride. And he's not a present for you, whatever you may think."

"I never thought anything of the sort", said Digory indignantly.

"I see you're telling the truth this time", said Mrs. Lefay "And I know you didn't expect to be given Coiny. A nice house this would be for a sensible, experienced rabbit and he a founder of a family! I only wanted to make you angry."

"Why, Godmother?", asked Digory.

"To see what you'd look like, of course. To see if you'd the right flash in the eye. And you haven't lost that, anyway, though I think you've lost something else

in the last day or so. And now, I don't want to waste any
more time. Here's my card with my address on it, and if
ever you want to see me, take in all these directions
because I don't mean to say everything twice over. You
can catch a tram outside this house that will take you to
Ravelstone Circus. Then look all round the Circus till
you see Little Antrim Street. Then go along that on the
left side till you come to Cuckoo Court. Then go down
the Court on the right side till you come to a furniture
shop that sells birds and pictures. Then you must go
into the shop and you'll see

See what? No one knows because the manuscript,
unfortunately, breaks off at this point. A pity, for
the matter-of-fact Mrs. Lefay was beginning to be
a very interesting old woman. But what kind of
woman? She appears indirectly in *The Magician's
Nephew* as Uncle Andrew's *bad* fairy godmother
from whom he "inherits" the Atlantean dust out of
which the Magic Rings were made. My guess is that
she would have been Digory's *good* fairy godmother.

I have said that this fragment "appears to be an
early version of *The Magician's Nephew*," but I
have it on the testimony of my friend Roger
Lancelyn Green that Lewis read the fragment to
him in June 1949—which means that it was almost
certainly written immediately after *The Lion, the
Witch and the Wardrobe*. When compared with
the four Narnian stories which were completed in
between *The Lion, the Witch and the Wardrobe*
and *The Magician's Nephew*, we see what Lewis
called the "Author's impulse" in him "pawing to get
out"[4] vividly illustrated in this "Lefay Fragment"

4. "Sometimes Fairy Stories May Say Best What's to be Said,"
op. cit., p. 35.

which runs to a little over twenty-six pages in one of his notebooks. Also of interest is the manner in which we see the ingredients of this single surviving manuscript finding their way into other stories:

1. After the Lefay fragment ends abruptly at the top of page 27 of the notebook, Lewis skipped a few lines and wrote an early version of Eustace's diary, which is found in *The Voyage of the "Dawn Treader."* So, even if we didn't have Roger Lancelyn Green's account, it would be clear that the Lefay fragment preceded the diary in time.

2. The picture of Aunt Gertrude with which the Lefay fragment opens is remarkably like the Head of Experiment House who, after the excitement at the end of *The Silver Chair*, was seen to be "no use as a Head, so they got her made an Inspector to interfere with other Heads. And when they found she wasn't much good even at that, they got her into Parliament where she lived happily ever after" (ch. XVI). The Head of Experiment House was, then, almost certainly modelled on Aunt Gertrude.

3. In the second chronicle of Narnia, *Prince Caspian*, we meet a talkative red squirrel named Pattertwig who offers Caspian a nut from his winter store. As he bounds off to fetch it, Trumpkin whispers in Caspian's ear, "Don't look. Look the other way. It's very bad manners among squirrels to watch anyone going to his store or to look as if you wanted to know where it was" (ch. VI). In the Lefay fragment Digory is offered a nut from a red squirrel, Pattertwig, and when the squirrel goes off to get it "Digory at once looked the other way; it is considered very [bad] manners among squirrels to watch anyone going to his hoard. To ask where it is would be simply outrageous." Pattertwig is yet

another winsome ingredient salvaged from the un-published manuscript.

4. While the name "Digory" does not appear in the first story of Narnia, it was Roger Lancelyn Green's belief before it was mine, that Lewis was, in the Lefay fragment, searching for the origins of Narnia. If the author *had* gone on from this Lefay beginning, I think Digory would still have been discovered (as he is in *The Magician's Nephew*) to have been the boy who later in the series becomes Digory Kirke and, by a tying up of loose ends, the old Professor of *The Lion, the Witch and the Wardrobe*. But Lewis went on to write *Prince Caspian* and so this was delayed. It is also worth noting that, in the end, Lewis decided against having talking animals and trees in England—thus causing, as I think he intended, a sharper contrast between our world and that of Narnia.

The Lefay fragment, then, was written soon after *The Lion, the Witch and the Wardrobe* and before the final draft of *Prince Caspian*, which contains one of its characters (Pattertwig). Lewis possibly wrote other such fragments—now lost. This one survived because the notebook in which it was written contains notes on English literature that Lewis made a point of preserving. I have thought it worth quoting in full because it reveals so much worth knowing about the workings of Lewis's imagination. The fragment is rather like a fuzzy ball of dandelion seeds which, when struck by the wind, were scattered in many directions. Some of the seeds, or "pictures," found root in other books, and some remained on the parent stem and became the basis for *The Magician's Nephew* as we now have it.

The five manuscript pages of Eustace's diary that

follow the Lefay fragment are essentially the same as the diary found in Chapters II and V of *The Voyage of the "Dawn Treader."* Still, as the differences between them are nevertheless very interesting, and to realise my intention of publishing *all* the Narnian manuscripts there are, it seems wise to transcribe the whole of the manuscript diary here:

Tue. Aug 20—This is positively the first day since we left L.I. on which it has been possible to write anything. We have been driven before the storm for 26 days and nights, as I know because I have kept a careful count: though the others all say it is 28. (Pleasant to be embarked on a dangerous voyage with people who can't even get a simple little thing like that right!). I have had an appalling time, up and down enormous waves hour after hour and week after week, usually wet to the skin, and of course without any chance of a proper meal even when I was well enough to eat. It all proves what I told them at the very beginning, the *madness* of setting out in a rotten little tub like this. It would be bad enough even if I was with *decent* people, instead of *fiends in human* form. Caspian and Edmund are probably the most selfish boys that ever lived. The night we lost the mast—there's only a stump left now—though I was *seriously* ill they forced me to come on deck and work like a slave. Lucy said that if she and Reepicheep could she supposed I could too. I wonder she doesn't see through Reepicheep: everything he does is for the sake of *showing off*. But of course a kid like her can't understand that.

To-day this beastly boat is level at last and the sun is shining and we have all been jawing about what to do. We have biscuit enough (beastly stuff, by the way) to last about 15 days. We shall have to kill all the fowl as quickly as we can eat them, because the muck they eat is nearly finished. That means about 10 days' food: say 25 altogether. The real trouble is water. On short rations, quarter of a pint a day each, we've got enough for 20 days. (There's still lots of rum and wine but that would only make us thirstier). If only we *could*, of course the sensible thing wd. be to turn W. again and make for L.I. But it took us 26 days (they say 28) coming with a gale behind us. Even if we got an E. wind it might take far longer to get back. And at present there's no sign of a E. wind, in fact there's no wind at all. As for rowing back, it would take months; and anyway, no one could row on ¼ pint of water a day.

The others all decided to go *on*, further E, in the hope of finding land. I felt it my duty to tell them that we didn't know there was any land to the E and tried to get them to see the dangers of *wishful thinking* and the importance of *facing the facts*. Instead of producing any better plan they had the cheek to ask me what I proposed. That was a bit too much, so I just pointed out, coolly and quietly, that I had been kidnapped and brought on this *idiotic* voyage without my own consent; and it was hardly *my* business to get *them* out of their scrape. Even the *clever* Caspian couldn't think of any answer to that, so they all just went on talking to one another as if I wasn't there. So it's settled we're to go on E. if we can.

Wed. Aug 21. Still becalmed. Roast fowl for dinner. All the good bits kept for the others as usual. Lucy for some reason tried to make up to me by giving me a bit of hers but that *interfering swine* Edmund wouldn't let her. Pretty hot sun.

Thur Aug 22. Still becalmed and very hot. Feeling very ill all day and sure I've got a temperature. *Of course* these idiots have come to sea without a thermometer.

Fri Aug 23. A horrible day. Woke up in the night *knowing* I was feverish and *must* have a drink of water.

Any doctor would have said so. Goodness knows, I'm the last chap to try to get any unfair advantage, but I never *dreamed* that this water rationing wd. be meant to apply to a sick man. I would have woken the others up and asked if I hadn't been too unselfish (much thanks I get for it! There are some people it is no good being decent to). So I just got up and took my cup and crept along to the beaker, very quietly of course because I didn't want to disturb the others. Some chaps, if they'd been feeling as bad as I was, wouldn't have bothered about that but I *always* try to behave properly to people even if they don't do it to me.

Well, I got to the beaker alright, but I'd hardly had more than a cupful when *that little spy* Reepicheep came along and caught me. I tried to explain but he had everyone up in a moment and there was the deuce of a row. I of course asked, as anyone would, what Reepicheep was doing sneaking about the beaker in the middle of the night. But he's such a *dear little pet* with them all that no one wd. believe *he* was trying to steal an extra drink: and when he understood what I meant he whipped out his silly little sword and wanted to fight me. By Gum, if only I hadn't felt so ill! As it was I had to apologise for peace sake. Then Caspian, who is a *brutal tyrant*, said that in future anyone found tampering with the beakers wd. get 2 dozen: and as if that wasn't enough went on in the most *patronising* way pretending to be sorry for me and saying that everyone felt just as feverish as I did and we must all make the best of it etc, etc. Beastly prig! Stayed in bed all to-day.

Sat. Aug 24th. A little wind to-day but still from the W. Made a few miles E.wards with the sail set on what Caspian (trying to be v. nautical) calls a jury-mast, made out of the bowsprit set upright and tied onto the old stump. Still terribly thirsty. I shall go quietly overboard some night soon and then perhaps they'll be *sorry* for the way they have treated me

Aug 25—Still going E. I stay in my bunk all day now and see no one but Lucy who tries to be decent in her kid's way.

Aug 26. Land in sight: a v. high mountain a long way to the S.E.

Aug 27 The mountain is bigger and clearer but still a long way off. Gulls again to-day for the first time since I don't know how long.

Aug 28—Caught some fish and had them for dinner. Dropped anchor at 7 p.m. in 3 fathoms in bay of this mountainous island. That *idiot* Caspian wouldn't let us put off in the boat to get water because it was getting dark & he was afraid of savages and wild beasts (he was supposed to be afraid of *nothing*). Extra water ration to-night

Aug 29. The most terrible and queerest day of my life but all's well that ends well (Here follows Bill Birdbittle's dragon story & the writer's change of heart)

This clearly is a rough draft of Eustace's diary which underwent various transformations as Lewis discovered not *one* Lone Island, but three. It would also appear that the author had originally planned for the "Dawn Treader" to dock at Narrowhaven for a shorter time than it actually does, and to have the ship brave a *storm* for twenty-eight days, rather than a *hurricane* for twelve. Perhaps the most significant change of all is that while Eustace's adventure as a dragon lasts, according to the manuscript, only a day, it is in the book lengthened to about six days.

Such then are the extant manuscripts from which we can learn something about the earliest "mental

pictures" and "deliberate inventing" behind the
Narnian stories. They are to be accepted for what
they are—and no more. Lewis believed that most
that survives from the past survives or perishes by
chance. "Is there," he asked, "a discovered law by
which important manuscripts survive and unimportant perish? Do you ever turn out an old drawer
(say, at the breakup of your father's house) without
wondering at the survival of trivial documents and
the disappearance of those which everyone would
have thought worth preservation?"[5] Anyway, it is
enough to say that I wasn't looking over the author's
shoulder as he wrote the Narnian stories, nor have
I seen any of the manuscripts which were thrown
away. But something warns me that if I begin to
conjecture about my conjectures someone other than
Prince Rabadash will turn into an Ass. So I sternly
draw rein and return to the more profitable realm
of fact: the seven Chronicles of Narnia which
Lewis meant for us to read.

5. C. S. Lewis, "Historicism," *Christian Reflections*, ed.
Walter Hooper (London; Grand Rapids, 1967), p. 109.

✗ VI ✗

Narnia Within

e mental picture of a Faun carrying an
and parcels in a snowy wood, Lewis went
agine a country which has become as real
liar to many people as the world we live
for some more dearly loved. After Miss
Pauline Baynes had been commissioned to illustrate
The Lion, the Witch and the Wardrobe, Lewis sent
her his own drawing of Narnia. On it are marked
the sites we come to know in all the stories set in
Narnia proper (Lantern Waste, the Castle of Miraz,
Beruna, Cair Paravel, etc.) as well as the fringes of
the Wild Lands of the North and Archenland,
which lies south of Narnia. Lewis had, apparently,
foreseen the story of *The Silver Chair,* for marsh-
wiggle country is clearly indicated on his original
map with a note to Miss Baynes pointing out that
"a future story will require marshes here. We
needn't mark them now, but must not put in anything inconsistent with them."[1]

Lewis's close observations of nature and his ability
to describe what he saw, heard, and smelled, are

1. For reasons which I am unable to explain, Miss Baynes's
re-drawing of Lewis's original map appears only in the
(British) Geoffrey Bles hardback and Puffin paperback editions
of *Prince Caspian.* The pictures of the Monopods in chapter
XI of *The Voyage of the "Dawn Treader"* are based on
drawings by Lewis of a Monopod asleep and a Monopod
standing. Lewis's map, his drawings of the Monopods, and
his letters to Miss Baynes are in the Bodleian Library, Oxford.

nowhere so evident as in the Narnian stories. His description of Narnian countryside, weather, and food are, I expect, more effective than we first realise in contributing to the astonishing sense of reality achieved in these books. Not surprisingly, they are based on the countries Lewis knew and liked best: the British Isles and the Republic of Ireland, which are the only countries he knew well.

In July 1964 Lewis's brother, Warren, or Warnie as he was affectionately known, and I went on a motor tour of Co. Louth in the Republic of Ireland. We stopped at what seemed the highest point in the Carlingford Mountains, a spot which, according to Warnie, his brother Jack Lewis "pronounced to be the loveliest place he had ever seen." I felt, as we walked through the heather with the sun on our faces, that I had been plunged into the quiddity of Narnia. There the grass is almost emerald green and the heather a delicate purple. Looking north you can see, down below, a narrow bay of water stretching inland to Warren Point. And visible beyond that is Rostrevor—a favourite resort of the Lewis brothers—and higher up are the Mountains of Mourne which really do appear to be "sweeping down" to the Irish Sea. It was Warnie's belief that his brother had to a great extent modelled Narnia on this beautiful aggregate of gentle mountains and windswept coastline. And certainly it comes close to fulfilling Jack Lewis's notion of ideal weather: cool, dewy, fresh. It is, however, worth noting that, while Lewis claimed to be impartial to weather in general, he once described himself to me as having the "constitution of a polar bear," and I have heard him complain of summer weather with temperatures in the high seventies as "suffocating," "blistering," "scorching."

No accident, then, that he placed Calormen in the *southernmost* region of his imaginary world?

Although I am about as indifferent to food as a man can be, I nevertheless feel that modern works of fiction have for a long time become less "homely" and "cosy" in neglecting to say much about what its characters eat and drink. Indeed, so-called realistic literature seems to have almost forgotten that food is one of the most steadfast pleasures in nearly everyone's life. While Lewis is not glaringly obvious in correcting this deficiency—if it be such— some of the finest "imbedded" pleasures of the Narnian stories are his descriptions of Narnian foods. Descriptions which somehow familiarise, without making dull, the strangeness of another world, and which quietly convince us that we are in a *real* world that we should enjoy living in if we could get there. Sumptuous feasts very properly follow coronations and victories, but I suspect most of us are more vulnerable to the descriptions of the more ordinary Narnian fare. There are many ex- amples to choose from, but there are two which are especially nice: the jug of beer and the freshwater trout which was "alive half an hour ago and has come out of the pan half a minute ago" in the Beavers' cave,[2] and the meaty, spicy sausages "fat and piping hot and burst and just the tiniest bit burnt" in the cave of the Dwarfs.[3]

As I pointed out earlier, it would be difficult to know what kind of "dressed animals" Lewis was writing about in his boyhood stories without the benefit of his illustrations. In the Narnian books his animals appear in their natural beauty and in- teresting differences. They are the real thing. While

2. *The Lion, the Witch and the Wardrobe*, ch. VII.
3. *The Silver Chair*, ch. XVI.

few people have seen Lewis's juvenilia, the chances
are that almost every reader has seen a Walt Disney
film. I find much of Walt Disney's work very
pleasant, but his dressed animals do not seem to me
much like the animals they are intended to represent. Perhaps they are not supposed to be. For
whatever reason, I don't think it could be claimed
that Mickey Mouse is very mousy, or Pluto very
doggy. On the other hand, the Narnian animals,
whether they can talk or are dumb, retain the
qualities that endear them to us. Anyone who has
owned a dog will recognise the realistic touch when
he reads about the adventures at the Giants' Castle,
where there are "wagging tails, and barking, and
loose, slobbery mouths and noses of dogs thrust
into your hand."[4] The Giants' dogs were dumb, but
even the Talking Dogs in *The Last Battle* "joined
in the conversation but not very much because they
were too busy racing on ahead and racing back and
rushing off to sniff at smells in the grass till they
made themselves sneeze" (ch. XIV). In the same
chapter everyone is waiting to hear what Aslan said
to Emeth the Calormene; and when "the Dogs had
all had a very noisy drink out of the stream they all
sat down, bolt upright, panting, with their tongues
hanging out of their heads a little on one side to
hear the story."

Excellent as Lewis's descriptions are, the books
are so enhanced by the illustrations of Pauline
Baynes that it would be an inconsiderate omission
not to refer here to her part in the success of the
Chronicles of Narnia. The combination of story
and illustrations is one of the happiest I know of,
and Miss Baynes, when I asked her in July 1978

4. *Ibid.*, ch. VIII.

who chose her to illustrate the books, told me that the idea seems to have originated with the author himself. Recalling her meetings with Lewis, she said "C. S. Lewis told me that he had actually gone into a bookshop and asked the assistant there if she could recommend someone who could draw children and animals. I don't know whether he was just being kind to me and making me feel that I was more important than I was or whether he'd simply heard about me from his friend Tolkien."[5]

Lewis had indeed admired Pauline Baynes's illustrations to Professor Tolkien's *Farmer Giles of Ham* (1949) and he told me that he had "endless admiration" for her illustrations to his Narnian books, particularly her drawings of his animal characters. It would seem, however, that Lewis was unaware of how formidable he appeared in the eyes of someone as modest and self-effacing as Miss Baynes, for he told me he found her "too shy" to talk with as frankly as he should sometimes have liked. But it is best to hear the story from Pauline Baynes who has kindly allowed me to reproduce a letter she wrote to me on 15 August 1967:

. . . Dr. Lewis & I hardly corresponded at all over the illustrations to his books; he was, to me, the most kindly and tolerant of authors—who seemed happy to leave everything in my completely inexperienced hands! Once or twice I queried the sort of character he had in mind—as with Puddleglum & then he replied, but otherwise he made no remarks or criticisms, despite the fact that the drawings were very far from perfect or even, possibly,

5. This came out in an interview with Miss Baynes in the documentary film *Through Joy and Beyond: The Life of C. S. Lewis* made by Lord and King Associates of West Chicago and released in 1979.

from what he had in mind. I had rather the feeling that, having got the story written down & out of his mind, that the rest was someone else's job, & that he wouldn't interfere. As I remember, he only once asked for an alteration —& then with many apologies—when I (with my little knowledge) had drawn one of the characters rowing a boat facing the wrong direction!

When he *did* criticise, it was put over so charmingly, that it wasn't a criticism, i.e. I did the drawings as best I could—(I can't have been much more than 21 & quite untrained) and didn't realise how hideous I had made the children—they were as nice as *I* could get them—and Dr. Lewis said, when we were starting on the second book, "I know you made the children rather plain—*in the interests of realism*—but do you think you could possibly pretty them up a little now?"—was not that charmingly put?

We had very few meetings—one, I think, in Geoffrey Bles' office, once over lunch at the Charing Cross Hotel [1 January 1951]—(rather a hectic affair with him watching the clock for his train)—and once when he invited me to lunch at Magdalen [31 December 1949] with an imposing collection of fellow guests, including Ruth Pitter. On all these occasions, being a self-conscious & stupidly introverted young girl, all I could think of was whether I was saying & doing the right thing, so that I didn't really register the important things like what Dr. Lewis said and did! He was invariably friendly & kind to me, but I suppose inevitably, I always felt overawed. I distinctly remember him picking the chestnuts out of the brussels sprouts with his fingers & saying it was a pity to waste them at the end of the Magdalen lunch! . . .

One remark he made somehow made a big impression on me—but I don't really see why it should have done so. At the time of the Charing Cross Hotel lunch, he looked through some of the drawings I had done—& it was of bears—& he said "This one is particularly nice— you have got the right feeling"—& I said "how funny, I find bears no trouble at all, very easy to draw"— whereupon he answered—"Things one finds easy are invariably the best." This took a lot of thinking about, for though it is of course logical, up till then I had thought that nothing could be worthwhile that had not been a battle, a difficulty overcome, & that good things could only come after a lot of hard work & rubbing out. Of course he was right: if one knows about something so that you can draw it effortlessly it will be fluent & direct.[6]

By the time Miss Baynes had completed the illustrations to the fifth book, Lewis was more satisfied than ever with the quality of her work. His enthusiasm is particularly evident in the letter he wrote to her on 21 January 1954:

Dear Miss Baynes

I lunched with Bles yesterday to see the drawings for *The Horse* and feel I must write to tell you how very much we both enjoyed them. It is delightful to find (and not only for selfish reasons) that you do each book a little bit better than the last—it is nice to see an artist growing. (If only you cd. take 6 months off and devote them to anatomy, there's no limit to your possibilities).

Both the drawings of Lasaraleen in her litter were a rich feast of line & of fantastic-satiric imagination: my only regret was that we couldn't have both. Shasta among the tombs (in the new technique, wh. is lovely) was exactly what I wanted. The pictures of Rabadash hang-

6. Bodleian Library, MS. Eng. Lett. C. 220, fols. 162–64.

ing on the hook and just turning into an ass were the best comedy you've done yet. The Tisroc was superb: far beyond anything you were doing 5 years ago. I thought that your human faces—the boys, K. Lune etc.—were, this time, really good. The crowds are beautiful, realistic yet also lovely wavy compositions: but your crowds always were. How did you do Tashbaan? We only got its full wealth by using a magnifying glass! The result is exactly right. Thanks enormously for all the intense work you have put into them all. And more power to your elbow: congratulations.[7]

Miss Baynes has undoubtedly shown that, of the many illustrators who over the centuries have drawn anthropomorphic beasts and fanciful creatures, she is very near the top of the list.

But we may well ask why Lewis chose to make so many of his characters Talking Animals and mythological creatures or *Longaevi* (longlivers)—a name borrowed from the classical writer Martianus Capella.[8] Would not people have done as well? Talking Animals and *Longaevi* such as giants, dwarfs, fauns, centaurs, dryads, naiads, and other creatures which are not human, but which behave in varying degrees humanly, are, Lewis believed, the "expression of certain basic elements in man's spiritual experience . . . the words of a language which speaks the else unspeakable."[9] He is, then, speaking the proper language of the fairy tale, the

7. Bodleian Library, MS. Eng. Lett. C. 220, fol. 155.

8. See the chapter on "The *Longaevi*" in Lewis's *The Discarded Image: An Introduction to Medieval and Renaissance Literature* (Cambridge, 1964), pp. 122–38.

9. C. S. Lewis, *A Preface to "Paradise Lost"* (Oxford, 1942), ch. VIII.

only language there is for the type of stories he was writing. To have used people instead, or to have given these creatures anything other than their traditional characteristics, would have been, he thought, *ungrammatical*. Besides this, Talking Animals and *Longaevi* are, he believed, "an admirable hieroglyphic which conveys psychology, types of character, more briefly than novelistic presentation."[10] For instance, Eustace, Jill, and Puddleglum have among the Northern Giants a quality of experience that would have been impossible among any other sort of creature. All those twenty-ton, earthshaking, unpredictable morons, just as likely to laugh as cry, are the only creatures who could have frightened and exasperated them in just that way. Could the greedy and vulgar Shift have been anything but an ape? Could any *person* have made us understand bravery so well as the gay and martial Reepicheep? Lewis was not fond of talking about his own books, but when he did, it was usually with as much detachment as when speaking of other writers' works. It was, however, his opinion that Puddleglum and Reepicheep were the best of the Narnian creations. Puddleglum, the marshwiggle, is modelled, Lewis told me, after his gardener, Fred Paxford—an inwardly optimistic, outwardly pessimistic, dear, frustrating, shrewd countryman of immense integrity. But unlike Paxford, Puddleglum is so much *more* the type of man of which Paxford is typical.

But here an example might be illuminating, though I must first point out that, while true, it is meant to show what was undoubtedly a loving side

10. "On Three Ways of Writing for Children," *Of Other Worlds*, p. 27.

of Paxford's character: if anyone thinks otherwise I can only suppose him to be of a congenitally acid disposition. Though very generous with what he had, Paxford was an adept at what is called "holding things together with a nail and a piece of string." During my stay at the Kilns I noticed in Major Warren Lewis's study an example of this. Once when a window in the major's study was broken, Paxford could not bring himself to buy a new, clear pane of glass to replace the broken one. He used instead an opaque piece, such as is normally used in lavatories, which was the only kind he happened to have handy. It is there to this day, and the effect is that, when glancing out the window, one invariably feels that something has gone wrong with one's eyes.

Occasionally Paxford did the cooking, and very good he was at it. We always ate simply, but well. The problem was that, as Paxford did the shopping, we could never be sure of having enough of some rather basic things. As Lewis's secretary, it was part of my job to arrange teas, and I was often worried as to whether there would be enough sugar in the house. This indispensable item, of which Lewis was so fond, comes in both two- and one-pound bags. It was typical of Paxford to buy only half a pound at a time if he could find someone to take the other half. As Lewis entertained a number of distinguished visitors, and as most used sugar in their tea, I was in constant fear of there not being enough. I talked this over with Paxford, who invariably said "Well, you never know when the end of the world will come and we don't want to be left with sugar on our hands. What'll we do with it then, eh?" In vain did I argue that it wouldn't make any difference what was in the larder when the End came. The point I particularly stressed is that we wanted "Mr. Jack's" guests to enjoy their tea—especially the one coming that very afternoon.

"He may not take sugar," said Paxford.
"But he *may*," said I.
"But he may *not*," replied Paxford, "and then where are we?"

As Lewis pointed out in his essay "On Stories,"[11] there is a convenience in making your characters animals and *Longaevi*. As they are not human, so many economic difficulties are avoided. They do not have to be either children or adults. There is no struggle for existence, no domestic worries. They come and go as they please. There is plenty of good eating in Narnia, but where does it all come from? The Dwarfs are very clever, but no one ever heard of their keeping pigs. Who, then, made the sausages? or the wine, beer, and cheese?

Lewis's ideas on animal immortality were mentioned earlier in the book, and it is now time that we noticed the application of those ideas in the Narnian stories. We must remember, however, that we are talking about imaginative fiction, and I think it would be unwise to push the analogies too far. It would appear that part of Lewis's purpose was to create a world in which the relation between men and beasts is as nearly as possible like that which might have existed before both were corrupted at the beginning of this world. He even gives us an idea of what the Narnian animal king-

11. *Of Other Worlds*, p. 14.

dom was like before men or evil came into their lives (the people are there only as witnesses at first). Instead of animals being subordinate to men, the dumb beasts are subordinate to the Talking Animals (see chapters IX and X of *The Magician's Nephew*). The biblical parallels are fairly obvious. After the Creation, Aslan chooses from the beasts (all of which are dumb) two of every kind and gives them speech and reason: Noah is commanded to take into the Ark "every living thing of all flesh, two of every sort" (Genesis vi: 19). Aslan then gives the Talking Beasts dominion over the dumb beasts: as God gave Man "over every living thing that moveth upon the earth" (Genesis i: 28). Aslan commands the Talking Beasts to treat the dumb ones gently lest they become like them and lose their reason, "for out of them you were taken and into them you can return" (ch. X). The nearest parallel to this—although, like the first, the context is not the same—is the curse that falls on Man after the Fall: "In the sweat of thy face shalt thou eat bread, till thou return unto the ground; for out of it wast thou taken: for dust thou art, and unto dust shalt thou return" (Genesis iii: 19).

However, after the Coronation of King Frank I, all Narnian beasts become subordinate to Man. Though Man is responsible for the corruption of Narnia—through Digory's having brought the evil Jadis there on the day of Creation—the Kings and Queens of Narnia must always be human. This is not their privilege, but their responsibility: "As Adam's race has done the harm, Adam's race shall help to heal it."[12] It is, then, part of Man's

12. *The Magician's Nephew*, ch. XI. Cf. Rom. v: 19 and I Cor. xv: 22.

redemptive function to help raise the beasts to their derivative immortality in the eternal Narnia. And— who can deny it?—the beasts play a not insignificant part in the redemption of Man ("Either other sweetly gracing").

Most of Lewis's children are quite unattractive before they visit Narnia, and they come back much improved. That is one of the reasons they are taken there. Some of their faults can be traced to their schools. "I wonder what they *do* teach them at these schools," Professor Kirke asks in *The Lion, the Witch and the Wardrobe* (ch. V). Eustace Clarence Scrubb, we learn in *The Voyage of the "Dawn Treader,"* "liked books if they were books of information and had pictures of grain elevators or of fat, foreign children doing exercises in model schools," and he also liked bossing and bullying other people (ch. I). When he takes shelter in the dragon's uncomfortable cave, the author says: "Most of us know what we should expect to find in a dragon's lair, but, as I said before, Eustace had read only the wrong books. They had a lot to say about exports and imports and governments and drains, but they were weak on dragons" (ch. VI). At the beginning of *The Silver Chair*, Eustace and Jill Pole are pupils at the same school: "It was 'Co-educational,' a school for both boys and girls, what used to be called a 'mixed' school; some said it was not nearly so mixed as the minds of the people who ran it. These people had the idea that boys and girls should be allowed to do what they liked" (ch. I).

Lewis's overt attack on the modern theory of "democratic" or "progressive" education in Great Britain and the United States is contained in two articles[13] criticising the Norwood Report.[14] It was continued in a later article[15] and reached its fullest expression in his *Screwtape Proposes a Toast*. In the last two instances Lewis reminded us of Aristotle's belief that democratic education ought to mean, not the education that most "democrats" like, but the education that will preserve democracy. Lewis believed that educators and parents had confused the two. They want an education that is "democratic" only in the sense of being egalitarian—one that smudges over the inequality of the intelligent and diligent boy and the stupid and idle one. There are, Lewis thought, two ways of doing this: one is to abolish those one-time compulsory subjects that show up the real differences between the boys; the other is to make the curriculum so broad that every boy is bound to find something he can do well. In either case the object is the same, which is that no boy, and no boy's parents, will feel inferior. This demand for equality, which is by no means confined to schools, and which grows more ravenous every day, results (he felt) in the inferior person's resentment of anything that is stronger, subtler, or better than himself. And, as Envy is insatiable, the more you concede to it the more it will demand.

13. "Is English Doomed?", *The Spectator*, CLXXII (11 February 1944), p. 121; and ["The Parthenon and the Optative"] "Notes on the Way," *Time and Tide*, XXV (11 March 1944), p. 213. (Lewis wrote titles on his private copies of "Notes on the Way," and I have reproduced them here within square brackets so that we can distinguish one essay from another.)

14. *Curriculum and Examinations in Secondary Schools: Report of the Committee of the Secondary School Examinations Council Appointed by the President of the Board of Education in 1941* (London: H. M. Stationery Office, 1943).

15. ["Democratic Education"] "Notes on the Way," *Time and Tide*, XXV (29 April 1944), pp. 369–70.

As Lewis has Screwtape say in his "Toast," it induces a man "to enthrone at the centre of his life a good, solid resounding lie"—a lie that is often expressed in the familiar and incantatory phrase *I'm as good as you.*[16]

Eustace Clarence Scrubb is the product of a social education and home that have made him the truculent, selfish coxcomb we meet at the beginning of *The Voyage of the "Dawn Treader."* Desperate diseases require desperate remedies. It is in the form of a dragon, the outward semblance of his inner spiritual condition, that he learns humility and the beginnings of self-knowledge. Afterwards, Aslan helps him strip off the "old Adam" and he emerges a much better person. This is one example of what is repeated throughout the books. None of the children simply "develops" into a better person. They are strongest when they are most dependent on Aslan, and it is all those Lion's kisses (imparting divine grace) that make the otherwise impossible possible.

It is Peter who, in my opinion, best fulfills the chivalric ideal. Lewis devoted an essay to this special contribution of the Middle Ages to our culture[17]—an ideal he found perfectly expressed in Sir Ector's lament over his dead brother Sir Launcelot: "Thou wert the meekest man that ever ate in hall among ladies; and thou wert the sternest knight to thy mortal foe that ever put spear in the rest."[18] The important thing about this ideal is the *double* demand it makes on human nature. "The

16. *The Screwtape Letters and Screwtape Proposes a Toast: with a new Preface* (London, 1961; New York, 1962).

17. ["The Necessity of Chivalry"] "Notes on the Way," *Time and Tide*, XXI (17 August 1940), p. 841.

18. Sir Thomas Malory, *Le Morte Darthur*, XXI, xiii.

Knight," said Lewis in his essay, "is a man of blood and iron, a man familiar with the sight of smashed faces and the ragged stumps of lopped-off limbs; he is also a demure, almost a maidenlike, guest in hall, a gentle, modest, unobtrusive man. He is not a compromise or happy mean between ferocity and meekness; he is fierce to the *n*th and meek to the *n*th." Unfortunately, it is not natural for a man to be both heroic and meek. Heroism is most often found in the noisy, arrogant bully: and meekness usually found in the weak, defenceless man. Though the two tendencies are difficult to bring together, it is, nevertheless, important that a man embody both. Further, it is this ideal, as embodied in Sir Launcelot, which Lewis believed "offers the only possible escape from a world divided between wolves who do not understand, and sheep who cannot defend, the things which make life desirable."

At our first meeting with the four Pevensie children in *The Lion, the Witch and the Wardrobe*, it is Peter whom we would choose as the meekest, the most courteous and fair-minded. But would he be any good at defending Narnia, to say nothing of himself? But then, what about the impetuous and cowardly St. Peter of the Gospels? If we had read nothing beyond the story of his denial, nothing of his part in the Acts of the Apostles, would we have believed that after the Resurrection he would become one of the most courageous defenders of the Faith the world has ever known? When Susan winds her horn, the slightest prompting from Aslan is sufficient to send Peter to her rescue. He feels sick at the thought of fighting the Wolf, but he rushes into battle. For a while it is all "blood and heat and hair" (ch. XII), but he slays the Wolf and is after-

wards knighted Sir Peter Wolf's-Bane. Then the
seed of courage is planted in all of them. Even the
one-time traitor, Edmund, after some words from
Aslan (which he never forgets), fights the White
Witch until he falls wounded.

In this and all the other Narnian books, the
greatest feats of arms are inseparable from the most
perfect courtesy. Some of the most thrilling are
recounted in *The Voyage of the "Dawn Treader."*
The young king, Caspian, overthrows the slave trade
in the Lone Islands by sheer pluck and courage.
How it must cheer the heart of anyone who has not
given himself body and soul to politics to see the
hideously complicated, lazy bureaucracy overturned
by Caspian who, an instant later, his naked sword
across his knees, is facing the bilious Governor.
" 'My lord,' said he, fixing his eyes on Gumpas, 'you
have not given us quite the welcome we expected.
We are the King of Narnia' " (ch. IV). Then follows
the all too familiar bilge from Gumpas about
economics, interviews, appointments, graphs, trade,
statistics, ending in the question, "Have you no
idea of progress, of development?" "I have seen
them both in an egg," Caspian replies. "We call it
Going Bad in Narnia."

It is on this same voyage that the adventurers
sight what appears to be a cloud of infinite black-
ness resting on the sea. It is decided that they will
not venture into the ominous Darkness, and all
speak with hushed voices as they prepare to avoid
this frightening enterprise. "And why not?" comes
the clear voice of Reepicheep. "Will someone explain to me why not." No one is anxious to explain
and so Reepicheep continues: "If I were addressing
peasants or slaves, I might suppose that this sugges-

tion proceeded from cowardice. But I hope it will never be told in Narnia that a company of noble and royal persons in the flower of their age turned tail because they were afraid of the dark" (ch. XII).

These and all other heroic achievements are centred around the castle of Cair Paravel, the hereditary seat of Narnian kings. It is modelled on a medieval court such as that of King Arthur at the beginning of that exquisite fourteenth-century poem *Sir Gawain and the Green Knight*. More than that, Lewis restored all the fragments of an old unity: coronations, feasts, rich clothes, courtly language, merriment, friendship of a high order, hawking. There is one detail of the medieval (indeed, even earlier than the medieval) court which Lewis, an enthusiastic reader of epic poetry, was certain to include.[19] Before Eustace and Jill set off in search of Prince Rilian, they are entertained in the great hall of Cair Paravel where after "all the serious eating and drinking was over, a blind poet came forward and struck up the grand old tale of Prince Cor and Aravis and the horse Bree, which is called *The Horse and His Boy*."[20] They are listening to a Narnian epic which is well over a thousand years old. Though the setting of all the Narnian stories is essentially medieval, it is *Narnian* medieval. Lewis has so perfectly blended the high court of Cair Paravel with the ancient *Longaevi* of Greek and Roman myths that we are hardly aware that it has a dimension no real medieval court ever had. It seems the most natural thing in the world to see a centaur come galloping up to court, and some of

19. See his chapter on "Primary Epic" in *A Preface to "Paradise Lost."*
20. *The Silver Chair*, ch. III.

Lewis's own marsh-wiggles doing most of the "watery and fishy kinds of work" nearby.[21]

Narnia is a monarchical society, one in which there is loyal and joyful obedience to those above one in the hierarchic scale of being. From top to bottom, the order of precedence would run something like this: The Emperor-Over-Sea and Aslan— the High King Peter—the Kings and Queens of Narnia—the lesser nobility—Talking Beasts and *Longaevi*—the dumb beasts. One would be very far out to suppose that because Narnia is monarchical it is a society of slaves. Before his coronation Frank, the first king of Narnia, promises Aslan that he will "rule and name all . . . creatures, and do justice among them, and protect them from their enemies," rule the creatures "kindly and fairly, remembering that they are not slaves . . . but Talking Beasts and free subjects," that he will not "have favourites either among his own children or among the other creatures or let any hold another under or use it hardly," and if enemies come against the land, to "be the first in the charge and the last in the retreat."[22] These solemn promises are binding on every king of Narnia and Archenland: Tirian, the last king, quite rightly offers his life in the service of his subjects.

Those who live under very different systems of government might, understandably, sense some seeming contradiction in the fact that Lewis made his Narnians free subjects, yet at the same time answerable to the Monarch. Aslan knows that evil is already at work on the day of Creation, and he is insuring Narnia against an absolute, tyrannical rule

21. *Ibid.*, ch. XVI.
22. *The Magician's Nephew*, ch. XI.

such as the Calormenes chafe at under their Tisroc. The "seeming contradiction" will, I hope, be cleared up by what I think is a fair summary of Lewis's political "position." (1) He believed that most people are democrats because they think themselves so wise and good as to deserve a share in the government. He was, he claimed, a democrat for the opposite reason: he believed that mankind is so fallen that no man can be trusted with unchecked power over his fellows. It follows from this that they ought to have equal rights (equal *rights* being a very different thing from the "good, solid resounding lie" that all men are equal beings). But having equal rights is not something we should be proud of having to have. It is, more properly, something we ought to feel a certain shame about, something to be regarded as a medicine for our fallen condition, rather than as a food. (2) Quite apart from the high, personal respect Lewis had for Queen Elizabeth II and her father, King George VI, he defended the ceremonial monarch on the grounds that it is, among many other advantages, a visual reminder that we are not equal beings:

There, right in the midst of our lives, is that which satisfies the craving for inequality, and acts as a permanent reminder that medicine is not food. Hence a man's reaction to Monarchy is a kind of test. Monarchy can easily be "debunked"; but watch the faces, mark well the accents, of the debunkers. These are the men whose tap-root in Eden has been cut: whom no rumour of the polyphony, the dance, can reach—men to whom pebbles laid in a row are more beautiful than an arch. Yet even if they desire mere equality they cannot reach it. Where men are forbidden to honour a king they honour millionaires, athletes, or film-stars instead: even famous prostitutes or gangsters. For spiritual nature, like bodily nature, will be served; deny it food and it will gobble poison.[23]

23. "Equality," *The Spectator*, CLXXI (27 August 1943), p. 192.

VII

Theological Parallels

C. S. Lewis believed that there are three elements
in all developed religions, and in Christianity one
more. The first is the experience of the *Numinous*.
If you were made aware that there is a mighty
spirit in the room with you, you would feel wonder
and a sense of inadequacy to cope with such a
visitant. This shrinking feeling which the numinous
object excites in you is *awe*. A good example is
Jacob's vision of a ladder reaching from earth to
Heaven upon which ascend and descend the angels
of God. When Jacob woke from sleep he exclaimed,
"Surely the Lord is in this place; and I knew it not.
And he was afraid, and said, How dreadful is this
place!" (Genesis xxviii: 16–17). The second element
in religion is the consciousness of a moral law, and
the third element appears when we realise that the
numinous power is the guardian of the morality to
which we feel an obligation. The fourth is an
historical event, such as the recognition that the
incarnate Son of God is the "awful haunter of
nature and the giver of the moral law."[1]

All these elements are vested in the person of
the great, golden Lion of Narnia, but it is the
Numinous, the dreadful, that at first strikes us
the most directly. When, in *The Lion, the Witch
and the Wardrobe*, the Pevensie children first hear

1. *The Problem of Pain*, ch. I.

the name of Aslan, something jumps in their insides (ch. VII). When they see him they know that they are face to face with one who is both good and terrible. The sight of his great, royal, solemn, overwhelming eyes causes them to go "all trembly" (ch. XII). He is a figure of immense power and beauty. When, after his resurrection, "he opened his mouth to roar his face became so terrible that they did not dare to look at it. And they saw all the trees in front of him bend before the blast of his roaring as grass bends in a meadow before the wind" (ch. XV). In *The Voyage of the "Dawn Treader"* the greed of Caspian and Edmund over the magical properties of Deathwater pool, which turns all that touches it to gold, gives way to fear and wonder when, across the grey hillside "without noise, and without looking at them, and shining as if he were in bright sunlight though the sun had in fact gone in, passed with slow pace the hugest lion that human eyes have ever seen" (ch. VIII). Two qualities Lewis told me he borrowed from various descriptions of the Holy Grail, that of brightness and a sweet odour, contribute to Aslan's numinous effect. Both are present in the manifestation of Aslan's glory to Shasta in *The Horse and His Boy*. When the boy fell at the Lion's feet, the "High King above all kings stooped towards him. Its mane, and some strange and solemn perfume that hung about the mane, was all round him. It touched his forehead with its tongue. He lifted his face and their eyes met. Then instantly the pale brightness of the mist and the fiery brightness of the Lion rolled themselves together into a swirling glory and gathered themselves up and disappeared" (ch. XI).

There is never any doubt in anyone's mind that Aslan is the Lord of that world. Even his enemies

believe this ("the devils also believe, and tremble,"
James ii: 19). If I had not read the Narnian
Chronicles, I could not have believed an author
could concentrate so much goodness into one being.
None of the soulful, overnice qualities we sometimes
find in people we feel we ought to like, but cannot.
Here, in this magnificent Lion, is absolute, thrilling
goodness beyond anything we could imagine. Qualities we sometimes think of as opposites meet in
him and blend.

He can be very stern. When the White Witch
questions whether he will keep his promise (to die
in Edmund's stead), his great roar sends her running
for her life. A particularly fine example is found in
The Silver Chair. After the rude and saucy Jill has
pushed Eustace off the cliff, she turns toward the
stream to get a drink. Her way is unexpectedly
blocked by the Lion, who she knows has seen her
"for its eyes looked straight into hers for a moment
and then turned away—as if it knew her quite well
and didn't think much of her." When she asks him
to move out of her way, she is answered by a look
and a growl. She knows she might as well have
asked a mountain to move aside for her convenience.
Nor will he bargain with her. Desperate for a drink
of water, she asks, "*Do* you eat girls?" "I have
swallowed up girls and boys, women and men, kings
and emperors, cities and realms," says Aslan. "I
daren't come and drink," replies Jill. "Then you
will die of thirst," the Lion tells her. When she
proposes to look for another stream, he tells her,
"There is no other stream" (ch. II).

It does not occur to Jill to disbelieve the Lion.
And Aslan's sternness, as she and all the other
children come to see in time, is the only thing that
could have helped them past their pride and

ignorance to some good which he planned for them. It is the proof, not the weakness, of his love. He always wants for them something so much better than they could have wanted, or thought they wanted, for themselves. As the master of an unwilling donkey knows when to apply the whip, and when the carrot, so Aslan in his omniscience knows when tenderness is best. At the end of the quest for Prince Rilian, recorded in *The Silver Chair*, the sight of Aslan causes Jill to remember all her snappings and quarrellings and how she muffed nearly all the signs he had given her. She tries, but is unable to say "I'm sorry." The Lion, understanding this, draws Jill and Eustace to himself, and touching their pale faces with his tongue, says, "Think of that no more. I will not always be scolding" (ch. XVI). In *The Horse and His Boy* Shasta did not know that Aslan had been caring for him since his birth. Nor does he realise that he would never have reached King Lune in time to warn him of Rabadash's treachery had not the Lion spurred him on. When the tired and dispirited lad complains that he is the unluckiest person in the world, he feels the warm breath of Aslan on his hands and face and the great Lion says "Tell me your sorrows" (ch. XI).

Nowhere in the Narnian books is the large, embracing love of Aslan for every creature in all worlds so poignantly felt as when Digory, anxious to draw the Lion's attention to the fact that his mother lies dying, blurts out:

"But please, please—won't you—can't you give me something that will cure Mother?" Up till then he had been looking at the Lion's great front feet and the huge claws on them; now, in his despair, he looked up at its face. What he saw surprised him as much as anything in his whole life. For the tawny face was bent down near his own and (wonder of wonders) great shining tears stood in the Lion's eyes. They were such big, bright tears compared with Digory's own that for a moment he felt as if the Lion must really be sorrier about his Mother than he was himself.

"My son, my son," said Aslan. "I know. Grief is great. Only you and I in this land know that yet. Let us be good to one another."[2]

There are others whom Aslan is unable to help. Like many of us in this world, the Dwarfs in *The Last Battle* are so determined not to be taken in that they stop their ears and close their eyes against anything that can do them good. When, for instance, a glorious feast is spread before them, they see and taste only such fare as they would expect to find in a stable. "The Dwarfs are for the Dwarfs," they constantly reiterate to their spurious comfort and to their eternal undoing. "They have chosen," says Aslan, "cunning instead of belief. Their prison is only in their own minds, yet they are in that prison; and so afraid of being taken in that they cannot be taken out" (ch. XIII). When, in *The Magician's Nephew*, the self-imposed blindness of Uncle Andrew erects a barrier between himself and the comfort Aslan longs to give him, the Lion says, "Oh Adam's sons, how cleverly you defend your-selves against all that might do you good!" (ch. XIV). Similar words were spoken by this same Lion over Adam's sons in the land of Judah centuries ago: "O Jerusalem, Jerusalem, thou that killest the prophets, and stonest them which are

2. *The Magician's Nephew*, ch. XII.

sent unto thee, how often would I have gathered thy children together, even as a hen gathereth her chickens under her wings, and ye would not!" (Matthew xxiii: 37).

Yes, the *same* Lion, for Aslan is Christ. It is, however, with reluctance that I mention this fact regardless of how well-known it already seems to be. I am reluctant because I do not want in any way to damage Lewis's success in getting "past those watchful dragons" which freeze many people's feelings about Christ and orthodox Christianity. I am sympathetic with those well-intentioned Christians who in Sunday schools, and writing for periodicals, draw attention to the fact that Aslan is meant to be the Son of God; and I know only too well the temptation, when all our evangelistic efforts seem to fail, to hand out to non-Christians the fairy tales with the comment, "Just you read these, and you'll know what I mean." Let us, by all means, give away as many copies of the fairy tales as we can afford: but not, please, with any explanation about who Aslan is. An "explanation" on our part is, I am convinced, very unwise, as it would very likely frustrate Lewis's purpose and blunt the effectiveness of the books. It is often precisely because many readers do *not* know who Aslan is that the Narnian stories have been so successful in getting into the bloodstream of the secular world. Hints about who is what and so forth have already caused many readers to regard the fairy tales as codes that need deciphering. They were written to give pleasure and (I think) as an unconscious preparation of the imagination. And this—it cannot be denied—they do most effectively without our extra efforts. If the fairy tales succeed in breaking down the partition of prejudices that prevent nonbelievers from even thinking about the Christian tenets (and they appear to be doing this), *then* our efforts will be very much needed.

"But why," you might well ask, "are you at this very moment talking about the forbidden subject?" The kind of book I am writing is not meant for children or those who enjoy only a nodding acquaintance with the stories, but for specialists— people deeply interested in C. S. Lewis himself. When I heard that the Narnian tales were, in some places, being taught as a kind of systematic theology, I felt that someone ought to attempt an explanation of why this is impossible: or for those who do think it possible, why they should proceed with the greatest caution. It is my belief that we will not find an exact, geometrically perfect equivalent of Christ's Incarnation, Passion, Crucifixion, and Ascension in the Narnian stories. We are not meant to. This is why we should not press the analogies too closely, or expect to find in the tales the same logic we find in the Christian story. If we do press the analogies too closely, we will, I think, go a long way towards spoiling our receptivity for what the stories have to give us. Here are some examples of what I mean.

1. First, in what way is Aslan the Son of God? I once thought we could say that he is the Son of God *incarnate* as Lion. This may have been because Lewis himself says that Aslan "is an invention giving an imaginary answer to the question, 'What might Christ become like, if there really were a world like Narnia and He chose to be incarnate and die and rise again in *that* world as He actually has done in ours?' "[3] Lewis is, however, using the

3. Letter of 29 December 1958 in *Letters of C. S. Lewis*, ed. W. H. Lewis (London; New York, 1966), p. 283.

term "incarnate" rather loosely here, for Aslan is never incarnate as Lion in the same way that Christ was Man. Let us consider what the Incarnation means.

According to the Athanasian Creed, Christ is: "God and Man; God, of the Substance of the Father, begotten before the worlds: and Man, of the Substance of his Mother, born in the world; Perfect God, and Perfect Man . . . Who although he be God and Man: yet he is not two, but one Christ; One; not by conversion of the Godhead into flesh: but by taking of the Manhood into God." This means that in some mysterious way the eternal Son of God is united with a natural, human organism so as to become one person; the union, as the Creed says, of Perfect God and Perfect Man. The Christian story goes on to say that, by His incarnation, Christ is able to taste death on behalf of all others, and by His rising to life again restores us to everlasting life. He then ascends into Heaven in His glorified Manhood—which Manhood He keeps for all time.

When Christ became Man, His divine nature was united with that of a natural, human mortal. But Christ as Aslan is never incarnate as a natural, dumb lion; never a cub suckled by a lioness. Indeed, He is not always found in the fashion of a Talking Lion, although if Chapter XIV of *The Horse and His Boy* were the only part of the fairy tales we possessed we might be led to think so. In that chapter Bree the Horse maintains that Aslan (whom he has never seen) is not a *real* lion, but resembles a lion only in his strength and fierceness. While Bree is expounding the nature of Aslan, the Lion walks up from behind and nearly startles the Horse out of his wits. "Now, Bree," says Aslan, "you poor, proud, frightened Horse, draw near. Nearer still, my son. Do not dare not to dare. Touch me. Smell me. Here are my paws, here is my tail, these are my whiskers. I am a true Beast" (ch. XIV). This episode is quite obviously modelled on St. John's account of the risen Lord's appearance to the doubting Thomas, and Aslan's answer to Bree is doubtless meant to stand as a parallel to Our Lord's answer to Thomas: "Then said he to Thomas, Reach hither thy finger, and behold my hands; and reach hither thy hand and thrust it into my side: and be not faithless, but believing" (John xx: 27).

The passage from St. John and the passage from *The Horse and His Boy* are remarkably similar, but they nevertheless mean something quite different. Thomas had been with Jesus for several years and he is saying (John xx: 25) that only by handling His physical body will he believe (a) that Jesus is risen, and (b) that the risen Lord is the same person as the incarnate and crucified Jesus. Bree, on the other hand, is more like the Bishop in *The Great Divorce* who thought of Jesus as "something purely spiritual."[4] The Horse even denies that Aslan has the body of an animal, for as he says "If he was a lion he'd have to be a Beast just like the rest of us" (ch. XIV). Aslan makes it quite clear that he is not a man, not a phantom, but—like Horses, Squirrels, Rabbits, Dogs, and so on—he is a true *Beast*. And *that*—and no more than that—is what Lewis meant when he wrote about Christ being "incarnate" in Narnia.

By taking upon Himself the form of a Man, Christ was (I presume) never free to change His nature into something other than a Man. Aslan is

4. C. S. Lewis, *The Great Divorce* (London, 1945; New York, 1946), ch. V.

not thus restricted. Quite obviously, it is as a Lion that Lewis thought of Aslan. John the Baptist, after all, thought of Christ as a Lamb ("Behold the Lamb of God"),[5] and in the same Gospel Our Lord speaks of Himself as bread, water, light, a vine—even a door.[6] But of course it is as a Lion that Christ is most often pictured, especially by the Old Testament writers—a choice of images on which I was favoured by the following note by my friend, the late Austin Farrer, sometime Warden of Keble College, using his own translations of biblical texts:

The Seer of Revelation is shown Christ as a Lamb, not a Lion. But it is to be observed that as his first appearance the Lamb-Christ is introduced as a paradoxical substitute for a Lion-Christ. "One . . . saith unto me, Weep not: behold, the Lion from the Tribe of Judah, the Scion of David, has conquered; he can open the Book . . . And I saw in the midst of the Throne . . . a Lamb standing as though slaughtered" (Rev. v: 5–6). A Jewish seer of much the same date presents the straight picture of the royal Aslan: "And I beheld, and lo, as it were a lion roused out of the wood roaring; and I heard him send forth a human voice . . . This is the Messiah whom the Most High has kept unto the end of the days, who shall spring up out of the seed of David" (II Esdras xi: 37; xii: 32). The Lion-Messiah of Jewish tradition derives from the Oracles of Jacob on his twelve sons. He praises Judah as the royal stem, a lion none does rouse, a hand from which the sceptre will never depart (Genesis xlix: 9).

Quite apart from the biblical parallels, Narnia is after all predominantly a world of animals, and

5. John i: 29.
6. John vi: 35; vii: 37; xii: 46; xv: 1; x: 7.

the Lion, the traditional King of Beasts, seems the most natural and appropriate choice for Lewis to have made. Still, the incarnation of Christ differs in yet another way from Aslan's "incarnation" in Narnia: Aslan does not *always* appear as a Lion. In *The Voyage of the "Dawn Treader"* Aslan takes the form of an albatross (ch. XII) and a lamb (ch. XVI). In *The Horse and His Boy* he assumes the form of a cat (ch. VI) and on several occasions that of an ordinary dumb lion. And, finally, in the "new Narnia" as envisaged in the last chapter of *The Last Battle*, "He no longer looked to them like a lion." What then? What else but in His resurrected Manhood. It is fortunate, I think, that Lewis does not actually say this, for that fact belongs to all the "chapters" that followed, of which the Narnian Chronicles had been "only the cover and the title page." There would have been no Narnian stories had there not been the great Original, but the stories being what they are, and the readers being what they are, there are undoubtedly others than myself who want to preserve in our memories as long as we can that magnificent leonine form.

2. In order to satisfy God's demand for perfect justice, Christ, the Perfect Man, died upon the Cross for the sins of the whole world. Aslan died on the Stone Table for Edmund Pevensie. We might deduce from this that Aslan would have died for the whole of Narnia, but we are not in fact told that he would or did do so. Try as we might, I simply do not see how we could work out a doctrine of the Atonement from Aslan's vicarious sacrifice for one boy—a boy, not from Narnia, but from this world. I should be very sorry to hear that anyone was attempting to do so, for I think he would have to read into the Narnian stories all sorts of things

that are not there, were not meant to be there. What Lewis tells us is that Aslan is obedient to the will of the Emperor-Over-Sea, and that he loves Edmund so much that he is willing to pay his penalty for him. It is moving and beautifully clear, easier for most untrained minds to grasp than the fact that Christ died for all mankind. *And* it gets "past those watchful dragons."

3. The Gospels represent Christ as passing after death into a life that has its own new Nature: He is still corporeal, can eat broiled fish, but finds locked doors no obstacle for Him (John xx: 19) and can ascend bodily into Heaven. He is related to Nature in such a way that Spirit and Nature are fully harmonized. Or, to use Lewis's analogy from his book on *Miracles*: "Spirit rides Nature so perfectly that the two together make rather a *Centaur* than a mounted knight" (ch. XVI). I tremble at the thought of what I should say if I were forced to explain how (if at all) Aslan's pre-resurrection body differed from that which he had after his death. In *The Lion, the Witch and the Wardrobe* we see the Lion undergoing something very like the Passion of Christ: "But how slowly he walked! And his great, royal head drooped so that his nose nearly touched the grass. Presently he stumbled and gave a low moan" (ch. XIV). What does it mean? It means exactly what it says. Nevertheless, I cannot see that any physical change is caused by his resurrection: he was omniscient and omnipotent both before and after the event. It is perhaps pointless to make such heavy weather of a theological problem not even posed, but my worry is—what happens if it *is* posed? In any case, the most reliable hints about the new, resurrected Nature are found, not in *The Lion, the Witch and the Wardrobe*, but in the final

chapter of *The Last Battle*, which will be discussed later.

However, accepting—as I do—that it would be unwise to try and maintain an artificial silence about biblical as well as non-biblical parallels which even Lewis has been accused of having made quite "obvious," I offer the following advice regarding what many others would now wish to open up to closer inspection.

Lewis himself gave us a very useful piece of advice on the dangers of imagining "parallels" which are not there. It is found in a passage from his essay on "The Genesis of a Medieval Book," the last two sentences of which I have italicized:

The text before us, however it came into existence, must be allowed to work on us in its own way and must be judged on its own merits . . . And while we are reading or criticizing we must be on our guard against a certain elliptical mode of expression which may be legitimate for some purpose but is deadly for us. We must not say that the Grail "is" a Celtic cauldron of plenty, or that Malory's Gawain "is" a solar deity, or that the land of Gome in Chrestien's *Lancelot* "is" the world of the dead. *Within a given story any object, person, or place is neither more nor less nor other than what that story effectively shows it to be. The ingredients of one story cannot "be" anything in another story, for they are not in it at all.*[7]

Thus, while it is true that "disguise" of a sort was part of Lewis's intention, it is nevertheless essential to see—as he points out above—that what is in one book or world cannot be the same in another book

7. C. S. Lewis, *Studies in Medieval and Renaissance Literature*, ed. Walter Hooper (Cambridge, 1966), pp. 39–40.

or world. Put another way, what "Miss T" eats does not remain as it was but *turns into* "Miss T." The instructions Aslan gives Eustace and Jill on how to discover Prince Rilian are meant, I think, to reinforce the importance of following Christ's commandments. On the other hand, if, while reading *The Silver Chair*, we are thinking only of Christ's instructions to the rich young man recounted in St. Mark x: 17–21, we'll have missed what we are meant to be attending to in Narnia. It's afterwards, minutes or hours or perhaps even years afterwards, that the two worlds are to be joined in our minds. (Pauline Baynes told me that while she was deeply moved by the sacrifice of Aslan, it was not until *after* she had illustrated *The Lion, the Witch and the Wardrobe* that it broke upon her Who he was meant to be.) But even if that juncture *never* takes place, we will have benefitted enormously from *The Silver Chair*, for it is part of the success of a great author that the sense of his book does not depend on the reader's knowing the original source of its ingredients.

Is there any good to be had from source-hunting? Whatever benefits the discoveries confer upon the hunters, there are some misuses I see resulting from too great emphasis upon this suspect "use" of literature.

Let us, for instance, and for the sake of argument, suppose that Lewis borrowed the black cloud resting over the Dark Island in *The Voyage of the "Dawn Treader"* from the similar black cloud resting on the sea in Rider Haggard and Andrew Lang's *The World's Desire* (1891). Lewis had read *The World's Desire* and for all I know he could have "got" his idea of the black cloud from that book. As, however, Lewis had just as fertile an imagination as did either Haggard or Lang, should we not assume that they "got" the idea from some other author who may have "got" it from some earlier writer? If all the literature ever written were available, and we had time enough to read it all, would we find that the idea goes all the way back to Adam? Or is it not possible that Lewis and the authors of *The World's Desire* (and no telling how many others) came at the idea completely independent of one another? In a letter to Arthur Greeves of 31 August 1930 Lewis admitted that one ingredient in his poem *Dymer* (1926) was in fact borrowed from George MacDonald's *Phantastes* but that another ingredient was already in *Dymer* before he read and found pretty much the same thing in MacDonald's *Wilfred Cumbermede.* "Don't you get the feeling," he asked in the letter, "of something waiting there and slowly being recovered in fragments by different human minds according to their abilities, and partially spoiled in each writer by the admixture of his own mere individual intentions?"[8]

Certainly there *is* something to be said for looking for and finding interesting "parallels," but my belief is that when a teacher comes across a pupil who rejoices in having solved a mere "puzzle" by discovering that Narnia is the name of an ancient Italian city, that Arslan (which Lewis altered to Aslan) is the Turkish word for lion, that the name Puddleglum is John Studley's sixteenth-century translation of two Latin words from the *Hippolytus,*[9] the teacher should lead him away from the suspect realm of anthropology to true literary pleasures by showing him how one thing becomes

8. *They Stand Together, op. cit.*
9. See C. S. Lewis's mention of this in his *English Literature in the Sixteenth Century* (Oxford, 1954), Bk. II, ch. ii, p. 256.

a *different* thing in another book. It is, for instance, not enough to say that the immediate source of Shakespeare's *Romeo and Juliet* is Arthur Brooke's extremely ugly *Tragical History of Romeus and Juliet*: we need to show him what a completely different use Shakespeare made of the story if we are to help him appreciate the latter's genius.

Even those likenesses which seem to bear the closest resemblance to historical events in this world can be so similar without being the same. Yet these similarities required nothing of mature analysis for their perception; indeed, children, whom Lewis regarded as the most aware of his readers, were the first to respond to the ultimate likeness. And then, invariably, Lewis would be courteous in his reply. Like the one he offered to a little girl, Patricia Mary Mackey, who was living in Bedford. She had written to Lewis and told him exactly what he meant in the Narnian stories. So, typically, Lewis replied:

> Magdalene College,
> Cambridge.
> 8 June 1960

Dear Miss Mackey

All your points are in a sense right. But I'm not exactly "representing" the real (Christian) story in symbols. I'm more saying "Suppose there were a world like Narnia and it needed rescuing and the Son of God (or the Great Emperor Oversea) went to redeem *it*, as He came to redeem ours, what might it, in that world, all have been like?" Perhaps it comes to much the same thing as you thought but not quite.

1. The creation of Narnia is the Son of God creating *a* world (not specially *our* world).

2. Jadis plucking the apple is, like Adam's sin, an act

of disobedience, but it doesn't fill the same place in her life as his plucking did in his. She was *already* fallen (very much so) before she ate it

3. The stone table *is* meant to remind one of Moses' table

4. The Passion and Resurrection of Aslan are the Passion and Resurrection Christ might be supposed to have had in *that* world—like those in our world but not exactly like

5. Edmund is like Judas a sneak and traitor. But unlike Judas he repents and is forgiven (as Judas no doubt wd. have been if he'd repented).

6. Yes. At the v. *edge* of the Narnian world Aslan begins to appear more like Christ as He is known in *this* world. Hence, the Lamb. Hence, the breakfast—like at the end of St. John's Gospel. Does not He say "You have been allowed to know me in *this* world (Narnia) so that you may know me better when you get back to your own"?

7. And of course the Ape & Puzzle, just before the Last Judgement (in the *Last Battle*) are like the coming of Antichrist before the end of our world.

All clear?

I'm so glad you like the books.

Yours sincerely
C. S. Lewis

I think we can better appreciate the use Lewis made of biblical parallels when we consider the two opposite dangers into which he could have fallen. Had the parallels been very obvious, he would not, I think, have nearly so many readers. Nonbelievers would have felt they were being "got at" and rejected them at once. On the other hand, our imaginations would not have been attuned to the Everlasting Gospel had he been too subtle—

especially as so many people today have never read the Bible. Some middle way was needed. This *via media* came easily to Lewis because he did not begin with morals or the Gospels at all, but wrote stories in which those ingredients pushed themselves in of their own accord. This is understandable to those who spent some time in Lewis's company. He could talk about the saints as naturally and unembarrassedly as you or I could talk about next-door neighbours. "Poor Lazarus," I recall him saying, "he had to die all over again!" And because Lewis's primary intention was to tell a story, rather than get a "message" across, the biblical elements blend into the stories. They are more like leaven in dough than raisins in a cake: it is difficult to say where they begin and where they end. Indeed, sometimes the "parallels" elude our discovery by the sheer multiplicity of them, blended into what is a quite simple episode. A good example is found in chapter XIII of *The Voyage of the "Dawn Treader"* where the children find three Lords of Narnia asleep under an enchantment, round a table spread with exotic foods supplied by a beautiful Princess. On the table is the cruel-looking knife with which the White Witch killed Aslan. The Princess's father, Ramandu, appears but is unable to speak until a bird lays a live coal on his lips. Among the many possible "sources" for these elements, other than Lewis's own imagination, are those we all know about. There is Rip Van Winkle; there is the passage in I Kings xvii: 6 which tells how ravens fed Elijah with "bread and flesh in the morning, and bread and flesh in the evening." The Knife recalls King Pelles's sword which struck the Dolorous Blow. The bird takes us back to Isaiah vi:6—"Then flew one of the seraphims unto me,

having a live coal in his hand, which he had taken
with the tongs from off the altar: and he laid it
upon my mouth." It is inevitable that a man so
widely read as Lewis should have known all these
things—but they, as I have pointed out above,
neither collectively nor individually, are what *his*
story is about.

My next example illustrates, not so much a
multiplicity of elements which are fairly easy to
identify if one has read what Lewis would have
called the "Right Books," as what might be called
a theological overtone. The Narnian stories might
perhaps have succeeded just as well without any
mention of the Emperor-Over-Sea, but Lewis, it
seems, wanted to hint at the Trinity of Persons in
the Godhead. The Emperor-Over-Sea is meant, I
think, to suggest the Father. The Holy Ghost is
hinted at more subtly. In the Nicene and Athanasian
creeds we confess that the Holy Ghost *proceeds*
eternally from the Father and the Son. After His
resurrection, Christ "breathed" on the Apostles
saying, "Receive ye the Holy Ghost" (John xx: 22).
I believe Lewis meant to suggest something like this
when Aslan breathes on the children, imparting
strength for the tasks they are to undertake. A
broader hint is found in *The Horse and His Boy*:
"Who *are* you?" Shasta asks the Lion who has been
walking beside him. " 'Myself,' said the Voice, very
deep and low so that the earth shook: and again
'Myself,' loud and clear and gay: and then the third
time 'Myself,' whispered so softly you could hardly
hear it, and yet it seemed to come from all round
you as if the leaves rustled with it" (ch. XI). The
reader who knows some theology, and whose mind
is turned, as it were, in a certain direction when he
reads these words, may catch an echo of eternal

truth reverberating from Aslan's words: *Myself* (the Father) . . . *Myself* (the Son) . . . *Myself* (the Holy Ghost). If, on the other hand, the reader does not "know the doctrine," the passage will by no means be spoiled for him. He will take the Lion to mean what he says, even if he (the reader) does not know the depths of meaning behind the Lion's words.

Turning to the Old Testament, it will be remembered that while on Mount Sinai Moses asked to see God's glory, the full manifestation of Himself. Because no man can see the Lord's face and live, the Lord said, "There is a place by me, and thou shalt stand upon a rock: And it shall come to pass, while my glory passeth by, that I will put thee in a clift of the rock, and will cover thee with my hand while I pass by: And I will take away mine hand, and thou shalt see my back parts: but my face shall not be seen" (Exodus xxxiii: 21-23). At the end of *The Silver Chair* Aslan comes with Caspian, Eustace, and Jill into this world to visit Experiment House. "They shall see only my back," says the Lion. After he caused the wall of the school to fall down, "he lay down amid the gap he had made in the wall and turned his golden back to England, and his lordly face towards his own lands" (ch. XVI). The bullies from Experiment House rush toward them, but when they see the back of the Lion and the figures in glittering clothes they are filled with terror. After they are given a sound thrashing they run and get the Head who, when she sees the Lion and the others, becomes hysterical. All this eventually results in Experiment House becoming a better school. God's manifestation causes Moses to worship and pray for the Israelite nation. The golden back of Aslan strikes terror into the hearts of the children and the Head, who had previously been not unlike those "stiff-necked people" for whom Moses prayed.

But such parallels, variously transfigured as they are in Narnia, are not what the books are *about*. Indeed, I do not think it is specially the identifiable biblical elements which cause us to regard the Narnian stories as Christian books. Almost every page of every book is suffused throughout with moral substance of a quality which I don't believe anyone, whatever his beliefs, could fairly object to. As pointed out earlier, the tales are not built around moral themes which were in the author's mind from the beginning: these themes grew out of the telling and are as much a part of the narrative as scent is to a flower.

I heard a specialist on children's literature say recently that writers are "going back" to moral themes—and he cited "pollution" as the supreme example. None of us objects to a clean world, but the morality of Lewis's books goes far deeper and touches on levels of human understanding rarely attempted even by those who write for adults. An especially good example occurs in *The Voyage of the "Dawn Treader"* (ch. X). As Lucy searches the Magician's Book for the spell which will make the Dufflepuds visible, she comes across a spell which will let you know what your friends say about you. Not even wishing to avoid this dangerous thing, Lucy says the magical words and hears her good friend, Marjorie, say very unkind things about her to another girl. Later, when Aslan discovers what poor, heartbroken Lucy has done, he says, "Spying on people by magic is the same as spying on them in any other way. And you have misjudged your friend. She is weak, but she loves you. She was afraid of the older girl and said what she does not mean." "I don't think I'd ever be able to forget what I heard her say," answers Lucy. "No, you won't," replies Aslan.

Are there many of us who have not found, like Lucy, that such a dangerous course, once taken, forbids return? I've never seen the enormous difference between what our friends *say*, and what they really *think*, about us so unforgettably portrayed.

Finally, before we move onto *The Last Battle*, which deserves separate and special consideration, it is right that we see how the Narnian stories answer so many of the questions raised by Lewis as he progressed from atheism to Christianity. Paganism, as Lewis came to see, had been only a "prophetic dream" of that which became Fact in the Incarnation. But just as God, by becoming Man, underwent a certain humiliation, so the old, richly imagined myths, Lewis believed, must succumb to rational analysis: they must undergo a kind of death before they can be reborn in glory. But "those who attain the glorious resurrection," Lewis wrote in *Miracles*, "will see the dry bones clothed again with flesh, the fact and the myth re-married, the literal and the metaphorical rushing together" (ch. XVI). In his interplanetary novels Lewis attempted to bridge the gap that, in this world, exists between fact and myth. On Malacandra (Mars), Lewis's hero, Ransom, meets creatures who use the same method of shepherding as did the Cyclops in Homer.[10] He sees on Perelandra (Venus) the Garden of the Hesperides, mermaids, mermen, Mars and Aphrodite, and realises that the "triple distinction of truth from myth and of both from fact was purely terrestrial—was part and parcel of

10. *Out of the Silent Planet* (London, 1938; New York, 1943), ch. XV.

that unhappy division between soul and body which resulted from the Fall. Even on earth the sacraments existed as a permanent reminder that the division was neither wholesome nor final. The Incarnation had been the beginning of its disappearance."[11] At the end of the third novel, *That Hideous Strength*, the Planetary Intelligences come down from their spheres to destroy a modern Tower of Babel in England. And in his short story, "Forms of Things Unknown," the astronauts discover something on the Moon that, on Earth, they had dismissed as "mere mythology."

But nowhere in all of Lewis's fiction are we so likely to forget that there ever has been an estrangement between fact and myth as in the Chronicles of Narnia. This is, I should think, especially true of those young readers who are brought up on the Narnian stories before they know there are such things as "ancient myths"; they will consider the *Longaevi* just as much a part of Aslan's original creation as are the animals. But Lewis had been closing the gap between fact and myth in ways other than his interplanetary novels. A good example is found in his chapter on "Miracles of the Old Creation" in which he pointed out that when Our Lord made water into wine at the wedding feast in Cana He was doing "close and small and, as it were, in focus what God at other times does so large that men do not attend to it." This miracle, he said, "proclaims that the God of all wine is present. The vine is one of the blessings sent by Jahweh: *He is the reality behind the false God Bacchus*. Every year, as part of the Natural order, God makes wine. He does so by creating a vegetable organism that

11. *Perelandra* (London, 1943; New York, 1944), ch. XI.

can turn water, soil, and sunlight into a juice which will, under proper conditions, become wine."[12]

But if Christ (Aslan in Narnia) is the *reality* behind the false god, why does Lewis bring into *Prince Caspian* Bacchus, Silenus, and the Maenads? Because now that we know who the God of wine really is, there is no danger of confusion: Bacchus "can do nothing of himself, but what he seeth the Father do" (John v: 19). Now that we no longer *need* Bacchus, it is *safe* to have him. Besides this, how else could we have a proper romp before the Battle of Beruna Bridge if we forego such a wealth of imaginative experience as we get from Bacchus and his madcap followers? Although Lewis divested him of his power to cause madness and murder, the god retains his essential wildness. In his retinue is his old tutor, Silenus, who "began calling out at once, 'Refreshments! Time for refreshments,' and falling off his donkey and being bundled on to it again by the others, while the donkey was under the impression that the whole thing was a circus, and tried to give a display of walking on its hind legs. And all the time there were more and more vine leaves everywhere." After the festivities Susan says to Lucy, "I wouldn't have felt very safe with Bacchus and all his wild girls if we'd met them without Aslan." "I should think not," replies the sensible Lucy (ch. XI).

Thus, without enfeebling his own power, Aslan does through Bacchus that which he did "close and small" centuries ago in Cana of Galilee. "Here you are, mother," said Bacchus, dipping a pitcher into the cottage well and handing it to the little old woman. "But what was in it now was not water but

12. *Miracles*, ch. XV (italics mine) .

the richest wine, red as red-currant jelly, smooth as oil, strong as beef, warming as tea, cool as dew." The same is true of the other mythological creatures in Narnia: all are extensions and expressions of the power and fecundity of their Creator. "Hail, Lord," says the River-god to Aslan (ch. XIV). That gets it just right: there never has been a permanent divorce between fact and myth.

VIII

A Rebirth of
Images

"You all know," said the Guide in the first work Lewis wrote as a Christian, "that security is mortals' greatest enemy."[1] But unlike some of the ancient Stoics, as well as a great many of the modern ones, Lewis was not putting on a "brave face" because he thought death either terrible or final. Indeed, it was for him the reverse. Even in his wild, atheistical youth he seemed undaunted at the prospect of death: and by the time he became a Christian he had already come a long way towards seeing that "Joy," the deepest longings of all men is, at bottom, a desire for Heaven. While he disliked the "Liturgical Fidget" which has overtaken the Anglican Communion, I think the one expression Lewis would have heartily approved of in the new Roman Rite is the prayer for the "Pilgrim Church on earth." But to put into perspective his thoughts on "mortals' greatest enemy" and the inevitable destination of either Hell or Heaven for everyone, I quote a passage from the last book Lewis was to write, the final sentence of which has possibly become the most famous he was ever to pen:

I do *not* think that the life of Heaven bears any analogy to play or dance in respect of frivolity. I do think that while we are in this "valley of tears", cursed with labour,

1. *The Pilgrim's Regress*, op. cit., Bk. X, ch. i.

hemmed round with necessities, tripped up with frustra-
tions, doomed to perpetual plannings, puzzlings, and
anxieties, certain qualities that must belong to the
celestial condition have no chance to get through, can
project no image of themselves, except in activities
which, for us here and now, are frivolous. For surely we
must suppose the life of the blessed to be an end in itself,
indeed The End: to be utterly spontaneous; to be the
complete reconciliation of boundless freedom with order
—with the most delicately adjusted, supple, intricate, and
beautiful order? How can you find any image of this
in the "serious" activities either of our natural or of
our (present) spiritual life?—either in our precarious and
heart-broken affections or in the Way which is always, in
some degree, a *via crucis* . . . It is only in our "hours-off",
only in our moments of permitted festivity, that we find
an analogy. Dance and game *are* frivolous, unimportant
down here; for "down here" is not their natural place.
Here, they are a moment's rest from the life we were
placed here to live. But in this world everything is
upside down. That which, if it could be prolonged here,
would be a truancy, is likest that which in a better
country is the End of ends. Joy is the serious business
of Heaven.[2]

While we know that Lewis wavered occasionally
in ordering some of the events in the first six
Chronicles, and that he had to do a little "deliberate inventing" here and there, no one can say
that he gave no inklings of the "twist" he was to put
into *The Last Battle*. Hint after hint is thrown out
in all the other stories that no one may camp
forever in Narnia, just as no one may camp forever
in this world. If we feel too great a shock at having

2. *Letters to Malcolm, op. cit.*, ch. XVII.

the old, familiar Narnia crumble beneath our feet,
how are we to endure the shock when the real
thing happens here? But it would not be fair to
suggest that anything remotely like despair is what
Lewis was after. Every hint of impending separation
from the old Narnia is underpinned by persistent
intimations of how great a loss it would be to lose
the royal and all-loving Aslan, how complete would
be our happiness to enjoy him forever.

It is difficult to select from the many passages in
which Lewis attempts to woo our hearts from all but
Aslan the ones that do this best, those which might
be called the most typical. I am, thus, obliged to
become autobiographical. After numerous readings
of the Chronicles the passage which stabs me with
the sweetest and sharpest desire comes from the last
chapter of *The Lion, the Witch and the Wardrobe*.
After the White Witch is dead, Aslan leads the
children to Cair Paravel. The castle towered above
them and "before them were the sands, with rocks
and little pools of salt water, and seaweed, and the
smell of the sea and long miles of bluish-green
waves breaking for ever and ever on the beach. And
oh, the cry of the sea-gulls! Have you heard it?
Can you remember?"

Taken in their context, these words—especially
the questions—set me yearning for that "unname-
able something" more powerfully than any bluish-
green waves and the cry of seagulls in this world
have ever done. In this particular instance I do not
feel sorry for the children in Narnia (they remain
there for five years) but for myself. I can tell from
the feel of the book in my hands that for me the
adventure is almost at an end. And, forgetting the
other stories momentarily, how can *I* live never to
meet Aslan again? I am suggesting that for both the

reader and those who make it into Narnia, the joys of that world (the place, the inhabitants, the castles, the landscapes) are inseparable from the greater joy of knowing the Lion. We want to be there because *he* is there. We desire the Lion because—well, not only because Aslan is in himself desirable, but because the desire is one of the things he has implanted in us, one of the things of which we are made.

From what we are told about Experiment House in *The Silver Chair*, it seems unlikely that any of the pupils there would have read the kinds of books that evoke a desire for anything outside this world. In any event, Jill is certainly puzzled when Aslan speaks of "the task for which I have called you and Eustace here out of your world" (ch. II). She explains to the Lion that nobody called them into Narnia, but that it was their own wish to go there, hoping that "Somebody" would let them in: to which Aslan replies, "You would not have called to me unless I had been calling to you." At the end of their quest for Prince Rilian, Jill and Eustace are taken to Aslan's Country where they see Caspian X resurrected from the dead. Longing to be, like Caspian, forever united to Aslan, "A great hope rose in the children's hearts." "No, my dears," said Aslan, reading their thoughts. "When you meet me here again, you will have come to stay. But not now" (ch. XVI).

There is a particularly moving example of the children's love for Aslan in *The Voyage of the "Dawn Treader"* (ch. XVI). When they learn that they must return to their own world, the truth dawns upon them that it is not so much the change in *worlds* they dread, but separation from the lion:

"It isn't Narnia, you know," sobbed Lucy. "It's *you*. We shan't meet *you* there. And how can we live, never meeting you?"

"But you shall meet me, dear one," said Aslan.

"Are—are you there too, Sir?" said Edmund.

"I am," said Aslan. "But there I have another name. You must learn to know me by that name. This was the very reason why you were brought to Narnia, that by knowing me here for a little, you may know me better there."

That, I think, is as frank a statement as Lewis makes anywhere about his evangelistic purpose in writing the Narnian stories.

The English children are, I suppose, from a Narnian point of view, "Gentiles" from an unknown world who become Narnians by adoption. There are, however, native Narnians who, when they see the Lion for the first time, feel a natural and spontaneous devotion to the person of the divine Aslan—as, for instance, Caspian's old nurse in *Prince Caspian*, who when she sees Aslan bending over her sickbed says, "Oh, Aslan! I knew it was true. I've been waiting for this all my life" (ch. XIV). Hwin, the mare in *The Horse and His Boy*, on seeing the Lion, trots up to him and says, "Please, you're so beautiful. You may eat me if you like. I'd sooner be eaten by you than fed by anyone else" (ch. XIV). But from here we move on to the culmination of the triumphant theme of Joy as the "serious business of Heaven."

The Last Battle, which won the Carnegie Medal for the best children's book of 1956 is, in my opinion, the best written and the most sublime of all the Narnian stories, the crowning achievement of the whole Narnian creation. Everything else in all the other six stories finds its ultimate meaning in relation to this book. One can read the other stories in any order, but *The Last Battle* must be read last because, as Lewis would say, you cannot possibly understand the "play" until you've seen it through to the end. Lewis insisted on taking us to the end—and beyond.

If *The Last Battle* is re-read less often than the other fairy tales—and I don't know that it is—this is probably because the first eleven chapters, which take place in the old, familiar Narnia, are so extremely painful to read. Almost everything we have come to love is, bit by bit, taken from us. Our sense of loss is made more excruciating because we are allowed—even encouraged—to believe that things will eventually get back to "normal." We feel certain that the King, at least, will not be deceived by Shift's trickery: but he is. When Eustace and Jill arrive we know it will only be a matter of time until all is put right. Yet, despite their willingness to help, there is so little they can do without the help of Aslan. And where, by the way, *is* He? Our hearts warm within us as Jewel the Unicorn recounts the centuries of past happiness in which every day and week in Narnia had seemed to be better than the last:

And as he went on, the picture of all those happy years, all the thousands of them, piled up in Jill's mind till it was rather like looking down from a high hill onto a rich, lovely plain full of woods and waters and corn-fields, which spread away and away till it got thin and misty from distance. And she said:

"Oh, I do hope we can soon settle the Ape and get back to those good, ordinary times. And then I hope they'll go on for ever and ever and ever. *Our* world is going to have an end some day. Perhaps this one won't. Oh Jewel—wouldn't it be lovely if Narnia just went on and on—like what you said it has been?"

"Nay, sister," answered Jewel, "all worlds draw to an end; except Aslan's own country."

"Well, at least," said Jill, "I hope the end of this one is millions of millions of millions of years away." (ch. VIII)

So do we all. Yet a few minutes later Farsight the Eagle brings word that Cair Paravel, the high seat of all the Kings of Narnia, has been taken by the Calormenes. And, as he lay dying, Roonwit the Centaur asked the King to remember that "all worlds draw to an end and that noble death is a treasure which no one is too poor to buy" (ch. VIII).

Lewis's didactic purpose ought to be clear to those who are conversant with orthodox Christianity. He uses his own invented world to illustrate what the Church has been teaching since the beginning, but which is becoming more and more neglected or forgotten. Namely, that this world will come to an end; it was never meant to be our real home—that lies elsewhere; we do not know, we cannot possibly know, when the end will come; and the end will come, not from within, but from without.

Most of the events in *The Last Battle* are based on Our Lord's apocalyptic prophecies recorded in St. Matthew xxiv, St. Mark xiii, and St. Luke xxi. The treachery of Shift the Ape was suggested by the Dominical words found in St. Matthew xxiv: 23–24:

If any man shall say unto you, Lo, here is Christ, or there; believe it not. For there shall arise false Christs, and false prophets, and shall shew great signs and wonders; insomuch that, if it were possible, they shall deceive the very elect.

The Ape almost—so very, very nearly—succeeds in deceiving even the most faithful followers of Aslan, first through trickery and, later, when he becomes the tool of Rishda Tarkaan and Ginger the Cat, in propounding his "new theology": the confusion of Aslan and the devil Tash as "Tashlan." As the monkey Shift is a parody of a man, so his "theology" is a parody of the truth. We are prepared for ordinary wickedness in an adventure story, but with the advent of the "new theology" we move into a new and dreadful dimension where ordinary courage seems helpless.

When it seems quite certain that Eustace and Jill will soon die fighting for Narnia, they speculate as to whether, at the moment of their death in Narnia, they will be found dead in England. Frightened by the idea, Jill begins a confession which she breaks off mid-sentence. "What were you going to say?" asks Eustace. She answers:

I *was* going to say I wished we'd never come. But I don't. I don't. I don't. Even if we *are* killed. I'd rather be killed fighting for Narnia than grow old and stupid at home and perhaps go about in a bathchair and then die in the end just the same. (ch. IX)

From that point onward Lewis lets go the full power of his imagination, and we are carried relentlessly forward into what is truly the *last* battle of Narnia, in front of the Stable. There King Tirian, the children, and the remnant of faithful Narnians are either slain or make their way inside. The Stable has become none other than the way into Aslan's Country and, drawing out this brilliant piece of symbolism, Lewis has Jill say in a moment of selfless appreciation: "In our world too, a Stable once had something inside it that was bigger than our whole world" (ch. XIII).

What is a little confusing, but which is partly explained in chapters IV and V, and fully cleared up in the last chapter, is that all (except one) of the "friends of Narnia"—Digory Kirke, Polly Plummer, Peter, Edmund and Lucy Pevensie, Eustace Scrubb, and Jill Pole—died together in a railway crash in England. They are reborn in glory and, inside the Stable, Eustace and Jill meet all the others. The exception is Susan Pevensie who, "no longer a friend of Narnia" (ch. XII), has drifted of her own free will into apostasy. Liberal clergymen and other "kind" but mistaken people, preferring the temporary passion of Pity to the eternal action of Pity, have found the absence of Susan a reason for calling Lewis "cruel." But they are well answered in *The Great Divorce* where, explaining why those who have chosen Hell shall not be allowed to veto the joys of Heaven, he says: "Every disease that submits to a cure shall be cured: but we will not call blue yellow to please those who insist on still having jaundice, nor make a midden of the world's garden for the sake of some who cannot abide the smell of roses" (ch. XIII).

Numbered, however, among the blessed in the eternal Narnia is Emeth the Calormene. I have never heard any denunciation of Lewis for allowing him this beatitude, but it might be worthwhile seeking some justification. "Is it not frightfully unfair," Lewis asked, "that this new life should be confined to people who have heard of Christ and

been able to believe in Him? But the truth is God
has not told us what His arrangements about the
other people are. We do know that no man can be
saved except through Christ; we do not know that
only those who know Him can be saved through
Him."[3] Like the Pagans in *The Pilgrim's Regress*,
the "pictures" the Calormenes received probably
contained the divine call, but through a passage of
time they were all but overgrown with Calormene
inventions. The fact remains that Emeth, stung with
desire, acted on as much truth as he could perceive
through the "dirty lens" of the Calormene religion.[4]
He sought Aslan with all his heart even when
circumstances made it all but impossible to find him.
And though he did not know Aslan *until* he went
through the Stable door, it is Aslan, nevertheless,
who became his Saviour *there*. The beautiful
retelling of Emeth's meeting with Aslan echoes
many Dominical utterances, but one passage I
believe Lewis almost certainly had in mind is: "And
other sheep I have, which are not of this fold: them
also I must bring, and they shall hear my voice;
and there shall be one fold, and one shepherd"
(John x: 16).

With a terrible beauty that makes the heart ache,
and which is perhaps only matched by Dante's
Paradiso, Aslan goes to the Stable door and holds
His Last Judgement. Those who are worthy pass
in, the others turn away into darkness. Inside, the
children watch as Aslan, fulfilling the apocalyptic
prophecies of the New Testament, destroys Narnia

3. C. S. Lewis, *Mere Christianity* (London; New York, 1952),
Bk. II, ch. v.

4. "Horrible nations have horrible religions: they have been
looking at God through a dirty lens." *Mere Christianity*, Bk.
IV, ch. ii.

by water and fire and closes the Stable door upon it forever.

After this dazzling feat of the imagination, one might reasonably expect that Lewis could not help but let us down in "unwinding" his story. He knew that the merest slip of the pen could have cast a shadow of incredulity over all that went before, and he proceeded very cautiously in opening the children's eyes to where they are. The question was how do you portray Heaven? How make it *heavenly*? How "unwind" *upwards*?

The answer lay in finding—and then trying to describe—the difference between the earthly and the eternal world. In order to stride the pitfalls into which so many critics of the Narnian stories stumble, it is necessary to do a little demolition work here. First, it's about as natural as sneezing for moderns to call something an "allegory" when it has a meaning slightly different from, or other than, the one the author gives it. In this sense you can "allegorize" practically anything. The reason why Lewis claimed that neither his Narnian stories nor his interplanetary trilogy are allegories is that he was using the traditional definition of the term: by allegory he meant the use of something real and tangible to stand for that which is real but intangible. Love can be allegorized, patience can be allegorized, anything *immaterial* can be allegorized or represented by feigned physical objects. But Aslan, for example, is already a physical object. To try and represent what Christ would be like in Narnia is to turn one physical being into another physical being—and that, of course, does not fall within Lewis's definition of what constitutes an "allegory." On the other hand, there is much in the Narnias, and specially in *The Last Battle*, which would fit Lewis's own description of symbolism:

The allegorist leaves the given—his own passions—to talk of that which is confessedly less real, which is a fiction. The symbolist leaves the given to find that which is more real. To put the difference in another way, for the symbolist it is we who are the allegory. We are the "frigid personifications"; the heavens above us are the "shadowy abstractions"; the world which we mistake for reality is the flat outline of that which elsewhere veritably is in all the round of its unimaginable dimensions.[5]

Symbolism, as described here, was not for Lewis a fanciful bit of intellectualism. He believed that Heaven is the real thing of which earth is an imperfect copy. His problem was not only of finding some way to illustrate this, but to describe the heavenly life in such a way that it would not seem a place of perpetual negations. In his essay "Transposition," he suggests that we think of a mother and son imprisoned in a dungeon. As the child has never seen the outer world, his mother draws pencil sketches to illustrate what fields, rivers, mountains, cities, and waves on a beach are like:

On the whole he gets on tolerably well until, one day, he says something that gives his mother pause. For a minute or two they are at cross-purposes. Finally it dawns on her that he has, all these years, lived under a misconception. "But," she gasps, "you didn't think that the real world was full of lines drawn in lead pencil?" "What?" says the boy. "No pencil-marks there?" And instantly his whole notion of the outer world becomes a blank . . . So with us. "We know not what we shall be";

5. C. S. Lewis, *The Allegory of Love: A Study in Medieval Tradition* (Oxford, 1936; New York, 1958), ch. II.

but we may be sure we shall be more, not less, than we were on earth.[6]

Lewis had a knack of making even the most difficult metaphysical concepts understandable and picturing the otherwise unpicturable. In order that his readers will feel as comfortable in the world beyond the Stable door as the children in the book, he brings in homely details such as the fact that Narnian clothes feel as well as look beautiful and even the very comforting news that "there was no such thing as starch or flannel or elastic to be found from one end of the country to the other" (ch. XII). Then, as the children and many of the animals they have come to love follow Aslan further into the country, their sense of strangeness wears off until it eventually dawns upon them that the reason why everything looks so familiar is because they are seeing for the first time the "real Narnia" of which the old one had been a "copy." As they rejoice in this discovery, Lord Digory, whom we first met as old Professor Kirke in *The Lion, the Witch and the Wardrobe*, explains the difference between the two, adding, "It's all in Plato, all in Plato: bless me, what *do* they teach them at these schools!" (ch. XV). He is referring in the main, perhaps, to Plato's *Republic* and the *Phaedo* in which Plato writes about immortality and the unchanging reality behind the changing forms.

One very important detail, overlooked perhaps by the majority of readers as it is blended so perfectly into the narrative, concerns the manner in which resurrected bodies differ from earthly ones. The children discover that they can scale waterfalls

6. In *They Asked for a Paper* (London, 1962), p. 178.

and run faster than an arrow flies. This is meant
to be a parallel to the Gospel accounts of Christ's
risen body: though still corporeal, He can move
through a locked door (John xx: 19) and ascend
bodily into Heaven (Mark xvi: 19). But whereas
Christ had been the "first fruits" of the Resurrection, *all* now share in this mighty and glorious
immortality as prefigured by St. Paul when he wrote,
"We shall not all sleep, but we shall all be changed,
in a moment, in the twinkling of an eye, at the last
trump: for the trumpet shall sound, and the dead
shall be raised incorruptible and we shall be
changed" (I Corinthians xv: 51–52).

When the children reach the Mountain of Aslan
they are joined by all the heroes of the other six
books, Reepicheep the Mouse, Puddleglum the
Marsh-wiggle, and a host of other old friends.
There another surprise awaits them. Lewis had
earlier, in his novel *That Hideous Strength*, defined
Arthurian "Logres" as the permanent and enduring
heart of Britain. So now, without bending any
Apostolic teaching so far as I can see, he extends
this analogy further by showing the children that
"no good thing is destroyed" and that all the
countries that were worth saving have become parts
of the whole—"spurs jutting out from the great
mountains of Aslan" (ch. XVI). Uneasy, nevertheless, that their joy may yet be snatched from them,
and that they may be sent back to earth, they turn
to Aslan who answers the question in their minds:
"Have you not guessed?" he says, "The term is over:
the holidays have begun. The dream is ended: this
is the morning."

And as He spoke He no longer looked to them like a
lion; but the things that began to happen after that were

so great and beautiful that I cannot write them. And for us this is the end of all the stories, and we can most truly say that they all lived happily ever after. But for them it was only the beginning of the real story. All their life in this world and all their adventures in Narnia had only been the cover and the title page: now at last they were beginning Chapter One of the Great Story which no one on earth has read: which goes on for ever: in which every chapter is better than the one before.

There has never been a book written, I fancy, in which the assumptions of the author were not present, implicitly or explicitly. Even the most blameless stories of child-life have at their base beliefs about something or the other. There is no such thing as not believing *anything*. One who does not agree with the central premises of the Narnian Chronicles must agree with some others. Will they lead to better ends than those of Lewis's books? I have read many modern works of literature about which I am forced to say "I admire the workman-ship, but deplore the sentiments"; but only of the Narnian Chronicles can I unhesitatingly say, "This is beautiful, and this is right."

IX

Our True Home

IN WHAT is perhaps an unnecessary, but I hope not an unworthy Epilogue, I have chosen to end on a personal note. There has not been, there should not be, any attempt to read the Chronicles of Narnia as Lewis's "autobiography." It nevertheless seems to me perfectly natural and legitimate for the reader of the Narnian stories and Chapter VIII of this little study to wonder if the author of the Narnian stories took the most serious parts of it much to heart. He did.

Writing about the desire for Heaven as part and parcel of the desire for God, Lewis once said, "The proper rewards are not simply tacked on to the activity for which they are given, but are the activity itself in consummation."[1] The old Narnia, as we have observed, flowed into the "real Narnia." In the penultimate chapter of *The Last Battle*, Jewel the Unicorn, arriving on the other side of the Stable door, expressed the feelings of all the others. He stamped his hoof, neighed, and cried, "I have come home at last! This is my real country! I belong here. This is the land I have been looking for all my life, though I never knew it till now."

The Unicorn's words recall for me Lewis's own reaction to death at a crucial time in his life. After years of illness, Lewis was taken on 15 July 1963 to

1. "The Weight of Glory" in *Transposition and other Addresses*.

the Acland Nursing Home in Oxford. Immediately upon arrival, he went into a coma and the doctors expected, and in fact said, that he would die at any moment. After a priest had given him Extreme Unction, I, along with other friends, waited close by for the sad news. To our astonishment and delight, Lewis awoke and asked for his tea, completely ignorant that he had been so close to death. During the weeks that followed, I sat by his bed talking with him about many things. His conversation was as lively and interesting as I ever remember it. I can still hear his great, booming voice quoting the English poets, joking with his friends, and taking me to task for deficiencies in my logic.

Despite Lewis's high spirits, I began to feel that I was wrong in not telling him how close he had come to dying after entering the nursing home, especially as the doctors felt he might not live much longer. I was tortured as well when I remembered Screwtape's belief that it is better for us to die *unprepared* in costly nursing homes amid friends who lie about our condition, than for a soldier to go, *prepared* for death, into battle.[2] In the end I gave in and told him about the coma from which it was not expected that he would recover, his anointing—everything I knew. And all the while I attempted to comfort him as best I could. He listened spellbound, his eyes glowing with excitement. "Dear Walter," he said when I finished, "I am glad you have not left me a stranger to that which concerns me most deeply." And then, seeing how afraid I was that he might die soon, he set about comforting *me*.

Although Lewis's illness caused him little pain

2. *The Screwtape Letters and Screwtape Proposes a Toast, op. cit.,* Letter V.

at this time, he knew he would never be completely well. And knowing that this is a world in which none of us tarry long, he yearned for those "lenten lands" beyond which something better and permanent awaited him. Observing his peaceful acceptance of death—there was nothing regretful about it—I said, "You know, you really do *believe* all the things you've written." His eyes opened wide with surprise. "Of course!" he said. "That's why I wrote them." I know he was tantalised by the fact that he had almost passed the last frontier separating him from our true country, and after he came home he dictated many letters describing his feelings about the experience in the nursing home. He began one: "The door was open, but as I started through it was closed in my face." Then, turning to me, he added, "I would rather have died, but apparently it is my duty to live. I am happy to do either, but—oh, I would like to have gone through that door." A few months later—the same day, and I think the same hour, that John F. Kennedy was killed in Dallas— the door opened again. This time he went through.

INDEX